Praise for *The Whisper of Leaves*

'An impressive debut novel which combines assured writing and well-paced storytelling. K.S. Nikakis is a welcome addition to the ranks of Australian fantasy authors.'
  Juliet Marillier

'[*The Whisper of Leaves*] is strong on its arboreal setting, and promises further complexity. For the genre fantasy fans.'
  The Age

'Nikakis . . . weaves an enthralling story with characters you care about.'
  The Sydney Morning Herald

'This excellent book is filled with adventure and mystery, tragedy and love, with power struggles, the thrill of success and the crushing weight of defeat. A definite recommendation . . .'
  Daniel Habashy, *Newcastle Herald*

'This is great fantasy.'
  Cairns Post

'Here's a strong new voice in Australian fantasy writing. It will be a pleasure to watch as this tale unfolds in future instalments.'
  Good Reading

'Follow the lovely, vibrant Kira every step of the way in this fast-paced, epic story from a brilliant new Australian writer.'
  Toowoomba Chronicle

D0681270

KAREN SIMPSON NIKAKIS grew up in the alpine region of north-eastern Victoria. She spent her childhood riding horses around the surrounding countryside, developing a keen interest in landscapes.

After starting out as a teacher, Karen worked in adult migrant education, teacher education and business communications. Taking leave from work to spend time with her young children, she pursued further education, becoming interested in fantasy, mythology and Jungian theory. As well as doing a PhD on Joseph Campbell's hero path, she wrote short stories, poetry and novels during this period.

Karen lives with her family on acreage near the western edge of Melbourne and lectures in business communications at Deakin University.

The Whisper of Leaves is Karen's first novel.

the
WHISPER
of LEAVES

K.S. NIKAKIS

ARENA
ALLEN&UNWIN

For Libby Ferri, lifelong friend,
28 November 1954 – 29 November 2006

This edition published in 2008
First published in 2007

Arena Books, an imprint of
Allen & Unwin
83 Alexander Street
Crows Nest NSW 2065
Australia
Phone: (61 2) 8425 0100
Fax: (61 2) 9906 2218
Email: info@allenandunwin.com
Web: www.allenandunwin.com

Cataloguing-in-Publication details are available
from the National Library of Australia
www.librariesaustralia.nla.gov.au

ISBN 978 1 74175 504 6

Internal design by Kirby Stalgis
Map by Ian Faulkner
Set in ITC Legacy Serif by Midland Typesetters, Australia

This book was printed in December 2009 at
McPherson's Printing Group
76 Nelson Street, Maryborough, Victoria 3465, Australia
www.mcphersonsprinting.com.au

10 9 8 7 6 5

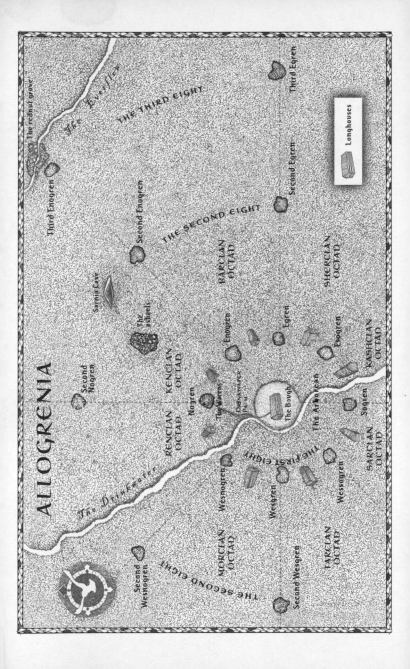

ALLOGRENIA

The rednut grove

The Everflow

THE THIRD EIGHT

Third Enogren

Third Enogren

Second Enogren

Second Egren

THE SECOND EIGHT

BARCLAN OCTAD

SHORCLAN OCTAD

Spirit Lave

The shield's

Second Nogren

KENCLAN OCTAD

Enogren

Egren

Esogren

KASHCLAN OCTAD

RENCLAN OCTAD

Nogren

The Green's

Osogren

The Atwell Well

Sogren

Longhouses

The Bough

The Arlen'con

SARCLAN OCTAD

The Drinkwater

THE FIRST EIGHT

Wesnogren

Wesgren

Wessogren

MORCLAN OCTAD

THE SECOND EIGHT

Second Wesnogren

Second Wesgren

TARCLAN OCTAD

The Tremen

THE BOUGH-DWELLERS

Maxen (Leader, Kira's father, of Kashclan) + Fasarini (of Sarclan)
Merek (eldest son of Maxen) + Kesilini (of Morclan)
Lern (second son of Maxen)
Kira (Kiraon, daughter of Maxen)
Kandor (youngest son of Maxen)
Sendra (helper, of Sarclan)

KASHCLAN
Descended from Kasheron
Miken (Clanleader) + Tenerini (of Barclan)
Tresen (son of Miken)
Mikini (daughter of Miken)
Brem (experienced Healer and Protector)
Arlen (learner Healer and Protector)
Paterek (learner Healer and Protector)
Werem (learner Healer and Protector)
Kertash (Protector Leader)

SARCLAN
Descended from Sarkash
Berendash (Clanleader)

TARCLAN
Descended from Taren
Farish (Clanleader)
Kemrick
Sarkash (Protector Commander)

MORCLAN
Descended from Mormesh
Marren (Clanleader)
Kest (Protector Leader)
Kesilini (Kest's sister)
Feseren (Protector) + Misilini (of Barclan)
Penedrin (Protector)

RENCLAN
Descended from Renen
Sanden (Clanleader)
Pekrash (Protector Leader)
Sanaken (Protector)

KENCLAN
Descended from Kentash
Tenedren (Clanleader)
Senden (Protector Leader)

BARCLAN
Descended from Baren
Ketten (Clanleader)

SHERCLAN
Descended from Sheren
Dakresh (Clanleader)
Sener (elder son of Dakresh)
Bern (younger son of Dakresh)
Bendrash (Protector Leader)

The Shargh

Erboran (Chief) + Palansa
Arkendrin (younger brother of Erboran)
Tarkenda (mother of Erboran) + Ergardrin

Loyal to Erboran
Erdosin
Irsulalin
Ormadon
Erlken
Irmakin

Loyal to Arkendrin
Irason
Ermashin
Urpalin
Orthaken
Irdodun
Urgundin

Founders of the Four Shargh Peoples
The Shargh: Artmenton
The Soushargh: Urchelen
The Weshargh: Irkardin
The Ashmiri: Ashmiridin

Prologue

Death pervaded the cavern, crusting the walls and rising in clouds to the top of the chamber. Was it the air's long confinement that caused the accompanying stench, or the bitterness of those whose lives had been snatched away, leaving only their voices imprisoned in the dreams of Shargh Tellers? Or was it something else?

Whatever the cause, darkness added to the sense of oppression, the fire in the chamber's centre giving little light.

Ordorin wasn't perturbed by the stench, attributing it to the tailings from some wolf lair deeper in the labyrinth or the rotting carcass of a stray ebis that had crashed through the ceiling from the Cashgars above. The world of dreams and Tellings, and of the shades of those who'd already gone to the Sky Chiefs' realm, held no interest for Ordorin. His world was that of the he-wolf in flight, the straight-thrown spear, the men he could bring to his side and the women he could coerce to his bed. He'd come to the cavern only because the Teller's summons had hinted at power – and power interested Ordorin very much.

Ordorin's hand went to his dagger as he strained to make out the hunched shadow waiting for him. Crouched next to the fire, the Teller's body was more bone than flesh, his eyes dark pools despite the firelight.

'This will be my Last Telling,' said the shadow.

Ordorin wondered whether the Teller was playing at trickery, reaching his own fist towards the chiefship. Perhaps the Teller's call had been a ruse to get Ordorin away from the Grounds and the blood-ties that might help him. It was said the Tellers drew their dreams from human flesh.

The Teller's lips curled in a macabre imitation of a smile. 'Perhaps you're wondering why I summoned you,' his voice rasped again. 'Perhaps you're wondering why I've chosen to favour you above all others with the last and most important of my Tellings.'

Ordorin's grip tightened on his dagger. Could the Teller pluck the very thoughts from his head?

The Teller's bony hand groped at the skin bag at his waist and he dropped a clutch of leaves into the fire, the stench in the cave becoming the rank sweetness of rotting fruit. Abruptly Ordorin's blood took on the same ragged pulse that came with the cornering of a he-wolf or the sight of the naked flesh of his rival's join-wife. He was to be privy to something denied other warriors. Already he was wondering how he'd be able to use the information to their cost.

'Ordorin!' came the Teller's voice, jerking his attention back to the cave. 'How many ebis have you stolen this season from your neighbours?'

Ordorin's brows lowered, his eyes probing the darkness, judging the Teller's intent, but the air around him had thickened and his head swam.

'How many, Ordorin?' insisted the Teller.

For Ordorin, the Teller's voice had slipped into the same slow rhythm as the swirling, over-sweet smoke, the cave rippling in front of his eyes.

Ordorin felt the answer drawn from him. 'Eleven,' he said.

The Teller dropped another handful of leaves in the fire, turning the smoke white and sending shadow wraiths along the walls. They stretched and shrank, towering over Ordorin, then drawing back into the darkness. Ordorin watched them with heaving chest, unable to withdraw his gaze. Sweat slid down his back, then a new acrid odour filled his nostrils, making him forget his dagger and all memory of why he'd come.

'How many sons and daughters who bear their fathers' names carry your blood, Ordorin?' said the Teller, his voice seeming to come from far away.

Ordorin stared down at his massive hands. He'd used them to crush the life from a writhing neck more than once, but now they lay slackly against his knees as if they belonged to someone else.

'Seven,' he heard himself say.

'Tell me who fathered your grandfather, Ordorin.'

'Orkarnin.'

'How many sons did Orkarnin bring forth?'

'Four.'

'The third of these sons. Who was he joined with?'

'Marzeka.'

'And how many sons did Marzeka birth?'

'Five, but the second was ill-formed and died in his birthing-bag.'

The Teller nodded and his eyes gleamed, the following silence broken only by the flitter of bats hunting bessel moths high in the cavern. Ordorin had the unsettling sensation of gazing down at the shell of himself crouched beside the fire. The darkness was no less intense but his vision was more acute, so he could clearly make out the bony body of the Teller and his own stolid form. He craved his dagger, flatsword and spear.

'I did not bring you here for your wit *or* for your morals,' the Teller went on, 'I brought you here for your memory. This will be my last Telling, and the last Telling of the Shargh. No more Tellers will walk the Grounds or go where I go in dream. I am the last.'

The last? thought Ordorin, dazed.

The white smoke lit the Teller, making him burn brighter than fire but colder than death.

'What . . . what is it you would have me do?' said Ordorin, his tongue thick and unwieldy.

'Listen, then be my mouth.'

'Your mouth? But who am I to tell?'

'Your memory will carry on in your blood, as your appetites and lusts will. Take your first-born son and instruct him as I instruct you. In turn, his first-born son will be *his* mouth.'

'But . . .'

'Be silent and listen! I give you the story of the doom of the Shargh . . . and the power to undo it.'

The Teller's hand moved and the smoke blushed red, causing Ordorin's eyes to sting and weep. The shadow of the Teller stretched like a vast serpent around the cavern walls, imprisoning him. Ordorin's brain screamed at him to be gone, but his body was as heavy as stone.

Then a wailing filled the cavern, driving him before it – a reedrat under talon shadow – fleeing along the ways beyond the realm of sleep, beyond the earth times of light and darkness, to the realm of the Teller. This was the place of the impossible made possible, of the unimaginable given shape, of the void of beginnings and endings.

Abruptly the wailing stopped and Ordorin became aware of his thundering heartbeat, and above it the chant of the Teller, imprinting his body and mind and memory.

If Healer sees a setting sun
and gold meets gold, two halves are one.
Then Westerner with silver tongue
will love and lose the golden one
but bind a friendship slow begun.
If horses graze in forests deep
where trees their summer greening keep
then fire will be the flatsword's bane
and bring the dead to life again.
Deeds long past will hunt the Shargh
and funeral smoke consume the stars
until the thing that draws no breath
devours the dark that feeds on death.

Silence suddenly reasserted itself and the heaving shadows became the blank walls of the cavern. The light that had illuminated the Teller was gone too, leaving nothing more than a broken old man.

'Thus speaks the last of the Tellers,' the man whispered, his voice as sere as summer grass. 'Sleep now.'

Ordorin's head sank forward and he knew no more until roused by the dim light of day. His neck ached and his legs were no better, cramped and bloodless. He cursed as he massaged feeling back into them before staggering upright.

The cavern was empty but the Teller's message remained.

Many seasons later, deep in the south-west, wind rippled the canopy of an immense forest. High in a sever tree, Kira was showered with medallions of light, and a sweet mix of sever, castella, ashael and lissium scents were released into the air. From Kira's vantage point, the forest was a vast gleaming ocean, chattering as twigs clashed, locked, then broke free again.

'Don't be more of a fool than you already are, Kira!' came a voice from below.

Kira climbed even higher, partly to spite Tresen and partly to get a better view of the canopy. The intense blue of the sky made her squint after the muted light of the forest floor. If she were in an alwaysgreen she'd be able to see to the Third Eight, but the sever tree was smaller and more finely limbed, the branch she was on already protesting.

Tresen shouted again but his voice was lost in a cacophony of birdcalls as a flock of springleslips skittered away. Kira watched the yellow and blue flashes of the springleslips disappear among the branches and heaved a sigh. If only *she* could fly, up and away from the confines of the Bough, her father's disapproval and the squabbles of the Tremen, over the canopy to its very edge and beyond.

The thought brought the familiar shiver of fear. Far to the north, beyond the forests of Allogrenia, were the vast mountains and plains that the Writings spoke of: the terrible landscape of Kasheron's journey and the brutal haunts of the Terak Kutan. How could Kasheron, whose blood flowed in her own veins, be so different from his twin brother Terak?

The branch Kira was on creaked again and she swung herself down to a sturdier one, then descended hand over hand until she'd left the bright world of the leaf-ocean behind and was back in the cooler green-lit world below. It seemed an age since she'd last climbed high into the canopy, as she spent more time in the Warens now, exploring the Writings stored there. In the last few moons she'd ventured into the further caverns, finding Writings that spoke of Kasheron's journey, how he had established Allogrenia, named his people the Tremen and brought healing into being, using new herbs they had found beneath the trees.

Kira grinned at Tresen, still staring up, hands on hips, feet planted wide. From her vantage point, he looked so full of his own importance. Since he'd begun Protector training with Commander Sarkash in the Warens, he thought he knew everything, but she knew more about the Writings and could still jump better than him, *and* from greater heights, if she chose.

'Kira! Come down!'

By the 'green, he was turning into a nag, she thought, strolling to the end of the branch and lowering herself into a crouch. No doubt he thought her still too high to jump but she'd done so from these heights before, and so had he before the Protectors had curbed his freedoms and made him *sensible*. A honeysprite chirruped above her head, then the wind woke again, making the bough dip. Stinking heart-rot! Her arms windmilled and she grabbed at the foliage, slicing her hand in the process. Ow! They weren't called sever trees for nothing.

At least Tresen had given up bawling at her, she thought, sucking the wound and quickly scanning the forest floor. Where was Kandor? Surely Tresen hadn't let him wander off? Her clanmate was poking at a shelterbush with his sword, pretending to ignore her. She opened her mouth to shout but thought better of it. It'd be quicker to jump. Crouching carefully, she glanced back and forth between the ground and the branch, estimating her height and visualising her landing. It was a long time since she'd made such a jump and doubt stirred, but she dismissed it. Taking several deep breaths to loosen her muscles, she pushed off.

For a wonderful moment she was flying, the fragrant air an intoxicating mix of sunlight and shadow, birdsong and silence. Then, too soon, she hit the ground with a terrific impact. There was an explosion of leaf litter as she relaxed her knee joints and dipped her shoulder into a roll. But instead of coming up and over and back onto her feet, the force of the landing threw her forward again and onto her belly, slamming the air from her lungs. There was a horrible moment of suffocating panic, then the blessed relief of a lungful of air.

'Not one of your more skilful efforts,' observed Tresen dryly.

Kira spat the leaf litter from her mouth and struggled to her feet, ankles throbbing and pain spearing her back. Breathing was difficult too, and she remained bent, as if her only concern were brushing the litter from her breeches.

'Wh . . . where's Kandor?' she asked, when she had enough breath.

'I've sent him back to Enogren.'

Kira's head jerked up, sending another spasm of pain through her back. 'On his *own*? What in the 'green for?'

'He's nearly thirteen seasons, Kira.'

'I *know* how old he is.'

Tresen frowned, making him look like his father Miken, in one of Miken's sterner moods. 'He's old enough to get to the First Eight without you, and I judged the risk of him journeying alone less than the risk of remaining here.'

'What mean you?'

'We both know that jump was too high,' said Tresen, his finger stabbing skywards. 'And if you're going to take idiotic risks, it's only a matter of time before he will too.'

Kira bit back a retort, not wanting to argue with her clanmate. He was barely two seasons older than her and they'd been companions for as long as she could remember. But she'd scarcely seen him lately and she didn't want to spoil this time together.

'I would forbid Kandor to jump,' she said, picking up her gathering-sling.

Tresen threw back his head and laughed. 'Forbid him? Just like your father forbids you to go beyond the First Eight?'

'It's not the same,' said Kira, colouring. 'When I tell Kandor not to do things, he knows it's for a good reason.'

'True, but example is a more powerful teacher than words. Whereas your father . . .' Tresen paused. Despite his long friendship with Kira, he didn't have the right to say the words poised on the tip of his tongue. Kira's eyes had already dulled to moss green, a change he knew only too well.

Forcing a smile, he plucked a twig from her hair. 'You look like you've been in a fight with some sour-ripe and the sour-ripe won,' he said. 'Sit down and I'll salve your back and ankles.'

'They're not paining me. I'd rather we started back,' said Kira, anxious to find Kandor. 'I've gathered all the sorren I need.'

Tresen stepped in front of her, blocking the way. He was a good head taller than her now, and no longer the shortest of the new Protectors. In another season, he might even be able to look Commander Sarkash in the eye – if he dared. Kira jiggled impatiently, trying to get round him.

Tresen's smile became genuine. 'Oh come now, Kira, credit me with *some* Healer-knowing. We're both Kashclan after all, even though you're mightier than me, oh Healer Kiraon, dweller of the wondrous Bough, heart of all learning and healing.'

Kira grinned, some of the gold returning to her eyes, and Tresen relaxed a little. She was still the uncomplicated clanmate he'd spent his childhood roaming the forest with, despite this Turning making her a woman.

He thought of Seri and his smile faded a little as he recalled their latest quarrel. It was a shame she wasn't more like Kira.

'Has anyone ever told you how bossy you're becoming?' muttered Kira, plonking herself down.

'No one important,' said Tresen equably, raking about in his Protector pack for some salves and offering up thanks for Kest's pedantry. *Protector Leader* Kest, he corrected himself. He could almost feel the Protector Leader's ice-blue eyes on him as he fumbled about. It was a Protector rule that a basic healing store be carried at all times, and it was one Kest enforced rigorously. All Protectors' packs were supposed to contain icemint, bluemint, sickleseed, sorren, falzon bandages and stitchweed. It wasn't much compared with the Healer's pack Tresen used to carry, but then Healers didn't have to lug food around for five- or six-day patrols, nor sleeping-sheets, knives or swords.

Kira eased off her boots, watching Tresen remove the cloth stoppers from pots of icemint and bluemint. He looked older suddenly, perhaps because his hair was cropped in Protector-style, and the fuzz on his upper lip she'd taken to teasing him about was missing. He'd obviously been using clear-root.

'And how's the beautiful Seri?' asked Kira, watching him carefully. Mikini had told her Tresen was heartsick for the pretty Sarclanswoman.

Tresen's rich brown eyes flashed to hers but his face remained determinedly expressionless. 'I wouldn't know; I've been busy with more important things. Now, what would you like on those ankles? Icemint for the strain or bluemint for the jarring?'

'Perhaps both.'

'Both? It must've been a *really* good jump this time,' he said, lathering a dollop of icemint onto her ankle and massaging it into her skin, his strong fingers seeking out the points where the pain was greatest, making Kira groan. The air soon filled with a sharp fragrance, reminding Kira of when she'd first gathered icemint. It'd been the first time she'd used a herbal sickle too, the first time she'd touched metal. How proud she'd been to lay the shoots in her sling, but also relieved to slide the sickle back into its ornate pouch, no longer having to touch its slippery coldness.

The hilt of Tresen's sword gleamed now in a dapple of sunlight as he worked, and a sense of repugnance surged back into Kira, her thoughts turning to the clash between Kasheron and Terak, the gold-eyed twin princes of the north. Their eyes had been remarkable enough, a gift from their mother, a powerful woman in her own right, who'd ruled after the death of her bondmate the King. It had only been the peoples' love for her – that had lingered after her death – that had staved off the catastrophe as long as it had. For what land could be ruled by twin kings – men who mirrored each other in looks, but whose hearts were as different as sunlight and shadow?

Kasheron had inherited his mother's love of healing, but Terak emulated his father's warrior ways. And so, the people had sundered. Kasheron left the northern lands to the savagery of his brother, and brought his followers south. Many generations later, the descendants of Kasheron and his followers made up the Tremen, eight clans who had established longhouses in a circle round the centre of the Bough. Because of the limited nature of the food the forest offered, the longhouses were a quarter-day's walk from the Bough, and nearly a half-day's walk from each other.

Kasheron had declared metal *prasach* because it could sever the green and growing, inflict terrible wounds, even end life. Metal cooking pots, eating knives, tree-axes, shaving-blades, buckets, buckles, bracelets, brooches and beads were all shunned in Allogrenia.

Yet Kasheron had retained some metal, including herbing sickles carried by the Healers; swords worn by the Protectors; and the Leader's ring of rulership – with its Tremen alwaysgreen and Terak Kutan running horse. Given Kasheron's hatred of killing, the retention of swords was the least explicable to Kira. Perhaps the blood he shared with his brother couldn't be entirely denied, or perhaps the seasons of fighting he'd endured in the north had imprinted his very being. Whatever the case, Protectors continued to carry swords long after Kasheron's death, despite the fact that no stranger had ever penetrated the vast forested depths of Allogrenia.

'I've not seen much of Merek recently, or Lern for that matter,' said Tresen.

'Father keeps them well occupied,' said Kira, Tresen's rhythmic massage making her drowsy. 'He has Merek and Lern out beyond the First Eight gathering the last of the spring shootings, and in the evenings they must study the Herbal Sheaf.'

'What of you? Why doesn't Leader Maxen demand the same of his daughter as he does of his sons?' asked Tresen.

'I already know the Herbal Sheaf by heart, along with the cycles and shootings of all the herbs listed there well beyond the Third Eight.'

Tresen's hands stilled. 'The Third Eight! It's not safe that you go so far.'

'You're starting to sound like father.'

'Perhaps he's right on this occasion.'

Kira jerked her foot away, eyes flashing gold. 'There's nothing in any of the Writings I've studied in the Warens that speaks of dangers greater than withysnakes and heart-rotted trees.'

'Yet we unmake paths and keep the ways of the Warens secret, and all men must train and do their duty as Protectors.'

'They're traditions from the Sundering, when the forest seemed as wild and dangerous as the north! Kasheron's people brought their fears with them but they were ill-founded. No stranger's ever found a way into Allogrenia.'

Tresen paused, considering a group of tippets squabbling over a nest of bark beetles, the tippets' sharp beaks snapping up the beetles with brutal efficiency. Since beginning Protector training, he too had gained greater insight into the Writings, which recorded things never discussed outside the Warens.

'We don't know that no one's found their way in,' he said carefully. 'Allogrenia's massive. Who's wandering in the east while Protectors patrol the west? Can you say? I certainly can't. The Writings merely tell us what common sense confirms: that no place can ever be entirely safe.'

'You sound just like a Protector these days,' grumbled Kira.

'Good, that will please Commander Sarkash. I fear the poor man has all but given up on me. He keeps scratching his head and comparing me unfavourably with my father.'

'That's unfair!'

Tresen smiled, pleased at her indignation. 'Perhaps, but it might be accurate. Protector Leader Kest's a lot kinder. He simply says I have much to learn. Now turn over and I'll salve your back.'

Kira rolled onto her belly. Tresen pushed up her shirt and scooped the bluemint onto her skin, making her wriggle.

At least Commander Sarkash and Protector Leader Kest were fair, thought Tresen, working the tightness from Kira's muscles. They might be scathing over his failures but they also acknowledged his small accomplishments. Kira, on the other hand, worked late into the night poring over the Herbal Sheaf and spent much time in the Warens, sorting through the Writings in the training rooms and in the rarely visited caverns beyond. Yet her father ignored her efforts, though he was quick to take her to task for any misdemeanour, no matter how small. Miken had once said that Maxen's coldness towards Kira stemmed from the loss of her mother, but it was beyond

Tresen how Kira could be blamed for her mother's death. Fasarini had died birthing Kandor, not Kira.

It seemed to him more likely that it suited Maxen to push Kira aside, especially now her healing skills were equal to his. He'd certainly made it clear that he favoured either Merek or Lern for the leadership after him, though what Maxen's scheming could achieve – apart from making Kira miserable – was beyond Tresen. The leadership wasn't passed from father to eldest son automatically, as had occurred during the cursed times before the Sundering. Instead it was gifted on the basis of healing skill, a blessing begun by Kasheron and enduring still. Each new generation of Tremen produced a Healer whose skills shone more brightly than the Guide Star and Kira was clearly the one, a fact that was increasingly whispered about.

Tresen wiped his hands on his breeches and tossed the salves back into his pack. The decision as to who the next leader would be was the Clancouncil's to make in any case, and fortunately wouldn't have to be made for many seasons. Maxen was a strong man, and hale, while Kira remained wayward. The Third Eight indeed!

Kira was busy pulling on her boots, her single braid as light as candle-flame where it caught the sun. Seri wore her hair like Mikini: intricately braided around her face, joining into a weave at the back and decorated with ashael beads. Tresen half smiled. Seri, with her slightly upturned nose, reddish brown hair and soft curves, was a typical Sarclanswoman. It was hard to believe she was only a season older than Kira. From a distance Kira looked like Kandor.

Tresen hefted on his pack, pushing his sword out of the way and wondering again how the more experienced Protectors managed to run at full speed without tripping over them. Then, catching Kira's hand, he pulled her upright.

'Ah, you Protectors are so strong,' said Kira, her eyes pulsing between green and gold, a characteristic that unnerved people who didn't know her well. She smiled up at him in the way Seri did, but without realising its effect.

'Shall we go back to Enogren, oh mighty Protector?'

'Yes,' he said, unnerved by the surge of attraction he'd felt. By the 'green, she was his clanmate! 'You lead,' he said tersely.

'Shouldn't you go first to protect me?' said Kira, still smiling.

Tresen busied himself adjusting his sword. 'I don't think you're in need of protection but *I* might be if I meet Protector Leader Kest or Commander Sarkash. I'm further east than I should be.'

'I remember a time when you didn't care about such things,' said Kira.

'Perhaps I've grown up.'

Kira saw that he was genuinely worried. 'If we meet any Protectors, I'll tell them you're aiding me in my important search for fireweed,' she said.

'Fireweed? I've never heard of it,' said Tresen.

'They won't have either.'

'Are you saying it doesn't exist?' There was no way he would lie, even to escape a humiliating punishment.

'Oh it exists all right and it's important. I'm just having trouble finding it.'

He stared at her in mystification but she'd already set off.

He started after her, taking a parallel course. The Protectors roamed as far as the Sentinels, yet never trod the same ground twice under the same moon. Nor did the Healers, whose seasonal collecting took them to the same gathering places over and over again. All lands beyond the Arborean had to remain unmarked by paths.

Kira went quickly, seeming to know where every boulder and hole lay hidden under the drifts of greygrass and simpleweed. Unfortunately Tresen didn't, and he stumbled often, coming close to rolling his ankle.

'Those salves seem to have worked wonders,' he panted.

'I don't like to think of Kandor alone,' said Kira apologetically.

Tresen pushed his sword out of the way for the umpteenth time and wiped the sweat from his face. The day was turning out to be hot, and though spring had yet to grow old, the air was heavy with the summery scent of russetwort. He was tempted to tell Kira again that Kandor was safe, but it would be pointless. While she was reckless of nearly everything else, she was almost too careful with her younger brother.

A leaf thrush erupted from the dense stand of shelterbush to his left but he scarcely noticed. Kira had all but disappeared among the trees, forcing him to lengthen his stride to catch her. The crash of their passing dwindled and the leaf thrush came back to its roost, but had scarcely begun preening again, when it was forced to quit once more.

A short, powerful figure emerged from the thicket, stood for a moment staring after Kira and Tresen, then slipped away to the north-east.

2

The Bough was the grandest building in Allogrenia and had long been the home of the Tremen leaders and their families. Set in the centre of the Arborean, it was the heart of the Tremen community, both geographically and in its focus on healing. The Bough had a large hall running its entire length – used for communal gatherings – and had sleeping and work rooms opening off along one side. The work rooms included a Herbery to dry and store herbs, and a Haelen to house the sick and injured. Apart from the Haelen, it was an internal design mirrored by the longhouses deep in the octads. The Bough's roof was more steeply pitched than the clan longhouses though, and its eaves, lintels and ceiling beams more heavily carved. Only the Morclan longhouse rivalled it in ornateness, for Mormesh's followers were known for their woodworking skills; indeed it had been Morclansmen who had executed the work on the Bough countless seasons past.

Kira wasn't thinking of the Bough's history as she sat at the massive table in the grand hall taking her evening meal with her father and brothers. Instead she was thinking about the sullen throb of her back. She'd have to get Kandor to salve it when her father had retired for the night or else she'd be in pain for the next moon.

She shifted uncomfortably on the unpadded chair, then peered up at the carved ceiling beams in an effort to distract herself. As a child they'd frightened her, their images transformed into leering Terak Kutan by the firelight. But now she found them beautiful, with their carvings of sour-ripe entwined with lissium; alwaysgreen, castella and fallowood leaves flowing in scrolls; and honeysprites, tippets and springleslips arced in flight.

Kira had only been to the Morclan longhouse once as a child and remembered little except the strange designs woven into the Morclan tunics. Yet she had a sudden yen to visit again. Any such visit was unlikely, however, as her father had developed an antipathy for all things Morclan.

'There's more metal in Morclan than the cursed city of the Terak Kutan,' he'd sneered recently.

Kira rubbed at her back surreptitiously. Another reason why she'd be unlikely to see the Morclan longhouse again was her father's recent prohibition on her journeying. 'The Bough must always have a Healer within,' he had said, eyes steely. But with him, Merek and Lern all able to heal, Kira failed to see why she couldn't be spared.

Maxen was in his usual position at the head of the table, talking about something or other. Kira caught Kandor's eye and he flicked one eyebrow up and down and contorted his mouth in comical shapes, while somehow managing to keep the side of his face nearest their father still. In spite of her aching back and gloomy thoughts, Kira struggled not to giggle. Their father forbade impropriety during meals.

Fortunately Maxen had turned to Merek and was now droning on about council business, Merek listening attentively and nodding in all the appropriate places. Not that it was any hardship for him;

Kira's eldest brother seemed to agree with most things their father said.

The conversation came to an end and Kandor straightened and assumed a dutiful expression, his fair hair catching the firelight. Kira hoped it wouldn't darken like her father's, or her other brothers', for Kasheron had been fair and it pleased her that their noble ancestor's blood showed more strongly in her and Kandor than in the rest of the family.

The talk at the table ebbed and flowed. Sendra's teeth clicked on a pile of pitchie seeds, a soggy collection of husks growing in front of the elderly helper. Kira had never liked pitchie seeds, but they contained enough sustenance to keep a traveller hale for many days, and without them Kasheron and his companions wouldn't have survived their first winter.

'If her cough doesn't ease, you'll need to concoct a syrup of three parts annin to one part brenna oil,' her father was saying to Merek.

Kira roused. 'What cough is this?'

Lern took a gulp of thornyflower tea and wiped the wetness from his lips. 'Thinaki, daughter of Lomarkon. She's been in the Haelen since this morning. Lomarkon says she's been coughing for three nights, and nobody in their longhouse can get any sleep.'

'So he's brought her here to rob us of ours,' grumbled Merek.

'Is the cough wet or dry?' asked Kira.

'Dry,' replied Lern.

'Then she should be having something more soothing than brenna oil.'

'Kiraon,' her father's voice cut in icily, 'you weren't in the Haelen this morning to examine her, so I fail to see how you can make such a judgement.'

'If the cough's dry, then it would be better treated with honey.'

'Lomarkon said they'd tried honey but it hadn't worked,' offered Merek.

'Lomarkon hasn't the wit he was born with,' broke in Sendra.

14

'I remember when his first bondmate Birishi gave birth. Lomarkon thought the babe would do better if nut oil were added to the wet nurse's milk. Nut oil! We had six days of scouring before your dear mother – may she rest easy 'neath the 'green – found out what the trouble was.'

Sendra placed her calloused hand over Kira's. 'She was a lot nicer to that fool than I would've been. He needed a good knock on the head with something solid to get his brain working. But your mother sat him down with never a harsh word, and explained to him that a mother's milk was like the finest draught of withyweed ale to a baby, and you couldn't improve on withyweed ale. He seemed to understand that and the baby thrived. Still, that was your mother all over. She always knew what to say and how to say it.'

There was a brief silence broken only by Sendra's sniffing, but Kira felt little sadness, remembering hardly anything of her mother and rarely thinking of her. It hadn't always been so. When she was younger she'd yearned to know everything: the colour of her mother's hair and eyes; her favourite bird and tree and flower; where she'd liked to roam and gather; and how she'd healed.

Her father had made his disapproval of her questioning plain, and in Kira's ninth or tenth season, he'd simply forbidden it. 'Your mother is at rest beneath the alwaysgreen, and shouldn't be disturbed,' he'd said.

Kira could still remember the cold finality of his eyes, and they were the same now, staring at her over the rim of his cup.

'And where have you been this day, Kiraon?'

Kira felt Kandor tense and avoided looking in his direction. 'I've been gathering,' she said, reaching for a piece of Sendra's special nutcake as if her only concern were hunger.

'I didn't ask what you'd been doing, I asked where you'd been.'

'I gathered in and around Enogren.'

'In and around Enogren,' her father mimicked, studying her unblinkingly. 'As I have specifically forbidden you to go beyond

Enogren, I'm assuming that "in and around" means only the land west of Enogren.'

Lern and Merek had stopped talking and Sendra's teeth had fallen silent.

'The stocks of sorren were exhausted. I needed to go a little way east to gather more.'

'You went beyond the First Eight?'

Kira's heart flapped like a broken-winged bird. Her father knew that sorren didn't grow within the First Eight; every Healer at the table knew it, just as they knew it was a powerful purifier that the stores in the Haelen must never be without. But her father wasn't interested in any of these facts; he was only interested in whether she'd defied his will.

'I went beyond the First Eight,' she admitted.

'And you took Kandor with you?'

'I left him at Enogren,' she said, the heat rising in her face, though she refused to drop her gaze. Let him prove her deceit if he could; he wasn't going to bully Kandor as well.

'And, in your judgement, it was safe to abandon your brother and go off as the whim took you?' His voice was silky, but his eyes were as hard as axe-wood.

Abandon Kandor? How dare he! 'The Protectors deem the First Eight safe and have never imposed any limitation on travel within them *or* to the longhouses. Of course, if you believe they err in this matter, perhaps you should discuss it with Commander Sarkash,' she said, gazing at him innocently, though inside a small voice crowed in triumph.

'In going beyond the First Eight, you disobeyed me,' said her father, abruptly changing tack. 'This flouting of my authority is not new in you Kiraon, and it becomes you less and less. You're nearing seventeen and as a resident of the Bough, it behoves you to set an example to others, and particularly to your younger brother. You're too old to go traipsing about dressed like some wild Terak Kutan

16

of the north, and too old to spend as much time as you do with Protector Tresen.'

'Tresen? But we're clanmates,' said Kira, staring at her father in astonishment. Did he know she had been with Tresen this day?

'Precisely!'

Kira searched the others' faces, at a loss to know what her father's objection was, but Merek was intent on his nutbread and Sendra sat with her eyes downcast, while Kandor looked as bewildered as she.

Only Lern was prepared to offer something. 'Father's saying that people might think you're courting,' he said uncomfortably.

'But we're *clanmates*,' repeated Kira, staring at her father in shock. Was he suggesting she'd break the Tremen law forbidding bonding between clanmates? Maxen's flinty eyes stared back at her and she realised he knew she and Tresen were only friends; he was simply using their friendship as a weapon against her.

'In penance, you will confine yourself to the Arborean for the next moon, and conduct yourself as a member of the Bough should,' said Maxen. 'You will wear clothing befitting your position and you will not go wandering about the forest gathering; there are sufficient gatherers within the Bough without you doing so. You may heal in the Haelen if you wish, though there is little enough to do there for myself and Merek and Lern. At the end of this moon, we will discuss this matter further.'

A whole moon! 'But father . . .'

Maxen's hand slammed down on the table, spilling Lern's tea and scattering Sendra's pitchie seeds. 'There will be no more discussion on this matter! Is that understood?'

Kira's eyes blazed but her father's were the harder and she was forced to nod.

Maxen relaxed back in his seat. 'Now, as you've finished your meal, Kiraon, you may go to your room.'

*

Kira gave up the struggle to sleep somewhere near the mid point of the night. She'd forgotten to get Kandor to salve her back and it was throbbing, but that wasn't the main thing keeping her awake. She felt as if something was sitting on her chest, crushing and suffocating her. Throwing back the covering, she rose and went to the window. The moon was full, silvering the sweep of grass and limning the trees fringing the clearing. The Bough was one of the few places where the moon could be seen unimpeded by a mesh of leaves and branches, for Kasheron's followers had cleared a large circle round the Tremen place of healing.

It had always seemed strange to Kira that though there were no trees, the Northerners had named the area around the Bough the Arborean. But in the last moon she'd stumbled upon the answer to the puzzle. She'd been testing her knowledge of the Warens by travelling with an unlit lamp when she'd missed her turn and come upon a small storage room. It was damp and most of the Writings had mouldered away, but there were a few tantalising fragments still readable.

... seed of the al ... ns ... something Kira had taken to be always-greens *... has grown well, and seed from these first eight ...* something *... planted a day's march ... cared for by the octads ... the first eight now make a fitting crown for the Arborean ... one greater than je ...* Jewels, Kira had guessed. The rest of the Writing had disintegrated, but the meaning she gleaned from it was that the Arborean was crowned with a circle of alwaysgreens, the First Eight, a crown made of the green and growing, not the hardness of the metal and gems of the northern crowns. So originally the Arborean had referred to not just the circle of land around the Bough but a greater circle of land stretching to the Warens' entrance, which meant that her confinement in the Arborean would actually allow her to continue exploring the Warens. No doubt her father wouldn't quite see it in this way, she thought resentfully.

Beyond the window, the moon illuminated the trees. Enogren

would be as bright as a candle and as easy to climb as a stroll to the Kashclan longhouse. Her fingers beat a rapid rhythm on the window-sill. If only her father weren't Leader she'd be living in the Kashclan longhouse with the rest of her blood: Miken and Teserini, Mikini and Tresen, the Healer Brem, old Tilda, Arlen, Paterek, Werem ...

She swung away, colliding with the chimes hanging there and releasing a burst of woody music that she quickly stilled. Every child had chimes of alwaysgreen in their sleeping rooms to ward off harm. Her mother had hung these ones for her: a sun, a moon, a star and a mira kiraon; simple shapes singing a simple song, not like the Morclan chimes Teserini had told her about. Those took the shapes of things beyond the forest, including the sinuous running horse of the north. Her father wouldn't be pleased!

There were six paces between her bed and her door, and she counted them now as she had so many times before. Six paces, six paces, six paces. Miken had once joked she'd wear out his floor with her pacing. He'd said she should take to withyweed ale when she was upset, like normal Tremen. Miken joked with her often but her father never joked. Perhaps it came with the burden of leadership, this necessity of weighing every word, of controlling, of crushing. The sense of suffocation grew again, as if the air had thinned.

Suddenly a cry sounded, the shock of it like frost on flesh. The mira kiraon was hunting in the canopy, wild and free. She was out the door and halfway across the darkened hall before she was fully aware of where she was going.

Then another sound brought her up short. A bark, almost like an owl, but not the mira kiraon this time. It was too harsh for a frostking or a hanawey. She looked round wildly, searching for a darker shadow to hide in, then abruptly realised that it was Thinaki coughing in the Haelen. Kira cursed herself. She'd meant to check on Thinaki earlier but the argument with her father had pushed it from her mind, and now the poor girl had been left alone half the night in a strange and frightening place.

Thinaki's eyes widened as Kira opened the door.

'It's only Kira,' she whispered, coming across to the pallet.

Thinaki's grip on the blanket loosened as another bout of coughing took her. Kira laid her hand across Thinaki's forehead, feeling a moist heat. Her father had said nothing about fever. Thinaki's pulse was fast too.

'Do your bones ache?' asked Kira.

Thinaki nodded. 'And my head.'

'Did you tell the other Healers?'

'I told my father,' said Thinaki shyly.

And no one had questioned her further, thought Kira.

Thinaki was a summer younger than Kandor and had the dark hair and beautiful long-lashed eyes common among Barclan, but right now her hair was damp with perspiration, and her eyes over-bright.

'I've some salve that will take the ache from your bones, and a tincture to soothe your cough and cool you down,' she said, smiling reassuringly and patting Thinaki's hand. 'I won't be long.'

She went to the Herbery, not bothering to light a lamp. The room, which was drenched in moonlight, was filled with the smell of beeswax seals, and of the herbs hanging in bunches from the ceiling.

Kira worked quickly, returning to find Thinaki bent double over the pallet, another bout of coughing racking her body. She eased Thinaki back and began massaging the salve into her joints, inhaling deeply as she worked, the scent releasing her own tension.

'That feels good, Leader Kiraon,' said Thinaki.

'I'm not the Leader, Thinaki, that's my father.'

Thinaki flushed. 'Th . . . those of my longhouse call you Leader. They say you're the best Healer in Allogrenia since Kasheron himself.'

Such a sentiment was hardly likely to please her father! thought Kira. 'That's very nice of them, Thinaki, but not true. Now, I'm going to give you a tincture to soothe that cough and let you sleep. No, it's not evil tasting,' she added as the girl's nose wrinkled. 'You have my word as "the best Healer since Kasheron"!'

Thinaki drank it and settled back into the pillows. Her work done, Kira collected up the salve pot and empty cup and started to the door, Thinaki's eyes following her.

'Would you like me to sit with you until you go to sleep?' asked Kira.

Thinaki nodded and Kira came back, settling beside the pallet and smoothing Thinaki's hair from her forehead with long gentle strokes.

'Ah, Healer Kiraon, that feels nice,' murmured Thinaki drowsily. 'It takes away the pain.'

3

In the lands below the cave where his ancestor Ordorin had long ago received the Last Telling, Erboran bent and scooped the muddy water of the Thanawah into his mouth. The low sun threw his shadow across the grass as he scanned the dusty pasturelands and cloudless sky.

In the Older Days, the sorchas would've already been dismantled and the long trek north begun, following Nastril, burning low and bright on the horizon. In the Older Days, the young and the women who were large with child would sit astride the ebis, the sorchas and cooking pots lashed behind them as they skirted the Cashgars' eastern flank, journeyed across the Mahktan Plain and rounded the Braghan Mountains, to enter the rich pastures of the north.

In the Older Days! he thought, his eyes flashing and the muscles rippling under his skin. The tales of his people's dispossession were fresh in his mind despite the long seasons since Tarkenda had told them to him. The northern tribes had come together and taken all the lands north of the Braghans for their own, butchering the Shargh like fanchon. The fighting had been long and bloody, but in the end the Shargh had been forced beyond the Braghans' southern foothills. The defeat had broken them into four peoples.

Urchelen had led his remaining blood-ties deeper into the south looking for new pastures, and the Soushargh still dwelt there. Irkardin's people had become the Weshargh, taking their name from the western lands they'd retreated to. His own forefathers had settled here, in the shadow of the Cashgars, under Artmenton's rule. They'd been the only ones to keep the name – of the Shargh – the Sky Chiefs had granted them. But Urchelen and Irkardin had had more honour than Ashmiridin. *They'd* never dirtied *their* knees to the cursed Northerners to keep their grazing tracts, as Ashmiridin had. And Ashmiridin's blood-ties had honoured his treachery by continuing to use his name!

He scooped more water to his mouth and spat it back into the river, reminding himself that all that happened upon the earth, this dawn and a thousand dawns past, was the Sky Chiefs' will and couldn't be gainsaid, despite the carping of some on the Grounds. Even thinking such thoughts risked seeding past evils into the present.

He touched his palm to his forehead, begging the Sky Chiefs' indulgence. Then, for good measure, he tossed a handful of water over his head, cleansing himself of the memories. Shaking himself like a reedrat, he sloshed his way up the bank and settled into a loping run, head lowered, black hair streaming in the wind. The Grounds stretched away east and west, dotted here and there with ebis, while in front of him a single spur rose, set with sorchas glowing in the westering sun.

Yrkut the First had bequeathed them sorchas after he'd risen from the dust and spat his essence into the air, bringing the Shargh into being. As well as these shelters, he'd given them the wolves and the grahen; the moorats and the fanchon to hunt; and he'd given them the ebis' hide and hair, bone and sinew, meat and milk to feed and clothe themselves so that they might have the strength to give thanks and honour to those who watched over them.

Erboran brought his palm to his forehead in a habitual gesture, but he didn't alter his pace or vigilance. To the west, thirty-two ebis grazed with twelve ebi at their feet. In the next few days, the ebi would number twice that if the birthings went well, the rains came and the grass grew green again. Away in the stone-trees, an ebis bull bellowed and a shrill squawking erupted overhead as a flock of marwings broke from the trees, clashing and squabbling, before coming together in the shape of a spearhead. Erboran smiled and some of the tension lifted from his shoulders. The sky might be bereft of clouds and the air as warm as fire coals, but the marwings' flight augured well.

Erboran ran on, his long stride bringing him to the roots of the spur, but he didn't lessen his pace as the land steepened, for he was Chief of the Shargh and could run with equal strength over flat land or hilly. He continued to scan the surrounding lands as his muscles propelled him up the slope, his eyes confirming the dryness of the pasture, the grazing places of the ebis and the manner of bird flight. After a time he came to the first of the sorchas.

Dugeda, Irsulalin's join-wife, sat outside, busy fashioning a carrier from horiweed. She brought her palm to her forehead on seeing Erboran and he acknowledged her. Irsulalin's sorcha was low on the spur but he and his blood-ties were loyal to the first-born chiefs. Ermashin's sorcha was next, but it was deserted, as was Orshenkon's. It was possible the two were north of the Shunawah, hunting wolf or fanchon in the Cashgars, or wood-gathering in the burrel and stone-trees, though he doubted it. He grimaced, exposing a set of perfect teeth, knowing that Urgundin and his blood-ties would be absent too.

He veered across the spur's back and down its eastern slope, where the lowest sorchas were set, mirroring their owners' status and lack of Voice, noting without surprise the absence of Urpalin, Orthaken and Irdodun, although Urpalin's join-wife Morsuka and his elder son were there, and acknowledged him respectfully. Doubtless they would mention his visit to Urpalin.

Ignoring them, he loped back up the slope, his legs carrying him forward while his mind roved over the blood-ties of his people.

Blood-ties could work for or against him, and for or against his dear brother Arkendrin. All Shargh palmed their foreheads to him, as they must, but who would be loyal to Ordorin's line of first-borns, and who would hover like marwings over grahen nests, waiting for an opportunity to break their way, was yet to be tested. There were certainly those who were attracted by Arkendrin's wild talk of reuniting the Shargh and taking back the northern lands; those who chattered like chipbirds with memories as short as summer storms.

Erboran pounded past Urgundin's empty sorcha and up to his brother's, empty too. He continued to the highest sorcha, his own. The Chief of the Shargh lived above the Shargh, both figuratively and literally.

It was dim inside, for the vent was shut, and he let his eyes adjust before peeling off his shirt and tossing it on the bed. It was saturated, the sweat adding to the odours of smoked meat, cheese, slitweed and air too long confined. Taking a drinking bowl from the shelf beside the firepit, he drew a draught of sherat and gulped it down as his gaze flicked around the room to make sure all was as it should be.

His spears stood next to the bed, the leather circlet of chiefship with its metal horns lay on the table, his spare daggers and flatswords were propped next to the door. Under the table, cured meat and last season's cheeses lay tumbled together in broken baskets, while his cape and other spare clothes were tangled on the floor. Tarkenda was right; it did lack a woman's touch, and his thoughts drifted to Palansa, daughter of Ordaten, son of Orkandon, son of Ermamandin, son of Arpapan the One-Arm. Her mother was sister to Irsulalin's join-wife, but it was not the long loyalty of the line that attracted him. He'd watched Palansa for several moons now. As well as her beauty, there was a containment about her and a pride in her bearing that hinted at thoughts beyond the chatter of many of the young women on the spur. He'd told his mother that he had no intention of taking a

25

join-wife yet, despite her insistence that it was time he fathered an heir, for why tether his ankle to a single woman, when the whole spur was his to be had? But now as he thought of Palansa, he wondered if he'd spoken truthfully.

He sucked the dregs from the bowl, feeling the liquid warm and loosen his muscles, and drawing a second draught, wandered back into the cooling air outside. The setting sun was painting the pasture gold and staining the sky the colour of blood. The springer-bugs were beginning their evening chitter.

He sipped the sherat slowly, staring down the slope to where several women had gathered, his eyes searching out Palansa. His heart quickened as he caught sight of her holding a basket on her hip while she talked to the other women.

Something flickered on the edge of his vision and his gaze jerked west. Shargh warriors on the run. Even as he watched, they split into two groups, one turning at the Thanawah and following it down, the other fording it and heading straight towards the spur. His brother ran in front. Judging by the sudden sundering of the group, he had no wish to be seen with his company. Erboran swirled the sherat in his mouth, his hand drifting to the cool metal of his flatsword. His younger brother's greed for the chiefship was mostly a small irrita-tion, like the blackflies of summer, but if Arkendrin had coerced the likes of Urgundin and his blood-ties into following him, then . . .

Erboran watched them with eyes as hard as ebis horn. He was the first-born son of Chief Ergardrin, the last in a line of first-borns that stretched back to Ordorin, the Mouth of the last of the Shargh Tellers. Ordorin had been a man of strong memory but stronger hands and Erboran had inherited both traits, as had Arkendrin, although Arkendrin had also inherited Ordorin's faithlessness and lust for power.

Dismissing thoughts of his brother with a shrug, he turned his attention back to the gathered women, watching Palansa moving down the slope towards the Thanawah, her hair swinging in rhythm

26

with her hips. Draining the sherat, he tossed the bowl back towards his sorcha and sauntered down the slope. Palansa was of an age where she could have had several lovers, yet she hadn't come before him in a Joining Ceremony, and he knew from his mother, Tarkenda, that she hadn't slipped away to lie in the targasso stands either. Tarkenda was privy to all the doings on the Grounds, most little more than gossip, but Erboran had learned early in his chiefship that it was useful to know the small private acts and moments of unguarded speech of those he ruled.

Palansa disappeared over the lip of the spur but Erboran continued his leisurely pace, enjoying the prospect of his coming meeting with her. He glanced about as he went, the sherat coupled with the pleasant ache in his muscles from the long run home making him unusually content. Smoke spiralled from the cooking fires he passed, carrying with it the smell of roasting meat, and his people lounged in front of their sorchas exchanging news of the day's doings.

In the great arc of darkening sky, Wistrin suddenly winked into being. Erboran watched it as he walked, for it was the eye of the Sky Chiefs, who commanded birth and death and the fortunes of every Shargh warrior in the long day in between. No one knew when they might be summoned to leave the earth and join the Sky Chiefs in the cloudlands above. His own father had been scarcely older than he was now, when he'd been called home. Erboran came to an abrupt stop. What if the Sky Chiefs were to call him home now, *without sons*? All this would be Arkendrin's.

His contentment dissipated like spit on firestone. No secondborn would break Ordorin's line! No secondborn would have what was his! His gaze flashed over the sorchas, seeing nothing. His blood already flowed in sons owning others as fathers, but that was all for naught if none carried his name. The next Chief must be indisputably his, the firstborn of a firstborn, growing in the belly of a join-wife who'd lain with no other. His face relaxed and he smiled.

*

Palansa lay curled in her bower of slitweed, her head propped on her hand, listening to the distant lowing of ebis and watching the follow-star Nastril burn in the sky. Wistrin, Maghin and Sonagh glittered nearby, firing as the sky darkened to purple. After a while she rolled onto her back, absently stripping the seeds from a stem of slitweed. What other peoples were being silvered by the stars now lighting her? Soushargh, Weshargh, Ashmiri, perhaps even the savages in the north. The Sky Chiefs were mighty and their children many, and she had long harboured a yearning to tread Grounds strange to her.

She sat up, hugging her knees. The Thanawah muttered softly as it flowed away, but what lay at its end? She'd heard tell of vast forests in the south-west, trees so thick they swallowed the sun. Did they also swallow the Thanawah? Her father had joked with her when she was small that if she wandered too far the trees would eat her as well, but her mother had assured her it wasn't so. Still, the idea of the world beyond the Grounds was intriguing. Perhaps she'd send a message. Using slitweed, she fashioned a little boat, tucking the stalks under carefully and setting it gently on the water. For a moment it wobbled, tangled in the detritus at the river's edge, then the current took it and spun it out of sight.

'Where have you gone, little boat?' she murmured.

The slitweed crunched with the unmistakable sound of foot-steps and she scrambled upright, staring around wildly. Surely Arkendrin hadn't returned? Semika had told her he'd gone off with the warriors, or else she'd never have risked coming here alone. Many welcomed Arkendrin's attentions, anticipating improving their fortunes by rising up the slope. Palansa wasn't one of them and so far she'd managed to turn his attentions aside without insulting him. But what tale could she spin him now? It was almost as if she'd chosen this place to tryst.

The reeds were thrust apart and she gasped. It was Erboran! She dropped her head and brought her hand to her forehead, her heart thrashing in her throat.

'Who's your lover?' he demanded, his eyes boring into hers.

'I don't have a lover, Chief Erboran,' she replied, flattening her wet palms against her skirt.

'You were speaking to someone,' he said.

'I was speaking to myself. I came here to watch the stars and listen to the river, that's all.'

Erboran's expression eased a little. 'So you're not waiting here for your lover?' he said softly.

Palansa's mind began to work. The possibility of her having a lover had clearly angered him. Surely he wasn't jealous? Maybe he knew that Arkendrin sought her and wanted to spite his brother by taking her first. The last thing she wanted was to be his temporary prize, cast aside as soon as his goading was complete.

'I have no lover,' she replied, keeping her eyes down, 'but often now I am followed . . .'

'By Irpurlin?' asked Erboran, naming one of the younger Shargh whose preening has earned him the ironic title of chipbird.

'By someone . . . higher on the spur.'

'Is it Arkendrin?' he asked.

Palansa hesitated and the slitweed crunched as he came nearer. He was more handsome than Arkendrin, taller and leaner, his skin smooth, his lips finely shaped.

'And has my brother been satisfied?' he asked.

'I'll go to no man's bed unless as his join-wife,' she said.

'And of course, Arkendrin has offered only his flesh,' murmured Erboran.

He was so close to her now that she could smell the sweat on his skin and the sherat on his breath, but there was more to him than just the odour of a long day. Power clothed him like a wolf-cape, and there was a sinuous grace in the curve of his shoulder, in the muscles under his skin and in the tendrils of hair curling on his neck.

'So, the beautiful Palansa has her pride,' he said, bringing his hand to her face. His rough fingers caressed her cheek, turning her face to his, then his mouth fastened on hers. His lips were salty, his kisses hardening as his hand slid to her neck, finding the opening of her shirt. Palansa felt the heat flare in her own body as his hand moved over her breast, gently flicking her nipple till it stiffened. Her breath scoured her throat and she had to stop herself clinging to him.

'Would you come to the Chief's bed?' he asked.

Palansa swallowed. 'The honour is great, but I must think of my sons.'

'As my join-wife?'

His join-wife? The blood pounded in her head. To be the Chief's join-wife and mother of the next Chief was second only to being the Chief himself. The thought was wild, intoxicating. But was Erboran merely toying with her? There was desire in his face but no mockery. She nodded.

'It's done then,' said Erboran, his hand lingering on her breast. 'I'll announce it at the morrow's Speak.'

Erboran strolled back up the slope, well pleased with his evening's work. The urge to take Palansa there and then had been strong, but the sons she'd bear must be unquestionably his, and so his pleasure must be postponed until the morrow's night. His blood quickened again in anticipation. Palansa's full mouth hinted at a passionate nature, and her flesh had responded to his quickly, nor was she dull-witted like some of the women who'd come to his bed. Her answers to his questions had been respectful, but clever.

There was also the delicious irony of announcing their joining at a Speak his brother had called. He smiled, then threw back his head and laughed.

4

The highest sorcha on the spur was stifling, despite the sun having slid beyond the sweep of grasslands some time ago. Heat lay trapped by the skin walls, heavy with the sweat of the assembled Shargh. Despite an oppressiveness hinting at summer storms, there were no purple-black clouds boiling above the Braghans; there'd been none for many moons.

Tarkenda sat quietly, her shirt sticking to her skin, her eyes on her sons at the front of the gathering. In the dim light they looked similar, but the shadows were deceiving. Despite being younger, Arkendrin was broader in the shoulder, carrying his father's heavier brows and straighter hair. He also shared his father's impatience with the delay thinking imposed on action. Erboran, by contrast, was both taller and more lightly built, and content to wait until things were more thoroughly known.

Tarkenda pushed the damp hair from her brow, silently thanking the Sky Chiefs she'd birthed Erboran first. There had been many Chiefs like Arkendrin before the loss of the northern pastures, their recklessness having fuelled the Shargh's defeat. Arkendrin's fieriness

31

still attracted many of the warriors who hadn't experienced the long seasons of privation following the fighting, with the hunters and the herders dead, the ebis scattered and the wolves ravening. Only old women like herself remembered such tales.

Her face remained impassive, despite her thoughts, as she gazed around the sorcha. Arkendrin had ensured many of his cronies were present, even those low on the spur. Urgundin was there, his eyes sliding everywhere, along with his Voiceless blood-ties, Irdodun among them, puffed up with their own importance. Also in attendance were those loyal to Erboran: Erdosin; Irsulalin, with his level head and willingness to question; Ormadon and his son Erlken; and Irmakin and his blood-ties, some of whom linked to Irsulalin.

There was a clear division in the warriors gathered under the hide roof, a rift seeded by Arkendrin's jealousy and fed by the privations of the rain-starved earth. While the final schism might not come this night, its arrival was as certain as an ebi's birthing after ten moons. Tarkenda reminded herself that whatever came was the Sky Chiefs' will and not hers to question. There'd been a time, though, when her acceptance hadn't been so freely given.

Erboran had still been at her breast when her belly had grown large again, and she'd offered sweet shillyflower and cakes of honey and squaziseed to the Sky Chiefs, entreating them for a daughter. But they'd decided otherwise.

Worse was to come, for scarcely had Arkendrin joined Erboran at her breast, than the Sky Chiefs had called Ergardrin home. For twelve long seasons she'd acted as the Shargh Chief, waiting for Erboran to grow, until finally he'd taken his father's circlet from her hand and placed it on his own head. In that time Arkendrin had grown too, as had his envy of his brother and his hatred of their birth order.

Erboran sat on the hide of chiefship facing the gathering, the metal horns on the circlet of chiefship winking in the firelight, his flatsword and spears lying crossed in front of him, the blades pointing outward. Though Arkendrin was speaking, Erboran's eyes were fixed on Urgundin, seated before him, who fidgeted under his gaze, dribbles of sweat migrating slowly down his neck. Erboran watched their progress with a slight smile, before finally transferring his attention to his brother.

'. . . and so we come to you, our Chief, as is our right, to share our voices with you and to seek your wisdom,' said Arkendrin, finishing the traditional Speak of Greeting and bowing his head to just the required depth.

Erboran regarded him in silence, extending the moment Arkendrin must remain bowed, before beginning the Response.

'I, Erboran, Chief of the Shargh, *first*-born son of Ergardrin . . .'

Tarkenda watched, heavy-hearted. Each Speak had to begin with this exchange. How many times had Arkendrin gathered a Speak to badger his brother about this or the other, and then been forced to endure the public reminder of his lesser position? If only Arkendrin could accept the reality of his birth order, thought Tarkenda, he could garner the glory he craved by supporting Erboran in his tasks. Instead, they were like blackflies stuck in a web, with the struggles of each threatening to bring the sucking-spider scuttling to destroy them both.

Erboran's response drew to an end. '. . . *first*-born son of Ordesron, *first*-born son of Ordorin, Mouth of the Last Teller of the Shargh, will hear you.'

With the ceremonial part of the meeting dispensed with, Arkendrin straightened his back, all semblance of humility gone.

'I bring to this Speak that which the Shargh have long dreaded,' he began, then paused theatrically, his gaze sweeping the gathering. 'In seasons long past, the last of the Shargh Tellers predicted our ruin. It is fitting that I, Arkendrin, who carries the blood of the great Ordorin, the first Mouth of the Last Teller, should be the bearer of bitter tidings.'

Fixing his eyes on Erboran, he announced, 'The first part of the Telling has come to pass; a gold-eyed Healer haunts the forests to the south-west. If we do nothing now, the rest of the Telling will unfold and doom will overtake us.'

Arkendrin's followers had clearly known what he was going to say, but Erboran's hadn't, and a storm of speech erupted among them. Irsulalin and Ormadon looked to Tarkenda as if seeking guidance, but her face remained impassive, a skill she'd acquired during her time as Chief to help her survive the sneering opportunism of those who preferred a broken bloodline to a woman's rule, however temporary.

After a while, the noise ebbed and attention focused on Erboran's response.

'The Telling does not speak of a *gold-eyed* Healer,' he said pleasantly, ignoring the import of his brother's announcement.

Arkendrin's expression remained unchanged, obviously expecting this objection. 'The Telling speaks of a Healer. This woman is of the people who live in the forests. They keep no animals but spend their time gathering things no man can eat: bark, seeds and leaves. They can have no other use for them but healing. The Telling speaks of gold, Chief Erboran, and she has golden eyes. No one has golden eyes. Even the cursed goatmen and horsemen of the north, with their hair of dry grass, don't wear the sun in their faces. No, this woman is the creature of the Telling.'

'You forget that the Last Telling only comes into being *if* the Healer sees a setting sun,' said Erboran, his smile brittle. 'Would you bring her out of the trees and ignite a fire to devour us all?'

'The dead see nothing.'

There was another torrent of discussion, much of it based on the garbled versions of the Last Telling that flourished lower on the slope, for the Last Telling was known in its entirety only by Ordorin's line. It no longer mattered though; Arkendrin had captured the hearts of those present and that demanded action by the Chief.

Erboran remained motionless, refusing to be swamped by the debate raging around him. Arkendrin might be at his most dangerous when he raged and blustered, but the opposite was true of her eldest son. He would be digesting Arkendrin's words, sifting his intent, weighing his strengths, finding his weaknesses. Finally his voice rang out, powerful and hard, slicing through the hubbub like a flatsword.

'Arkendrin! You have indeed brought us a message of immense import, and we offer thanks to the Sky Chiefs that they've chosen *you* to send us this warning. We are grateful, indeed, that it was *you* who was gifted with the sight of this cursed gold-eyed Healer, possibly the bane of which the Last Teller spoke.'

Arkendrin faltered. 'I . . . I haven't seen her.'

The assemblage muttered.

'*You* have not seen her?' said Erboran coldly. 'Then who might we thank for this warning?'

'It was Urgundin's blood-tie Irdodun who was granted the sight.'

'In that case, I'm surprised you judged the matter worthy of bringing before me, and before the other warriors present.'

Tarkenda watched Arkendrin struggle – and fail – to regain control of the Speak. He'd thought the import of his message would be enough to bring the gathering to his cause, but he was wrong. Irdodun was the lesser blood-tie of Urgundin, and had no Voice. Arkendrin, like his father before him, had failed to think beyond the moment.

'She's the creature of the Telling,' asserted Arkendrin, straining to be heard above the growing rumble of speech.

'Then bring me proof.'

'Proof?' Arkendrin's gaze flicked to Urgundin.

'I can do nothing to protect my people until I have proof. Bring me this gold-eyed Healer, alive and blinded or dead.'

The sorcha hushed and the gathering turned expectantly to Arkendrin, but for once he hesitated, his face now oily with sweat, his body rigid.

'Is the task too difficult for you?' goaded Erboran.

'The forest is endless, its stinking trees clothed in darkness whether the sun's risen or set, but *our* people will have their proof, Chief Erboran.'

Erboran inclined his head. 'It's urgent they have it soon Arkendrin, for you might carry our doom in your hands. However, I recognise your *difficulties*. You have until the full moon after this to complete what you've pledged.'

Erboran turned back to the gathering. 'It's fortunate my brother has called a Speak at this time,' he began, 'for there's another matter of great import to the future of the Shargh that I wish to announce.'

The sorcha hushed, the only sound the call of mawkbirds away on the Grounds.

'Let it be known that I take Palansa, daughter of Ordaten, son of Orkandon, son of Ermamandin, son of Arpapan the One-Arm, as my join-wife, and that my first-born son will be Chief of all the Shargh, to rule in the time after I pass to the lands of the Sky Chiefs above,' he said proudly.

There was a ripple of surprised approval. Palansa was a good choice, despite her family's lack of Voice, thought Tarkenda, possessing an intelligence and confidence that augured well for the future of the chiefship. But Arkendrin's anger and frustration were palpable. Tarkenda's head swam, then the sorcha walls were ripped away. It was as if she were floating, looking down at snow-capped mountains above a golden plain. Shargh warriors were being cut down by men on white horses, and funeral pyres were piled high with Shargh dead.

The vision dissipated as quickly as it had come, leaving Tarkenda sweat-soaked and reeling. Breaking convention, she stood, and stumbled outside, clinging to the side of the sorcha while she sucked air into her lungs. No woman was a Teller, and no Tellers had walked the Grounds for countless seasons. So why had the Sky Chiefs chosen her, and why now? Other questions even more terrible burned too. Had her vision been the backwash of something already passed, or something yet to come? The sky in her vision had been as starry as the one above, but without beauty, promising only suffering and death. Stifling a groan, she made her way unsteadily down the slope.

5

The mira kiraon arced through the predawn darkness, a leafmouse dangling from its beak. Alighting on a castella branch, the owl's eyes flashed gold as it watched a figure pass beneath. It waited till the forest was silent again before beginning to eat.

Kira went quickly, oblivious to the owl hidden above her, the dew-laced air beading her cape and filling her senses with silversalve and icemint. The forest canopy was chinked with moonlight but Kira's stride would have been equally swift had the night been cloudy. Tremen were keen-sighted, their vision honed by seasons living in muted light, and Kira's sight was particularly acute. Some said it was a trait passed from her forebear Kasheron – a man renowned for his surefootedness – but others argued it was a natural counterpart to her healing ability. Certainly Healers had to see the smallest herbs hidden in litter or shadowed by shelterbush, as well as recognise the subtlest changes in leaves and stems denoting ripeness and potency. Whatever the case, in all her growing, Kira had never lost a game of find, much to Tresen's and Kandor's annoyance.

She rushed on without pause, scarcely aware of the world

turning back towards the sun, the air beginning to lighten and the castellas and chrysens shrugging off their night-time browns and blacks. Her belly growled, forcing her to chew on pitchie seeds. Her father had gone to the Clancouncil at the Kashclan longhouse and she hadn't wasted time breakfasting, needing all of the day to reach the Warens, explore the Writings, and return before him.

The shrill calls of springleslips finally penetrated Kira's thoughts and she smiled in delight. *Dawngreeters*, Kasheron's folk had called them, and it was apt, their joyous voices announcing that the sky was now ripe for flying. The branches whispered under the dart of their blue and yellow plumage. After a while there came the sound of water, too, and the trees gave way to a stream lined with stones as round as tippet eggs. Tossing down her pack, Kira settled on the bank, letting the chill water run through her fingers.

The Drinkwater rose north-west of the Renclan longhouse and exited the Arborean through the Kashclan octad. It had once serviced all the octads, the clans carting water for drinking, cooking and bathing. It must have been hard, thought Kira, hauling buckets through the stands of shelterbush and bitterberry, through the tearing grip of sour-ripe vines, up and down stony slopes and drifts of leaves. Even bucketing water the short distance from the roof-barrels was a chore children bickered over. Kira snorted as she recalled the rumour that Morclan brought water inside using hollow branches. Whoever had spread that tale must've imbibed too much withyweed ale!

Cupping her hands, she drank deeply, the water clean and bright and tasting faintly of cinna, a welcome change from the moss-tainted water of the Bough. Emptying her waterskin, she refilled it from the stream, then started back along the path.

'Kira! Kira! Wait!'

By the 'green! Kandor must've run all the way to have caught her here. She watched him dashing towards her, the scatter of sunlight and shadow painting his hair honey-gold then brown, his face red with running. When he was almost upon her, Kira gave a whoop and set off in a mad sprint, tunic clutched high, leaf litter spurting from her feet. Trees flashed by and Kandor's voice wailed in the distance.

'Kiraaaa . . .'

Taking pity on him after a while, she came to a halt – breath scouring, chest heaving – and flopped down on a sever log. How quickly her muscles were softening during her confinement!

Finally Kandor came plodding up, collapsing beside her. 'That was . . . a mean trick,' he panted.

'You're just annoyed because I can run faster than you.'

Kandor's head came up. 'That's not true and you know it. I'll race you the rest of the way to the Warens.'

'It's not behaviour behoving someone of the Bough,' she said, mimicking her father's clipped tones exactly.

'Neither's this,' said Kandor, rolling off the sever with theatrically flailing arms and lying prone in the leaf litter.

Kira laughed.

Kandor's dive into the leaves had roused the scents of russetwort and redreed, summer herbs, despite spring having not yet ended. 'It's going to be a dry season,' said Kira.

'That's what Tresen says too,' said Kandor, tucking his hands behind his head.

'Oh, does he now? It must be true then, if a mighty Protector says it. And when did you see Protector Tresen?'

'At the Kashclan longhouse yesterday. Father sent me with some of Sendra's nutcakes for today's Clancouncil. Tresen came home as I was leaving.'

It was nearly a moon since Kira had seen Tresen and she missed him more than she liked to admit. Between her father's prohibitions and Tresen's Protector training, their jaunts together seemed a distant memory.

'And what else did he have to say?' she asked, hauling Kandor upright.

'Oh, that he's been on patrol beyond the Third Eight for a moon quarter, and that he's now such a fine swordsman that Commander Sarkash does nothing but heap praise upon him.'

Kira rolled her eyes, plucking another sprig of pitchie as she walked.

'He asked where you were, and said to tell you his patrol came back past the starstone and the rednuts are almost ripe. He's on leave for the next moon quarter and suggested we can pick them together. We can go and get them, can't we?' said Kandor, catching her arm. 'It seems an age since we were there.'

Kira hesitated. The starstone; she couldn't remember whether it had been her or Tresen who'd named it. It was just an irregularly shaped pale boulder really, not star-shaped at all, perched right on the edge of the Everflow and shrinking in size each time they visited it. Yet it remained special. The rednuts grew on either side and they would sit on the stone at the end of the day's harvesting, gorging themselves and telling wild tales of what they'd do when they were all full-grown.

The groves were in Kenclan octad, just beyond the Third Eight, well over two days' journey from the Bough. The rednut trees were prolific and Kenclan had never objected to their occasional harvesting by other clans. From her tenth season and Tresen's eleventh, they'd gone there. Filling their packs with dried osken, beggar leaves and fruit, they'd set off through the trees, taking turns to carry Kandor when he was very small, and setting their sleeping-slings high in the ashaels at night.

'Can we go, Kira?' asked Kandor, blocking her way, his eyes almost level with hers. At this rate he'd be as tall as Merek by the end of the season.

Kira considered quickly. Her penance in the Bough was almost finished, and she'd been to the rednut groves many times before. Her father couldn't possibly have any objections. And it would be so good to be there again, just the three of them.

41

'Yes, we'll go,' she said, grinning.

Kandor whooped and capered, pulling out his pipe and playing a lively tune more commonly heard in the training rooms than in the polite company of the Bough.

'Your playing's certainly improved,' said Kira, laughing. 'Can you manage "The Parting"?'

Kandor nodded and, carefully adjusting his fingers on the pipe, began to play. His efforts were faltering, and now and then he hit a wrong note, but the air was filled with the poignant melody. 'The Parting' told the story of when the northern peoples had been broken, with Kasheron bringing his followers south. But Kira always thought of it as Birika's song, not Kasheron's, for Kasheron's bondmate had left her father and brothers in the north, never to see them again.

What must it be like to lose everyone? she thought, her eyes filling with tears.

Kandor's arm came round her, his face creasing in a crooked smile. 'My playing's not that bad, is it?'

'It's beautiful,' said Kira thickly.

The entrance to the Warens was so close to Nogren's bole that Kira and Kandor had to edge round it in single file. Kasheron's people had probably planted the alwaysgreen there to disguise the fissure in the rock, thought Kira, or maybe they simply hadn't realised how big the tree would grow. Kira let Kandor go first, pausing to look up into the alwaysgreen's heavy, dark foliage, a favourite haunt of the mira kiraon. The trees of the First Eight were massive and far older than the Bough; Kasheron had brought the seeds from the north and planted the great circles of the Eights long before the longhouses and the Bough had been built.

There were no gold eyes winking down at her today, and with a sigh she followed Kandor into the first cavern, chill after the summery air outside and filled with an instantly recognisable odour of wind-blown leaves, twigs, dry blossom and the stone's peculiar scent.

The Warens were gloomy, and in parts damp, ignored by all but the Protectors who lived there during their training and service, and organised the storage of each season's excess gathering there. Still, Kira found a certain enjoyment in their solitude, away from her father's chilly disapproval and the Tremens' sideways glances and whispers about her eyes. Lately she'd found more time to read the decaying Writings in the further caverns. Had they been left to moulder because they spoke of Terak ways? She didn't know and she daren't ask her father in case he forbade her from going there.

'Ah, the lovely gold-eyed Healer of the Bough.'

Kira started, irritation rousing. She didn't go round greeting people by commenting on their eyes, or hair, or ears for that matter, yet people felt perfectly free to do so with her.

'I'd thought this day dreary but I see now that fortune's smiling on me,' the speaker continued.

He was very tall and Kira had to tilt her head back to look at him; Morclan, she guessed, for no other clan had hair as white as hoarfrost. He also had the blue eyes common among Morclansmen and women. His self-assured manner was no doubt due in part to the Protector Leader insignia he wore at his shoulder.

'I have no idea who you are,' she said bluntly.

His smile didn't falter. 'Ah, I am disappointed, Kiraon.'

She glanced beyond him to the tunnel Kandor had disappeared into, regretting her delay at Nogren. This man, whoever he was, was wasting precious reading time.

'I'm Protector Leader Kest, of Morclan,' he said, noting the direction of her gaze.

Tresen's commander. Was that why he expected her to know him? She couldn't recall him coming to either the Feast of Turning or Thanking, and with eyes like those, she'd surely remember him. Not that all Tremen made the journey to the Bough, choosing instead to celebrate in their own longhouses.

'Ah, you lead my clanmate Tresen,' she said politely.

He remained intent on her but she didn't know what else to offer, and with a brief nod went to pass on. Annoyingly, he fell into step beside her.

'You go to the stores?' he asked.

Kira hesitated, caught between the wish to be free of him and a reluctance to lie. 'No, beyond the training rooms.'

Kest frowned. 'It's unwise to go further than the lamps. Not all of the Warens have been mapped and it's easy to become lost.'

This was all she needed: a man as bossy as her father! 'I've been well beyond the lamps many times, Protector Leader Kest, and I can assure you, I've never been lost.'

He looked at her doubtfully and she softened her voice. 'Please don't be concerned on my behalf. I'm a Healer and healing requires an excellent memory. I could stand here and recite the entire Herbal Sheaf to you, and every cavern and tunnel turning between here and where I'm going . . . if I had time,' she added, smiling sweetly.

Kest hesitated, clearly unconvinced. 'I request you report to one of the Protector Leaders on your return so that we know you've come out safely. Protector Leaders Kertash, Pekrash and Dekren are within today. You'll find them in the training rooms.'

Kira nodded, quickening her steps, and he gave a small, informal salute, watching her until she'd disappeared into the gloom.

Kiraon of the Bough, he mused, Tremen Leader Maxen's only daughter. He hadn't seen her for two seasons, not wanting to 'enjoy' Maxen's company at the Turning celebrations. She'd certainly changed, even if she did still wear her hair like a child. How old would she be now? he wondered. Merek was coming up for twenty-six at Turning and Lern must be twenty-two, having finished his Protector training a season ago, which must make her close to seventeen. His men regularly reported seeing her wandering about beyond the Third Eight, which was baffling considering Maxen's propensity for controlling Allogrenia and everyone in it.

Kest followed in Kira's direction, taking several more turnings before coming to the Water Cavern. The spring that surfaced through the stone gave the cavern its name but also its moisture, making it useless for anything other than filling the water barrels for the training rooms, and occasionally replenishing the waterskins of Protectors who'd either forgotten or were unable to visit the Drinkwater.

Commander Sarkash had asked him to check the flow, something Kest did regularly, but which most Protectors saw little point in. The amount of water in the subterranean river was a good measure of rainfall north-east and north-west of Allogrenia and therefore of the likely growth of forage plants in the northern octads. What he saw now didn't augur well, for the level was lower than last moon, and that had been lower than the moon before. It was news that Sarkash would pass on to Maxen at the Clancouncil, not that Maxen would welcome it, Kest thought, as he made his way back towards the entrance. Maxen didn't welcome anything he didn't have control over.

Kira travelled quickly, habit rather than necessity making her count the caverns to either side. Lamps flickered on the walls, set in wooden brackets driven deep into the stone, some lighting empty caverns to confuse any would-be attackers. Not that an enemy had ever found their way into Allogrenia, nor a friend for that matter, but Kasheron's legacy of care and caution endured long after other ways he'd brought south had been forgotten.

The echo of voices heralded the stores and she took a deep breath as she plunged into a brightly lit cavern, crowded with Protectors busy stacking the season's growth of osken. The cavern was well suited to storage, with straight walls and deep crevices in the ceiling bringing in draughts of dry air from above. Kira had expected to find Kandor here, lurking between the bags of beggar leaves, pitchie and nutmeal, begging blacknuts or dried mundleberries. But he was nowhere to be seen. He must have gone on to the training rooms, or at least she hoped he had; it would be annoying to have to waste time searching for him.

The Protectors greeted her cheerily as she hurried on, the smooth floor of the tunnel descending and the air growing moist. Three more cavern entrances passed, dark slashes in the stone, then the sound of clashing metal reached her ears, running along the stone walls. The noise grew, with gruntings and thumpings joining the screech of metal against metal. Kira's heart quickened.

Before Tresen had begun Protector training, they'd slipped in here to use the practice swords, sometimes with each other, sometimes on the sawdust-filled effigies hanging from the cavern's ceiling. Tresen would pretend he was the mighty Kasheron, and Kira his bondmate Birika, fighting off foes on their epic journey south. It had been quiet then, but it wasn't now, Protector Leaders bawling instructions to men in the full throes of fighting practice, the air filled with the thud of battle and the acrid odour of sweat.

Kandor was perched on a side bench, his eyes bright with excitement as he watched two men practising with real swords. The fight looked genuine, the blades flashing in the lamplight, their points slicing dangerously close to each man's unprotected flesh.

Kira screwed her eyes shut, reminding herself that the Protectors didn't embrace killing any more than she did, and honed their skills only to keep the Tremen safe. The practice ended and there was a scatter of applause. Kira opened her eyes in time to see the combatants embrace and begin towelling themselves dry.

'I lost you in the tunnels, so I thought I'd wait for you here,' said Kandor, springing lightly from the bench.

'I was held up by Protector Leader Kest of Morclan. He seemed to think I should know who he was.'

Kandor assumed an expression of solemnity. 'Really, Kiraon, I am most disappointed. It behoves you to greet your future bondbrother graciously.'

'What?'

'Merek's pledging to Kest's sister at Turning.'

Kira gaped at him. Was he playing at trickery?

'Father's said nothing,' she said, eyeing him.

'That's probably because he knows nothing. Merek has been careful to keep it to himself,' said Kandor.

'Obviously not careful enough,' said Kira, recovering enough to start searching for a lamp among the clutter on the shelf behind him. 'How is it you know?' she asked, checking the box of flints she'd found.

'Oh, I don't spend my days buried in mouldy Writings in dark caves. Merek and Kesilini needed a messenger to carry their little love notes. I've been happy to oblige, since Morclansman Jadek is a wonderful piper and happy to teach anyone who shows an interest. Love is a wonderful thing,' he said, glancing at her sideways. 'Kesilini is as beautiful as her brother is handsome.'

'So it's been a fair trade,' said Kira, ignoring his teasing, and checking the nut oil in the lamp. 'Music training for scouting.'

'I might stay here, Kira, if you don't mind. Mendrin said he'd have a turn with me when the men have finished.'

'But only with practice swords,' she warned.

Kandor's face crumpled in mock disappointment. 'Oh, I was planning on using a real sword like our mighty clanmate, *Commander* Tresen.'

Kira made her way along the darkened tunnel, the unlit lamp in one hand, the other hand skimming the wall. She'd told Kest she had an excellent memory, and so she did, but it had to be worked at, and the best way of doing so was to find her way in the dark. The cavern floor was mainly smooth, so she was able to make good time, counting the openings as her hand trailed into nothing, and noting the occasional pools of warmer air telling of vents in the roof. These dwindled the further she went, the air becoming closer and wetter until she came to the cavern she'd discovered on an earlier jaunt. Setting down the lamp, she fumbled through the pots and pouches of pastes and herbs in her pack for the flints; it took a considerable time and she'd gone through every curse she knew before the wick smouldered into life. *Patience, Kiraon, is not one of your virtues*, her father's admonishment echoed in her ears, adding to her ill temper.

The Writings were as she'd left them, spread out on the musty floor, and her frustration was forgotten as she crouched over them, mould transferring to her tunic without her noticing. Miken had told her many peoples lived beyond Allogrenia, using different tongues, and that even the Terak Kutan didn't share a single language, which was why Onespeak had come into being. None of this mattered in Allogrenia, except to the Healers, for the Herbal Sheaf was written in Onespeak as well as Tremen, and Kira had spent much of her childhood struggling with it.

She'd complained bitterly about learning everything twice, but as she'd grown she'd come to understand that healing didn't belong to a single people, nor should it. It was a gift to be given freely, her knowing gifted to her from all the Healers who'd gone before. Still, it had been difficult learning Onespeak, and while her knowing of the healing words was thorough, she struggled when the language spoke of other things, as it did now. Her eyes skipped over the page, searching for references to healing and herbs, especially the mysterious fireweed she'd read about on an earlier visit.

Finally she sat back on her heels, shoulders aching and eyes burning, her early excitement a dry ash of disappointment. There was much in the Writings about the brutality of the world beyond the trees, of a people called the Shargh, of their flatswords and of the wounds they inflicted, but nothing of any use to her, such as information about fireweed.

Dusk must be settling on the world outside and her father would soon be returning to the Bough. She got stiffly to her feet, hating to leave the Writings in the damp darkness but unwilling to take them with her in case her father confiscated them. With one last look, she went back to the tunnel, faced the way she must go and extinguished the lamp.

6

The sever had been pushed over by last winter's storms, but it wasn't dead, its roots still searching the earth for nourishment, its canopy forming a snug and private bower. Merek and Kesilini lay together, their eyes on the window to the sky the falling sever had punched through the canopy, and on the brightwings flashing iridescent in the moonlight.

'I love it when the moon's big,' murmured Kesilini.

'So do I,' said Merek, 'for I can see you so much better.' His fingers stroked the exposed skin of her shoulder.

Kesilini wriggled closer, drawing in his scent. 'You're supposed to say how beautiful it is, and then compare me to it,' she chided.

Merek continued tracing the curve of her shoulder and she loosened the lacings of her tunic further. 'You *are* beautiful and you know I love you. Must I include glib talk of the moon?'

'No,' said Kesilini, though she wished he would. Merek had no time for the frivolities of other couples nor did he share their views on lovemaking, making it plain early in their courting that they'd not be sharing a bed until after they were pledged. She willed his hand to stroke lower, but he continued to caress her shoulder. Kesilini sighed and Merek's hand paused.

'What troubles you, my love?'

'I was just wishing that Turning had passed and you were coming home with me.' He kissed her on the lips and she pulled him closer, kissing him hungrily. 'Come to my longhouse this night,' she said thickly.

'Soon, soon we'll be together,' he whispered, caressing her cheek, 'but in the Bough, not your longhouse.'

Kesilini looked at him, startled. 'But . . . I thought you'd be coming with me to the Morclan longhouse. Surely there's no need for you to stay at the Bough, not with your father and Lern and Kiraon all able to heal.'

A hoarse, barking cry sounded away in the canopy and for a moment Merek was silent, listening. 'A hanawey, I think,' he said, tucking a tendril of Kesilini's hair back into one of the ornate plaits circling her head. 'You should teach Kiraon how to dress her hair properly.'

Kesilini said nothing and Merek sighed. 'I don't think Lern's heart is in healing,' he said. 'It wouldn't surprise me if he went back to the Protectors.'

Kesilini couldn't see Merek's expression, but he sounded put out.

'Will your father be angry?' she asked.

'Lern makes his own decisions,' said Merek shortly.

The tock of a bark beetle started above their heads and Kesilini moved restlessly. 'Even if Lern leaves the Bough, your father and Kiraon can heal and maybe Kandor, too, when he's grown a little. Kest's seen him gathering with Kiraon. Surely that's enough? It's said your sister's skills are so great she'll be Tremen Leader one day.'

'That's for the Clancouncil to decide.'

Kesilini snuggled back, trying to reassure herself with the familiarity of Merek's presence, but she was troubled. Their own Clanleader, Marren, had said Kiraon's skills were as great as Kasheron's, and Marren was not a man easily impressed. Surely there'd be no debate about her becoming Leader? Perhaps Merek wanted the leadership for himself. The idea was as shocking as it was unexpected.

'What think you?' asked Merek after a while.

'Nothing,' she said, lacing her top.

Merek tweaked one of her braids. 'Come now, Kesilini, we're almost pledged. Do you think I can't tell when you're upset?'

She stopped and turned back to him. 'Would you put yourself before your sister for the leadership?' she said, heart skittering.

'It's the council's decision, Kesilini.'

'What about your father?' What had Kest said? *Maxen's arrogance is exceeded only by his ambition.*

'What about my father?'

'Would he have the council overlook Kiraon for the leadership?'

Merek slipped his jacket back on and helped Kesilini to her feet, bringing his arm around her as they walked.

'How many female Leaders have there been in Allogrenia, Kesilini?'

'Two.'

'Sinarki and Tesrina,' confirmed Merek. 'And how old were they when they died?'

Kesilini shrugged helplessly.

'Let me tell you. Sinarki was eighteen seasons and Tesrina twenty-three. The first Kiraon, whose skills, it's said, exceeded those of her son, didn't live to see her twenty-seventh season.'

'What are you saying?' said Kesilini, stopping. It seemed to her suddenly that naming their own Kiraon after Kasheron's mother, the great northern Healer-Queen, was a bad omen.

'I'm saying, my love, that healing exacts a price, and that the greater the healing gift, the greater the price.'

Kesilini remained staring at him and he took her hand. 'Come.'

They walked on in silence, picking a path through the moon-iced trees, carefully stepping round the occasional tangles of sour-ripe. Bitterberry blossom rambled through the shelterbush, spilling its perfume into the air, and moon moths hovered, attracted by its scent.

'But surely male Healers suffer in the same way,' said Kesilini after a while.

'The Writings suggest not. They've enjoyed much longer lives than their female counterparts. Perhaps because they're less skilled,' he added dryly.

'Is that what your father believes?'

Merek laughed. 'By the 'green, no! And I doubt anyone in Allo-grenia would have the nerve to suggest it.'

'So what you're saying is that it's best that Kiraon's *not* Leader, or even heals?'

'I want Kiraon to live a long and happy life.'

Kesilini laid her head against his shoulder. 'But maybe it's not the same thing,' she said softly. 'Everyone knows she loves healing, and I'm sure she'd be miserable if she didn't do it. Kest says the Protectors have come across her gathering beyond the Third Eight.'

'I've no doubt they have. But Kiraon's almost seventeen, and soon she'll raise her eyes from the ground and see that there are young men in Allogrenia, not just herbs. I know father feels that Clanleader Farish would make her a worthy mate, but whoever she chooses, there will come a day when she will bond, live in her bond-mate's longhouse and bear his children.'

'You think it's better so?'

Merek raised her hand to his lips. 'Do you dispute the importance of love?'

'No, of course not.' She paused. 'Nor the importance of a large moon, which means your father will be taken up with council business and not wondering where you are.'

'So, the moon is good for something apart from highlighting your beauty?' teased Merek.

'Of course; it shows us the way home.'

*

It was dim in the Bough, the only light a gentle orange pulse from the fire. It gilded the oil casks and pots of beggar leaves, nutmeal and osken lining the shelves, also lighting up Kira's face as she sat curled in a chair deep in thought. She was scarcely aware of the fire or the piping drifting from Kandor's room, for her mind was on a passage in Onespeak she'd translated earlier that day.

She'd realised partway through reading it that it had nothing to do with healing, but she'd persevered, finally being rewarded with a description of silver horses racing across a golden plain. The only horse Kira had ever seen was the one graven on the Tremen ring of rulership her father wore, yet the picture in her mind was potent, rousing a strange, nameless yearning.

Abruptly the Bough door clicked and she sprang from the chair, hurriedly smoothing her tunic and noticing the mould for the first time. Stinking heart-rot! She brushed at it, feverishly rehearsing the version of her day's doings she'd formulated, which avoided lying to her father without actually revealing where she'd been.

'If this is all the welcome a noble Protector gets for trekking through the night in your service, then the hospitality of the Bough is lacking indeed.'

Kira laughed in relief. 'Tresen! How is it you're here?'

Tresen dumped his pack on the floor and pulled a chair to the fire. 'Well, as our fathers are presently engaged in Protector training using their tongues as swords, I thought it would be a good time to escape.'

Kira shifted a pot of simmering water deeper into the coals and retrieved the thornyflower tea from the shelf. 'What were they discussing?'

'Discussing? Bickering more likely, about the gathering rights of Morclan and Tarclan beyond the Third Eight, of all things.' Tresen jiggled the pot, watching the bubbles begin to rise.

'But no one gathers beyond the Third Eight.'

'Precisely. The fact that the whole thing is pointless is irrelevant to them both.'

It was typical of Tresen to blame both men equally for the quarrel, but Kira knew who'd probably started it, and who'd be refusing to let it go.

He poured the water onto the thornyflower, nodding appreciatively as Kira added a spoonful of honey to his. Tresen's sweet tooth had earned them many a bee bite in their growing, and the daring tales of how they'd managed to rob bees' nests high in the canopy had grown with each telling.

Tresen took a long sip of his tea and sighed, then settled back into his seat. 'It's a long walk to the Bough and I'm a little hungry,' he said, eyeing the cooking place hopefully.

'Fortune smiles upon you,' said Kira, straight-faced. 'I collected some scavengerleaf on the way back from the Warens. I'll get you some.'

'I said hungry, not starving and desperate.'

'Hoping for some of Sendra's nutcakes, were you?'

'There were scarcely any left at the council by the time I got there,' grumbled Tresen. 'They're always the first to go.'

Kira fetched the basket and emptied the last few onto a platter. 'It looks like they're the first to go here too.'

Tresen picked one up and took several large bites. 'Actually, the reason I'm here is not Sendra's nutcakes,' he said, cheeks bulging.

'Oh, really? It must be her pitchie seeds then.'

Tresen choked and Kira watched him in amusement. 'That nutcake doesn't seem to be doing you much good, Protector Tresen.'

Tresen finally managed to swallow, pouring himself a second cup of thornyflower tea and adding another generous dollop of honey. 'The reason I've come,' he said, ignoring her teasing, 'is for us to go to the starstone.'

Kira stilled. She'd told Kandor that they'd go, but that had been under the trees, not here in the hall, with her father's straight-backed chair looming out of the shadows. She bit her lip. 'I don't think I can.'

'Kandor told me your father's forbidden you to leave the Arborean until the moon's full. It's full tomorrow.'

Kira shook her head, unable to meet his eyes. 'That's tomorrow, not this night. I doubt father will give me permission in any case.'

'When did you ever wait for his permission?'

Kira's head came up, eyes flashing. 'You don't know what it's like! He's . . .' she stopped abruptly, swallowing several times. 'He can be very harsh with Kandor.'

And with you, thought Tresen, leaning forward and catching her hands. 'Dakresh was late again and the council didn't get under way till past noon, so they've decided to stay over and finish the council business tomorrow. No doubt your father will follow his usual practice of ensuring every discussion ends with his words, so he's unlikely to be back until the dawning after next. The moon will be well and truly full by then and his prohibition ended.'

Kira said nothing and Tresen's voice gentled. 'I've food and sleeping-slings in my pack. Come with me like you used to. It was so good, walking and talking together and sleeping in the ashaels, just you and me and Kandor.'

'Did I hear my name?' said Kandor, appearing from his room, eyes on the platter of nutcake remnants.

'No, you didn't,' said Kira.

'If you're talking about going to the starstone, I'm coming too,' said Kandor, dabbing at the crumbs.

'You know father's forbidden me to leave the Arborean,' said Kira tersely.

'Well he hasn't forbidden *me*,' retorted Kandor. 'Tresen and I could bring some rednuts back for you if you want to stay here, or you could come and harvest your own and risk our dear father's wrath. I don't think you've searched that way for fireweed, have you?'

Tresen stifled a smile at Kandor's guile.

'So, are we travelling as a twosome or a threesome?' asked Tresen casually.

'A threesome,' snapped Kira.

Kandor capered around the cookingplace, clapping his hands and whooping.

'Save your strength for the journey,' said Kira dourly. Then, turning to Tresen, she said, 'Give me a moment to change.'

As Kira headed towards her room, Kandor's smile vanished. 'There are times when I hate father,' he said, dropping his voice. 'He's never happy unless he's making Kira unhappy.'

Tresen stared at him in surprise. Having his own thoughts echoed was far from comfortable. 'Perhaps he has reasons for wanting her close,' he suggested diplomatically.

'Close? He can hardly bear to have her near him, or me for that matter. But it's worse for Kira because she's a Healer, and not just any Healer, the best in Allogrenia. I know it, you know it, and most of the clans know it, and that's what father can't stand.'

Tresen's surprise deepened. Kandor was the chubby-faced babe Kira had carried on her hip, the little boy with the serious brown eyes who'd trotted at her heels, the gangly youth with an easy smile whose wrists and ankles were now always too long for his clothing, not someone to utter unpalatable truths.

'I . . .' began Tresen, but at that moment he heard Kira's footsteps returning and she reappeared, clad in breeches and shirt, and carrying a gathering-sling.

'Do you have a waterskin?' she asked Kandor. 'And something warm to wear at night?'

'It's almost summer,' protested Kandor.

'You'll need a cape,' said Kira, filling her waterskin from the cask and checking the contents of her pack.

Kandor sighed and headed off towards his room.

Tresen watched Kira pull her pack closed and flick back her

plait. In the close-fitting breeches and shirt, she looked very much like Kandor, and more boy than girl . . . until she turned.

'*He can hardly bear to have her near him,*' Kandor had said. Kira didn't look like Maxen, nor for that matter, did Kandor, so they must look like Fasarini. Maybe they reminded Maxen of his bitter loss all those seasons past. This might be the explanation for his coldness towards them. Then again, so might Kandor's assertion that Maxen was jealous.

'Which way do you want to go?' asked Kira, heaving on her pack.

'You choose,' said Tresen, unsettled by his thoughts.

'If we journey more northerly first, we can spend the night in the ashaels, before swinging north-east,' said Kira, putting another piece of wood on the fire and pushing an errant coal back into place with her foot. 'I'll need to see Lern first, if he isn't sleeping. Wait for me on the edge of the Arborean.'

Tresen and Kandor made their way out of the Bough and through the scatter of espins and castellas, Kandor playing his pipe but Tresen silent, his mood of happy expectation dampened. If Kandor were right about Maxen, Kira's future held only misery.

They came to a halt where the espins and castellas gave way to denser stands of fallowoods, Kandor settling on a stump, but Tresen wandering up and down at the edge of the trees. The moonlight limned the great sweep of the Bough's roof, picking out the intricate carvings on the eaves and windows and lending them the fragile beauty of an ice-crusted web.

Kandor's breathy tune came to an end and he pocketed his pipe and began poking at the twigs around him, impatient to be gone. 'If father weren't Leader, we'd be living in the Kashclan longhouse with you and free to come and go as we wished,' complained Kandor. 'I hope Lern's not being difficult about staying.'

Not since Kasheron's folk had turned their backs on the

northern lands and entered the trees had the Tremen been without a Healer in the heart of their settlement. Gales might blow and even snow fall, and in the early days, wolves ravage and maim, but the Healer always endured, in a crude wooden shelter at first, and later in the magnificence of the Bough.

Tresen's fingers beat a tattoo on a nearby castella as he wondered if Lern were indeed being difficult. It seemed unlikely, for Maxen's second son was more like Kira than Merek in temperament. Merek was a stickler for rules, protocols and processes, especially when they suited him.

'What's Merek doing nowadays?' he asked Kandor suddenly, realising he hadn't seen Kira's eldest brother for some time.

'He gathers a lot with father,' mumbled Kandor, plucking at a stem of pitchie seeds, 'and he spends a fair bit of time in the Haelen updating the healing records.'

'Does he . . . ?' began Tresen, then forgot his question as Kira came swiftly through the trees. 'All's well with Lern?' asked Tresen.

'He's more than happy to remain as Healer . . . for his share of the rednuts.'

'Oh, that can be arranged,' said Tresen cheerfully. 'The first windfall is always plentiful.'

Kira giggled. The first windfall was notoriously small and the nuts often bitter. 'And Sendra gives you this,' she said, handing him a package.

'What is it?'

'Freshly baked nutcakes from the drying room.'

'They're for sharing,' broke in Kandor.

'Of course.' Tresen stowed them and reached for Kira's hand. 'I'm glad you've come.'

The warmth of Tresen's hand chased away the last of Kira's dread and she took a long, slow breath, pleased to be journeying again, Kandor on one side, Tresen on the other.

'I'm glad too,' she said.

2

Erboran dropped the load of washwood onto the floor and looked around his sorcha, still surprised by how different it seemed with the floor clear of his clothing and the air full of the clean scent of plateflower blooms, instead of sweat and soured food.

'Shelving for my join-wife, or it will be,' said Erboran, dusting himself down.

Palansa smiled delightedly, drawing him a bowl of sherat before settling at the table opposite him.

'Did you have to go far?' she asked.

'Nowhere is too far for my join-wife,' said Erboran, enjoying seeing her colour slightly. Her hair was loose, as he liked it, and glistened where it caught the light shafting in from the smoke-vent.

'Not drinking?' said Erboran, knowing full well that Palansa's parents disapproved of sherat.

'I'm not thirsty,' said Palansa, flicking back her hair and exposing the curve of her throat.

Erboran let the potent liquid swirl in his mouth. 'I think it's more likely you're still under your father's hand,' he teased.

'I'm less Ordaten's daughter than your join-wife,' she said, smiling.

'All of my join-wife,' said Erboran, rising. Palansa stood also and he came to her, slipping open the first button of her shirt. Her breathing quickened as his fingers moved to the second button, then the third.

He'd never bothered undressing a woman like this before, content for them to unclothe themselves before taking themselves to his bed, or simply pushing up their skirts and taking his pleasure as quickly as possible. But it was different with Palansa. Even the Grounds felt different to him. When he stood gazing over them now, he thought of Palansa by his side and later, their sons there too.

Erboran reached the last button and peeled the shirt from Palansa's shoulders, exposing her breasts. Her breathing had quickened, her mouth already searching for his. He tasted the sweetness of her breath and felt the insistence of her body as she pressed against him. His kisses moved down her neck to the hollow of her shoulder. She was clinging to him now, so that it was no effort to lift her onto the bed.

Erboran began to struggle out of his shirt, but Palansa stilled his hands. 'Let me,' she said with a grin, clambering up on him and easing him out of it.

Her hair fell over her breasts and he could feel her hot moistness as she sat astride him, her fingers on the lacings of his breeches intensifying his need of her. With a groan he pulled her close again, her hair cool against his skin as he rolled her gently beneath him.

Arkendrin plunged his blade into a tree, jerked it sideways, and sent another gouge of wood spinning into the undergrowth. He strode forward, counting under his breath and forcing his way through a dense stand of grasping tendrils before slashing down again. Sweat stung his eyes as he hacked bad-temperedly at a spongy plant crowding his feet. It was stifling under the tangle of stems and branches, and he pulled out his waterskin once more and drank greedily.

It seemed an age since he'd seen more than a fragment of sky, or felt the clean bite of wind on his face; an age since he'd left behind the open spaces of the Grounds.

'This forest has no end,' said Urgundin, coming level. 'And it eats the wind.'

Arkendrin stared about grimly. He'd waited most of a moon before he'd set out, refusing to jump to his brother's command, like an ebis running before a herder's stick. They were now into their fourth day of travel under the trees, the sixth since leaving the Shargh Grounds, and the only gold eyes they'd seen belonged to an owl. An owl wouldn't satisfy Erboran. Oh no, the great Chief must have proof to prop up his chiefship! Under his brother's rule the Shargh were directionless, watching the pasturelands wither and die, the ebi tug at their mothers' empty milkbags, content to eke out an existence in the desiccated ebis pen the battles of the Older Days had confined them to! Erboran was even happy, it seemed, to wait for the creature of the Last Telling to stroll onto the Grounds and destroy them all!

Well, there'd be no waiting for Arkendrin! He'd take back proof of the gold-eyed creature and then Erboran would be forced to act as a Shargh Chief should – *or lose the chiefship*.

He brought his dagger down through the bark of another tree, thinking that if it had been Erboran's throat, his work would have been far more pleasurable. Urgundin was right; the forest was endless. Bole upon bole as far as the eye could see; green and brown and grey and black; no sunlight, no air and no paths. Irdodun had sworn that he'd seen the gold-eyed creature *and* treemen as well, but how did they walk and not mark the ground with their passing? Were they as birds? Arkendrin glared up at the trees, scratching at his six-day beard.

Irdodun was a strange man, given to wandering far beyond the ebis pastures, and he was also low on the slope. If Urgundin hadn't vouchsafed him, Arkendrin would never have left the Grounds. Still, for all Irdodun's strangeness and lack of Voice, at least one of his claims was true; there *were* immense trees running south-west, roughly a day's march apart. He had no idea how Irdodun had come to notice such things, for the land was an unremittingly dreary mix of alien growth, but it was useful. It had made his and Urgundin's route into the forest easier. All he needed now was the gold-eyed creature Irdodun claimed to have seen.

What if finding the creature of the Telling was impossible in a single journey? What if they never found it? Arkendrin's knuckles whitened on his dagger. Irdodun had seen her and other treemen as well, but he'd come here many times over the past seasons, finding his way through the rank tangle in his strange moorat way.

Arkendrin hacked wildly at the fronds again and wiped the sweat from his eyes, furious at toiling here while Erboran took his pleasure with Palansa! Behind him, Urgundin slowed, letting the gap between them widen.

Erboran should be here, not him! It was the Chief's task to protect the Shargh, not his! The task of the mighty Chief Erboran; the task of the firstborn! Yet he'd demanded proof! But proof could take many forms; it need not be the creature itself. Arkendrin stopped mid slash. It would be easier to capture a treeman, for there were many of those, and once back in the Grounds, with Irason's help, it would take neither time nor skill to wring the truth from his lips. Then Erboran would have to leave his warm bed and come here to slay the creature himself.

Arkendrin's mind worked feverishly. They had been in this dirty green world nearly four days. If Irdodun were to be trusted, one of the treemen's long wooden sorchas must be close. He didn't want to stumble into it and find himself in battle. The *tesat* on his flatsword was deadly but it wouldn't kill all of them, and fighting would delay their search.

Time to turn back. The chances of stumbling on a treeman were just as great journeying north-east as they were south-west. And if he didn't, he'd return at his convenience, not Erboran's.

He swung round to Urgundin, waiting several lengths behind. 'We head north-east,' he said, and strode off through the trees.

8

The air in the Water Cavern was oppressive, the lateness adding to the sense of foreboding that lay like a heavy hand over the gathered Protector Leaders. They exchanged nods as their comrades entered the cavern, but no one spoke.

Commander Sarkash had ordered they assemble in the Water Cavern with all possible speed and discretion. It took little wit to guess the news was bad, for why else would they have been ripped from their beds? To be called together was unusual, and in the middle of the night and in the least hospitable of the Warens' many caverns, unheard of.

Their Commander stood before them, poorly lit by the single torch. Sarkash rocked back and forth on the balls of his feet, trying to ease the tightness of his muscles as he mentally ticked off each new arrival. Only Pekrash and Dekren were absent now, and he knew where they were. Pekrash and his men had been so exhausted that he'd sent them straight to their beds, and Dekren's patrol was too far out to be called back, even *if* he were willing to risk sending more scouts. A fresh wave of fear broke over him and he tried to comfort

63

himself with the knowledge that Dekren's patrol was further west in Renclan octad and probably safe.

The Water Cavern was uncomfortable, but far enough from the main caverns for there to be little chance of his words reaching the ears of the younger Protectors before he had time to properly prepare them. The last thing he wanted was panic sweeping through the Warens or the news reaching the longhouses before he had a chance to speak with the Clancouncil. He was breaching protocol already by speaking to his Protector Leaders first, but he had no choice. His first duty lay in securing the safety of the Tremen, and that meant Maxen and the council would have to wait.

Kest stood with the rest of the Protector Leaders, his gaze on the tense face of his Commander. He was not far from where he'd met Kiraon that morning, and he hadn't expected to be here again so soon, and certainly not in the middle of the night. Kest's unease grew as he watched Sarkash's hand brush at his face, a mannerism that appeared only when Sarkash was at his most discomfited. What was he waiting for? Was this to be an exercise in patience, like their endless tramps through the trees? At dawn he must be out in the Sarclan octad again, and that meant he should be sleeping now.

'I thank you for your prompt attendance,' began Sarkash at last. 'Protector Leader Pekrash has just returned from the Kenclan octad with the grave news that beyond the Third Eight, running parallel with the Kenclan Eights, he came upon a line of trees, slashed at twenty-pace intervals.'

Kest jerked towards his comrades, seeing the same mixture of incredulity and dread that clawed at his own guts. Allogrenia had been breached! Someone had come in and was marking a passage to find their way out again. But the idea was ludicrous, impossible! His eyes fixed on Merenor, whose white face gaped back at him.

'Pekrash returned at speed,' continued Sarkash, 'a course of action for which I've commended him.'

Kest's mind reeled. Surely it would've been better to have pursued the invaders and found out their purpose? Then again, if there'd been many of them, Pekrash and his men could've been killed, and then there'd be no warning, or at least, none in time. The Protectors learned swordplay and patrolled, but Allogrenia's safety was built on the premise that the vastness of the forest protected them. No Tremen contemplated they'd ever actually have to fight.

'I've decided to forbid travel beyond the First Eight,' Sarkash continued, 'and will assign each clan a patrol so that gathering is conducted within the Eight under our protection.'

If the Protectors were confined within the First Eight, thought Kest, the intruders would be free to roam anywhere in Allogrenia, slashing their paths and laying their plans. It was absolute madness.

'Commander Sarkash!' The words were out of his mouth before he had time to stop them and all eyes turned to him expectantly.

'Yes, Protector Leader Kest?'

Kest dredged around for something to say that was more acceptable than his thoughts. 'There's insufficient sustenance within the First Eight to support a longhouse.'

'I'm aware of the quantity and quality of the gathering in Allogrenia, Protector Leader,' said Sarkash, with studied politeness. 'It's an interim measure until the Clancouncil decides upon our best course of action.'

Kest nodded but his thoughts tumbled about like storm leaves. Surely Sarkash wasn't going to put their people's welfare in the grasping, arrogant hands of Maxen – or worse, in the doddering hands of Dekrash and his ilk. Only Miken of Kashclan, and Kest's own leader, Marren, saw beyond their own prestige and power, or the small matters of their daily existence. And their voices were too often drowned by the rest of the Clanleaders, with all their shortcomings.

'. . . and Protector Leader Kest, you're to go to the Bough and see that all's secure there,' came Sarkash's voice.

'The Bough?' repeated Kest, snatching at his scattered wits.

'You needn't take a patrol with you at this stage,' went on Sarkash, 'simply ensure that the Healers are safe and that they remain within the Bough.'

Kest nodded. There was no need of a patrol because to reach the Bough invaders would have to fight past the longhouses and their guarding Protectors. It was one of the advantages of the scattered food sources that had forced the Tremen to build their longhouses apart. His role would be more ceremonial than practical. Was Sarkash punishing him for questioning his authority? He stared at the lined face of his Commander and dismissed the thought. Sarkash had his faults, but vindictiveness wasn't one of them.

The Protector Leaders groped their way back along the tunnel, Kest following them to the training rooms to collect his sword and pack, then returning alone to the outer cavern. Whereas his fellow Protector Leaders had to gather their patrols, his trip would be solitary. He edged round Nogren's trunk and started along the Drinkwater Path, eyes scanning the trees. He'd prefer to be heading out to one of the longhouses with his men, than journeying in to the Bough. Whatever way he looked at it, he was little more than a scout, and the bearer of bad news to boot. He quickened his pace, his shadow leaping along the leaf litter before him. It was a good night for travel, for both him *and* the intruders.

A torrent of curses escaped him, then he forced himself to think of what he must say to Maxen. If it had been Lern or even Merek he must deal with, rehearsal would be unnecessary. But Maxen was not an easy man at the best of times, and these were *not* the best of times. The Tremen Leader would be far from amused that news of such magnitude was being delivered by a lowly Protector Leader rather than by Commander Sarkash himself, and would no doubt make his displeasure known at length.

Kest strode on, stopping only to wrench off his sweaty jacket and thrust it into his pack. He'd had little to do with Maxen, knowing him more by repute and through Maxen's dealings with

Sarkash. Kest was far more familiar with Merek. His scowl deepened as he thought of his sister's plans, but he resisted the urge to swear again; Kesilini would be twenty at Turning and well able to choose a bondmate without his help. Still, he would have wished for a warmer, more sociable man for her. Merek was too much like Maxen for his liking, not just in his containment but in his arrogance. Maybe it was a family trait; the daughter was certainly deaf to all advice, roaming wherever the whim took her.

The night grew older before the trees finally gave way to the cleared circle round the Bough. Kest came to a stop in the shadows, catching his breath and scanning the open space, his gaze moving back and forth between the Bough and the trees surrounding it. It was the most beautiful building in Allogrenia, but now all he saw was its horrible vulnerability. The sides were lined with windows, and the large double doors opening into the central hall would be easy to breach.

As he made his way over the open ground, he noted that no lamplight was visible through the shutters. He rapped on the door, scanning again as he waited. Maxen was likely to be even more humourless than usual, dragged from the warmth of his bed. Kest readied the speech he'd prepared but there was no creak of footsteps from within. He rapped again harder, stinging his knuckles. The ashael behind him exploded and Kest's sword hissed from its scabbard, only to see a bird flapping away, eyes flashing gold. The door opened and he spun back, sword still raised high.

Lern's sleep-drowsed face froze. 'Kest,' he croaked, eyes on the sword.

Kest sheathed his weapon and straightened. 'Protector Leader Kest,' he said, with a bow. 'I'm here on Commander Sarkash's orders to speak with Tremen Leader Maxen. Is he within?'

'My father's still at Clancouncil. We've heard from our clanmate Tresen that my father will be there till the morrow. It's at Kashclan longhouse this moon.'

Kest managed to keep his face expressionless. Sarkash hadn't mentioned the Clancouncil because even the smallest child knew council meetings took place near the full moon.

'Who's within?' he rasped out.

'Just me,' said Lern.

'But where are the other Healers?' said Kest, alarmed.

'Merek was here earlier but he's probably at your longhouse by now, and Kira and Kandor have gone nut-gathering. I'm here, so there's a Healer within the Bough, if that's what's concerning you, Protector Leader,' added Lern tartly.

Kest scarcely noticed. His orders were to secure the Bough and to ensure the safety of the Healers there. But what if most of the Healers were elsewhere? He took a steadying breath, calculating quickly. Maxen was at the Kashclan longhouse with Miken and Marren, as well as other men who'd completed Protector training. No doubt it was where Sarkash was going too. Maxen would be safe.

Merek was at Kest's own longhouse and by first light a Protector Leader and patrol would be there to secure it, so Merek would be safe too. Lern was here alone, but any attack aimed at the Bough would have to pass the Protectors moving out into the octads, so there was no real threat to him either. That left the two youngest Healers and their cursed nut-gathering. It seemed ominous suddenly, that they'd been out all night.

'When did Kiraon and Kandor leave?' he asked.

'At moonrise.'

'Moonrise? They went nutting at night?'

'They gather rednuts. The grove's beyond the Third Eight. They're usually away four or five days.'

'Beyond the Third Eight?' said Kest, shocked.

'Perhaps Protector Leader, you should come in,' said Lern politely. 'It would be a better place to speak.'

Kest nodded and followed him across the darkened hall towards the cooking place, his footfalls echoing. Lern put another log on the fire and sat, gesturing Kest to sit also. But Kest remained standing, wondering what Commander Sarkash would want him to do.

Lern cleared his throat. 'Kira and Kandor often go rednut harvesting this time of year. They . . .'

'They go to the rednut groves in Kenclan octad? Those on the Everflow?'

'Yes.'

'By the 'green!' The best Healer the Bough had ever birthed was out in the same octad as the invaders, with only her younger brother for protection. What ill chance was this? thought Kest.

Lern came to his feet again. 'Will you tell me why you're here, Protector Leader?'

'Slashed trees marking a path have been discovered in Allogrenia,' said Kest.

Lern's face drained of colour and he sat down heavily. 'Where?'

Kest said nothing and Lern's horrified eyes came to his. 'Not . . . not in the Kenclan octad?'

Kest nodded.

'Do they mean us harm?' asked Lern hoarsely.

'We don't know,' said Kest, 'but until we find otherwise, we must assume they do. Each longhouse is being assigned a patrol, and there will be no travelling beyond the First Eight for the time being. I've been sent to ensure the safety of the Healers here. Unfortunately Commander Sarkash didn't foresee that most of them wouldn't be here.'

He took several steps to and fro. 'It surprises me Leader Maxen allows his children to stray so far alone.'

'Kira's always gathered widely,' said Lern. 'She knows Allogrenia better than many who've lived twice her seasons, and Tresen's with them.'

'Tresen of Kashclan?' asked Kest, eyes widening.

Lern nodded. 'Clanleader Miken's son.'

'He's been in training only a short time,' said Kest. 'He won't be much use if . . .' He cut the sentence short and straightened. 'Healer Lern, I'm returning to the Warens to gather a patrol. I'll send half back here but in the meantime I ask that you bolt the doors and identify all visitors before allowing entry.'

'What of Kira and Kandor?'

'I'll take the other half of the patrol and go after them,' said Kest, already striding down the hall. 'Do you know which part of the octad they're intending to travel through?'

'They didn't say, but I know they've got sleeping-slings and that Kira likes to sleep in ashaels. There's a large stand west of Second Enogren.'

'I know it,' said Kest. 'If they're journeying slowly, we might be able to catch them. Why does your sister like sleeping in ashaels?' he asked, stepping out into the cool night air and pulling on his pack.

'She says they sing in the wind.'

'Sing in the wind,' muttered Kest, shaking his head as he strode off into the darkness.

Lern stood staring after Kest long after he'd disappeared among the trees, unwilling to return to his bed despite the weariness dragging at his limbs. This night, when he'd gone to sleep, the world had been as it always was, but now . . . Surely Kest was mistaken. Surely no stranger could find their way into Allogrenia. It was too vast, too tangled, too . . . It was unthinkable!

'A line of slashed trees', that was what Kest had said, and it was exactly how a stranger would mark their way. Lern shivered as he thought of Kira, Kandor and Tresen. Surely there'd be no risk to them?

He pulled the door shut, struggling to slide the bolts into place and having to rub nut oil on them before they'd budge. More decorative than functional, it was the first time he'd ever used them.

He slumped into a chair, briefly considering whether to wake

Sendra, but there was no point in ruining her night's rest as well. The flames died down and the log crumbled to a pile of coals but still he sat there. The Bough creaked and groaned and it seemed that he could hear footsteps in one of the storage rooms, and the sly testing of shutters. If only Merek or his father were here. If only Kira and Kandor were tucked in their beds, warm and secure. 'By the always-green which Shelters us,' he muttered, 'let them be safe.'

9

The night grew old, settling into the deep silence that comes before the earth turns back towards the sun. Tresen slowed, then stopped in a dense stand of terrawoods, his enjoyment of the forest replaced by a preoccupation with sore shoulders and aching legs. He dropped his pack and flexed his shoulders.

'Time to rest,' he called, shivering as the night air penetrated his damp shirt.

Kandor came level, throwing off his pack and collapsing onto a log. 'I'm ready for bed,' he mumbled, yawning hugely.

'So am I. We'll stay here,' said Tresen. The air was warm and still. It would be a good place to spend the rest of the night.

'We always sleep in the ashaels,' said Kira, striding over and making no move to take off her pack.

'They're too far,' said Tresen, rummaging in his pack for the sleeping-slings. 'Kandor's all but dead on his feet.'

'He can go further,' insisted Kira.

'He's too tired.' Tresen pulled out the first of the bundles. 'The terrawoods are a good tree to sleep in.'

'I don't remember agreeing that you should lead this expedition,' said Kira.

Kira's cold tone made Tresen look up. He and Kira rarely quarrelled and when they did it was mostly over her cosseting of Kandor, not the reverse. Now her hands were planted on her hips, and her chin tilted. She'd been unusually quiet on this trip too.

'What troubles you, Kira?' he asked.

Her eyes flashed in the last of the moonlight and he braced himself. 'I'm not going to be bossed about on this trip as well as in the Bough. You sleep here if you want, but we're going. Come on, Kandor.'

'It's not what *I* want,' said Tresen steadily. 'It's clear Kandor can journey no more this night.'

'I'm a better judge of that than you'll ever be, *Protector* Tresen. Let's go, Kandor.'

Kandor sat unmoving, his gaze on the ground. 'Can't we stay here and sleep in the terrawoods just for once?'

'We *always* sleep in the ashaels.'

'Yes, but we didn't leave the Bough till moonrise this time. It's too far to the ashaels and my legs ache. Please, Kira?'

Kira straightened, flicking back her plait. 'Stay if you want, but I'm going on.'

Tresen jumped to his feet. 'Don't be a fool! It's not safe to travel alone.'

'Not safe, not safe?' she mimicked. 'What's there to harm me? You've been spending too much time with Commander Sarkash. It's *his* task, not yours, to make shadows into monsters to give Protectors something to chase. Tell me what's dangerous in Allogrenia. The withysnake's deadly to the littermouse, but I'm no littermouse; the barkspider's painful certainly, but nothing more. Wolves don't come within the Sentinels and heart-rotted trees don't grow where I go. So what else is there, oh mighty *Protector* Tresen?'

'There's ignorance and arrogance,' snapped Tresen. 'Both can be fatal.'

73

'Of all the big-headed . . .' started Kira, turning on him.

'Don't!' cried Kandor, leaping between them. 'Don't argue, *please*! This was supposed to be a happy trip, not like home, not like the Bough!'

There was an uncomfortable silence. Kira took a deep breath, struggling with her disappointment. 'I'm sorry, Kandor. I suppose we can spend the night here if you're tired.'

'This tree looks good,' said Tresen briskly, patting the trunk of a nearby terrawood, 'but we'll need a volunteer to see if there's enough room for all of us.'

'I'll go,' said Kandor, with a sudden burst of energy.

Tresen gave Kandor a leg-up, for terrawoods set their branches some distance off the ground and their knobbed trunks provided few footholds. Kandor scrambled into the canopy, making the boughs shake and creak, and its leaves spill down like snow. Kira kept her face skyward, avoiding Tresen's eyes.

'Commander Sarkash said that the Northerners used to call these "sanctuary trees",' said Tresen.

'Yes.'

'You knew that?' asked Tresen.

'There are Writings stored beyond the training rooms that speak of it.'

'I didn't know you were allowed that far,' said Tresen. 'They're known to the Protectors, of course, but I thought they'd be too mouldy to read.'

'They're readable.'

'It's strange that they're not more safely stored,' said Tresen. 'What do they speak of apart from sanctuary trees?'

'Herbal lists, fighting in the north, the alwaysgreens . . .'

The branches rattled and Kandor's face appeared through the foliage. 'It's wonderful,' he said excitedly. 'There are three great branches quite close together, and it even feels warm in here once you go up a little. You'll love it, Kira.'

It was indeed warm in the foliage and they fixed their slings and clambered into them. They were the same type of slings as those used by Kasheron, with straps at the head and foot to secure them to branches and an envelope of material sewn into the bottom for the sleeper to crawl into. Commander Sarkash said that the pocket was for safety, so that even in a high wind, the sleeper couldn't fall out, but Tresen thought it unlikely. The sides of the sling were high, and the body weight of the sleeper made them higher still. The pocket was more likely for warmth.

There was only room for two slings side by side, so they fixed the third a little higher. Kandor climbed into this one and in no time his sling stopped jiggling. Kira lay for a long time staring at the leaves above her face, her roiling thoughts keeping her wakeful.

'We were right to stop,' she said finally. '*You* were right.'

Tresen reached over and took her hand. 'Are things so awful in the Bough?'

Kira's throat tightened, making speech difficult. When she thought of the Bough, all she could see was its confining walls and her father's cold, measuring eyes.

'I'm just tired,' she muttered.

Tresen's hand squeezed hers and, with a final pat, withdrew. 'Sleep then,' he said gently.

But, despite her weariness, Kira couldn't sleep. The forest seemed to have come alive again, with hanaweys sweeping through the canopy and skinks and leaf lizards scuttling along the branches above her head. As a child she'd lain deep in the forest and listened to the whisper of leaves, finding their voices deeply comforting. But now Kira tossed this way and that, until finally, in an attempt to distract herself, she began to list the foods that could be gathered in the octad. When she'd exhausted those, she started on the herbs, and was about midway through them when she felt sleep steal over her.

*

Kira woke with a start. It seemed only a moment ago she'd been mulling over herbal lists, but the air was cooler now and the leaves above her were rimmed with dew. Why had she woken? Her eyes searched the branches for owls, but they were empty. Then she heard voices; Protectors, no doubt. They came closer and their words grew more distinct. She froze. The language wasn't Tremen or Onespeak. The blood roared in her ears. It was a language she'd never heard before!

There were strangers in Allogrenia! But no, it was impossible! Then the speakers stopped directly below. Kira could scarcely draw breath, terrified Kandor would wake and call out, or that some demon's face would appear through the leaves.

Branches snapped as the strangers blundered about below. There was a harsh exchange of words and then, after an excruciatingly long time, the speakers moved off. There was one final thwacking noise and then silence.

Kira lay rigid, doused in sweat, not daring to move lest the rustling branches draw them back. No stranger could find their way into Allogrenia. It was unmarked. *Allogrenia was unmarked*. The thought lodged in her brain and she couldn't move beyond it. Eventually the frantic beating of her heart calmed and her weariness caused her to slip into an uneasy slumber, not fully rousing again until the sun was high and the terrawood alive with birds. She watched them dart about her, bright flashes of yellow and green, squabbling and singing. In the blue of day, the night voices seemed remote and unbelievable, nothing more than echoes of a dream.

Tresen and Kandor were nowhere to be seen and Kira's fear surged afresh, then she heard them chattering below. Hauling herself upright, she bundled up the sling and made her way down through the branches, staring about through the leaves before swinging herself down.

Tresen was tending a small fire, a pan of boiling water set on it, the smoke lacing the air with spiciness.

'Awake at last,' said Kandor cheerily, his cheeks bulging with nutcake, his lap filled with crumbs.

'We thought we'd let you sleep,' said Tresen, pouring the water expertly into a cup. Flakes of thornyflower swirled on the surface, the water quickly staining a deep green. 'Breakfast is served,' he said, handing it to her with a flourish. 'There's dried sweetberries and blacknuts to go with the nutcake, and fresh sour-ripe.'

Kira pushed the hair from her eyes. Tresen and Kandor were busy laying out more nuts and fruit, and Allogrenia looked as it always did in the mornings: golden with light and full of birdsong. Should she speak of what she'd heard? But what indeed had she heard?

'What is it?' asked Tresen, seeing her expression.

'I heard voices in the night,' said Kira.

'Protectors? I didn't think there was a patrol scheduled for this octad.'

'Not Protectors,' said Kira, 'strangers.'

Tresen looked sceptical. 'It's not possible. Surely you were dreaming?'

'I don't think I was dreaming,' said Kira, sitting beside Kandor and hugging her knees.

'But no one can find their way into Allogrenia. You must have been dreaming,' said Kandor. 'You're not thinking of going back, are you, Tresen? I don't want to go back yet.'

'Maybe it *was* a dream,' said Kira.

Tresen shrugged, thinking of what he'd learned since beginning Protector training. Kasheron had decreed that Allogrenia remain pathless and, apart from the Drinkwater Path, it had. The vastness of the trackless trees formed a formidable defensive barrier. He had never heard the Protector Leaders question its effectiveness, not even Kest, who the others looked to for guidance.

'I don't think there's any need to turn back,' said Tresen slowly. 'After all, if there had been voices, surely Kandor or I would have woken.'

77

Kandor heaved a mighty sigh of relief. 'Good. Now have your breakfast, Kira, before Tresen eats the rest of the nutcake.'

The Protectors moved swiftly through the trees, their breathing harsh and their faces slick. The sun was at its zenith, the air under the canopy stifling, but they continued on without complaint, their shirts and breeches grimy and sweat-stained. Finally an order rang out and they came to a halt, throwing themselves down in the deeper pools of shade and drinking deeply from their waterskins.

Only Kest remained standing, palming the stinging wetness from his eyes and squinting at the trees about him. The tang in the air told him a change was coming but it was too far off to bring them relief now. He tossed his pack down, arching his back in relief, then dragged his waterskin out. It was too hot for the pace he'd set, but his men had travelled faster and further than he dared hope possible. There were just ten of them; the other half of his patrol had been sent to the Bough. He took a swig of water, wondering again whether he'd done the right thing in splitting their strength.

Ordinarily he would have sought further orders, but things were far from ordinary. To have followed Sarkash to the Kashclan long-house would have cost him half a day, and time was already against him. Would Sarkash agree with him or deem him completely lacking in judgement – like Lern? Lern had suggested the nutting party would sleep in the ashaels, but his patrol had reached the ashaels just after dawn and there had been neither sight nor sound of them. Where in the 'green were they?

Kest had an overwhelming impulse to bolt on through the forest but forced himself to dredge his brain for every possibility first. If the nutting party hadn't gone to the ashaels after all, they'd have no reason to be as far west as he was. They would probably be taking the more direct, north-easterly route to the rednuts instead. No doubt they would be travelling more slowly than he was too, for they had no reason to rush. In which case, he was probably further

78

west than they were, and perhaps further north. He must strike east immediately!

He shouted an order and his men scrambled to their feet, struggling to get their packs back on. There was no need to explain the necessity of speed, or the possibility of battle at the end. They knew that there were strangers in Allogrenia, that trees had been slashed, and that the Leader's daughter and youngest son were likely in the same octad as the intruders. Kest shouted again, and they set off at speed through the trees.

A chill blast of air whistled through the undergrowth and the sunlight vanished from the forest floor, causing Kira to stare up in dismay. Beyond the sudden thrash of trees, clouds scudded across the sky, driven by a wind with a damp, keening edge. She pulled out her cape and put it on, drawing the hood close round her face to shut out the wind, then peered back to make sure Kandor had done the same. She didn't want him catching a chill.

Tresen was no longer in sight, though he'd been only a short way ahead a moment ago. He was eager to reach the groves, even though they were still a long way off. She grinned, remembering their little competitions as to who could gather the most. Tresen nearly always won, not only because he was the eldest and strongest, but because he was the least inclined to be distracted. Kandor usually spent too much time eating to pick quickly, and she'd inevitably spy some herb or other and go off to investigate.

Not that it mattered. They ended up sharing anyway, sitting on the starstone and using the river stones to crush the shells and release the nuts' pink flesh, feasting long into the night. Her mouth watered at the thought, and she quickened her pace. It seemed a long time since she'd last been there.

Arkendrin grimaced as he stared into the thickening gloom, considering the nights since he'd left. No doubt Erboran's glee at his absence had grown with each passing day, till it was as bloated as yesterday's moon. He spat and wiped at his greasy brow. At least the suffocating heat of morning had given way to a cooling wind; the Sky Chiefs be praised for that! And they were now journeying north-east, towards the Grounds, not deeper into the reek. The trees groaned against each other, and every now and then the tangled branches broke, letting shafts of cool air penetrate to the forest floor. He touched his hand to his forehead; surely the Sky Chiefs favoured his quest by sending him their sweet breath?

Urgundin's hand on his arm brought him up short, and he turned angrily, but his companion's gaze was fixed on a point to the south. There was a treeman there, carrying a pack and wearing a flatsword at his belt, but no dagger or spear, Arkendrin noted, as he slid soundlessly behind a straggly bush.

They were poorly hidden, but it didn't matter; the treeman moving as unwarily as a milk-blind ibis, easy to take. Irdodun had said that sometimes the treemen wandered solitarily, and sometimes in groups strung out through the forest. Marking the treeman's direction, Arkendrin waited. The man disappeared among the boles and, shortly after, another appeared. This one was more of a tree*boy*, thought Arkendrin contemptuously. He was narrow-shouldered and went with his hood drawn close, carrying a pack like the first one, but no sword. All the better.

Abruptly the smaller treeman stopped and looked back. Arkendrin froze, but the treeman's gaze moved beyond his hiding place, back in the direction from which he'd come. The treeman hesitated, as if about to turn back, but then he seemed to think better of it, continuing in the same direction as the first treeman.

Arkendrin's breath hissed between his teeth, and he unclenched his hand from his sword. There must be more treemen following, he guessed, for the second treeman had clearly been looking for someone else. It was as Irdodun had said. They didn't journey together, but spread throughout the forest. It was a strange way to travel, as if they

80

had no blood-ties with each other, or maybe they simply didn't have the wit to keep in step! It was useful though, making the taking of a lone treeman easy. The treeman's companions wouldn't even know he was gone.

A brown smudge emerged from the trees and Arkendrin smiled. This one was little more than a boy too, and like the second one, carried a pack but no sword. His travel was more erratic than that of his companions, plucking at the passing foliage, and putting whatever he picked into his mouth. Only the Sky Chiefs knew what filth the treeman was eating, for Arkendrin had found no food in this cursed place of wooden skies. The boy wandered on, intent on the things about him, not looking back.

Did that mean he was the last? Arkendrin's gaze flicked between the retreating back of the boy and the direction he'd come from, but no one else appeared. If he delayed much longer he might lose him in the trees. Gesturing to Urgundin to wait, he started forward. It wasn't possible to run as he did on the Grounds, but even so, he moved quickly in a half crouch, fronds whipping his face and trailing plants dragging at his breeches, his gaze fixed on the brown-caped back of the boy. The distance between him and his prey closed swiftly, the heavy leaf fall masking his steps.

The boy had stopped under a tree with heavy foliage. Arkendrin shortened his stride, judging the distance to his quarry with a hunter's precision, then lunged. One hand snaked round the treeman's nose and mouth, the other round his neck, a technique Arkendrin had found worked well. If smothering didn't bring submission, choking would. He wrenched the boy backwards into the shrubby bushes and there was a high-pitched shriek as a bird broke from the tree and winged away.

Kira turned at the cry of the mira kiraon, watching it arrow towards her, eyes alive with fire. It arced overhead, bright against the purpling dusk. Kira threw back her head and laughed in delight. No doubt Kandor had disturbed it. Her gaze dropped and the laugh choked to silence as she glimpsed a stranger, a flash of metal, and Kandor being dragged backwards. The world stopped. Then the void of disbelief gave way to a jumble of fragments: tales of Kasheron's battles and alien voices from the night. She sped back towards the terrawood.

Arkendrin thrust the half-conscious boy from him as Urgundin sprang to his feet and drew his flatsword. There was no need to tell him that they'd have to kill this treeman too, not that it was a problem; he was as heedless of his safety as the first had been. The treeman had slowed now in his headlong flight towards them, unsure of the whereabouts of his companion. Arkendrin stepped from his hiding place and the treeman jerked to a stop. His hood had come loose, revealing a long fair plait. A woman! The killing would be easier but no less enjoyable.

Then the woman's eyes came to his and his breath failed him. 'The creature,' hissed Urgundin.

Arkendrin swept his flatsword backwards. Should he kill her or blind her? Which would most discomfit his brother?

'Kiraon!'

The shout came from behind and Arkendrin spun in surprise. The other treeman had been to his right; what foul chance was this?

'Treemen . . . with flatswords,' grunted Urgundin.

Arkendrin dropped into a fighting stance and drew his dagger with his other hand. There were two to his left, one closing quickly, another beyond; too many to fight and still take the creature with them. Curse Erboran!

'To the Grounds,' he hissed, slashing sideways as he plunged away through the tangle of twigs and fronds, searching for gouged trees to his right, the treemen now coming from all directions. Metal struck metal and he cursed again; Urgundin had never been fast and he was paying the price.

The pounding of running feet was all around him and he slashed again, his flatsword finding flesh and flicking scarlet drops onto the leaves next to him, but he didn't stop. If he were on the Grounds he would be far away by now, but the earth here was littered with rotting wood, the air full of its foulness. Then someone shouted and the sounds of pursuing feet ceased.

Arkendrin ran on. The last of the light waned and the wind dwindled, but it had swung east, carrying with it the faintest scents of targasso and burrel. He kept his face to it as he ran, not even stopping when utter darkness descended, counting his steps and fumbling for slashes over the trees' coarse flesh as he went. And all the time his mind was filled with the image of the creature of the Telling; of the words he would use at the Speak, and of what his brother would now be forced to do.

10

Two fires flickered, blots of orange in the darkness, and voices drifted with the smell of roasting nuts. Kest's patrol sat around one fire, preparing their evening meal, and Kira crouched next to the other, tending the wounded.

She was aware of nothing but the terrible wounds confronting her. She'd sewn gashes from flint-stone and axe-wood before, and hurts caused by fires and falls, but never injuries such as these. These were sword wounds, wounds made with metal.

Feseren lay unmoving, the pink of his face a trick of the fire-glow, for in daylight Kira knew his face would be as white as mickle-fungus. Even so, with his single wound he was more fortunate than his comrade Sanaken, who had many, the muscle and sinew severed where the sword had plunged and twisted over and over again.

The sun hadn't set when Kira had begun stitching Sanaken, but the moon had risen before she'd finished, and now he slept the deep, death-like sleep of everest, while she stitched Feseren's wound.

Finally Kira tied off the stitchweed and unrolled a bandage, bringing it up and over, firmly and smoothly, until she could tie off its ends too. Feseren's shirt was blood-sodden and cold, and would need to be replaced.

She'd given Feseren sickleseed to dull the pain, but it dulled the senses too, and he was clumsy with it. If she'd been in the Bough, she could have given him cindra to counter the effect, but she carried none in her pack.

'Let me help, Healer,' said Brem, supporting Feseren's limp body.

Brem's strong arms slid Feseren expertly out of his soiled shirt and into a clean one, then lowered him back onto the sleeping-sheet and tucked it over him securely. It was fortunate that Brem had been in the patrol, for he was Kashclan like Kira, and carried Kasheron's passion and skill for healing.

'If you have no more need of me, I'll return to guarding,' he said rising.

'I thank you for your help,' mumbled Kira, her gaze on Sanaken. Kandor lay next to him, sleeping now, his swollen throat livid with bruising. How had he managed to escape the terrible wounds of the other young men she tended?

Kira's stomach lurched as the darkness was rent again by images of flashing swords. So much blood! Her hands were crusted, her shirt stiff with it. She must wash. Struggling to her feet, she staggered away from the fire, but a Protector suddenly materialised in front of her, blocking her way.

'Where is it you go, Kiraon?'

He was only a dark outline but she recognised his voice. Protector Leader Kest, the last person she wanted to deal with at this moment.

'To wash,' she muttered, eyes on the ground.

'You aren't to leave the fire.'

'What, not even to relieve myself?'

'Not even for that.'

She turned back and sat heavily, refusing to acknowledge him, as he settled beside her.

'Here,' he said, uncapping his waterskin and holding it out.

Grudgingly she put her hands out so he could pour water over them. She rubbed them together then dried them ineffectually on her breeches, suddenly feeling shamed. Kest had saved her and Kandor's lives and she was behaving like a sulky child.

'I thank you for the water, and . . . earlier . . .' she forced herself to say, raising her eyes at last. Kest looked very different to her memory of him; his hair matted with sweat, his face etched with weariness.

'I've spoken with Protector Tresen, but he was unaware of the attack until we arrived,' said Kest. 'I need to know what you saw, what the attackers did, and whether they spoke. I need to know everything that happened for my report to Commander Sarkash.'

'Must I speak of it now?' mumbled Kira.

'It's better to, while it's fresh in your mind.'

Fresh in her mind? She couldn't imagine a time when it *wouldn't* be fresh in her mind. It was as if the stranger still stood before her, sword raised, face filled with hatred – a hatred even more shocking than the sword. Her hands began to shake and she gripped her knees.

'Tell me,' he said more gently.

Haltingly she recounted each stage of the attack, Kest interrupting now and again to ask questions, but mostly letting her speak.

'And so,' he said, when she finally fell silent, 'you heard nothing at all, right up until they appeared.'

'I . . . I heard them in the night.'

'Protector Tresen said that was a dream.' The flames illuminated one side of his face and she could see that he was both puzzled and angry.

'I agreed with Tresen it was a dream, but later, I didn't think it was.'

'Why in the 'green didn't you tell him?' he demanded.

'I *wanted* it to be a dream.'

'But if you'd told Tresen, he would have brought you back to the Bough and none of this would have happened,' he clipped, voice tight with fury.

Kira scrambled to her feet. 'Do you think I don't know that? Do you think I would've risked Kandor? But Allogrenia's unmarked, remember? Allogrenia can't be breached; Allogrenia's *safe*.' Her voice was shrill and she felt like she was going to be sick again.

Kest rose too, regretting his show of anger. The girl had seen her brother nearly killed and had come close to death herself, and she'd spent every moment since dealing with Sanaken and Feseren's injuries.

'Protector Tresen will be finished guarding duty soon, then I'll send him to you,' he said. 'Then you're to sleep. We'll be leaving at dawn.'

'We have to stay here,' she said.

'We leave at dawn,' he repeated.

'I've given Sanaken everest. He won't be able to travel.'

'Everest?'

'It numbs pain and brings sleep. He *must* have rest for healing to begin.'

'He can be roused.' Not that it would make much difference. Sanaken and Feseren would probably have to be carried anyway. Four of his men with bearers in their hands, not swords, thought Kest.

'Everest brings a sleep which can't be broken, but I wouldn't allow it, even if it were possible to wake him,' said Kira, hands on hips.

'*I wouldn't allow it.*' She was as arrogant as her father! Well, he was the Protector Leader, not her. They couldn't afford to spend another night here with only ten Protectors to look after four people, one of whom slept like the dead. They must look to the living, for the wounded might well be beyond all care.

'You shouldn't have given him anything,' he snapped. 'It was obvious that we couldn't stay here.'

'Stitching Sanaken without everest would've killed him. I'm a

87

Tremen Healer, Protector Leader, not a barbaric Terak Kutan! Besides, the danger's past. One of the strangers is dead and the other's fled.'

'You're assuming, *Healer*, that there were only two. How many voices did you hear in the night?'

'Two . . . I think.'

'Two . . . you *think*. And there's no proof that the ones you heard were the ones who attacked you. Nor do we know who else wanders the trees, in this octad or in another. All we *do* know is what you've pointed out: Allogrenia's no longer safe.'

Fear suffused Kira's face, her remarkable eyes catching the fire-light. 'Were they Shargh?' she said.

Kest hesitated, caught off guard by her sudden change in direction. 'Yes, they were Shargh.'

Kira's shoulders sagged.

'How is it you know of the Shargh?' he asked, curious.

'Healers read many things, not just Writings on herbs.'

She might read many things, but Kest doubted Maxen did. He'd rarely seen the Tremen Leader in the Warens, and never beyond the storage rooms.

'The Protectors don't speak of the Shargh outside the Warens,' he said. 'There's little point creating fear of an enemy who's not been sighted or heard of since Kasheron entered the forest.'

'I read things that I don't speak of also.'

He went to turn away but Kira touched his arm.

'There's just one thing I would know about the Shargh, Protector Leader.'

Kest sighed. He was bone weary and ready for sleep. 'What?'

'Do the Protectors know of Shargh wounds or the salves Kasheron used for them?'

'There's nothing in the teachings, except . . .' He shrugged.

'What?'

'It's just a meaningless rhyme.' Meaningless *and* useless.

'Nothing in healing is meaningless, Protector Leader. Please tell me.'

'"Fire with flatswords brings the bane; fire without brings life again." Now sleep, Healer Kiraon.'

But sleep Kira couldn't, for Kest's words tumbled about in her mind long after he'd gone. Rhymes had once been used to teach all healing in Allogrenia, for Kasheron had brought Writings from the north, but no paper to record any more. It had taken them a long time to discover how to concoct a type of paper from patchet weed and longer still to devise an ink that didn't fade. In the interim, they'd used rhymes to keep herbal lore alive.

Kest's rhyme had to date from those early days, when the memories of Shargh wounds and their cures were fresh. It therefore *had* to hold meaning. But what? Kira yawned and rubbed at her gritty eyes. She must gather sorren and cindra, and snowflower too, to help with the scarring. Sanaken in particular was going to be disfigured, although at least his face had been spared. There should be sorren nearby, which was her main priority, for the slopes here were gentle and eastward-facing, ideal for its growth. Maybe she should gather now.

'You should be sleeping,' said Tresen, settling beside her. He looked around at the motionless bodies nearby and the shadowy forms of Protectors moving methodically through the trees. Brem had told him of the breaking of the patrol, of their desperate flight in search of them, and of the men who'd stayed behind to guard the Bough. The Bough! Surely Commander Sarkash didn't expect their attackers to penetrate to the very heart of Allogrenia?

'What news of the world beyond the fire?' asked Kira. 'Protector Leader Kest orders I remain within its light.'

'So he should, for he's sworn to protect,' said Tresen, taking a sever log from the windfall gathered earlier, and hefting it onto the fire, then watching with satisfaction as the flames took hold.

The new pulse of light clearly showed his clanmate's exhaustion. 'Sleep, Kira.'

'But I need to gather sorren.'

'Not this night; you need to rest.'

'I might need it this night.'

'Do you think they'll worsen?'

Kira shrugged helplessly. 'I've done as I would for any other type of wound, but these are Shargh wounds and I know nothing of Shargh wounds.' She dropped her head.

'Kira?'

She was weeping. She only cried when she was at her most distressed, and always soundlessly. He had wondered whether it was simply the way she was, or whether she'd learned to hide her misery from Maxen. Tresen pulled her close, feeling her tears wetting his shirt.

'You're safe now,' he murmured, 'we're all safe.' But even as he said it, his eyes searched beyond the thin line of guarding Protectors, and he wondered whether his words were really true.

Kira woke to the rattle of sever leaves, so unlike the ashael's soothing, whispered melody. She shivered as she realised that if they'd slept in the ashael groves, the Shargh would have seen them and they'd probably be dead. Pulling the sleeping-sheet over her head, she brought her arms round herself. As a child she'd hidden beneath her covering when winter gales sent lightning dancing over the canopy, tearing limbs from trees and blasting boles in half. She'd hidden there too, when her father's sharp-edged tongue had sent a sunny day into shadow, or his cold eyes had found fault with her gathering, or concocting, or healing. But there was no hiding now from the horror that had overtaken them.

She sat up. At least the wounded hadn't roused in the night, even when she'd checked them, and that was a good sign. But the unmistakable tang of rain in the air wasn't. She stared up through the sever branches at the chinks of leaden sky. If it rained they'd have to find some way of sheltering Sanaken and Feseren.

A Protector emerged from the trees, his eyes the intense blue

Kira remembered from the Warens and the dawn light making his hair white again. She scrambled to her feet, acutely aware of her crumpled, bloodstained clothing. Not that Kest looked much better. His face was smudged with grime and, judging from his expression, his night's rest had done little to improve his temper.

'Healer Kiraon, you slept well I trust?'

Kira nodded, avoiding his eyes.

'Rain comes,' said Kest. 'We must seek shelter for the wounded. There are caves less than a day south-west. Do you know of any others that are closer?'

'The Healers don't speak of caves in this area,' she said. 'I agree the wounded must be sheltered, but if they're to heal, they mustn't be moved. The terrawood will keep the worst of the rain off, and we can rig sleeping-sheets above them.'

Kest peered back up the slope towards the denser canopy of the terrawood, determined not to lose his temper with her again. Espins and castellas crowded close, providing excellent hiding places, which was why the Shargh had probably chosen here for their attack. No, he wasn't going to risk any more of his men.

'We'll carry the wounded to the caves,' he said.

'They must stay here,' insisted Kira.

Here they were again, in exactly the same argument as last night. 'The land around the terrawood is too heavily treed,' he said evenly. 'Shargh could be on us before the guards even knew they were coming. We must go to the caves.'

'Protector Leader –'

'I *won't* lose any more of my men, nor will I continue to waste time justifying my every decision to you, *Healer* Kiraon. I'm in command here, and you'll do as I bid!'

'Shifting the wounded could kill them!'

'And staying here could kill us all! We're leaving as soon as bearers are prepared, so I suggest you use the time left to do what you can to ease their journey.'

Kira stood fuming as he strode off.

'Are we leaving?' Kandor's voice croaked from behind her. Kira turned, trying unsuccessfully to smile. At least he could speak now.

'The weather's turned and Protector Leader Kest says we're to go to some caves.'

'What about the wounded? Didn't you tell him they can't be shifted?' rasped Kandor.

'What do you think?'

'I suppose Kest pointed out that he was the Leader of the Protectors, not you,' he said.

'More or less. How did you guess?' asked Kira.

'Ah,' Kandor whispered, snuggling back into his sleeping-sheet, 'I'm a man of much wisdom, dear sister.'

'A man of much wisdom, eh? I beg your pardon, sir. In the dim light I mistook you for my little brother.'

Kandor chuckled hoarsely. 'Merek's soon-to-be bondmate is sweet, but she has been known to complain about her bossy brother.'

'Yet she's willing to bond with Merek,' muttered Kira. 'She'll just be trading one arrogant man for another.'

Kandor rolled over and began poking at the fire with a sever twig. 'Oh, Merek's all right, especially when he's away from the Bough.'

'Away from father, you mean.'

A soft veil of rain started falling as they were readying to leave and Kira helped Kandor don his cape before putting on her own. The Protectors had fashioned bearers from sever saplings and sleeping-sheets, and Kira had supervised the lifting of the wounded onto each. Sanaken was pale, with the slow regular breathing caused by everest, and would probably sleep for another day; Feseren slept too, though his sleep was from injury and shock. Kira had decided against giving him everest for the journey, as it didn't mix well with sickleseed. It was going to be a difficult and painful time for him.

'Healer Kiraon,' said Kest, coming alongside, 'you will walk directly behind the bearers with your brother. We will stop regularly to change carriers, and rest for a short time at midday to eat. If all goes well, I expect to be at the caves by dusk, then we can stay there for as long as you deem necessary.'

He paused, as if waiting for Kira to acknowledge his concession, but when she said nothing he continued, clearly irritated. 'I want it understood, Healer Kiraon, that you are not to walk ahead, drop behind or diverge to either side. The configuration I've devised is the safest for all.'

Kira got no pleasure from Kest's annoyance. She fell into line behind the bearers but for a while nothing happened. Stinking heart-rot! If they must shift the wounded, let them get on with it! But having browbeaten her into submission, Kest appeared to be in no hurry to move, standing stolidly at the rear of the patrol, his attention on two of his men who were busy in a small clearing to his left.

Wood cracked and presently a plume of black smoke rose, bringing with it the smell of burning fat.

'What are they doing?' she asked the Protector behind her.

'Burning the Shargh.'

Kira felt a surge of disgust. Surely the dead deserved to be treated with respect, even if they were the enemy? She strode back to Kest, ignoring his obvious displeasure at her breaking of formation.

'He should be buried, Protector Leader, not burnt like firewood.'

'Would you poison the earth with those who would murder you?'

'I would not become as barbarous as they,' she retorted.

'You know much of healing, Healer Kiraon, but little of the Shargh. The Shargh gods live in the clouds, not in the earth, and they join their gods through fire. Would you rather we carried him back to Second Enogren, and buried him next to the Kenclan dead? I don't think Clanleader Tenedren would be very pleased, do you?'

Kira's face flushed, and she looked away.

'I take it that's a no,' said Kest more softly.

Kira opened her mouth to retort but Kandor had appeared and was tugging at her arm.

'Don't,' he croaked, drawing her back behind the bearers. 'Kest's tired and anxious, that's why he's behaving so.'

'Kest's insolent and overbearing, *that's* why he's behaving so,' hissed Kira, not caring whether the Protector Leader heard her or not.

If Kest had heard her, he made no sign, waiting impassively for the smoke to dwindle before ordering his men back into line. He gave a second order and the Protectors carefully picked up the wounded, then the small procession moved off.

11

Miken sat in the hall of his longhouse, contemplating the disorderly array of chairs around the table and the remains of his meal. His only companion was Maxen, the other members of the council and their escorts having departed some time ago to their own longhouses.

Commander Sarkash had gone too, after receiving a message that Kest hadn't remained at the Bough as ordered, but had set off in pursuit of Kira, Kandor and Tresen.

Sarkash had been disconcerted by Kest's actions, despite the Protector Leader leaving half his men guarding the Bough. He'd wandered about the hall in a dither till Miken eventually suggested he go back to the Bough to inform himself more fully of the happenings there.

None of it augured well, thought Miken. Kest had done the only thing possible, given that his orders were to safeguard the Leader and his family, and it worried Miken that Sarkash hadn't recognised this. Sarkash was methodical and hardworking and the men liked him, but what if that were no longer enough? What if the arrival of strangers in Allogrenia portended fighting? Leading men during warfare was very different to overseeing training and organising the storage of provisions.

Maxen's chair grated from the table, jerking Miken from his reverie. The Tremen Leader had received the news of the incursion with less outward emotion than the other Clanleaders, and he'd greeted the news of his children's predicament equally calmly, more calmly than Miken, in fact. But Miken knew his clan-kin better than to think this denoted acceptance. Maxen had a habit of long, slow digestion of things that displeased him, a habit which seemed to increase the vitriol of his final response. Now, as he drew himself up, Miken braced for the tirade to come.

'Undisciplined, undisciplined, undisciplined!' the Tremen Leader spat.

'I agree that Protector Leader Pekrash should have pursued the intruders rather than coming back to the Warens,' responded Miken evenly. 'It shows a gap in our defensive strategy that must be addressed.'

'I don't refer to Pekrash,' snapped Maxen, 'but to Kiraon.'

'Oh,' said Miken, watching Maxen pace to the window and back, reminding Miken of Kira at her most upset.

'I expressly forbade her to leave the Arborean before the full moon but as soon as my back is turned, she sneaks away. And now she's caused this,' went on Maxen.

'I don't think Kira can be blamed for intruders coming to Allo-grenia,' said Miken.

Maxen's lips tightened. 'I've never expected your support in matters concerning my daughter, Clanleader, and on that score I've never been disappointed.'

Miken's dislike of his clan-kin rose like gorge in his throat but he managed to swallow it down. 'Perhaps Kira would benefit from female guidance,' he said. 'Many girls are wayward at that age. Maybe she should come and live here in her clan longhouse for a time. She's always got along well with Tenerini, and she's close to Mikini.'

'Not as close as she is to Tresen.'

Despite Miken's best efforts, his voice sharpened. 'What mean you?'

'I need hardly remind you that they're clanmates, Clanleader, and that he's part of this jaunt as well,' said Maxen, his face frigid.

'Are you suggesting that their relationship goes beyond friendship?'

Maxen shrugged and flicked his cape over his shoulders. 'It's no longer seemly that she goes about with him. She'll be seventeen at Turning and needs to accept her responsibility for the smooth running of the Bough.'

'But not for healing?'

'I heal at the Bough,' said Maxen, hefting on his pack, 'ably assisted by Merek and Lern. There's no need for a fourth Healer.' He moved to the door. 'I bid you goodnight, Clanleader.'

'Commander Sarkash asked you to remain here until he could send an escort for you,' Miken reminded him.

'I'm the Tremen Leader. I have no need of an escort and no inclination to wait,' said Maxen, then nodded curtly, pulling the door shut behind him.

Miken went to the window and stood with his hands on his hips, watching Maxen's hawkish form until it disappeared among the trees.

'Undisciplined, undisciplined, undisciplined,' he muttered.

The small band of Protectors marched south-west, the scouts slipping through the trees ahead. The patrol moved faster than Kira liked and more slowly than Kest wanted. The land in this part of the Kenclan octad was hilly and heavily wooded, and where the trees thinned, bitterberry and tagenwort formed barriers, impeding their progress and making manoeuvring the bearers awkward. To add to their difficulties, the rain had grown heavier throughout the morning, trickling down their necks and slicking the windfall littering the slopes so that, despite their best efforts, the Protectors carrying the wounded slid and stumbled, jerking Feseren and Sanaken this way and that. Sanaken remained in his everest-induced stupor, but Feseren's groans grew louder as the journey progressed.

Every fibre of Kira's being rebelled against what was happening. How dare Kest treat injured men like this! But there was nothing she could do other than trudge on, glaring at Kest's back *and* at his face when he occasionally turned around. But Kest seemed completely oblivious, his gaze passing over her impassively. In an effort to distract herself, she began searching the land about her for herbs. There were few, just the occasional rosette of serewort and some straggly annin; too dry, she thought glumly.

The leaf-fall was the deepest she'd ever seen, in places akin to walking in river-sand, and yet as they were coming down a particularly steep slope, she spied a tall clump of withyweed, its slender heads nodding and dipping. It didn't make sense, she thought; withyweed needed a good supply of moisture. Distracted, she slipped on a mossy stone, almost rolling her ankle and yelping in pain.

Kest ordered the patrol to halt and his footsteps thwacked towards her as she knelt to rub it.

'Have you injured yourself?'

'No.'

'I'd stop for a rest but this rain isn't getting any lighter and it's best we press on,' he said wearily.

Kira squashed any feelings of sympathy. Kest had chosen to journey, the wounded hadn't.

They continued, the land rising and falling in a series of ridges, the trees on the slopes low and bent, their roots gripping the earth like old men's hands. Kira had never been here before and she looked about in wonder. In some places the earth gave way completely, revealing shards of pale stone like those lining the Everflow. On past nutting expeditions, they'd used the Everflow's stones to crush the rednuts, lifting them cool and dripping from their watery beds and replacing them each day when they'd finished feasting. But not this time.

The day wore on, the rain plinking through the trees, foliage slapping at them as they passed. Finally they came to a grove of bluenuts and Kest called a halt. It was probably past midday, even though the fragments of sky visible beyond the canopy were the same dull grey as earlier.

Kira's legs and back ached from toiling up and down the slopes, but at least the land under the bluenuts was fairly flat. Bluenuts weren't nut trees at all, but bore crops of large, tough-skinned berries, bluish-black when ripe, and too sour to eat even then, though honeysprites and chatterbirds found them rich pickings. The trees' broad, low-set branches provided good shelter and the formation broke, Kira forcing her tired legs to Feseren's side, and using her spare shirt to dry his face. His cheeks were flushed and she laid her hand on his neck. He was hot, his pulse skittering like a littermouse's.

'How is he?' asked Kest from behind her.

'Feverish,' she snapped.

'Will you give him everest?'

'No.'

Kest crouched beside her and lowered his voice. 'Surely it would ease his pain? Sanaken slept all the way here, whereas Feseren . . .' he trailed off.

'You may know a great deal about the Shargh, Protector Leader, but very little about healing,' said Kira.

Kest grunted and moved away.

'You're not being very nice to him,' rasped Kandor, settling on the ground and wringing out his cape. His voice was a little clearer.

'I'm simply giving him back his own words.'

'He saved us.'

'I know, I know,' muttered Kira, standing and pushing the wet

99

hair from her eyes. 'But I can't forgive him this journey! I can't forgive what he's doing to Feseren. He needs rest, not this constant bumping and jarring. And now he's feverish and I've got no sorren left.' She stared up at the canopy, dangerously close to tears.

'Do you think the wound's infected?' asked Kandor.

'I don't know. It shouldn't be. I cleaned it as I would in the Haelen so there *shouldn't* be any infection.'

'Then there will be none,' Kandor assured her.

'There shouldn't be any,' muttered Kira again.

The Protectors were spread out among the bluenuts collecting fuel, their capes blending perfectly with the bark and foliage. If it weren't for the clunking of axes and the drift of voices, she'd hardly have known they were there.

After a little, Brem came with an armful of wood, dumping it beside the wounded men and quickly building a fire. Kira watched, admiring his deftness as he struck spark from his flints. Soon the twigs began to smoulder.

'Aren't you going to check Feseren's wound?' asked Kandor.

He was as anxious as she was, realised Kira. He hadn't shown any interest yet in becoming a Healer, but he'd accompanied her on enough gathering expeditions and seen enough healing in the Bough to know when things weren't as they should be. The problem was that everything was wet and dirty here. Her breeches were slick with moss, her hands stained with sappy juices.

'I'll give him an infusion to cool him down and help him sleep, but I won't change the bandages until the caves.' Hopefully there'd be a stream nearby; if not, she'd send Protector Leader Kest out to fetch water.

'Will you be wanting water, Healer?' asked Brem, slipping the flints back into his pack and rising. The fire was burning strongly, despite the dampness of the fuel.

'Just . . . just a cupful of boiling water Brem,' said Kira, disconcerted that he seemed to have picked up her thoughts.

'There's a pan set on the other fire,' he said, brushing the leaves from his knees. 'I'll fetch some.'

Kest had set two fires again, keeping Kira and the wounded men separate from the rest of the Protectors. Was it because he didn't want them to be upset by the sight of their injured comrades, or because she was Maxen's daughter? She hoped the former. After all, come this Turning his sister would be her bondsister. How strange to have a sister, especially one she'd scarcely met. It also meant she'd be clan-linked to Morclan, *and* to Kest. He'd be her bondbrother.

As Brem returned bearing a steaming cup, Kira busied herself rummaging in her pack for the winterbloom and beesblest, struggling to subdue the surge of laughter that threatened to erupt. Kest a bondbrother? Impossible!

'What is it?' asked Kandor.

'Nothing,' said Kira, mixing the draught and relieved to feel the bubble of mirth begin to disappear. She left the herbs to steep, then stretched her legs to the fire and yawned. Her cape had kept the worst of the rain off, but her sleeves and lower breeches were saturated.

'Are you hungry?' asked Kandor. 'I've got some mundleberries.'

She shook her head and watched him cram the berries into his mouth. Bruised and swollen his throat might be, but it took more than that to dint his appetite. The air under the trees was warm and she yawned again. Beyond the ripple of smoke, guarding Protectors were pacing along the rim of an imaginary circle, backward and forward, their faces turned away from the comfort of the fire, to where any threat might come from. Was Tresen among them? Their capes and hoods made it impossible to tell them apart.

She'd scarcely seen Tresen since the attack. He was no longer part of their failed nutting expedition, but a Protector, owing his allegiance to Kest, not to Kashclan, or to her. The understanding was like a knife-blade against her skin.

'The infusion's ready,' said Kandor, his mouth full of berries.

'Support his head,' instructed Kira, as she guided the liquid

101

carefully down the wounded man's throat. He swallowed but didn't rouse; the heat from his skin was almost as warm as the fire.

'He's so hot,' said Kandor.

'I know,' snapped Kira, flicking the dregs into the flames and scowling at the empty cup. She forced herself to retrace each of the steps in his healing. She'd been taken up with stitching Sanaken, so Brem had given him sickleseed and staunched his wound. He'd used a torn shirt, which was standard Healer practice, for shirts, like bandages, were made of falzon, a plant whose purifying properties remained potent long after it was woven into cloth. It couldn't have been the shirt. What of the sorren? She'd ground it herself only two days earlier from leaf Merek had gathered at dawning. Dawn-gathered herbs were powerful and sorren lasted many months; it couldn't be the sorren.

The journeying then? The constant disturbance would have hindered Feseren's ability to fight the infection, but it was unlikely to have caused it. In all honesty, she couldn't blame Kest for something that, in the end, must be her fault. At least Feseren had had the strength to swallow the infusion, she comforted herself, and by the time they reached the caves, his fever should have eased. Winter-bloom was a reliable antidote in such cases.

Kest had promised they could stay at the caves as long as necessary, and she'd hold him to that. Three or four days of rest would allow both Feseren and Sanaken to recover a little before enduring the final part of the journey home. She'd still need sorren, though, just to make sure, and for that she'd have to gather. She'd have at least one more argument with Protector Leader Kest before this journey was over.

Night seemed to come suddenly, an abrupt absence of birdsong leaving behind the rattle of the canopy bending under a chill wind.

Kira had spent the last part of the journey scanning for sorren, despite knowing that the land here didn't favour it. It was too stinking dry! She kicked at the leaf litter in frustration and glimpsed a flash of red, startling in the thickening gloom.

'What the . . .' she began, then stopped, causing the Protector behind to cannon into her.

'Don't lag, Healer Kiraon,' ordered Kest.

'But . . .' She twisted round but was jostled forward, able to see nothing more than the grim faces of those following.

'Praise the 'green,' one of them muttered, 'the caves at last.'

They'd come out of a stand of espin and sever, and the land was beginning to rise again, rougher than before, with fewer trees and more gashes of stone where the soil had lost its grip altogether. Now that the trees had thinned, the wind was stronger, adding to the discomfort of the struggling carriers, and flicking Kira's cape across her face in stinging slaps.

She toiled on, using her hands when her feet gave way, until it seemed that the slope had disappeared into the black gulf of the gusting sky. With heaving chest, she scrambled over the last lip of land and straightened.

Deeper slashes of shadow marked the mouths of three caves, two partly blocked with boulders, the third open and massive. She followed Kest in. The pale stone glimmered, seeming almost white and very smooth, the cavern arching upward to a great sweeping ceiling so high that darkness ate the top. There was a rhythmic gurgling, too, quite different to the sluice of the rain outside. Kira stared around in bewilderment.

'Haven't you been here before?' asked Kest, shaking the water from his cape.

Kira shook her head.

'I thought that Healers foraged widely.'

Kira looked at him sharply but there was no antagonism in his face, just relief. He was as pleased to have ended the journey as she was.

'There's nothing in this part of the octad to gather. It's too dry.'

'Usually,' said Kest, palming the water from his face. 'There are fifteen caves that we know of in the surrounding slopes, but only two that are habitable, this one and one further west. The stone in these parts is soft and easily gouged away by rivers. If you listen you can hear it under our feet.'

Kira looked at him in astonishment.

'Further on there's a break in the floor where you can see it too, if you require proof.'

'What's it called?' asked Kira, refusing to be baited.

'The river? It's unnamed.'

'No, the cave.'

'Sarnia.'

'Sarnia,' breathed Kira. She'd heard the word before, but couldn't recall where. 'Did the Protectors name it?'

'It was named by Kentash's people after a settlement in the north. They lived here on and off for three seasons, until their long-house was finished.'

Kira moved her boot experimentally over the gritty floor. It was hard to believe anyone had ever been here before, let alone *lived* here. How would it be to have stone floors and walls and ceilings, instead of wood?

'Feseren slept for the last part of the journey,' said Kest. 'Whatever you gave him seems to have soothed him.'

Kest was trying to mend the breach between them, but fear held Kira silent.

Feseren had slept because the fever had stolen his strength, not because of her healing skill, and now she was going to have to clean the wound again, and use sorren. She glanced up in time to see Kest's face become bland, an expression she was coming to realise masked irritation. Nodding briefly, he strode back to his men, and she followed to where Feseren and Sanaken had been set down.

Brem was already building a fire. Kira had no idea where he'd got the fuel, but she was grateful. The cave was beginning to take on the comforting smell of espin and shelterbush smoke, replacing the dry scent of the stone. There was no reason to worry about water now, not with a river under their feet, so she could use her drinking water to wash her hands, and her spare shirt for clean bandages.

'Do you wish for aid, Healer?' asked Brem.

Kira nodded. She'd known Brem all her life and liked him, even though he'd once threatened to thrash her and Tresen for jumping from an espin onto the longhouse water barrels, and cracking one. His had been a hollow threat, for every child in Allogrenia knew that violence was *prasach*, the domain of the barbarous Terak Kutan, not the Tremen. Back then he'd called her *Kira-si*, after the owlings that had yet to fledge. Now he used the formal title of Healer.

Let's hope it's warranted, Kira thought, as she began undoing the bandage. Then the stench hit her, as powerful as a blow, making her reel back. The wound was slimed and reeking. Not even carrion in summer putrefied this quickly. Brem was rigid, his face filled with horror.

'He was slashed first,' he said thickly.

Kira struggled to make sense of his words and gave up, having no time for anything but ridding the wound of rot.

'Boil water,' she instructed, scrambling to her feet and swinging her pack back on, 'and fill the wound with cloths as hot as he can bear.'

Grabbing her cape, she ran back to the cavern's mouth, fastening the cape as she went, and barging between Kest and the Protector he was conversing with.

'Feseren's wound's poisoned. I must gather,' she barked. In her mind, she was already sprinting towards the Barclan octad where the land was kinder *and* moister.

'I don't know how many times we must have this conversation Healer, but –' started Kest.

'I must have sorren now! Feseren's worsening as we speak!' She tried to push past him but his hand fastened on her arm.

'You'll remain here.'

'You have no right . . .' gasped Kira as his grip tightened, then felt another, gentler restraining hand.

'Kira . . .'

It was Tresen and she turned on him furiously. 'You betray your Healer-blood!'

'You need to *explain* your urgency to Protector Leader Kest.'

Kira's gaze jerked between them, and she gulped down a lungful of air. 'Sorren's the most powerful purifier known in Allogrenia. It kills infection, but I used all I had after the attack.'

'If sorren's so powerful, why has the wound worsened?' asked Kest. 'Has the journeying caused it?'

Kest's voice was as calm as Tresen's, but his face was haggard, and for a moment she was tempted to lay the blame on him. 'The journey might have made it worse, but it hasn't caused it. My healing's been poor,' she forced herself to add.

'I don't believe that,' interjected Tresen.

Kira kept her gaze on Kest. 'I don't ask that you risk your men, Protector Leader. I'll go alone.'

Kest's face took on the look of weary exasperation she'd seen before. 'You don't seem to understand the nature of my job, Healer Kiraon. It's *you* I'm bound to protect. I can't let you go.'

Kira's voice sank to a fierce whisper. 'Feseren's dying, Kest! If you're to keep me here, you'd better get some rope ready, because I won't sit idly by and watch it happen.'

Sarkash's orders were clear, thought Kest. Protect the Leader and his family. Protect, not bind her hand and foot! But he owed his men protection too. Despite what the Writings said, he must fight to save the wounded among his men. To lose any of them was unthinkable, but Feseren! His bondmate, Misilini, was heavy with their first child.

'We'll go together,' he growled, wrenching his pack back over his wet shirt.

The Healer was already at the cave entrance, and he bawled at her to wait, then shouted orders to Penedrin. Kira hesitated for a moment but then disappeared from view. He ran after her, the rain-edged air chill against his face as he plunged down the slope. So much for the warm meal he'd been promising himself, not to mention the blessedness of sleep. The Healer was leaping recklessly from stone to stone, and he copied her as best he could, finally landing with a thud in the leaf litter at the bottom. By then she was already just a smudge among the trees and, smothering a curse, he set off in pursuit.

12

There was no rain on the Grounds, the night as dry as the day that had preceded it, the air heavy with the sere scent of the grass and the husks of dead things. Nothing moved, as if the heat that had stripped the moisture from the targasso and burrel stands had even stilled the rivers within their banks.

In the highest sorcha on the spur, Palansa lay naked on top of the bed-covering, watching the moonlight slide over the curve of Erboran's shoulder. She never tired of watching him, of touching him, of listening to the rhythm of his breathing as he slept.

The moon was big again, spilling in around the door flap and pooling on the wolf-pelts beneath the smoke-vent, painting the sorcha as bright as day. The food baskets Palansa had woven sat in a neat row on the shelves Erboran had built for her. Alongside them were the earthen bowls she'd baked, their rims imprinted with the flowers and targasso leaves she'd pressed into the wet clay. All she needed now were some new pelts for the floor and the sorcha would be as she wanted it.

She craned forward and wrinkled her nose in disgust. The pelts had been hunted in the days of Erboran's father, and were bald in places and torn about the edges.

'What is it?'

Palansa started, still surprised by how quickly Erboran went from sleep to alert wakefulness. 'I was just thinking about pelts for the floor.'

The bed rustled as he turned to face her. 'First I must hunt along the Thanawah for shelf-wood for my join-wife, now it seems I must hunt the Cashgars for wolves. Is she never to be satisfied?' His face was in shadow but his voice lightly teasing.

'I'm well satisfied,' she said.

'Ah, so the Chief is to her liking?' His hand slipped to her thigh, stroking gently, waking her passion again.

'Yes,' she said, forgetting the wolf-pelts and the moonlight. His skin was warm, his hair in soft curls low over his belly. She caressed it, feeling him harden. He pulled her close and they were both wet with sweat before they fell back panting. They lay for a while, letting their breathing steady and listening to the night sounds beyond the sorcha.

'And am I to the Chief's liking?' she asked finally.

'Every woman is to my liking.'

'Ah then, as you've already loved me twice this night, I'll seek another for your enjoyment,' she said, swinging her legs from the bed.

Erboran caught her arm. 'Stay.'

'But Chief Erboran, there are many women who'd be pleased to lie where I now lie.'

'I chose you.'

'Because Arkendrin sought me?' There, it was said, the thought that had haunted her in all their days together. Was she a fool to raise it even now?

But when Erboran spoke, there was no anger in his voice. 'Let us say, Palansa, that the fact that my dear brother also desired you was a bonus.'

She jerked her arm away and Erboran's voice softened. 'I'd chosen you before I knew of Arkendrin's desires. I'd been watching you. The way you walked, the shape of you through your dress, the way the light caught your hair.' His hand stroked the thick fall of her hair down her back. 'And I knew you were capable of more than idle chatter. I could have had nearly any woman on the Grounds, Palansa, but I wanted more than a chipbird to share my bed, to share my life with.'

Palansa's eyes glistened and she lay back down into the crook of his shoulder, her palm on the fine hair of his chest, her ear to the beat of his heart. 'I love you, Erboran.'

'You should,' he said, teasing again, 'as I'm your Chief.'

Ebis lowed out on the Grounds and hunting bats chittered above the sorcha.

'My father says that if rain doesn't come soon, the herders will have to take our ebis beyond the stone-trees,' murmured Palansa.

'The Dendora Plain is Weshargh grazing, as he well knows.'

'But they're blood-tied,' said Palansa.

'The Dendora's had as little rain as we have,' said Erboran.

'What of south then?' pursued Palansa.

'The same. The Soushargh suffer also.'

Palansa sighed. 'I don't understand why the Sky Chiefs don't send rain. Father says the ebi will die soon.'

'Your father forgets the days of plenty, as do many others on the Grounds. The herds grow when the pastures are lush, and shrink when they become bare. The Sky Chiefs follow their own ways, but they've never let the ebis herds dwindle to where they can't grow large again. The rains will come, Palansa, when the Sky Chiefs see fit.'

Erboran fell silent, his breathing sinking to a steady rhythm, and Palansa had just begun to drift into sleep when two high-pitched shrieks tore the darkness. Erboran sprang from the bed, jerking on his breeches as he snatched his spear. There was a third piercing cry and he was gone.

Palansa gripped the cover to herself, rigid. Three cries of the marwing. For Yrkut's sake, let there be a fourth. She strained for sound, but there was nothing. The bats had fled; the ebis were silent.

Lower on the slope, Tarkenda had also risen, throwing on her cape and going to the door to survey the Grounds. The sorchas glimmered in the moonlight but she could see and hear nothing amiss. No lamps burned and no one shouted or wailed. If death had come, it hadn't been here. She turned reluctantly and gazed south-west to where Arkendrin and Urgundin had gone. Had death visited them in the murky land of trees?

The grass whispered and broke and Erboran emerged from the shadows, the moonlight glancing off his spear and gilding the naked skin of his shoulders.

'Is there sickness in the Grounds?' he asked.

'Ermashin's father coughs like the Thanawah in flood and Marenka's babe refuses to suckle. Neither death would be unexpected.'

The cries of the marwing portended death of a more violent nature and Erboran's gaze swung south-west too. Tarkenda knew he wouldn't grieve if Arkendrin were lost; his brother's greed for the chiefship had long ago robbed them of any familial feeling. Tarkenda ducked back into her sorcha, and Erboran followed, settling at the table and taking the honeyed water she offered.

'How does Palansa?' she asked, sitting opposite him and sipping her own drink.

'Well.'

'Has she bled?'

'On the first night, but not since.'

The question was far from idle. The Shargh must know that Palansa had spilled only first-joined blood and might already be carrying the next Chief. Tarkenda hoped it was so, for sons born to a young Chief could grow to manhood under his protection, sparing Palansa the fight Tarkenda had endured to bring Erboran to manhood.

'And how does having a join-wife suit you?' she asked.

'It suits me very well,' said Erboran, smiling.

Indeed it seemed to, for Erboran had an air of contentment Tarkenda had never seen before. Perhaps the match had the good fortune to contain affection. Unexpectedly, her thoughts turned to Ergardrin, to their early days together, awaking an ache of yearning, deep and keen as pain. Then Erboran's bowl clicked back on the table and she was back in the sorcha.

'Time will show what the marwing tells,' he said as he went out.

Tarkenda watched the door flap still, her thoughts on the land of trees again. If there *had* been death there, the news wouldn't reach them for many dawnings.

'Time will show,' she muttered, as she went to her bed.

13

Deep in the forest, Kest was thinking no further ahead than surviving the night. The rain drowned the moon, blinding him to any Shargh who might be near, no matter how many times he wiped his sleeve across his eyes. The Healer had stopped again and was bending down at the bole of a tree. Kest sucked in air in a vain attempt to quiet the roar of his heart. He had no idea what she was looking at and was almost past caring.

Keeping her within vision range was hard enough, for although it was dark she ran as if chased by wolves and with an astonishing sure-footedness. He was well used to rough travel but he'd slipped several times, whereas she hadn't stumbled once.

She turned back to him, her face a pale smudge, hair plastered to her forehead.

'I think we're near Barclan octad,' she said.

'If we are, I don't see anything I recognise,' he admitted. In this light, he couldn't even tell whether the trees were castellas or fallo-woods.

'I've gathered here before,' she continued. 'If we keep westerly, we'll come to espins on a westward-facing slope. There should be sorren there.'

'Should be?' Didn't she *know*?

'Espin's friendly to sorren and western slopes catch the last of the sun,' she said. 'There are terrawoods there, which break the wind, and the ground's spongy and catches run-off; both things suit sorren.'

'How far is this grove?' he asked.

'If we *are* near Barclan octad, we should be there before the night turns.'

'Is there nowhere closer?'

'Do you think I'd be stumbling about in this stinking night if there were?'

'I didn't mean . . .' he began, but she'd set off again and he was forced to follow; weaving between branches, tripping over roots, dodging pale stones and stumbling over darker ones. Fronds whipped his face and scamper vine and sour-ripe tore at his clothes.

After a time the land began to rise and Kira came to a halt again, her breathing as harsh as his, a dark line under her eye appearing and disappearing with each wash of rain.

'You've scratched your face,' he said, but she ignored him, staring at a deeper darkness ahead.

'Espins?' he asked, hope surging.

'By the 'green, I hope so.'

The desperation in her voice lessened his own feelings of inadequacy. As they drew nearer the grove, the tang in the air was unmistakable, heightened by the glove of water each leaf wore. It was drier here too, the rain reduced to irregular plinks, so that he was able to clear his eyes. The Healer dropped to her knees.

'Sorren?' he asked.

She nodded, intent on extricating her herbing sickle. The plant didn't look much different to slipper grass, common enough around the Morclan longhouse, and he watched her cut the stems slowly and carefully. He would have simply ripped it up. She wrapped it in her sling and stowed the sickle.

'Will that be enough?' he asked. She'd gathered very little, considering the effort it had cost them.

'Its potency isn't increased by quantity, and it's important to take only what's needed.'

She set off again, but now her gait was awkward, as if the desperate strength that had propelled her forward earlier had deserted her. He felt scarcely better, his muscles having stiffened in the short time they'd stopped, his belly rattling with hunger. They'd journey better if they stopped, rested and ate; the rain was dwindling now so it wouldn't be quite as miserable. He was about to suggest it when she stumbled, then pitched forward, falling heavily and lying unmoving.

Stinking heart-rot, that's all he needed: an unconscious body to lug through the night. Forcing his aching legs up the slope he dropped beside her and turned her gently.

Her eyes were shut and blood oozed from a cut on her brow, mixing with the leaves and mud coating the side of her face. He wiped it away and her eyes flickered open, then she muttered a word he'd only ever heard very disgruntled Protectors use.

He smiled in spite of himself. 'How do you feel?' he asked.

She struggled into a sitting position, her head in her hands. 'Wonderful, Protector Leader, wonderful.'

He sat on the soggy ground beside her, feeling the wet soak through his breeches. 'I think we can dispense with the title. Just call me Kest.' She looked at him sideways, blood trickling down her cheek. 'You look terrible, Healer Kiraon.'

'You don't look so grand yourself,' she muttered. 'And my friends call me Kira.'

The night was quiet, the only sound the delicate music of droplets falling from the leaf-roof. Nothing moved or gave voice, yet the night held a sense of expectancy, as if the water-washed light of the new day secreted itself behind every bole.

'Dawn's close,' she said softly. 'We've been away too long.'

'We need to rest and eat.'

'We don't have time.'

'Travel is swifter and surer with food in the belly. We'll be back in the caves sooner if we rest and eat now.' He pulled some dried mundleberries from his pack and passed her some. 'Eat,' he ordered, 'then I'll clean that cut.'

'Later,' she said, cramming the berries into her mouth and struggling to her feet.

'*Now.*'

Her mouth set but she bent her head and he gently washed away the mud and leaves. 'You need some bluemint; you don't want it to scar.'

'My scarring concerns me less than Feseren.'

'Bluemint,' he repeated. Why did the best Healer in Allogrenia have to be the stubbornest?

Kira grunted and pulled bluemint from her pack.

'Scarring might concern you when you're older,' added Kest, smoothing it on.

'Healers don't need to be beautiful,' she retorted.

At that age, thought Kest, Kesilini hadn't worried about the neatness of her hair or the brightness of her eyes either. These days she spent half her time peering into the quieter pools of the Drink-water and lamenting that Kasheron hadn't brought any of the fabled looking-glasses south. The Healer was close to her seventeenth Turning, and no doubt would soon be similarly obsessed.

They went on, the rain drifting away and finally silvery fingers of light stealing between the trees making the going easier. Instead of quickening her pace, Kira slowed. Nothing around her looked familiar.

'I don't know this part of the octad at all,' she confessed.

Kest stopped, offered Kira his waterskin, then took a swig himself. His eyes were more grey than blue in the early morning light, but no less intense as he scanned their surroundings, his gaze moving methodically over slope, stone and tree as he turned. 'Ah, we're further north than I thought,' he said, an uncharacteristic grin on his face. 'We can strike south from here to the caves.'

'South?' said Kira. That made no sense at all.

'We approached the caves from downslope yesterday because of the bearers. We can reach them from the spur above, and climb down. It's very steep,' he said.

'Is it quicker?'

Kest nodded.

'Then we'll go that way,' agreed Kira.

Kest took the lead and after a time, the slopes gave way to stone-strewn cliffs. Some of the stones were massive, others small and treacherous. Kest occasionally passed Kira his waterskin and she gulped down the chill water, but they didn't stop and they didn't rest.

Finally, Kest announced, 'We're almost there.'

For a moment he looked as if he were being eaten by the canopy, then he disappeared. She could see nothing but a wall of castellas leaning crookedly into space. Kira scrambled after him. Kest was far below her, bracing himself against the curve of the land, using the scrubby bushes to steady himself as he descended. Kira's heart gave a nauseating jolt.

Once she and Tresen had climbed onto the roof of the Kashclan longhouse, pretending that they were travelling on one of the legendary ships of the north. The game had been fun until it was time to descend, when she'd frozen completely, unable to move. In the end, Miken had had to climb up and bring her down on his shoulders. Tresen had teased her unmercifully but she'd gained her revenge by winning every tree-climbing and jumping game since.

Feseren and Sanaken were both at the bottom awaiting her aid, she kept telling herself as she pushed one faltering foot after the other. In the end she squatted, using her backside more than her legs, her knees trembling with the strain, muddy water soaking her to the skin. Finally Kest came into sight again, standing waiting for her. Gripping her wrists, he half lifted her the rest of the way down.

They were back on the shelf of land rimming the caves, smoke from the campfires purpling the trees. Kira stumbled into the dimmer coolness of the cave, barely aware of Penedrin's salute to Kest or Tresen's shocked eyes on her face. The cavern was warm and smoky, but the wound's stench was worse than she remembered; Feseren's head was rolling from side to side, his breathing as harsh as sand on stone.

'I've kept the wound packed with hot cloths,' said Brem, materialising from the gloom and squatting beside her, 'but he's worsened and will take no water. Have you got the sorren? I've found some stones for grinding.'

'Make enough for Sanaken too,' said Kira, intent on unbinding the second man's wounds. Everest had held Sanaken quiet, but his wounds were as rotten as she'd feared they'd be.

'I can dress the wounds, Healer, you should rest,' said Brem, hovering over her with the sorren, his kindly face creased with concern.

Kira shook her head and tore up the rest of her Protector shirt, her gaze on the thrashing form of Feseren. It was her poor healing that had caused the infections and now she must make amends. She smoothed the sorren into Feseren's wound. Then Brem held him while she bound him up again. She did the same with Sanaken, the task taking far longer, for his wounds were many.

Leaving Brem to wrap each man back into his sleeping-sheet, Kira limped back to the cave's entrance and squinted out. It was past the mid point of the day now, the sun fiery on the white stone and glancing off the water-filled crevices. Squatting by one of the deeper pools, she washed the reek from her hands, then doused her face, gasping as the water opened the cut. Blood dribbled down her cheek and dripped onto her breeches, adding to the sour-ripe stains and crusted mud. Oh to wash in the warm water of her bathing bowl, to slide beneath her sleeping-cover, to know that Feseren and Sanaken were healed, she thought dazedly.

'Kest says you're to rest,' said Tresen, suddenly appearing and hauling her to her feet. 'Kest sleeps now himself,' he added, tightening his grip as he felt her sag, and guiding her back to the cave.

The men taking their meal watched in silence, and Tresen felt a surge of protectiveness. She'd carried out her healing well; none of this was her fault!

Inside, Brem had laid Kira's sleeping-sheet ready, and Tresen lowered her down and tucked it over her. 'Are you hungry?' he asked.

'I need to watch the wounded.'

'Brem and I will watch them and waken you if they worsen,' said Tresen.

'I healed poorly.'

He took her hand in his. 'You've done all you can.'

Her eyes jerked past him and she half roused. 'Where's Kandor?'

'Foraging with Nandrin and Jonkesh. They haven't gone far, he's quite safe,' he said, settling next to her and smoothing the hair back from the cut on her face. 'You look like you've had a fight with a thicket of sour-ripe and the sour-ripe won.'

'It was a hard journey,' she said.

A hard journey; how true that was. He'd chosen not to believe there were strange voices in the night, and so she'd chosen not to believe it too. If they'd both chosen differently, none of this would have happened. But they hadn't wanted to believe that the web of protection they'd woven around themselves was as fragile as a mothcase; no one did. He wondered how Maxen would react. Not well, he suspected.

Once Kira's eyes were shut and her breathing steady, Tresen rose, standing for a moment looking down at her. The firelight glimmered on her hair and lit the planes of her face, honed by exhaustion. For a moment he glimpsed another Kira: older, wiser and sadder. Outside the day was bright with birdsong, but in here, death waited.

Merek stared out of the Bough window. The sun was high, the dew long gone. He should be out gathering, or netting, or blacknutting, or better still, with Kesilini. Even collecting pitchie seeds for Sendra was preferable to being cooped up here. He stuck his head out the window, watching the brown-caped smudges of Kest's men moving on their predictable paths through the trees.

That was the trouble with men who lived their lives under orders; not a single thought of their own. The whole exercise was a complete waste of time in any case. Even if there were intruders in Allogrenia, and they were hostile, they'd never reach the Bough. He'd said as much to the Protector in charge, but the man had simply told him to return to the Bough. He may as well have conversed with a chuff beetle for all the sense he'd got out of him.

Even dealing with Kest would've been better, despite his stiff-necked ways, but Kest was *not available*. He'd gone off after Kira and Kandor, no doubt on Sarkash's orders, for it was the kind of mean-ingless activity the Protector Commander delighted in. After all, even if the intruders were in the same octad as Kira and Kandor, the size of the octad meant that the chances of the intruders stumbling upon them were minuscule. Grunting, Merek threw himself into a chair beside the all-but-dead fire. Sarkash had been closeted with his father in the Herbery for most of the morning, Sarkash probably badgering him about locking everyone away in the clan longhouses until the danger had passed. But how were they to judge that the danger *had* passed if they were all skulking behind their shutters?

Suddenly, the outer doors burst open, but it was only Lern, his arms loaded with windfall. Merek watched him drop his burden into the fire-basket and dust off his shirt.

'What news from the world beyond the door?' asked Merek ironically.

'Who knows?' said Lern, raking the coals back into life and positioning the new log. 'I've spent most of the morning getting Barash's permission to gather wood. He doesn't seem to know what's going on. I don't think the Protectors have organised messengers between the patrols yet.'

'Hardly surprising given that Sarkash is in control.'

'Oh, Sarkash's all right,' said Lern, poking at the new log until flame spurted.

'All right for stacking scavenger leaves and storing water barrels.'

'You've never got along with him,' teased Lern, settling beside Merek, 'just because he thinks the Warens are more important than the Bough.'

'He's certainly ignorant of protocol, if that's what you mean. His first duty was to inform the Bough of the intruders, not send Protectors scuttling all over the forest.'

'He's Commander of the Protectors, Merek, his first duty is to –'

The Herbery door flew open and their father strode out. 'You need to remember, Commander, that *I'm* the Tremen Leader, and it's *I* who'll decide our course of action . . . after due consultation with the council, of course.'

Sarkash followed him across the hall, almost jogging to keep up, his hand brushing at his face. 'I assure you that's not in dispute, Leader Maxen. I simply request you call no Clancouncil until Protector Leader Kest has returned from the Kenclan octad. Apart from anything else, it's unwise to require the Clanleaders to travel from their longhouses until we have a better understanding of the intruders.'

Maxen turned on him. 'And will Kest be able to provide us with that? I think not. He's unlikely to report anything that we don't already know from Pekrash. It requires only one pair of eyes to see slashed trees, Commander.'

'With respect, Tremen Leader, if Protector Leader Kest had only slashed trees to report, he would have returned by now.'

'He may not have located my daughter and son, or if he has, they'll slow him down, neither Kiraon nor Kandor having the strength or discipline of his men,' said Maxen.

'We don't know what Protector Leader Kest has encountered, which is why I urge you to wait.'

'I won't wait, Commander. You will send messages to each of the longhouses that the council will meet tomorrow dawning at the Bough. Provide each Clanleader with an escort if you will, I leave that to your discretion,' he said, drawing himself a draught of ale and drinking deeply.

'I'll provide escorts, as you wish, Tremen Leader Maxen,' said Sarkash heavily. 'I bid you good day.'

Maxen nodded curtly, waiting for the door to shut before saying, 'That man is a fool.'

Lern kept his eyes on the fire. He'd never enjoyed his father's imperious moods, and drinking an ale while not offering Sarkash the barest of hospitality was churlish and embarrassing. Merek seemed to be suffering no such discomfort, drawing himself an ale also, and saying, 'Sarkash should've been retired seasons ago. He seems to be under the delusion that Kasheron came south to establish the Warens, not the Bough.'

Lern glanced from his brother to his father, noting their similarity as he'd done many times before. Why was he so different? Different from them, *and* Kira and Kandor. He felt a surge of envy for his sister and younger brother, for their closeness, then a shiver of apprehension. If only they were safely back here.

His father and Merek were still discussing Sarkash's shortcomings, and didn't notice Lern make his way outside, and towards the guarding Protectors. Just as well his father and Merek were engrossed in denigrating Sarkash; the last thing Lern wanted to do was to have to explain his overpowering need to escape their company. He took a deep breath and felt the tension drain from his shoulders. The forest was full of sunlight and birdsong, and the easy camaraderie of patrolling; not like the Bough, with its endless power plays.

Lern's feelings of frustration weren't new. The realisation that he no longer wanted to live in the Bough – or even to heal – had crystallised slowly over the last few seasons until now, he realised, it was as hard as fallowood sap. All that was left was for him to find the words – *and* the courage – to tell his father.

14

Tenerini lifted the baking boxes from the coals, the lids rattling as her hands shook, and tipped the loaves onto the stone at the side of the hearth to cool. Nutty steam rose and Miken's mouth watered, despite his churning thoughts. The Kashclan hall was quiet, most of the clansmen and women having already breakfasted and returned to their rooms to begin their daily tasks.

'Where's Mikini?' asked Miken suddenly.

Tenerini was taking out her anxiety on the dough, her flour-covered hands slapping and punching. 'She's gone with Sherine and Mira to collect redwort.'

'Not beyond the castellas?' said Miken sharply.

'Of course not. They know Protector Leader Senden's orders as well as we do.' She worked for a moment in silence, folding and refolding the dough, then half shook her head.

'What?' asked Miken.

'The girls have finished a length of cloth and simply *must* have redwort for the dyeing. So many young men stationed so close to the longhouse! I suppose there has to be some compensation for all Senden's prohibitions,' she said, her hands thumping up and down. 'I think the Protectors appreciate the company too. It can't be very interesting treading the same piece of forest over and over again.'

'Not as interesting as pretty girls,' agreed Miken, his thoughts on the rednut groves in Kenclan octad.

Tenerini wiped her hands on her apron and lifted the bread crock from the shelf. 'At least they've taken Mikini's mind off Tresen.' She faltered and bit her lip.

Miken sighed. He could add nothing more to what he'd said last night as she'd lain weeping in his arms. Tresen and Kira and Kandor were beyond their reach and beyond their aid. All they could do was to put their trust in Kest and wait. And waiting was always the hardest.

'They should've been back by now,' she said hoarsely.

They'd been through that too. 'We don't know how long it took the patrol to find them. They might've missed them at the rednuts and have had to double back to search the octad. It's not easy in Kenclan, given the terrain, and if one of them has turned an ankle or something, which is possible in the stonelands, it'd slow the whole group down.'

'The first batch is ready,' said Tenerini, when her voice was steady again.

Miken selected the largest one and broke it in two, inhaling the doughy odour, but her words had sharpened his own worry again, robbing him of enjoyment. She was right; the nutting party should have returned by now. And he'd been so busy with the Clancouncil, he hadn't even farewelled Tresen properly when he'd left.

May the alwaysgreen Shelter you, and guide your way; may its shadow bring you home again, lest you stray. Home again . . .

Tenerini's eyes were upon him and he took a bite from the loaf. 'Fit for a feast. Let's have some tea, too,' he said with forced cheeriness, going to the thornyflower bin. Beyond the castellas, he could see Senden's patrol moving backward and forward through the trees. Where in the 'green was Kest's?

He hoped with all his heart that all was well, but it was useless pretending; it mightn't be. The Shargh and their kin were the only people south of the Azurcades and their brutality was well known. Tresen wouldn't even be able to protect himself – his training was too short – and he was with Kira and Kandor. Tresen wouldn't leave Kira, and she'd never abandon Kandor. One sword for three people, against how many Shargh?

A figure emerged from the trees, and Miken froze. It was Sarkash, stoop-shouldered and grim-faced.

'What is it?' asked Tenerini.

'Commander Sarkash,' said Miken slowly. 'I'll get another cup.'

Tenerini's stricken gaze remained fixed on Miken's face.

'We'll need some platters for the nutbread,' added Miken, 'and some sweetfish and sour-ripe. The Commander probably hasn't eaten.'

There was a knock at the door but Tenerini remained rooted to the spot.

'Don't keep the Commander waiting on the doorstep,' said Miken gently.

Tenerini took off her apron and went to the door while Miken set the platters on the table.

'Kashclan welcomes you, Tarclansman Commander Sarkash,' said Tenerini formally, her voice betraying only the slightest tremble.

'Tarclan thanks Kashclan,' returned Sarkash, his gaze already seeking out Miken.

'Commander Sarkash,' said Miken. 'You have news?'

Sarkash's hand fluttered over his face. 'I regret, Clanleader Miken, that Protector Leader Kest has yet to return. When he does, you will, of course, be informed.'

Informed! It was his son and his clan-kin who were out there; Sarkash was behaving as pompously as Maxen. Miken quelled his irritation, reminding himself that the man was a guest in his longhouse.

'You've eaten, Commander?'

'Not yet.'

'Please join us.'

Sarkash nodded and some of the strain eased from his face as they settled at the table and Miken filled their cups. Tenerini served the fish and added bowls of sour-ripe, riddleberries and honey, then pulled the last batch of nutbread from the coals and tumbled it steaming onto a platter.

For a while they ate in silence; the only speech the offering of food and polite acceptances or refusals. When they had finished, Tenerini collected the platters and brought a jug of withyweed ale and a small bowl of rednuts before muttering an excuse and withdrawing.

The door clicked behind her but for a moment neither man spoke. The hall remained empty too, as if word of Sarkash's presence had spread, and the Kashclansmen and women were reluctant to disturb them.

'I'm sorry I couldn't bring you news of your son and clan-kin,' began Sarkash.

'But that's obviously not why you're here,' said Miken curtly.

'No, it's not,' said Sarkash. 'I've been in discussions with Tremen Leader Maxen, and he requests your presence at the Bough, for a council meeting, tomorrow dawning.'

'Surely it's a waste of time meeting before Kest returns,' he said in surprise, studying Sarkash's impassive face. 'You told him this?'

'I . . . Tremen Leader Maxen and I discussed a number of things.'

More like Maxen blustered and you were forced to listen, thought Miken, his sympathy rising. 'Did you discuss what we should do now our defences have been breached?'

'That will be decided at the council.'

'It will be pointless discussing anything at council without your presence, Commander. It's the Protectors who ensure our safety, not the Bough.'

'That's not the Tremen Leader's view,' said Sarkash carefully.

Miken took a handful of rednuts and rolled them slowly between his fingers, considering the older man thoughtfully. Sarkash could have sent a messenger with news of the Clancouncil meeting, yet he'd chosen to come himself.

'The relative authority of the Bough and the Warens has never been clearly delineated,' said Miken at last, 'because what's affected one hasn't really affected the other, until now . . .'

Sarkash said nothing, watching him intently.

'Of course,' went on Miken, 'in one sense, the Warens' responsibility is essentially the same as the Bough's, namely to ensure the safety and well-being of the Tremen. Kasheron's passion for healing didn't blind him to the realities of what he'd fled in the north, and he clearly intended the Warens to be of equal importance to the Bough, or else he wouldn't have established it as a separate entity with its own Leader.'

'I'm hoping that's the view the council will take, Clanleader Miken. The Warens don't wish to usurp the power of the Bough, but it needs to be remembered that Kasheron established the Protectors as well as the Bough, and obviously foresaw a role for both of them.'

'I take your point, Commander,' said Miken, offering to refill Sarkash's cup. The older man declined, pushing his chair from the table. 'I'll send extra men to escort you to the morrow's council,' he said, moving towards the door.

'There's no need –' began Miken.

Sarkash raised his hand. 'I think it best that we err on the side of caution, Clanleader Miken, at least until Protector Leader Kest returns and we know more fully the nature of the threat.'

Long after those of his clan had gone to their beds, Miken sat alone in the hall, dread keeping him wakeful. Outside, the forest looked as it always had, yet the churn in his guts told him that somehow, somewhere, things had changed. He feared that his old life, *their* old life, was coming to an end. Was it just their peace of mind that had ceased with the arrival of the intruders, or the long peace of Allogrenia? One thing at least was plain: the uncomplicated coexistence of the Bough and the Warens was no more.

Miken's gaze drifted round the hall. Kasheron's followers had laboured long and hard to establish Allogrenia: building the Bough and longhouses, planting the great circles of alwaysgreen, filling the pages of the Sheaf with Healer knowing, imprinting each new generation with a hatred of metal. Axe-wood was fire-hardened for cutting, pots fired for boiling and beards removed with clear-root instead of blades.

And yet Kasheron and his folk had worn swords at their belts when they'd entered the forest, carrying more on their packhorses, *and* Kasheron had established the Warens, with its systems of Protector training and patrolling. Had Kasheron brought part of his warrior twin Terak with him, or was it simply that a lifetime of fighting couldn't be so easily cast aside? And was the coming confrontation between the Bough and the Warens to play out Kasheron's and Terak's conflict all over again? Was that what the heave of his stomach portended?

Miken rose and wandered round the hall, creaking boards following his footsteps. Maxen had already struck the first blow by demanding the Warens bow to his authority. If tomorrow's council acquiesced, the Tremen would be forced to invest all their futures in the wisdom of a single man – and one whose judgement had already been shown to be significantly clouded in relation to his daughter.

Miken stopped at the window, staring out into the darkness. Sarkash had come here tonight seeking his support, but he was only one of eight councillors. What of the others? As young men they'd all served as Protectors, but that was many seasons past for most of them, and none had returned to the Warens, concerning themselves with gathering rights, the exchange of surplus for lack, and the provisioning of their longhouses.

Miken frowned. Yes, the other Clanleaders attended every Clancouncil, as indeed they must, but they rarely disputed anything Maxen said. Only his own voice and Marren's were ever raised in challenge. Not that there had been a major issue to disagree on. Life in Allogrenia had long been ordered and predictable: the seasons came and went, marked by the celebrations of Turning and Thanking, bondings and birthings, and the lying to rest of the old among the roots of their clan's alwaysgreens. There had never been a need to debate the relative authority of the Bough and the Warens, let alone resolve it.

Snapping the shutters closed, he stomped back to the table, a single lamp burning on it. Maxen was his clan-kin but he had to admit that he'd never had much liking for him, nor respect for his skills. Fasarini had been the better Healer of the two, despite being a Sarclanswoman, but she'd died young and no one had challenged Maxen for the leadership. In retrospect, that had been a mistake.

Menedrin of Sarclan could have challenged, for his healing skills were equal or superior to Maxen's, but Menedrin had been a shy man and unwilling to put himself forward, and so Maxen had continued in the Bough. His healing skills hadn't grown over the seasons, but his arrogance certainly had.

Miken snuffed out the lamp and made his way out of the hall into the passage. Whichever way you looked at it, the morrow's Clancouncil could bring only ill news.

15

Kira jerked awake as a hand gripped her shoulder. A dark shape loomed over her and she felt a moment of confused terror until she realised it was Tresen, his eyes hollow pools, the cavern beyond him bathed in yellowy light. It was almost dusk.

'The fever's eased but his breathing's changed,' he whispered urgently.

She focused on the sounds around her and a memory of pretty stones came back to her. She'd spent the day at the Drinkwater collecting stones, carrying them home in a wooden bucket, swinging it as she went. They'd rolled together and rattled, and that's what she could hear now: rattling.

She struggled out of her sleeping-sheet and hurried to Feseren, laying her hand on his forehead. He was definitely cooler, but his chest rasped and heaved as if he were drowning.

'He's got worse and worse,' said Tresen, crouching by her side. 'Brem and I think we should raise him to help his breathing.'

Kira glanced to the Kashclansman, grim and silent on the other

131

side of the fire. None of it made sense. 'The fever's less. He shouldn't be struggling to breathe. Maybe –' she started.

'We have to raise him!' interrupted Tresen. He heaved the unconscious man half upright, and thrust his pack under his shoulders, but Feseren continued to gasp. Brem rose and left the cave.

'He can't bear to witness my failure,' said Kira.

'Why do you always think it's about you?' snapped Tresen. 'Brem's been stuck here all day. He's gone to stretch his muscles, that's all.' Tresen envied Brem's escape from the death-filled cave.

'You should go too,' said Kira.

Tresen coloured. 'I'll fetch you food. It's too long since you've eaten.'

Kira stared down at Feseren, barely aware of Tresen going. Feseren shouldn't be struggling to breathe. The thought congealed in her head and she couldn't move past it. Footsteps approached and she glanced up, surprised that Tresen had returned so soon, but it was Kest.

'Tresen's got food for you,' he said. 'Come and eat outside.'

She shook her head.

He squatted beside her. 'There's nothing more to be done here.'

His gentleness was harder to bear than his anger. 'I thought we agreed you weren't a Healer, Protector Leader.'

'Have you seen death before Kira?'

'I . . .' her eyes burned and she dropped her head.

Kest took her arm, guiding her across the cavern until the pale stone beneath her feet was replaced with earth and simpleweed. He lowered her onto a broad stone a little apart from the Protectors and settled by her side.

'Here,' he said, giving her a double handful of sour-ripe and rednuts.

For a long while Kira sat looking down at them, as if from far away.

'Eat, Kira.'

She put a sour-ripe in her mouth and tart juice squirted down her throat, waking her appetite. She ate another and another, finally raising her head and looking around. The Protectors were eating too, Kandor sitting next to Penedrin, his face alight as he listened to the men around him. Beyond him she could see the tops of castellas, severs and fallowoods bending in a soft breeze. Everything was the same as she remembered, yet unutterably altered.

'There were two deaths in my longhouse last season,' said Kest quietly. 'One was my father.' Kira looked at him startled.

'I wasn't called.'

'No Healers were.'

Kira nodded. The death of the aged was a matter for each clan. Kashclan used healing to prolong the lives of their old, but not all the clans did. Kira remembered that when Menini's mother had died, the helper had refused Maxen's offer to accompany her to her longhouse. 'In the end, even the alwaysgreen must fall,' she'd said.

Kest sat watching her. At least she was eating now, and a little colour was coming back to her face, though she still looked ill: the cut on her brow dark against her skin, her eyes more green than gold. And what he must say now wasn't going to help.

'I know the pattern of death,' he said, as matter-of-factly as if he were discussing the weather. 'The way Feseren's breathing . . . it's the way my father breathed at the end.'

Her eyes flashed to his. 'Feseren's young.'

'I know.'

'You're wrong. His fever's eased, he can't be dying,' insisted Kira, every fibre of her being screaming denial.

Kest had heard many tales of Kira's healing skill: of how she'd saved Narini and her babe when both seemed lost, how she'd cured old Barenen's cough when even Maxen had despaired of it, how she'd set Dernash's smashed hand so that it was as whole and fair as the other. She hadn't failed, ever. Healing meant life, not death. He sighed. Dusk was invading the trees again, and soon darkness

133

would hold the forest. Had the Shargh been alone, or were there others who waited now, as he did, for the ending of the day?

'Keep Kandor with your men this night,' she muttered.

He felt a stab of surprise. Had she accepted the inevitable after all?

'I'll share the watching with you.'

'I'll do it alone.'

'Feseren's my clanmate.'

Her head jerked up, a mix of emotions flicking across her face: shock, fear, shame. 'I didn't know . . .'

'I'd watch in any case. The men are under my care, regardless of clan,' he said, looking towards the Protectors clustered round the fire. He'd be the first Protector Leader in the history of Allogrenia to lose a man; *men*, he amended grimly.

The birdcall faded and the Protectors settled down in their sleeping-sheets, their mood sombre. Deeper in the cavern, the fire turned from bright flames to glowing coals, Penedrin coming to replenish the wood and exchange quiet words with Kest. Kira sat motionless, her attention fixed on Feseren. A long wrenching inward breath, an agonising hiatus, then a hoarse exhalation. His eyes were shut and his head had ceased its rolling. Kira took his hand in hers, feeling as if she'd stopped too, as if everything had stopped. She had no sense of a time before the cavern, and no hope of anything after. Feseren was dying; all her Healer senses told her, yet her heart refused to accept it.

She'd cleansed the wound, stitched the wound, bound the wound. The sorren had been pure, the falzon bandages the same as those she'd bound Sherendrin with, Mihrin, Jerid . . . They'd healed, they'd lived . . .

Feseren exhaled and there was absolute silence: no murmur of voices, no crackle of fire, nothing. Kira had stopped breathing too, all her strength focused on him, willing his chest to move, his heart to beat again. Firelight moved, but not flesh. Suddenly the pain in his body surged into her fingers and palm, burning her like flame. Gasping, she dropped his hand and sprang back, gaping at her hand and expecting it to be as charred as firestick, but it was unmarked.

'It's done, Kira, it's over. He's at peace,' said Kest softly.

She was overcome with nauseating weakness. The world she'd known had been torn apart and rebuilt in an alien mix – the air was too thin, the stone closing in and crushing her. With the last of her strength, she scrambled to her feet and fled.

'Kira!'

Kest's feet pounded behind her and his hand skimmed her shoulder as he lunged, but she was already plunging down the slope, her legs having collapsed beneath her, the world turning over and over, scraping and gouging her. Finally there was an immense wrench as Kest halted her descent.

'Are you hurt?' He was panting almost as harshly as Feseren, his hands moving over her, testing for injury. 'Are you hurt?'

She couldn't answer him. The fall had smashed the air from her lungs and she was dying too, going with Feseren into the dark cold places under the earth. Kest's arms jerked her upright, pressing her against his heart, and her senses were flooded with the scent and sense of him, dragging her back to life.

Kest felt her convulse against him, felt the wetness soak through his shirt as she sobbed. It was a long time before her shudders eased and she drew away from him, standing with bowed head. Kest didn't speak. What was there to say? That this nightmare was over? That he could undo death? Brem had told him that Sanaken's wounds were now as rotten as Feseren's.

'We need to go back,' he said, staring into the darkness, acutely aware that his sword was still in the cave.

'No.'

A figure appeared on the cave ledge above, dark against the wash of wood smoke, then disappeared as it made its way down. Thank the 'green for a clanmate, thought Kest, as Tresen approached.

'Stay with your clanmate for a little then bring her back to the cavern,' said Kest. 'Don't delay too long, Protector,' he cautioned.

Tresen bowed and watched his Leader make his way back up the slope. Kira's face was tear-stained but calm, and for the first time in all their seasons together he didn't know what to say. The silence stretched between them, and still he was held mute. And then, off in the west, a bird gave voice.

'The mira kiraon,' he said. 'Your namesake.'

'The first Kiraon's.'

'It's said she was a great Healer, yet even she couldn't save everyone,' said Tresen.

Kira said nothing.

'We need to go back to the cave. It's not safe here,' said Tresen.

'I'm not going back.'

'Kandor's there.'

'How can I go back when I've killed their friend?'

'It's not about you, Kira. The Shargh killed him.'

Kira turned on him furiously. 'I'm a Healer! Yet I couldn't heal him!'

Tresen sighed. 'No one could.'

'My father could have.'

'You know that's not true. You know you're a better Healer than him.'

'No!' Her hands had balled into fists and she was glaring at him.

'Maybe there's some things that can't be healed,' he said, glancing nervously into the dark.

'All things can be healed!'

'There are stories told by the Protectors that aren't to be spoken of outside the Warens.' He shivered slightly. 'The Shargh blades . . . there's something about them.'

Kira froze. Kest had said the same thing, two days and a lifetime ago. *Fire with flatswords brings the bane . . .*

Understanding hit her like a falling tree and she faltered. Feseren had *burned* with fever. The world swayed and Tresen caught her arm.

'Back to the cave,' he said firmly.

16

Miken scowled down at the table, his thoughts boiling. No sign of Tresen, or Kira, or Kandor, and yet Maxen seemed to have nothing better to do than engage in politicking. Everyone was seated and ready to start except Maxen, who stood apart, deep in conversation with his eldest son. What was so important that Maxen must tell Merek now? Nothing! Maxen was simply taking the opportunity to underline his authority by keeping everyone waiting. *And* to push Merek forward by keeping him in the hall for the Clancouncil, where he had no right to be. It might even suit Maxen if Kira didn't return, thought Miken bitterly.

Sendra appeared at his elbow, pale-faced and shadow-eyed, bearing a pot of steaming thornyflower tea, and Miken sobered.

'Tenerini sends greetings,' he said, touching her hand. 'She's not sleeping much either.'

'We must hope that the alwaysgreen Shelters them all.'

Miken nodded, watching the elderly helper moving down the row of councillors, but his hopes lay more in Kest and his men. No sign of them and no word. Kest had taken only half a patrol, just eleven men including himself. If Kest *had* struck trouble he'd have no men spare to send messengers back. Miken sighed and directed his gaze to the carvings above. Castella leaves, lissium blossom, tippets and springleslips, but no mira kiraon. Perhaps Kasheron hadn't wanted to be reminded of the mother he'd lost.

Who'd succeed Maxen if their own Kiraon were lost too? Not Merek – Miken would see to that. The Bough wouldn't have another Leader whose passion lay in control rather than cure.

'Maxen should make a beginning,' grumbled Dakresh beside him.

Miken eyed the disgruntled Sherclan leader sourly; it was rare that the council wasn't waiting for *him* to appear.

'I'm sorry there's no word of your son,' added Dakresh.

'There's time yet.' Miken paused. 'I don't know why we're meeting today. It's hard to see what we can do until Kest's patrol returns.'

'His return will make no difference,' replied Dakresh, his grizzled brows settling lower. 'Strangers have found their way in. The only question is, what's to be done about it.'

'Or who's to do it.'

Dakresh's rheumy eyes came to his. 'It's the Protectors' task to keep us safe.'

'Under whose orders?'

'I . . .' began Dakresh, but was interrupted by Maxen calling the council to order.

Miken's gaze moved over his fellow councillors as Maxen started the opening courtesies. Dakresh usually agreed to anything to get his aching bones home, and the rest were just as bad. Even Farish, who was half the age of some of those present, merely mimicked his neighbour Berendash's views. Only Marren of Morclan would occasionally back him up.

'I won't waste time going over what's already known,' Maxen was saying, 'our task is to determine what's to be done. I've given the matter considerable thought and there's no evidence to suggest the intruders are hostile. There have been no attacks on the longhouses or reports of Tremen being approached. Therefore I see no reason to continue the prohibition on gathering beyond the First Eight. Such a prohibition is unsustainable in any case.'

Miken felt his mouth gape open and shut it.

'I'm glad to hear it,' said Berendash, rising. 'The blacknuts are ripening ungathered.'

Farish was the next on his feet. 'The feathergrass tubers are also wasting,' he added.

'We've all found the curtailing of gathering difficult,' said Miken tersely, as he rose. 'But as Clanleaders we're obliged to put the safety of our longhouses before convenience. Nor are we at liberty to disregard the instructions of those trained to protect us.'

'I think, Clanleader Miken, that we're all aware of the purpose of the Protectors,' said Maxen. 'But it's the council's role to decide the future of the Tremen.'

'In matters concerning the daily doings of the longhouses and the octads, perhaps. But I can't agree with you in the matter of our people's safety. Kasheron established the Protectors for that purpose.'

Maxen glanced around. 'It's hardly surprising to anyone here, Clanleader, that you can't agree with me.'

There were several guffaws and Miken's guts tightened. 'Are you suggesting the council ignores Commander Sarkash's advice?'

'Sarkash's *advice* is precisely that,' said Maxen. 'It's given to us to consider, as we consider other factors in discharging our duty.'

'In that case, let us be absolutely clear what these other factors are,' countered Miken. 'We don't know how many intruders are in Allogrenia, we don't know *where* they are, we don't know what their intentions are. Just because the intruders have so far not attacked individual Tremen or the longhouses – *as far as we know* – doesn't mean they don't intend to. What we *do* know is that trees have been slashed, leaving a path for others to follow. What we *do* know is that Commander Sarkash, *whose duty it is to protect us*, has asked us to temporarily limit our gathering to the areas where he can safeguard us.'

'Thank you, Clanleader,' responded Maxen smoothly. 'Has anyone else anything to contribute?'

Dakresh wedged himself upright, his knobbly hands gripping the table. 'Have you read in your Writings, Leader, who these intruders might be?'

'The Writings speak only of healing,' said Maxen, 'but everyone here is familiar with Protector-knowing. The Terak Kutan hold the north and the Illian and Terkirs traverse the plains south of them. The Shargh were scattered countless seasons past, but one branch, the Ashmiri, have long reaped the rewards of being peaceable, free to go where they will. As the Ashmiri are a restless people, given to wandering, it's most likely they.'

'That knowing is old,' broke in Miken, springing to his feet. 'It's the way things were when Kasheron entered the forest. Who knows what's happened since?'

'Who they are is of less consequence than why they have come,' said Maxen.

'Perhaps they're merely curious,' suggested Farish, half rising and glancing at Berendash.

Maxen steepled his fingers thoughtfully. 'That's my belief. After all, we keep no grazing animals and we meld nothing precious from metal. There's nothing of value here for them.'

Marren's chair squeaked as he rose and said, 'I find it strange that they haven't been *curious* in the past. As you've said, the Ashmiri roam both north and south. They must've come to our borders often. Why haven't they come in before?'

'They may have, but left no sign,' said Maxen.

'If the intruders are Ashmiri, they'll have no love for us,' said Miken.

'How know you this?' asked Maxen.

141

'The Ashmiri share blood with the Shargh, and *they* have a long hatred for the northern seed.'

Maxen smiled tightly. 'Our knowing is old, Clanleader, as you've already pointed out.'

'Some things don't change.'

The councillors moved restlessly and it was Marren who finally broke the silence. 'Perhaps, until we hear to the contrary, it would be safer to assume they *are* hostile.'

'We cannot disrupt the doings of the longhouses merely on an assumption,' said Maxen.

'Yet you would risk their safety on an assumption,' retorted Miken, barely rising.

'I think this is a pointless debate, Clanleader, like so many others you and I have engaged in,' said Maxen. 'Rather than waste the valuable time of the rest of the council, I suggest we call for a division now.'

'Any debate on the safety of the Tremen is far from pointless!' exclaimed Miken. 'Allogrenia has been breached! Strangers have invaded our land, could still be here, and we don't know their purpose. It was for this that Kasheron established the Warens, that he made Protector training part of what it is to be a Tremen man. To ignore the Warens is to ignore Kasheron's wisdom and foresight at our peril!'

Maxen drew himself up to his full height. 'Do not have the presumption to lecture *me* on Kasheron's intentions, Clanleader! He built the Bough as the centre of healing; he made *it* the heart of Allogrenia, not the Warens. He sundered a people to leave the stench of sword-death behind. It was his intention that we would never again be governed by the sword and, by the 'green, it's an intention I intend to keep! The Protectors *will* bow to the Clancouncil!'

'Are we to leave ourselves defenceless? Is that what you want?' demanded Miken, his finger jabbing the air.

'No one said anything about being defenceless,' broke in

Dakresh. 'The Protectors are there if we need them. Be seated, man, so we can get on with the council.'

There was a general murmur of agreement. 'I thank you Sherclan Leader for reminding us of our purpose today,' said Maxen. 'We will now decide, as is the right and duty of the council, whether we return to our normal gathering, or if we remain confined within the First Eight. Those who would declare for the former, move to my right hand, those for the latter, to my left.'

There was a scraping of chairs and a shuffling of feet, and when the room had stilled again only Miken and Marren remained on Maxen's left.

'The division is clear,' said Maxen. 'Ensure your longhouses know the council's will. Now, are there any further matters for discussion?'

Eyes slid towards Miken, but Miken's lips remained tightly closed. What was the point? The council had decided that no threat existed, and so no stinking threat existed! No doubt if his son and his clan-kin were dead, they would have somehow murdered themselves! Miken heard Maxen begin the words of closing but he was already striding towards the door and was halfway across the Arborean before a shout managed to penetrate his seething thoughts.

'Miken!'

He whirled; it was Marren. 'We need to speak.'

'Of what? Apparently all is well in Allogrenia and we can all go back to our slumbers,' he said sarcastically and went to stride on, but Marren caught his arm.

'When the Leader's a fool, then the protection of the Tremen comes back to those who aren't,' said Marren.

'The Bough's all-powerful,' said Miken. 'We can't gainsay it.'

'No, my friend,' said Marren urgently. 'But it's our duty as Clanleaders to protect our longhouses as well as those we love. That hasn't changed. We need to go to the Warens. We need to speak with Sarkash.'

Miken steadied. Marren was right. They needed advice on what might still be done to keep their longhouses safe – to keep the *Tremen* safe – and to plan for what might come. He nodded and together they set off swiftly up the Drinkwater Path.

Kest's patrol moved slowly, maintaining a tight formation, with Kira and Kandor in the centre and the lifeless bodies of Feseren and Sanaken borne at the rear. Sanaken had died a day after Feseren without ever rousing from his everest-induced sleep. The remaining men went without speaking, grim-faced and weary with travelling. They'd scarcely paused since first light but were nearing the entrance to the Warens and would soon be able to rest and eat.

Kest walked to one side, his gaze on the surrounding trees but his thoughts on his Commander. He'd fulfilled his orders in keeping the Healer and her brother safe, but it had cost the lives of two of his men. He replayed what had happened for the thousandth time. The flatsword had been poised above the Healer, and any delay would have brought it slicing down across her throat, yet he wondered again whether he'd erred, and whether Feseren and Sanaken had died because of it. He plucked a leaf of cindra and chewed on it, its pungency driving the tiredness from his brain. He must report to Sarkash and arrange an escort for the Healer and her brother back to the Bough. Then he must take Sanaken and Feseren back to their longhouses. He clenched his jaw. *Here's your bondmate, Misilini. Here's the father of your child. I'm sorry he's dead.*

He spat out the leaf and wiped his mouth. Misilini might not even stay at the Morclan longhouse, preferring to raise her child among her own. Sanaken was unbonded but not unloved. There would be much suffering among his kin too.

Kest shrugged off the thought. His men were exhausted, their faces etched with grief. The Healer was slumped against her clanmate, her eyes on the ground. There were many victims of this bloody encounter.

*

The Protectors came to a halt and Kira looked up at the alwaysgreen, for a moment struggling to think which one it was. Nogren, she realised numbly; they must be at the Warens.

'You can rest and eat here,' said Kest, 'while I arrange a patrol to take you to the Bough.'

Kira's sense of foreboding intensified. She'd disobeyed her father by leaving the Arborean and she'd not taken the night voices seriously. And, most terrible of all, she'd failed in her healing.

The formation broke as the men were forced to shuffle round Nogren, the Protectors having to tilt the bearers to clear its trunk. One of the bodies slid sideways and a white arm slipped from beneath the covering, swinging limply.

Kira faltered but Tresen's grip tightened. 'Almost there,' he said soothingly.

They cleared the entrance and moved into the cool moistness of the Warens, the Protectors quickening their pace again. For the first time on the return journey, they spoke to each other in muttered snatches. Other Protectors appeared, their greetings cut short as they took in the grim faces and bearers. Kira heard fragments of speech being passed to and fro: the Shargh attack, the woundings, the deaths. The news ran like a wave before them, silencing everyone it touched.

After a while, orders boomed and the patrol split, Penedrin leading Kira and Kandor off into one of the smaller eating caverns. The rest of the men, along with Kest and Tresen, continued, their gritty footfalls echoing into silence.

Kira collapsed at a table, laying her head on her arms, watching Penedrin in conversation with another Protector. His voice was low, but she had no doubt what he was saying. She shifted her gaze to the lamp. It was made in the old style, its bulb of glass-root crazed and all but empty. That was how she felt at the moment: empty, scoured out, bereft.

'I'm starving,' said Kandor, plonking down beside her, his face filthy and his hair wild.

'I think Penedrin's getting food for us.'

'I wish he'd hurry up.' His fingers tapped the table. 'I hope it's not more dried mundleberries.'

Kira looked up at him. 'You should wash your hands and face before you eat.'

'So should you.'

Kira straightened. She didn't need her brother to tell her that she looked terrible. 'You –' she began, but Penedrin was approaching with a platter of sweetfish, nutbread and dried sour-ripe.

'You've water still in your waterskins?' he asked, his face shadowed with stubble and grubby as Kandor's.

Kira nodded.

'There's no time to brew tea,' he said apologetically. 'As soon as Protector Leader Kest returns, we'll be leaving.'

Kira thanked him and he resumed his muted conversation with the other Protector. Protectors came and went, their gazes curious, and Kira forced herself to concentrate on the sweetfish.

'The men are worried about Kest,' mumbled Kandor, cramming a thick wedge of nutbread into his mouth.

'Kest?'

'He's lost men.'

The sweetfish balled in Kira's throat and she swallowed with difficulty. 'The fault's not his.'

'That's what the men say.'

'Is Sarkash so unreasonable?' She didn't know much about the Commander, only that her father and Merek thought him a fool.

'It's not Sarkash who's in charge.'

'What?'

'Weren't you listening to what the men were saying on the way in? There's been some sort of argument while we've been away. Apparently father now commands the Protectors as well.'

'But surely Sarkash knows more about the Protectors and keeping us safe than father?'

146

Kandor started on the pile of sour-ripe. 'Of course he does. But you've heard Merek on the subject, surely. *Kasheron turned his back on killing in the north to establish a centre of healing in the south. That centre is the Bough. All things, including the Warens, must serve the Bough. It's what the great Kasheron himself intended.*'

'But Kasheron set up the Protectors too. They've always been separate. Before Sarkash, Thendron commanded them, and before him Barek. They've never been commanded by the Bough.'

'Yes, but things are different now father's Tremen Leader. It's all about power,' he said and sighed.

Several caverns further on in the Warens, Kest stood before his Commander, his back rigid despite his aching muscles, his face determinedly expressionless. He'd finished delivering his report some time ago, but still the silence stretched; Sarkash's gaze was on a point beyond his shoulder. Finally the Commander's eyes refocused, and he gestured to a chair.

'Sit, Protector Leader, you've had a difficult few days.'

Kest settled opposite, the ache in his muscles lessening, but not the churn in his guts. He could hear the spit of moon moths caught in the lamp flame. Only a single lamp burned and it lit the planes of Sarkash's face, making him look old suddenly, and worn.

'You're sure they were Shargh and not Ashmiri?' asked Sarkash.

'They were armed with daggers and flatswords, and wore no patterning. Unless the Ashmiri have given away their arrows and stopped dyeing their faces, they were Shargh.'

'It's a long time since we've had any knowing of the world beyond the trees,' said Sarkash. 'Perhaps things have changed among our neighbours.'

'Do you think our isolation has become a danger to us?' asked Kest suddenly.

'I wasn't thinking that, but . . .' He half shrugged. 'It no longer matters what I think.'

'I've been a Protector for eight seasons and for two of those a Leader. Your thoughts have always mattered to me.'

Sarkash's expression eased. 'You've heard that Tremen Leader Maxen has assumed command of the Warens?'

'Yes.'

'He's authorised the clans to resume gathering beyond the First Eight.'

'But that's madness!'

'He has the agreement of the Clancouncil.'

Kest stared at him in disbelief. 'But that was before they knew of the attack. Surely now they'll reverse the decision?'

'Tremen Leader Maxen is not in the habit of reversing his decisions, no matter what the circumstances. He would see it as a backdown.'

'Did no one argue against it? Surely they could've waited for my return?'

'Miken of Kashclan spoke against it, and your own Clanleader,' said Sarkash, then paused. 'Their objections were to be expected.'

Expected and therefore discounted. 'You've spoken with Clanleaders Marren and Miken since?' asked Kest.

'They came here seeking advice directly after the council. They're keen to secure the safety of their longhouses.'

As well they might be, thought Kest, his mind going to Sanaken and Feseren.

'There's one further thing,' said Sarkash, brushing at his face. 'Tremen Leader Maxen will seek to attribute blame for what's happened. He's already assured the council that the incursion into Allogrenia was some sort of harmless chance by a people who mean us no ill will. He would see it as a weakness to revise such an opinion.' Sarkash hesitated. 'Miken tells me Maxen's already blaming Kiraon for going beyond the Arborean, suggesting she caused the attack through her actions. When he hears that Tremen have been killed . . .'

Maxen would blame her for their deaths too. Kest let his breath out slowly. 'Kiraon's not at fault. I launched the attack that caused the deaths of Protectors Feseren and Sanaken.'

Sarkash gestured dismissively. 'The Leader's son was unconscious and the Leader's daughter in grave danger. No, you did as you ought. We cannot afford to lose Kiraon,' he said, his voice steely. 'But as we both know, Protector Leader, it's not how I view these things that is important now, but how Tremen Leader Maxen views them.'

And Maxen would be looking for people to hold accountable, Kest realised. That's what Sarkash was telling him. If Maxen were to maintain his assertion that no threat existed to the Tremen, then the injury they'd suffered must've been brought about by their own ill-considered actions or, more precisely, by the actions of his daughter Kiraon and Protector Leader Kest.

'The night grows old,' said Sarkash. 'You should get some rest.'

'I beg permission to take Feseren home.'

'Granted, of course,' sighed Sarkash. 'I'll assign you a patrol for the task and another to escort Kiraon and her brother back to the Bough. Merenor can lead them. I'll have a patrol take Protector Tresen back to his longhouse too; I know his clan-kin are most anxious. Pekrash can take another patrol to bear Sanaken's body home, for he's clan-kin. You see, Protector Leader, I have plenty of men at my disposal now no threat exists to Allogrenia.'

17

Erboran strode up the steep, skreel-clad slope, barely aware of the wind rasping over stone, or the grasses rattling against the hard-baked earth. Mawkbird feathers rolled past his boots and caught in the bones of long-dead bushes, but he didn't notice, nor did he see the marwing corpse, as desiccated as the buttonweed and flatgrass, for his mind had been consumed by the same thought for over a moon now: the gold-eyed Healer lived.

The cave mouth loomed before him but he didn't go in, instead turning aside and staring out over the Grounds. He couldn't enter the Cave of the Telling with his head whirring like a dust squall. The Sky Chiefs demanded a quiet heart and a respectful mind in this, the place they'd once gifted words. It was near dusk, but the air was still warm and he took a swig from his waterskin, grimacing at the muddy taint. The land was eating the water, so long was it since the Sky Chiefs had sent rain. Did they withhold it because Arkendrin had given Urgundin no fit sending, leaving him to rot among the entrapping trees?

It was unlikely; the days of clear skies and scorching sun had started long before Arkendrin and Urgundin had set off on their ill-fated journey, before even he'd joined with Palansa. The tightness in his neck and shoulders eased and he smiled at the thought of her. Soon Palansa's belly would be as round as a button flower and the coming of the next Chief as plain to the Shargh as it was to him. His mother had already whispered it among the sorchas but there were many, such as his brother's cronies, who must have the proof of it under their eyes before they believed.

The next Speak was yet to be held, for a moon of mourning must first be given to honour Urgundin, but already Arkendrin strutted about with puffed chest, seeding the Grounds with the story of his heroic journey. Not that it would do him any good. Those whose allegiances were to the blood-born Chief had been swift in ensuring that Erboran was privy to all that Arkendrin said.

Arkendrin knew the Telling, but had spent little time pondering it, unlike Erboran. Their long confinement and the present lack of rain had made him consider, over and over again, how the Telling might reflect the Sky Chiefs' will. Was it that the Sky Chiefs were keeping them safe from the slaughter of their forefathers, for the cursed Northerners didn't bring their swords south of the Braghans? The withholding of rain was more difficult to comprehend, especially by those who thought of nothing beyond the boniness of their ebis. It might be that the pastures beyond the Braghans were even drier than here, but it might also be a test. The Sky Chiefs knew, as he did, that a people whose lives consisted of full bowls and bellies soon lost their strength, becoming too weak to defeat any future adversity. Arkendrin and his cronies understood none of this. For them, need was a thirst to be quenched immediately.

He stared at the last of the sun. *If Healer sees a setting sun and gold meets gold, two halves are one . . .*

Did the gold refer to eyes, as Arkendrin believed, or something else? The land before him was gold, scorched by the relentless sun and ungreened by rain, the herders having to take the ebis to the foothills of the Cashgars to find fodder and, despite their care, losing more and more to the Cashgar wolves. Ormadon had told him there was anger among the warriors at the losses and that Arkendrin fed this anger with tales of lush pastures beyond the Braghans.

Such talk was opportunistic and deluded, but the willingness of some of the warriors to believe it revealed their longing for action. He knew Arkendrin sought to use the Last Telling against him but Erboran could also use it to soothe the restlessness of many of Arkendrin's followers. If it were a hunt they wanted, ending with the killing of the Telling, then Erboran could certainly oblige them at small cost to himself.

The wind flicked the hair from Erboran's face and he raised his eyes to the purpling sky.

Soon the moon would rise, brilliant and full-formed, streaming into the cave of the Telling and lighting it as if with a thousand lamps. This had astonished Erboran as a boy, until Tarkenda had pointed out the holes hidden in the roof. The moon had been full, too, the night she'd brought him here and made him the Mouth of the Last Teller, and though it'd been late they'd gone back to the Grounds to sleep. He'd not be sleeping here this night either. The walls of the cavern spoke with the voices of the Tellers whose bones were now as dry as the dust beneath his feet, and it was well known that the dead resented the intrusion of the living.

He turned into the cave's darkness, the gritty stone giving way to fetid slime as he neared the roosting places of the chika bats, quick pulses of air past his face marking the departure of those late to their hunting. Then the walls disappeared and he was in the Cave of the Telling, the last shaft of daylight illuminating a blot of darkness in the floor's centre. The hair on the back of his neck stirred, despite having seen it before. Here lay the ashes of the very fire Ordorin had knelt beside to receive the Last Telling.

He touched his palm to his forehead and lowered himself to the pitted stone where his father and grandfather had knelt, and where one day his own son would kneel too. Erboran remained motionless until the first faint beams of moonlight penetrated the chamber, his mind calming and his thoughts beginning to crystallise. There was no doubt that a gold-eyed creature existed, for Arkendrin's Voice was second only to his own and must be believed. But was she the thing of the Telling, the Healer whose breath would rob them of theirs? *If Healer sees a setting sun* . . . Arkendrin had said that such was the murk created by the trees, that neither the sun's rising nor setting could be seen. She might well be the one, but would killing her prevent the rest of the Telling coming to pass?

What was the meaning of the meeting of gold and of halves? Of flatswords failing? The thought chilled his blood. In fact, the whole Telling was like trying to corner a shadow-wraith, a wolf that howled but had no substance. He felt blind, as if a cape had been flung over his head, his temples pounding, sweat starting on his brow. The answers lay beyond his warrior grasp, in the ever-moving cloudlands of Tellers! Curse the lack of Tellers! Curse the Sky Chiefs for taking the Tellers from them!

A gust of wind found the cave's entrance, picking up speed as it roared along the narrow ways under the earth, and hurtled into the cavern. It scoured the ash from the fire circle, sweeping it up into a moonlit column so that it hovered over Erboran like a vast, faceless figure. Erboran cried out and sprang back, then the wind died and the ash fell earthward, greying his skin.

Erboran threw himself forward, face pressed to the floor, dust filling his mouth and nostrils, his voice rising and falling in harsh incantations. It was a long time before he was able to stumble back to the entrance. The Grounds stretched away before him, silver under the hard, bright ball of the moon, and he staggered down the slope and back across the grasslands, his shadow rolling and jerking behind him.

Tarkenda paced round her sorcha, wincing and stopping now and again to rub her hip. The Speak had been in progress just a short time but it wouldn't last much longer. She had remained in her own sorcha, for the Speak had little to discuss. Arkendrin had returned with confirmation of the gold-eyed creature, but without Urgundin. Blood must be spilt to assuage his death.

Tarkenda stared sightlessly at the sorcha walls. There had been too much blood lately, staining her dreams and visions, and she feared there was more to come, not just in the south-western forests, but on the Grounds itself. Thrusting the flap aside, she stepped outside.

The stars arched over her in an immense dome and, more through habit than anything else, she sought out the stars that had guided the Shargh in the Older Days: Nastril, Wistrin, Maghin, Sonagh and Anghin. The light they gave was still clear and bright, but the Shargh no longer followed it, penned now like ebis, at war even with themselves. Thank the Sky Chiefs that at least this night was quiet, with no shouts of warning or marwing cries heralding misfortune. She stared down the slope to where the cooking fires winked, red against black, like funeral pyres.

There was no comfort to be found there either. Rubbing at her hip again, she turned back to her sorcha and had just lowered her bones to a seat when the flap stirred again and Erboran appeared. The metal ebis horns of his circlet of Chiefship flashed as he straightened and Tarkenda's breath caught in her throat. For a moment she was looking at her long-dead join-husband, then the shadows shifted and the illusion vanished.

Erboran settled opposite, stretching his long legs to the side of the table. 'We'll leave with the growing of the moon and return with its withering,' he said.

'Arkendrin knows the way?' she asked, drawing him a bowl of sherat.

'He's marked a trail and the moon will help us. Scouts left this night,' he said, and sat for a moment, contemplating the bowl's patterning. Then his dark eyes flashed to hers. 'Keep Palansa near you.'

'Does the babe still make her ill?'

'She fears for me,' he said. 'It's the way of carrying-women, I believe.'

'I'll keep her safe.'

Erboran nodded and rose and Tarkenda stood too, despite the protest of her joints.

'Erboran?' she said. 'Must you go to the forests?'

Erboran's brows narrowed. '*You* ask me this? You who've served as the Mouth of the Last Teller?'

Tarkenda's knuckles whitened on the back of the chair. 'What of the Speak?'

'We're of one mind. The gold-eyed creature must be killed and Urgundin honoured.'

'She might not be the thing of the Telling,' said Tarkenda.

'Arkendrin and his followers believe she is.'

'And you? What is it you believe, Erboran?'

Her son smiled but there was no warmth in his eyes. 'That sometimes warriors must hunt more than wolves.'

The flap hissed back into place and the darkness swirled again, but it had nothing to do with a vision. Trembling, Tarkenda lowered herself back to her chair, drawing herself a bowl of sherat and gulping it down. Then she drew herself a second. Whatever the Sky Chiefs sent couldn't be changed, age had taught her that. It had also taught her that troubles were better faced without a befuddled mind. Grimacing, she thrust the bowl aside. All that was left for her was to plan for what was to come.

18

Kira pushed the grinding stone backwards and forwards, a pile of nutmeat to one side, a bowl of nut oil to the other. Time slipped away as she worked, the deep stillness outside drawing to itself a mantle of dew, the mira kiraon returning sated to their roosts, the forest beneath them dusted with bone, feather and fur. The moonlight was spilling in through the shutters and slowly awareness woke that the moon was full again, the second since the attack. Surely it hadn't been two whole moons since she'd returned? The pain rushed back, bringing with it the memory of her father looming over her, his words falling like blows.

Your arrogance and wilful disobedience have brought about a clash with a people who have never meant us harm, and have caused the deaths of two of our own people. Your ignorance of healing has caused unspeakable suffering, not only to those who died, but to their entire longhouses. The very Bough itself has been dishonoured by your actions, and all that Kasheron fought for over the long seasons, betrayed . . .

Tears scalded her cheeks. It didn't matter how kindly Lern spoke to her or how much Kandor railed against their father, she knew in her heart that if she hadn't disobeyed him, Feseren and Sanaken would still be alive.

Blinking away the wetness, Kira emptied the last of the nut oil into the cask and slowly wiped the slipperiness from her hands, then covered the nutmeat and placed it on the shelf. The baking could wait until the morrow, for there was still a good supply of nutbread Sendra had prepared before she'd gone back to her longhouse. Kira drew a chair to the fire and curled up in it, glad to be alone.

Kandor had spent much of the evening wandering round the cooking place eating the nutmeat and trying to start conversations, but he'd eventually gone off muttering something about practising his piping. Merek had been in the Herbery, but when Lern and her father had gone gathering, he'd suddenly slipped on his cape and left.

The fire was all but out, but Kira was too disheartened to add wood from the collection of windfall laid near, or to satisfy her hunger with nuts or sweetfruit, or to go to her bed, despite her weariness.

A rap on the door made her jerk convulsively; then there was a second rap, more urgent. Where was Kandor? He should . . . A third rap forced her upright and across the hall to the door. Kira gaped at Kest, struggling not just with his sudden appearance but with his strangeness. It wasn't only that he was clean and relaxed, but that he was dressed in the distinctively patterned clothing of Morclan, not Protector garb.

'Healer Kiraon. It's good to see you again.'

'I'm just Kiraon now, not Healer Kiraon,' she said, coughing to ease the sudden constriction of her throat.

'We have a woman in childbirth in need of aid,' said Kest.

'I . . .' She stopped, a shocking realisation coming to her. 'There are no Healers within the Bough,' she blurted out. Why had Merek left when he knew Lern and her father had already gone out?

'She's asking for you, *Healer* Kiraon.'

'I . . .' Kira took a steadying breath. 'As I said, I'm no longer a Healer, Protector Leader. I don't have the knowing, or the skill, to serve those who are ill. Healer Lern will be returning soon. He's helped in childbirth before. It's best . . . he goes with you.'

Kest's gaze remained on her face. 'She'll have no other Healer but you. If you won't aid her, she must birth alone. It's her first babe.'

Kira dropped her head. 'I can't come.'

She felt Kest's hand on her chin and raised her face reluctantly. 'Do you fear your father's anger?' he asked.

'Don't ask me to come!' she exclaimed, jerking away. 'I've already disgraced the Bough and I daren't injure it further.'

'Would you deny her your healing?'

The question was brutal, despite the gentleness of Kest's voice. All her life Kira had gathered for healing, or read of healing, or healed. Healing was a gift, given freely without expectation of reward. *To deny healing was akin to wielding a Terak Kutan sword.*

'Healing must never be denied,' she said.

Kest nodded. 'Good. I'll be waiting for you on the western edge of the Arborean with my men. Be quick.'

Kest strode back across the clearing, his mask of politeness replaced with one of fury. So, Maxen had taken the opportunity to remove his daughter from her rightful place as his successor. He'd scarcely recognised her! Even in their most desperate moments he'd never seen her show such despairing acceptance. The man was her stinking father! Had he no love for her at all?

'Was Maxen within?' asked Penedrin.

'No,' said Kest, taking out his temper on a length of scamper vine that had lassoed his ankle. 'Nor Merek nor Lern. For once fortune's smiled on us.'

'Is it as we thought?'

The Morclansmen were close and for once Kest allowed himself to speak freely. 'Things are as we've heard. Maxen has stripped his daughter of her role of Healer.' There was an angry mutter and Kest raised his hand, waiting till the men had quieted. 'I've persuaded her to come, but she doesn't know –' There was the sound of a door closing and he turned back to the clearing, smiling pleasantly as Kira half jogged towards him.

There were close to fifteen men waiting in the trees, and Kira's puzzlement grew as she returned their nods and greetings. They wore swords and were clearly under Kest's control, but like him they were clad in Morclan garb, not the dull green of Protectors.

'Is this a patrol?' she asked as they moved off quickly.

'Tremen Leader Maxen doesn't authorise the use of Protectors within the First Eight,' said Kest blandly. 'These are men from my own longhouse.'

Kira watched them slip swiftly away through the trees, taking up flanking positions as they had on the journey back from the Sarnia caves. Swords whispered from scabbards and there was an occasional gleam as they caught the moonlight.

The Clancouncil had decreed that no threat existed in Allo-grenia and the Protectors were bound by the declaration as much as the Clanleaders. With a cold sinking feeling, Kira realised that Kest was breaking Tremen law, as was Morclan Leader Marren, who'd obviously agreed to the use of his clansmen.

'If the Clancouncil has decreed that no Protectors be within the First Eight, then they shouldn't be here,' pointed out Kira, having to lengthen her stride to keep level with Kest.

'They are here as Morclansmen. As you know, each Clanleader has the right to use his men to protect his clan, as he sees fit. You're coming to aid a woman in the Morclan longhouse, so your safety and her safety are one and the same.'

It was the sort of word-trickery Kira had often heard from her father; a clever answer except for one thing. 'Only Protectors are permitted to carry swords, Protector Leader.'

Kest smiled. 'Yes.'

Kira said nothing more, concentrating for a time on picking her way through a young growth of bitterberry without falling behind the swiftly moving men. Her healing was not all that had failed with the coming of the strangers. Marren of Morclan was openly defying the will of the Clancouncil and, in so doing, defying her father. Was Marren alone? She knew little of the other councillors, except Miken. He was probably doing the same.

'The Clancouncil hasn't seen what we've seen, Healer Kiraon,' said Kest after a pause. 'They agree with Tremen Leader Maxen that no threat exists because it's preferable to believing terrible things have happened and might continue to happen.'

Kira wiped the sweat from her forehead but said nothing.

'You're very quiet, Healer Kiraon,' said Kest after a while.

'I was thinking.'

'Of what?'

'Of the Bough, of the Warens,' said Kira, panting slightly in her effort to keep up.

'And?'

That everything has changed, that no matter what happens now, we can never go back, thought Kira But she couldn't say it, *wouldn't* say it, in case voicing her fears made them more likely to come true.

'How long has the Morclanswoman been labouring?' said Kira instead.

'Since noon,' said Kest. 'And she's Barclan.'

'Her bondmate's Morclan,' murmured Kira, thinking aloud.

'He *was*,' said Kest.

Kira stumbled to a stop, staring at Kest in dread, aware that the Morclansmen in the trees had stopped too.

'Her bondmate was Feseren, Kira. It's Misilini who's birthing.'

Kira felt like she'd turned to stone, overwhelmed by memories of her failed healing. 'I can't do this, Kest.' The words were choked out, as if a boot were on her throat.

'Would you desert her?'

160

Kira brought her shaking hands to her face. 'I killed her bond-mate!'

Kest took her by the shoulders so that she was forced to look at him. 'Don't you recall what I said about Shargh wounds? *Fire with flatswords brings the bane, fire without brings life again.*'

'I don't understand what it means!' she all but shrieked.

'No one does, beyond the fact that it's Shargh swords that kill, not Healers! *Not* Healers, Kira,' said Kest, giving her a small shake.

'I'm not a Healer anymore!'

'And I'm not a Protector Leader any more,' said Kest bitterly. 'I lost two men, the first Protector Leader ever to do so. Tremen Leader Maxen felt I was no longer fit to lead, or even to protect.'

For the first time Kira saw Kest's anger and hurt. 'The fault was not yours! It wasn't yours!' she cried.

'Nor yours,' he said, gently lifting a leaf from her hair. 'We're a good pair, are we not? A man who's no longer a Protector, escorting a woman who's no longer a Healer, to aid a woman who trusts us both.'

'There's no one I'd rather be escorted by,' said Kira thickly.

For a moment his hand lingered on her face, then he straightened. 'Then let us continue as quickly as possible, Kira of Kashclan, for Misilini has need of us.'

The night was old before a narrow path emerged from the trees and Kira sensed some of Kest's tension ease. The smell of woodsmoke was unmistakable and a hum of speech rose from the men as they came together. Ahead, a blotch of yellow light appeared as a door was opened and an imposing silhouette advanced down the path to meet them. Kira blinked up at him, guessing it was the Morclan Leader Marren.

'Morclan welcomes the Bough's Kiraon,' a deep voice intoned.

'The Bough thanks Morclan,' returned Kira hurriedly, as she followed him under the heavily carved lintel into the hall. It was warm and bright, filled with lamps and the savoury scents of food. Every member of the clan seemed to be there. It was closer to day than night, and yet a sea of hands were extended to shake hers, or to touch her gently in greeting.

'The Bough thanks Morclan,' she repeated over and over again, moved almost to tears by the warmth of the welcome.

'We have food laid ready, Healer, if you would join us,' said Marren, his face stern and very lined, with the same blue eyes that made Kest so striking.

'I . . . I thank you Clanleader,' said Kira quickly, 'but I must see Misilini first.'

'By all means,' said Marren. 'Pera will take you to her.'

An older woman elbowed her way forward, and Kira hurried after her through a large door into the cooler dimness of the passageway. The door clicked shut behind them and Kira heaved a sigh of relief.

'You'd think they'd never seen a Healer before, wouldn't you?' said Pera, advancing down the passage.

'It's a long time since I've been here,' mumbled Kira, striding after her. Morclan was one of the largest clans, and the passage connecting each family's rooms was long with not a single part uncarved. Walls, ceilings and floors were all adorned, and chimes hung in every window, each set beautiful and different to its neighbour.

'Nearly seven seasons,' Pera's voice floated back.

'Seven seasons?'

'Since you were last at Morclan,' said Pera. 'But we've seen your older brother Merek often.' She smiled knowingly. 'He was here earlier.' There was a pause. 'Still carrying that little brother of yours around on your hip, or is he carrying you now?'

'Almost,' said Kira, dragging her thoughts from Merek. 'Kandor will be thirteen at Turning.'

'Thirteen! Is he thinking of healing?'

'I don't know. He enjoys swordplay.'

'Ah, they all do at that age.' Pera came to an abrupt stop and knocked on a door. 'The room's well prepared,' she said, 'but if you need anything, send Kesilini. I'll be back later with some food for you.' Then, with a brief nod, she disappeared back down the passage.

The door opened and Kira was enveloped by a gust of warm air. A tall young woman blocked the doorway – Kesilini, judging from the blue eyes sweeping over her and the white-blonde hair, intricately braided.

Kesilini caught Kira's hands and drew her inside. 'Thank the 'green you've agreed to come,' she said, giving her a hug and kissing her on the cheek.

'I hope I can help,' said Kira.

There were two other women in the room, and Kesilini introduced each in turn. 'This is Arini, Misilini's mother, and Eser, Feseren's sister.'

Arini's face was filled with the same relieved gratitude as Kesilini's, but Eser's gaze was cold. At least Eser didn't resemble Feseren, Kira thought in relief, as she moved to the bed. Feseren's bondmate was distinctly different too, small and dark-haired, and too exhausted even to lift her head.

'Healer Kiraon,' she said hoarsely, and burst into tears.

Marren and Kest sat together in the hall, watching the crowd of subdued Morclansmen drifting back to their rooms. A few clansmen came in from patrol and settled further up the table.

'I must admit you've surprised me,' said Marren. 'I would've wagered a cask of ale that Maxen wouldn't have allowed her coming.'

'Maxen wasn't there.'

'Ah,' said Marren.

'Or his shadow, Merek.' Kest gulped down his tea and refilled the cup. The thornyflower had steeped too long, but he barely noticed. 'The damage might have been done, though. He's tried to convince her she can't heal.'

'That was predictable. It's long been clear he's marked Merek for the leadership.'

'It's a cruel thing to do!' exclaimed Kest, slamming down his cup and slopping the rest of his tea.

'Maxen views leading as one man standing apart from others, with a vision shared by him alone. Dissent he sees as a challenge to his authority and to the safety of Allogrenia,' said Marren.

'Yet he risks us all,' said Kest.

'The Tremen have long trusted in whoever holds the Bough,' said Marren, 'and still do, although it's obviously unwise to presume – as Maxen does – that the intruders mean us no harm, especially given what we know now. As for Kiraon –' he paused, sipping his own tea. 'Most men would be proud to have such a daughter, and maybe Maxen would be also, *if* she didn't challenge him where he feels most vulnerable – in his healing.'

'And so he seeks to destroy it in her,' said Kest.

'It's a dangerous thing to do,' agreed Marren. 'We can ill-afford to lose *any* Healer, let alone our best one. At least you convinced her to come.'

'Only by telling her we had a first-time mother threatening to birth alone. I guessed she'd even risk Maxen's wrath for that.'

Marren rubbed his chin thoughtfully. 'It'd be better if she were out of his reach altogether. Miken could suggest she goes to the Kashclan longhouse for a time. If she's no longer healing, Maxen can't have any objection.'

'Miken's already asked and Maxen's refused.'

'How know you this?' asked Marren, his eyebrows shooting up.

'Her clanmate Tresen told me. Maxen won't let her heal and he won't let her go.'

'It's a pity then that she's too young to bond. If she were to take a mate, Maxen would have no more say over her movements,' said Marren, picking up a slice of nutbread and idly turning it in his hands.

'She'll be seventeen at Turning.'

Marren's hands stilled. 'Seventeen? She looks less than fifteen.'

'Kashclan women are slight. It's said the first Kiraon barely reached her sons' shoulders.'

Marren took a bite of his nutbread, regarding Kest speculatively. 'You seem to have developed a sudden and particular interest in Kashclan women.'

'She'll be my bondsister after Turning,' said Kest, ignoring his meaning.

'The thought displeases you?'

'I welcome Kira but not her eldest brother.'

'Ah well, we know that women go their own way,' said Marren yawning. He rose and stretched. 'I'm to my bed. Are you sleeping?'

'I might sit a little longer,' said Kest.

In the birthing room along the passageway, Kira was busy wiping away the second lot of vomit from Misilini's face. First the labouring woman had thrown back the mallowflower tincture, and now the harkenweed.

'Your mixtures aren't aiding her,' said Eser.

Kira pushed the damp hair from her forehead, keeping her eyes on Misilini's pale face. It was hot in the room and she was sweating, but Misilini was racked with shivers.

'What will you give her now?' Eser's voice intruded again.

It must be close to dawn and still Misilini was no nearer to delivering her baby, thought Kira. Arini had said that Misilini had begun to labour around noon the previous day, and yet her exhaustion matched that of a woman who'd laboured twice as long. There was something wrong, but Kira didn't know what. Maybe it was *she* who was wrong, coming here, believing she could heal, letting those here believe she could heal. She should have waited for Lern, or her father, or even Merek. They wouldn't have failed.

'She's been like this since we heard the news,' muttered Arini.

Kira roused. 'What mean you?'

'At first we thought her sickness was from the shock, but it's been going on too long, as if she's forgotten all about the babe. She's not eating; not sleeping; not taking care of herself.'

'The fault's not Misilini's,' broke in Eser.

'Nor anyone else's in this room,' retorted Kesilini, glaring at Eser.

Misilini groaned and Kira forgot everything but her. The babe was low; it should have been born by now; and it *must* be born soon if it were to live. She slid her hands over Misilini's belly, feeling the tight warm skin, and then, without warning, the world turned to fire and she reeled back.

'What ails you?' demanded Eser.

Kira stared down at her hands, panting, overwhelmed by memories of Feseren in the Sarnia Cave. Her hands had burned then, too. A sudden understanding came to her, and with it, calmness. This was Feseren's bondmate, the babe the part of him that still lived; she wouldn't fail him a second time.

'I need morning-bright and a pan of boiling water,' she snapped.

'There's morning-bright in the hall,' volunteered Arini. 'I'll fetch it.'

'I need fresh.'

'I don't know where it grows around this longhouse . . .' Arini's gaze went to Eser.

'I'll go,' said Eser grudgingly.

'I'll fetch the water,' said Arini, following Eser out.

'I didn't know morning-bright aided childbirth,' said Kesilini.

'It doesn't, but the scent gives a gentle welcome.' *And the fewer witnesses I have now the better*, Kira thought. She pulled the blanket clear. 'Help me sit her up, Kesilini.' Misilini cried out as they eased her up and pushed more pillows behind her.

'You're going to have this baby right now,' ordered Kira.

'No,' shrieked Misilini. 'It hurts.'

'I'll help you with the pain, but you must push,' said Kira. Steeling herself, she placed her hands back on Misilini's belly, screwing her eyes shut as the sear surged up her arms.

'I want to die,' sobbed Misilini. 'I want to be with Feseren.'

'Feseren didn't want to die,' panted Kira, 'he fought to live.'

Kesilini was looking at Kira strangely but the scorch was so great that she could think of nothing else.

'Push, Misilini, push,' gritted Kira, sweat stinging her eyes, or was it the ash of her own burning? Surely she must be dying? 'Push,' she croaked, and then, just as she thought she could bear no more, the room receded and with it, most of the pain. She was in a tunnel much like the Warens, but it was clothed in flame. In the distance, she could see a figure, reeling and stumbling along. It was Feseren, she realised in horror, leading her along the path he'd already followed. Was this death? Or was death beyond the fire, in a place of peace, deep in the quiet earth?

It was Kesilini's cry of delight that drew her back, and the lusty cry of the babe. The flames ebbed and she glimpsed Misilini's face, calm and beautiful as she brought the child to her breast, then the darkness surged back, sweeping everything away.

19

Kest wedged open the door with his back, eased the tray through, then steadied the door with his foot so that it closed softly. Kira still slept, a small mound in the centre of his bed. He put the tray on the table and gently pushed the shutters open, the glow of late morning gilding the spill of her hair across the pillow. What would Maxen say if he knew his daughter were in the bed of a Morclansman? Of Kest himself? And yet Maxen tolerated the prospect of Merek's bonding to a Morclanswoman! It seemed he denied his wondrous oldest son nothing!

Kest settled on the end of the mattress and looked at the sleeping girl closely. She was beautiful, but not in the way Kesilini was. Kesilini had the full beauty of maturity, whereas Kira was still as awkward as a fledgling. She shared Kandor's straight brows, but her mouth was fuller and the bones of her face finer. One of her hands was flung across the pillow, palm upward, the fingers tapered, and he was reminded of one of the Writings in the Warens. The Terak Kutan admired such hands, accentuating them with rings of metal set with glittering stones. Her pale shoulder was exposed by Kesilini's too big sleeping gown. But even as his gaze lingered, Kira stirred, her eyes soft and unfocused and then suddenly wide and brilliant gold as they settled on him.

'Kest! How come you here?'

'You're in *my* bed in *my* rooms, and you ask me that?' he asked, then smiled. Another woman might have shown embarrassment or anger, but Kira simply looked bewildered. Was she so unworldly that she saw no compromise in her position, or was it just that she trusted him? He hoped the latter. She'd wedged herself upright, hair like a halo round her face, and he wished he *had* shared the bed with her.

'I remember being in the birthing room, then I think I must have fainted.'

Kest watched her eyes dull to moss green. Sadness or fear; he remembered the change well from their time in the Sarnia cave.

She dropped her head, and picked at the covering. 'The birthing room must have been overly hot,' she mumbled.

Kest retrieved the tray and set it carefully beside her. 'Kesilini came and fetched me and I brought you here. She put you to bed,' he said, pouring the tea and spooning in some honey.

'I seem to be making a habit of falling at your feet.'

'I'd like to claim credit, but this time you actually fell at Kesilini's. Here, drink this,' he said, handing her the cup.

Kira sipped at the tea and he spread more of the honey on the nutbread. She was too thin, the bones in her wrist sharp, her collarbones ridging through her skin. He'd noticed at the caves how careless she was of her own wellbeing. Was it because she'd grown with no mother? Kest had lost his mother young, but there were many in the Morclan longhouse to care for him. Kira had grown in the Bough, without her clan-kin. He handed her the bread and she took a small bite.

'Misilini – is she well?' she asked, her anxiety plain.

'Yes, Kira, don't trouble yourself. She has a strong little boy, judging by his bellowing. Now eat. I want to see all that nutbread gone.' By the 'green, he was beginning to sound like Pera. Kira nibbled at the bread, but her attention now on the chimes in the window.

'The chimes are lovely,' she said, abandoning her meal and scrambling from the bed. 'Springleslip, hanawey, mira kiraon, frost-king,' she counted off, 'but what's this one, and this?'

Kest joined her at the window, touching each shape in turn. 'This one's a dwinhir, a hunting bird of the north, and this a silver-jack, and this,' he said, holding a sinuous shape in front of her, 'you already know.'

Indeed she did; the same shape adorned the ring of rulership her father wore. 'The running horse of the Terak Kutan,' she breathed. 'Why carve the creatures of the north?'

It was the kind of question Maxen would ask. 'We came from the north, Kira, and I can't believe everything there is bad, no matter what we're taught.' He ran his fingers over the graceful sweep of the horse. 'Is this ugly?'

'It's beautiful,' said Kira in a small voice.

Kest felt greatly relieved at her answer, realising with a jolt how much he didn't want her to be like Maxen *or* Merek. 'But this one is definitely funny,' he said, fingering the silverjack. 'Big ears and a stubby tail.'

Kira threw back her head and laughed. 'Ah, so now you're claiming the north is beautiful *and* funny.'

Kest paused, taken with this new image of her. It was the first time he'd seen her relaxed and happy. Her eyes were luminous, the smile on her lips soft as she fingered the chimes. If he bent his head now, he could kiss her.

'And how do you know they really look like this?' she asked, her eyes dancing as she looked at him. 'Maybe they had stubby ears and a big tail.'

'They were here too when Kasheron's folk arrived. They hunted them down to the very last.'

'You're saying Kasheron ate meat?' asked Kira in astonishment.

'Of course. The people were starving when they first lived in the forest, and starving people eat anything. At least they got rid of the wolves, for once the silverjacks were gone the wolves were forced to hunt elsewhere.'

Kira's eyes had fluoresced to gold, clearly shocked by the revelations of the eating habits of her forebears, but Kest had ceased to be surprised by such things, knowing that some of the Writings lying neglected in the unused caverns spoke of even more bizarre practices. All that had happened was that the Tremen had been selective in what they'd chosen to remember – it was probably the same with all peoples, he thought.

A whoop made them both turn, and two little boys ran by the window, disappearing round the corner of the longhouse, then quickly reappearing for the chase back. Another joined them, slightly older, with a dark-haired child in tow, and all four darted away into the trees, explosions of giggling slowly fading.

'Morclan has many children,' observed Kira.

'Twenty-three at last count,' said Kest with a smile. 'The two little boys are Eser's.'

'Eser's? I didn't realise she was bonded,' said Kira, unpleasant memories of the other woman's animosity returning.

'She isn't, *and* her sons have different fathers. Eser's only a season older than you,' he felt bound to add. Kira was clearly shocked and his smile broadened. 'You're in the wild and uncouth Morclan longhouse now, remember.'

'Children are the blessing of the trees,' murmured Kira, recovering enough to repeat the phrase common at birthing celebrations.

'And vital, given that no one has entered Allogrenia since Kasheron's time, at least until recently,' added Kest.

There was a short silence as they both considered the intrusion of the Shargh, then Kest retrieved the tray from the bed and set it on the table. 'And now we have one more child to thank you for. Come and finish your meal, Kira.'

She started on the nutbread again, the chimes singing softly, the coming and going of children's voices almost as musical. How would it be to love not one man but two, *and* to birth a child to each. It was scarcely comprehensible.

'Kesilini tells me you took away Misilini's pain,' said Kest.

The sunny room vanished and the sear and smoke swept back, as vivid as in the birthing room, making Kira's fingers throb. 'That's not possible,' she said, surreptitiously flexing them.

'Misilini says you did too.'

Kira took another bite of the nutbread and struggled to swallow it.

Silence stretched and it was Kest who broke it. 'Now that I don't have any Protector duties, I've had time to explore some of the Writings in the remoter caverns.'

'You know of them?' The nutbread was a painful lump halfway down her throat, but at least Kest had changed the subject.

Kest nodded. 'But over the seasons the maps have been lost and few Protectors bother trying to find their way about unless they have a particular reason.'

The question was obvious but she refused to ask it.

'I've been looking for the answer to our riddle about Shargh flatswords,' said Kest at last.

Kira's heart leapt. 'Have you found anything?'

'Nothing of Shargh wounds, but much on Sinarki. Do you know of Sinarki?'

'Daughter of Bekash and Tarina, first female Leader of the Bough,' she rattled off.

'Anything else?'

'Her daughter Tesrina later became the second female Leader of the Bough. All Leaders before and since have been men.'

'Did you know both women bore a special title? They weren't just Leader Sinarki and Leader Tesrina, but Leader *Feailner* Sinarki and Leader *Feailner* Tesrina.' Kest's eyes held hers, reminding her of the Drinkwater's deepest pools, clear and intense.

'I've read it's so,' said Kira carefully.

'And have you read what it means?' asked Kest.

'It's an old word, neither Tremen nor Onespeak. I understand it to mean "woman" or "female Healer",' replied Kira.

'So do most of the Tremen, but I've come upon a Writing that explains it somewhat differently. It means "taker of fire".' The breeze outside quickened, whirling the chimes and making the running horse rear and plunge. 'Kesilini told me that when you first touched Misilini, you jerked back *as if you'd been burnt.*'

Kira swallowed several times but could think of nothing to say. Kest's hand closed over hers. 'It's a very great gift, Kira, not something to be ashamed of.'

'I'm not ashamed of it . . . it might be nothing, just a chance, a quirk of the situation, just . . .' She shook her head helplessly. 'I don't want it spoken of.' It was bad enough that her eyes drew the stares of others, but if they thought she could take pain too . . . And then there was her father. 'Pledge me that you won't speak of it!'

Kest was suddenly very close, his breath warm on her face. 'Is it your father's anger you fear?'

'I . . . I need time to understand what it is. Pledge me, Kest!'

'Very well,' he said slowly. 'I'll ensure that Kesilini and Misilini say nothing, and even if Eser's heard the news, she won't have believed it. But in return, you'll stay here and enjoy Morclan hospitality again this night. Then, in the morning, I'll escort you back to the Bough.'

'I need to go now.'

Kest had stood, and she had to crane her neck to look up at him. 'You know how to give, Kira,' he said gently, 'perhaps too well, but not to receive. Maybe it's time you learned.' His eyes glinted, not like the Drinkwater now, but blue as a summer sky. 'We're not just fine carvers here in Morclan, but also players and singers, and this night, thanks to you, we have another life to rejoice in.'

*

173

The celebrations that night had the warmth of the Turning festivities at the Bough, but none of their formality. The hall tables were simply pushed against the walls, the players took up their positions next to the cooking place and the dancing and singing began. The older Morclansmen and women were expert singers and Kira listened enthralled as their voices formed complex lays, each group blending harmoniously with the next, until the hall was filled with a continuous ripple of music.

'It's a herding song from the north,' explained Kest, as they perched on the edge of one of the tables. 'Those who spent their time alone in watch over their animals amused themselves by singing to other herders further afield or higher in the mountains, and the other herders continued the lay, sending it on until it came back to the first singer.'

'What did they sing about?' asked Kira, intrigued.

'The weather, lost beasts, lost love – the usual things,' said Kest smiling. 'The words weren't really important, just the sense of company, of knowing that they weren't alone.'

'I wonder if they still sing them,' said Kira, struggling to imagine solitary Terak Kutan huddled over their campfires. The image didn't accord with her usual picture of them cutting across the plains in bloodthirsty swathes.

Kest shrugged. 'We know nothing of how things are in the north now.'

For the first time in her life Kira felt a sense of lack. Half of their people were *out there*, beyond the trees, and most Tremen knew nothing about them. Did the Northerners also gather in celebration as Morclan were doing this night? Did they sing with joy at each birth, weep at death, court like Merek and Kesilini?

She could see Kesilini now, her fair hair gleaming as she lined up with a slightly shorter Morclansman in a dance, couples forming up in front and behind them as the players tuned their instruments.

'Would you –' Kest began, but at that moment Eser appeared, nodding briefly to Kira, her eyes on Kest.

'Will you do me the honour of accompanying me in the weave dance, ex-Protector Leader Kest?' asked Eser ironically.

It wasn't usual for women to ask men to dance but Kest smiled graciously. 'It would be a pleasure,' he said, with a polite bow.

Kira watched him escort Eser over to the assembled dancers and wait for the players to begin. Eser was standing close to Kest, talking animatedly, tilting her head as she looked up at him. Her hair was a dark reddish brown, similar in colour to fallowood bark and, like Kesilini's, arranged in a series of braids meeting in a thick weave at the back. Eser was wearing a dark brown tunic, which showed off her creamy skin and accentuated her full breasts and narrow waist. Kira looked down at her shabby tunic and bit her lip.

'Healer Kiraon,' a voice boomed, making her jump. 'Would you honour me by partnering me in the dance?' It was Morclan Leader Marren, his face still wearing its former stern expression, but his eyes kind.

'It would be a pleasure,' said Kira, mimicking Kest's earlier response, but felt her cheeks warm as he led her ceremoniously to the head of the dancers, the gaze of the assemblage following. As soon as Kira and Marren had taken their position, the music started.

Kira knew most of the Tremen dances well, for since the death of her mother it had been her task to act as the Lady of the Bough during the celebrations of Turning and Thanking. Kira had led the dancing on the arm of her father from the age of seven or eight, and more recently on Merek's arm, for her father now disdained dancing. The weave dance was the most intricate of the dances, requiring each pair to move back through the column of dancers in complex loops. The concentration the dance required served Kira well and, after a while, she forgot about the Morclan eyes upon her and simply enjoyed the music and the rhythmic stepping and swaying.

Occasionally she glimpsed Kesilini and her partner, and Kest and Eser, Kest easy to pick because of his height and fairness. Eser was dancing close to him and there was a familiarity in the way she touched him that caught Kira's attention.

Were they lovers? Kira wondered abruptly. The idea was so shocking that she almost missed her step. Kest and Eser were clanmates, Kira reminded herself, and clanmates couldn't bond. But Eser was a mother, despite being unbonded, and Kira knew that Kest must be twenty-six or seven seasons, given that he was older than Kesilini. She coloured, as her thoughts ran on.

The music came to a stop and Marren bowed to her before escorting her to the water jugs and courteously pouring her a drink before taking his leave. Kira sipped it, fanning her hot face and contemplating her own shortcomings. She knew little of the matters of the heart, even when they were happening under her nose. Merek had been on the point of bonding before she'd found out, and she only knew because Kandor had told her. She'd noticed nothing herself.

'You dance very well, Healer Kiraon of the Bough and Kashclan,' said Kest, coming to her side and pouring himself a drink.

'So do you, Protector Leader Morsclansman Kest,' said Kira, smiling. 'Will you be coming to Turning?'

'I will this time,' said Kest, leaning on the wall behind her with one arm, almost as if he were embracing her. 'You forget that Merek will be bonding to Kesilini and that you and I will soon be brother and sister. I hope that pleases you.'

Kira felt a new wave of heat move over her face. 'It pleases me that Merek is happy,' she said honestly, 'and of course, Kashclan welcomes Morclan.'

'So your father –' Kest began, but again was interrupted as the players sounded their instruments. 'I *would* dance with you this time,' said Kest, putting down his cup. 'That is . . . if you are willing.'

His eyes fastened on hers as he said the last words and Kira gulped down the last of her drink. 'Of course I'm willing,' she said, moving past him, 'I enjoy dancing.' The musicians had chosen thread-the-leaves as the next dance and there were squeals of excitement as the younger Morclan members dashed onto the floor. Dancers had to pass under a long archway of joined hands, a task that many of the Morclan children interpreted as a race. There was much shrieking as they sprinted to the other end, turning and linking hands to form the next part of the arch. The presence of children in the dance caused Kest particular problems, for he had to bend double to pass under their arms. Twice he was almost decapitated and every time his hair was scuffed upright. He groaned theatrically at each collision, so that in the end, Kira was laughing as much as the Morclan youngsters.

Finally the dance ended and Kest straightened and rubbed his back. 'That was worse than one of Sarkash's training sessions – apart from the beautiful company,' he added.

20

Kira smiled at the memory, then the ladder shuddered and she tightened her grip and peered up. Kandor was perched on its upper rungs, a lamp swinging from one hand and a wreath of sour-ripe blossom clutched in the other. Other lamps already glittered among the greenery festooning the walls and ceiling of the Bough in readiness for the celebration of Turning. The results of days of baking were arranged on the great table, next to jugs of withyweed ale, cordials and water.

'Fix the lamp first, then worry about the sour-ripe,' she called.

'And waste my valuable time?'

She watched him secure the lamp and weave the blossom around the remaining beam. All that was left to do now was to clear away the last few chairs to make space for the dancing, which would take place before and after the bonding ceremonies. Who would bond this Turning? There were often surprises: couples who'd managed to keep their courting secret from their longhouses. She smiled again as her thoughts turned to Merek and Kesilini.

'Thinking of Kest, were you?' asked Kandor as he descended.

'No. Of Merek, actually.'

'Really? Our dear brother doesn't usually make you smile, but I've noticed you've been smiling a lot since returning from Morclan.'

'Have you also noticed there's a bare patch on that beam?'

Kandor shrugged. 'No one will be looking up; they'll be too busy watching you bond with Kest.'

Kira laughed in spite of herself. 'Help me with this ladder, will you?' She swung it down and Kandor grunted as he took its weight, then together they manoeuvred it round the table and into the Herbery, setting it against the wall. The room was full of the rich scents of drying herbs, the walls and ceiling lined with bunches of cinna, silvermint, serewort and winterbloom, their seeded heads forming a brittle canopy. Next to the ladder, her pack hung on its usual hook, bulging with the pots and packets she'd replenished that morning.

'You *could* bond tonight, you know; you'll be of age,' said Kandor, perched on the edge of a workbench and plucking a sprig of cindra to chew.

'I know how old I'll be,' said Kira, wandering up and down as she tested the herbs for dryness.

'If you bonded, you could leave the Bough,' he said, his face a curious mixture of the boy he still was, and the man he would become.

'Escape father you mean?' said Kira.

Kandor nodded.

'To leave the Bough I'd have to leave healing . . . and you. You know I can't do that,' said Kira.

'Father won't let you heal anyway.'

'He will eventually. He didn't punish me for going to the Morclan longhouse, did he?'

'That was because you had to go, thanks to Merek leaving the Bough without a Healer. Father was *most displeased and disappointed*.' Kandor giggled. 'It's the first time I've ever seen Merek suffer father's temper.'

'Probably the last too,' said Kira.

'I wouldn't be too sure, not after Turning,' said Kandor, grinning. His face grew serious again. 'You'll have to bond one day though, Kira,' he said.

She raised her eyebrows in mock alarm. '*Have* to? You know how much I hate that word. Besides, there's no rule which says I *have* to bond with anyone.'

'Ah, Kest's going to be devastated.'

'*Relieved*, I believe, is the word you're looking for,' said Kira, sitting next to Kandor, who passed her a sprig of cindra. She didn't like cindra but popped it in her mouth anyway. She hadn't seen Kest since she'd danced with him at the Morclan birthing celebrations a moon ago. There had been smiling faces and laughter in the Morclan longhouse, and she'd enjoyed herself, her pleasure heightened by the knowledge that she could truly heal.

Kandor was jiggling beside her, his legs swinging back and forth as he hummed a dancing tune. 'I haven't seen much of you lately,' she said. 'Are you sure you've not been secretly courting someone yourself?'

'I'll be thirteen at Turning, not seventeen!'

'That gives you a good four seasons to ensure you're making the right choice.'

'Probably ten seasons too few.'

'Well, if you've not been courting, what have you been up to?'

'Ah, preparing a little surprise for you,' he said and flushed.

'For me? What?' she asked curiously.

'Patience, dear sister, patience,' he said, pushing off from the bench and landing a good length away.

'Patience? You of all people should know I have none,' said Kira.

21

Kira was glad to be outside in the cool evening air beside her father, Lern and Kandor, greeting the guests, as the hall was already crowded and uncomfortably warm. It had been a long day and Turning would continue until well after the midpoint of the night. She flicked her hair back, enjoying the clink and rattle of the treegems studding her braids, and silently thanked Tena for her efforts. The elderly Renclanswoman had spent a good part of the day dressing her hair, the tedium made bearable by her reminiscences of Kira's mother.

'I used to help her prepare for Turning,' she'd said, as she pushed the faceted beads onto each braid, 'and she wore these too, as you did, even as a green-shoot. Always on her hip you were, even while she greeted her guests. Not that your father approved.'

'What did she look like?' asked Kira softly.

'Why, like you my dear, except her eyes were brown.'

Like me, thought Kira, the thrill of it trilling through her again, even as she bowed to the Tarclan Leader.

'You will speak with Clanleader Farish later,' her father murmured as Farish passed into the hall.

'About what?' asked Kira, her thoughts still on her mother.

'Do not pretend stupidity, Kiraon. He's a Clanleader and unbonded, and Tarclan is aligned with Sarclan, your mother's clan . . . *if* you recall. It would be a useful alliance for the Bough, and Clanleader Farish a worthy bondmate for you.'

'I don't intend to bond.' The words were out before she could stop them.

Her father nodded pleasantly to one of Sendra's kin. 'It's hard to see your value to Allogrenia, then, being neither a Healer nor a mother.'

Kira forced a smile at the heavily ornamented woman passing in front of her, but she felt like mute chimes dancing to the winds of her father's will. He'd stopped her gathering and healing, now he would choose her mate. Nor would it end there. He'd never be satisfied, never leave her be. The realisation was like a wood grub boring into her heart. She sensed him stiffen and her heart raced. Had her face betrayed her? No, his attention was on the group making their way across the Arborean: Marren of Morclan, his bondmate Sirini, Kest, and Kest's sister Kesilini.

'Clanleader Marren,' her father said, with the briefest of bows, and then the Morclan leader was level with her, his sombre face breaking into a broad smile.

'Healer Kiraon,' he said warmly, 'it's good to see you again.'

Kira gripped his hand with real pleasure, and he was swiftly replaced by Kesilini, who kissed her briefly on the cheek, her hair glimmering like moonlight, her gaze already searching the hall.

'He's up the end, organising the players,' whispered Kira.

Kesilini nodded gratefully and disappeared into the crowd.

'Morclansman Kest,' she heard her father's icy tones, 'even *you* must know that swords are only permitted to Protectors.'

Kest's hair gleamed as brightly as his sister's and he wore a fine tunic with the characteristic patterning of adzes and chisels around the hems. 'I regret it slipped my mind, Tremen Leader,' he said, his smile firmly in place. 'Perhaps your beautiful daughter can show me where I might stow it?'

Her father's jaw tightened, but Clanleader Dakresh and his kin were fast approaching and he had no choice but to turn his attention to them. Kira led Kest up the side of the hall, skirting the edge of the crowd. Excited people were milling about, reacquainting themselves with those they'd last seen at Thanking.

'Where would you like to leave it?' she asked, raising her voice above the din.

'Nowhere. A sword's useless out of your hand.'

Kira stilled. 'You think there's danger? Here? This night?'

'Allogrenia's no longer safe. We need to remain watchful at all times.'

Memories of Kandor being attacked surged back. Kira had seen the sword poised above her head, had watched Feseren and Sanaken die, then had come back, and life had gone on as before. Her father had insisted there was no threat, and she'd chosen to believe it. But Kest was right. There *was* no safety.

'I've brought you a present,' said Kest, taking her hand and placing a small bundle in it. 'Open it,' he said softly.

Kira unrolled the cloth. It was a mira kiraon carved in intricate detail, wings as fine as lace outstretched in flight, the wood polished to a deep red.

'Two beautiful kiraons together,' he said, slipping the thong over her head.

'It's lovely,' breathed Kira, moved by the thoughtfulness of the gift. She owned few pieces of jewellery, just some beads that had once belonged to her mother. Kest was very close to her, the sense of him quickening her heart. 'Can you please thank whoever carved it?'

'People will think me strange if I go around thanking myself,' said Kest.

'I . . . I didn't realise you could carve.' *He* had carved it for her. The realisation was startling.

'Ah, I'm insulted Healer Kiraon. I am a Morclansman after all, and here you are suggesting that I don't have the skills possessed by my clan-kin.'

He was teasing her she knew, but it did nothing to lessen the heat in her face. 'Are others of Morclan coming?' she asked, managing to steady.

'They're here now, apart from those securing our longhouse.'

Kira looked about in puzzlement.

'They're outside, guarding the lands within the First Eight,' said Kest.

The First Eight! She hoped her father didn't hear of it. 'It's a shame they'll miss the feast, but at least you're here.'

'I escorted Kesilini. As soon as the bonding ceremony's complete, I'll join my patrol.'

Only Protectors were permitted to patrol, and yet Kest used the term about his Morclansmen, who weren't Protectors and were bound by the Clancouncil's declarations to continue normal clan activities. *And* Kest had worn a sword, opening flouting her father.

'Kashclan does as we do,' he added, as if guessing her thoughts.

Kira's mouth dried. She'd thought a number of her clan merely late, but now she realised they probably wouldn't be coming either. Yet Turning was now the only time she could openly mingle with Mikini and Tenerini without risking her father's displeasure.

'Miken won't leave his longhouse defenceless, but he intends to come, as does Tresen,' said Kest, nodding to Sendra as she went past with a group of Sarclansmen and women. 'They wouldn't miss seeing their beautiful clanmate.'

'I wish you'd stop calling me that.'

'I thought you admired the truth. And with your hair braided and gemmed, you look even more beautiful than usual.'

Kira's eyes sheened gold and she opened her mouth to reply, but thankfully, at that moment the crowd stirred and drew back and the shouted conversations began to quiet. 'I think the players are about to begin. May I get you a drink, Morclansman Kest?'

'Only if you stay to share it with me,' smiled Kest.

'I must resume my greeting duties, for I'm leaving the task unfairly to Lern and Kandor.'

'But not to Merek?' asked Kest.

'I rather think Merek has an excuse this night, don't you?'

Erboran crouched motionless in the shadows, watching the group of treemen gathered outside the wooden sorcha. Dozens of lamps wasted their light through the windows, their spill catching the eyes of the girl each time she turned to greet the treemen issuing from the forest. It was impossible to tell her eye colour from his hiding place, but he'd no reason to doubt Arkendrin's assertion that she was the creature they hunted. She was younger than he'd expected, but clearly of important blood, standing next to the Chief and the other men of his line.

He frowned. If she were of ruling blood, it might explain her escape from Arkendrin and Urgundin, and the determination of the treemen to protect her. The Telling spoke only of the creature, but it made sense that she was important *and* powerful. His gaze went to their Chief. The Sky Chiefs themselves were strengthened by having their blood-ties around them and the blood-ties between the dead and the living endured beyond the funeral flames, so the threat wasn't just in her, but in those of her line too. If she were to be truly destroyed, then her blood-ties must also be scoured from the earth. He whispered to the warrior next to him and watched him slip away. Arkendrin and his followers were secreted on the other side of the clearing, and it was important they understood the power of the creature's blood-ties too.

In the time he'd been watching, two of the creature's male blood-ties had gone back into the sorcha, but she remained with the Chief. A Chief with no weapon! More like an ebis cow than a man, and like a cow, ripe for the slaughter. None of the finely dressed treemen and women emerging from the trees carried weapons either.

His hand went to his flatsword, loosening it in its sheath.

185

'They've come to carouse and feast together,' Irsulalin whispered, 'and much sherat will be drunk.'

Erboran nodded, taking his point. If they delayed their attack until late in the night, the treemen would have spent their strength in celebration, and the accomplishment of their quest would be all the surer. The Sky Chiefs' sheltering hand was over them, but he didn't want to have to waste his strength in this musty tangle again, not with his son growing in Palansa's belly back on the Grounds. He settled back on his haunches, elbowing aside a fleshy-leaved plant and muttering a curse. The tree-world was just as Arkendrin had described it: a vast rank reedrat's nest, with no dawn and no dusk. *If Healer sees a setting sun* . . . The Sky Chiefs willing, she'd soon be seeing nothing.

Kest sauntered up and down the hall, skirting the dance floor and exchanging pleasantries with those he knew, but avoided being drawn into conversation. The whole building hummed with music, the players' faces shining with sweat as dancers called for 'thread-the-leaves', and 'the weave dance', time and time again. He could see the dancers' heads whirling beyond the spectators and feel the vibrations through the floor, but felt no inclination to join them.

There was still no sign of Miken or his kin, and despite his outward calmness, Kest's belly was churning. The lamps had grown dimmer as the nut oil sank in the bulbs, and he came to a stop at a window and loosened the shutters, peering through the crack. He should be out there with his clan-kin, not stuck here. Grunting, he pushed the shutters wider and thrust his head out, enjoying the relief of the cool air on his face. The ornate lamps were pretty, but they added to the hall's closeness.

A weave dance came to a halt behind him, and he turned to see Maxen's spare form begin a slow pace to the top of the hall. Thank the 'green; the bonding ceremony must be about to begin. The lower part of the hall was crowded with elders resting their bones and exchanging gossip, but beyond their grizzled heads he glimpsed Kesilini's bright hair, and Merek, following Maxen up the hall.

Kest's fingers tapped the sill impatiently as he lounged against the wall, one eye on Maxen's progress and the other on the night outside. Where was Miken? Marren believed that any new attack would come at the full moon, for strangers would be aided by the extra light, and he believed it too, for it made sense . . . to everyone except Maxen.

The Feast of Turning is always held on the last full moon of spring and this will not be changing, he'd said.

Marren had called Maxen's response intransigent, but it was more like blind stupidity. And Kesilini was to bond with this man's son! A drumming began and Kest groaned; surely there wasn't going to be even more music? A crowd had gathered round the players' platform, blocking his view. A single note of a pipe joined the drum, and the crowd murmured appreciatively and surged forward. Kest drew himself up to his full height, straining over the gathering. The piper was Kandor, the tune slow and sweet, and vaguely familiar. What was it? The name escaped him but it had something to do with the first Kiraon.

Their own Kiraon was somewhere close to Kandor, no doubt. He could see Maxen in conversation with Farish, the Clanleader of Tarclan, but most of the Tremen were intent on Kandor's performance. The piping came to an end and there was enthusiastic applause as Kandor stepped down from the platform. Kest lost sight of him for a moment, then the crowd parted and Kest glimpsed Kira throw her arms around her brother.

He'd called her beautiful before, and so she was – her hair braided and bejewelled, her tunic finely woven and patterned – but in that moment her love for her brother made her as luminous as the lamps. The crowd thickened, anticipating the bonding ceremony, and he lost sight of her, but the image stayed with him. He'd seen her fight to save Feseren and watched her as she'd slept, her face still etched with Misilini's pain. He'd travelled with her and spoken with her since, but he was still at a complete loss to know how Maxen could have produced a daughter so unlike himself.

The Tremen Leader had mounted the players' platform and the ring of rulership flashed as he raised his hands in a grand sweeping gesture. He was completely at ease, his voice rising and falling, his gaze moving over the crowd solemnly, seemingly not at all concerned that his chosen heir was about to bond to Morclanswoman Kesilini, sister of the contemptible Morclansman Kest. Then an appalling thought occurred to him. Surely Merek had told his father of his intentions? Maxen's welcome had been icy, hardly surprising given their recent dealings, but the Tremen Leader had paid no special attention to Kesilini.

Kest launched himself into the throng, sliding through gaps when he could, and excusing himself when he couldn't. He could see his sister's fair head next to Merek's darker one, standing with the rest of Maxen's children to the side of the players' platform, but the first couple had finished their bonding pledge before he'd managed to reach them. Lern welcomed him with a smile but he couldn't catch Kesilini's eye, her attention fixed on those bonding. He willed her to turn, but the second couple completed their pledge and the hall erupted with clapping and cries of good wishes. Then she and Merek stepped forward.

Maxen looked as if he'd turned to stone. At any other time Kest would have welcomed Maxen's discomfiture, but not when his sister's happiness was at stake. Merek completed his declaration and then Kesilini began hers.

'I, Kesilini of Morclan, daughter of Mesan, daughter of Kirini, sister of Kest, speak now at Turning, that I choose Merek of Kashclan as bondmate and Shelter, until leaf-fall and branch-fall shall end all my days.'

Maxen hadn't moved. Someone unfamiliar with him could have mistaken his stillness for calmness, but Kest knew better. Why hadn't Merek warned his father? Then, as his gaze moved between father and son, he understood. They were equal in pride and arrogance, neither willing to bow to the other or share confidences. How could such a bonding possibly bring Kesilini happiness?

Applause erupted again and there was a brief hiatus while the crowd waited to see if others intended to bond, then the platform was engulfed with well-wishers as the bonded couples were congratulated. Maxen had already turned away, his conversation with the Sherclan leader giving him an excuse not to greet his new bond-daughter.

Kest forced a polite smile as he lined up behind Lern to wish Merek and Kesilini well. At least if Kesilini were utterly miserable she could break the bonding, he consoled himself, even if such actions were frowned upon. Lern embraced Kesilini and moved on to Merek, and then it was his turn. 'May your love be as strong and enduring as the alwaysgreen,' he said, kissing her on the cheek.

'And may you find love also,' she replied, her face radiant.

He nodded and turned to his new bond-brother, but even on this happy occasion, Merek's smile didn't quite reach his eyes.

'I welcome you to Morclan,' said Kest formally.

'And you to Kashclan,' returned Merek.

The bond could be broken, Kest reminded himself as he moved away, but the thought brought him little comfort. The players started up again and the dancers swirled across the floor led by the newly bonded couples, spiralling in then out again, as smooth and rhythmic as ripples in the Drinkwater. Kest searched the crowd for Kira. The tightness of his guts told him his time would be better spent outside, investigating the non-arrival of Miken and his kin, but he'd had a yen ever since Kira's visit to the Morclan longhouse to dance with her again.

Kira watched Merek and Kesilini dancing. Kesilini was holding Merek close and laughing up at him, and Merek looked the happiest she'd ever seen him. There was joy in the faces of the other bonded couples too, and Kira felt a twinge of envy.

189

'I beg one dance with the beautiful Kiraon before I leave.'

Kira started. It was Kest, his intense blue eyes holding hers.

She shook her head.

'You don't know the steps?' asked Kest.

'I know the steps, it's just that . . . it's for bonded couples.'

'The wreath dance is for anyone who enjoys dancing and I know that you enjoy it as much as I, unless, dear bond-sister, you've changed since we last danced together.'

'No, but –'

'Good,' said Kest smoothly, catching her hand and drawing her onto the floor.

The dancers ebbed and flowed, taking Kira with them, up the length of the hall, then round and back again. She whirled, carried along with the pulsing music, catching glimpses of Kandor making comical faces at her, and then of Kest, curiously intent. She was glad that she couldn't see her father.

Finally the last sweet note of the pipe died away, and the dancers came back into line, Kest bowing and she nodding, as was customary. 'I thank you, Kiraon of Kashclan,' he said, bringing her hand to his lips.

Then he was gone and Kandor was beside her. 'You're looking rather hot or are you flushed with regret that you've missed this year's bonding ceremony?'

'You were right the first time.' She fanned herself as she poured a drink. 'I didn't see you dancing,' she said between gulps.

'The handsome Kest didn't ask me,' said Kandor.

Kira choked and Kandor grinned, then the smile drained from his face.

'I would have speech with you, Kiraon,' said her father. 'In the Herbery,' he added, his eyes colder than sleet.

Kandor's shoulders straightened and he stepped forward.

'The jugs on the lower table need refilling,' said Kira quickly, holding Kandor's gaze. 'I'll be back in a moment to help you.' She willed him to go and finally he nodded, then she moved away quickly before Kandor had a chance to change his mind.

The Herbery door shut behind her, cutting off the bright light and cheery hubbub of the gathering, a single lamp illuminating the harsh planes of her father's cheeks and jaw. Somewhere behind her a moon moth fluttered against the shuttered window.

'Earlier this evening I asked that you speak with Clanleader Farish. Not only have you failed to do so, but you've made a point of denying him the barest of courtesies. As if that weren't enough, you've chosen to make an exhibition of yourself by dancing a bonding dance with Kest of Morclan, a man who's proven to be both incompetent and disloyal.'

'But Kest's not –'

'Kest initiated the attack,' gritted Maxen. 'And you failed to heal the wounded that resulted from it! By aligning yourself with him, you've insulted everything Kasheron stood for.'

Kira stared at him in bewilderment. She'd never seen him so angry. 'I've not insulted –'

His hand slammed down on the table. 'Don't contradict me! Morclan flouts the Bough daily. This very night Morclansmen usurp the role of the Protectors and defy *my* authority by sending out their own patrols.'

His voice sank to a harsh whisper, and abruptly his face was a hand span from hers. 'By favouring Kest, you've humiliated me in front of the entire gathering!'

Kira's heart was pounding in her throat, making speech difficult. 'I haven't –'

There was a flash as his ring caught the lamplight, and then the shock of a blow, sending her sprawling backward, cracking her head on the floor. Darkness imploded then receded, leaving behind pools of nausea. Then her father spoke again, his voice still resonating with anger. 'You *will* obey me in the end, Kiraon.' Then the lamplight dwindled and she drifted away.

22

Awareness came slowly, creeping back with the smell of dust, not the fine dust of herbs, but wood dust, filling her nostrils with grit. The smell was puzzling and she turned, waking a vicious throb in her head. A blinding shaft of light sliced the darkness, visible even through her closed lids as a door creaked open, and the sound of music and voices was suddenly loud, then muffled again as it clicked shut. The surface under her face vibrated as footfalls moved nearer.

'Kira?'

It was Kandor, reaching for the lamp. The full memory of what had happened surged back. Using the table leg, she hauled herself into a sitting position, the throb in her head trebling and making her retch. Kandor's lamp swung nearer, the yellow light sending shadows scuttling like littermice. *Go back to the hall.* The words formed in her head but dissolved into a meaningless mumble as they came out of her mouth.

'Kira!' hissed Kandor as he saw her face.

She caught his arm, forcing her numb mouth into action again. 'Do nothing.'

'I'll kill him! He has no right to do that . . . He has no right!'

He was shaking. She could feel it through his embroidered shirt. 'If you love me you'll do nothing.' By the 'green, she was going to be sick. Bile filled her mouth and she turned her head aside, vomiting onto the floor. Kandor's tears splashed down on her, warm and wet, sobs racking his body.

If the Tremen knew her father had struck her; if they knew the Tremen *Leader* had used violence . . .

'I'll leave and come back when everyone's gone,' said Kira. She'd have to find somewhere to hide until the Bough was empty of guests. No one must know. 'You . . . you must stay here, Kandor . . . say nothing.'

'No!'

Taking his face in her hands, she brought her forehead to his. 'Don't spoil Merek and Kesilini's night.'

He jerked away. 'Spoil *their* night? What about *your* night, Kira? What about *your whole life*!' He was all but shrieking; in a moment, someone would come to investigate the disturbance.

'I'll go to Miken,' she said hurriedly.

'You pledge?' said Kandor, between tearing sobs, his tear-stained face suddenly full of determination. 'Pledge me, Kira!'

She hesitated, regretting her words. The last thing she wanted was trouble between the Bough and the octads.

'Pledge or I'll tell everyone in the hall what he's done!' said Kandor.

'I'll go to Miken if you stay here and remain silent.'

Kandor flung his arms around her but she pushed him away and pulled herself upright. The room was swaying and she had to hold on to the edge of the table to stop herself falling.

'Pass me my pack, will you.' Once she was away, she could take some sickleseed to still the nausea.

Kandor handed her the pack and she slid it on, her head pounding so badly that she vomited again and had to wait for a while before being able to walk to the window. Kandor helped her clamber onto the sill, and steadied her as she lowered herself to the ground.

The shutters to either side were wide, throwing slashes of light onto the ground but the single lamp in the Herbery barely sheened beyond the room, leaving a path of darkness to the trees.

'Let me come,' pleaded Kandor, leaning out the window, the lamp behind him lighting his hair like a halo.

'We agreed you'd stay,' she said, dragging her hands from his. Then, crouching low so that those within the hall wouldn't see her, she followed the stripe of darkness across the Arborean. Once in the trees, she kept to the densest blots of shadow, barely aware of her direction, her face throbbing, her legs scarcely able to carry her.

It was a long while before she became aware of where she was. She was in the Kashclan octad, in the lands she'd trod a thousand times on her way to see Tresen, Miken, Tenerini and Mikini – to see those who loved her. Her throat thickened, and this time she let the tears come. All she wanted now was some hollow to creep into, to sleep away the shock and to give the pain in her face time to calm.

Finally, unable to go on, she dropped to her knees and pushed her way into a stand of bitterberry and shelterbush, ignoring the scratches as she forced her way forward, letting the mesh spring back behind her. It was quiet inside, sheltering, safe. She brought her arms around herself and curled into a ball, giving herself up to sleep.

She had no idea how much later it was when she jerked awake. A flowerthief whirred overhead, and then a springleslip, its wings thrashing like a drumbeat. Kira's numb brain grappled with the disturbance of the roosting birds, then branches tore and broke and the earth vibrated with the thump of running feet. Kira froze. There was a scream – gurgling, horrible, cut short – and then fighting was all around her: men shouting and cursing, and metal squealing against metal.

Shargh ran past, pursued by the taller shapes of Tremen, but most stood their ground, shouting to each other in their harsh tongue as they fought. The Tremen also shouted as they fought: *Behind you! 'Ware left! Hold fast!*

Moonlight flashed along the swords as they slashed and jabbed, and occasionally lit the faces of the combatants. Kira could scarcely bear to look at the Shargh, their guttural cries waking the terror of the first attack, but she recognised the garb of Morclan. The fighting surged backwards and forwards without any obvious order and then, somewhere behind her, there was a harsh scream. Several of the Shargh broke off their combat and ran in the direction of the scream, chased by Tremen.

Some Tremen remained, bent over the wounded, and she heard Brem's voice, bawling instructions on how to staunch bleeding. There was a brief moment of stillness, punctuated by the sobbing groans of those on the ground, and Kira scrabbled into a crouch, fingers gouging the earth. Then feet pounded back towards them and she heard Brem curse and the rasp of his sword being drawn. Her shelter was smashed sideways as Shargh burst through, a boot finding her thigh and an elbow skimming her head. There were four of them, the two in front slashing at any Tremen who challenged them, the two behind bent under the burden they shouldered. They must have seen her but they didn't stop, crashing away through the trees.

The Shargh were gone but Kira's dread grew, threatening to overwhelm her. Sweat started on her brow and she searched for movement. Nothing and then . . . a soft blurring of the canopy. Her nose caught the scent first. Smoke was coming from behind her, *from the Bough*! With a nauseating shock she realised the Shargh had come that way too.

Kira sprang away, the smoke thickening with every stride until the air was crackling and the trees ahead vivid with orange light. The forest thinned then gave way, and she slewed to a stop on the edge of the Arborean. The Bough was burning, great gouts of flame gushing skyward, the heat beating at her skin in waves. Silhouettes ran back and forth, fighting and dying against a lurid backdrop, joining the shapes already littering the ground. She could see Sendra, huddled on her side; her father, prone; Lern, his head at an impossible angle. She reeled backwards, grabbing at a tree for support as a flame-clothed figure staggered screaming into the trees.

Then a tableau appeared at the side of the Bough, the heavier shapes of two Shargh dragging a struggling figure, forcing him to his knees, crimson light running along the blade as it swung back. Kandor!

The world disintegrated, jagged pieces of everything Kira had known sucked into a void of horror, taking her with it, her lungs devoid of air, her heart stopped. Then, just as abruptly, the world reassembled itself and she screamed and sprang forward. In the same instant her legs were smashed from under her and she was hurled face down to the ground. A hand clamped over her mouth, another pinioned her arms and she was dragged backwards, her heels scrabbling for purchase and finding none. Then she was wrenched off the ground completely as her captors began a mad flight through the trees, bushes clawing at her clothing and branches whipping her face. Her captors said nothing, their silence as relentless as their speed. There was blood in her mouth but her mind was empty of everything except the appalling image of the descending blade.

23

Tarkenda dropped the spindle between her knees, drew the ebis fleece taut, then flicked it round her hand and set the spindle flying again. It grew fat with yarn but she barely noticed, her ears straining for sound, her gaze darting between her spinning and the door flap. She was weary. Sleep had been as scarce as rain in the days since Erboran and Arkendrin had gone to the south-western forests, her nights filled with images of blood and the endless cries of marwings.

Palansa sat beside her, carding, her lapful of ebis fleece hiding the bulge of her belly, and Tarkenda offered up thanks again for new life even as she shifted on her stool, trying to ease her back.

Palansa looked at her sympathetically. 'Your bones pain you?'

Tarkenda nodded. Once they had ached only when the ebis pastures were green, but it was a long time now since they had been other than brown.

Palansa put aside her carding brushes and rose.

'Where are you going?' asked Tarkenda sharply.

'To fetch your seat. It's more comfortable than Erboran's stool.'

'It would be best you stayed here,' said Tarkenda.

'There's fleece enough for spinning. I won't be long,' said Palansa.

'Stay, Palansa!'

'I –' Palansa began, surprised by Tarkenda's vehemence. Abruptly a high-pitched wail sounded down the slope.

Tarkenda closed her eyes as the wailing grew, surging up towards the sorcha like the Grenwah in flood. The sound of running feet was unmistakable and Palansa's horrified gaze jerked between Tarkenda and the door.

'Get the circlet of chiefship,' ordered Tarkenda.

'What?'

'Get the circlet! Erboran is dead. You must protect your son.'

Palansa gripped her belly and swayed, but Tarkenda forced her bones into action, catching Palansa by the shoulders and shaking her savagely. 'Arkendrin will kill the babe – you must protect the next Chief!'

The words were scarcely out of Tarkenda's mouth when the flap was thrust aside. Tarkenda whirled, throwing herself between the intruder and Palansa, but it was only Irdodun, his face scarlet from running, but his air of triumph unmistakable. Beyond the sorcha, the day was filled with screaming and shouting.

Irdodun wiped the sweat from his face and bowed. 'I bring grievous news, Chief-mother. The Sky Chiefs have called your first-born home. Your secondborn, *Chief* Arkendrin, asks that you prepare the ceremonies to speed his brother's passing.'

Palansa gave a shuddering groan but Tarkenda stared at Irdodun without speaking and his colour deepened. Arkendrin had made the mistake of sending one of his cronies ahead, rather than coming himself. Finally, with an awkward bow, Irdodun turned back to the door, Tarkenda following him, head held high, back straight as a spear. Shargh were massing round the sorcha, forming an ever-thickening circle, moaning and wailing.

Tarkenda stood motionless outside the sorcha, and slowly they quieted. 'The Sky Chiefs have chosen to call Chief Erboran home,' she began. 'He has been a great Chief, caring for us well, and while he will rest in the cloudlands, I grieve for his passing. Yet my sadness is balanced with joy, for the Sky Chiefs – in their wisdom – have ensured that the Shargh's ways, the ways that he, *the firstborn*, followed, can go on. The Chief is gone, but his son, who carries his blood and the blood of all first-born sons back to the Mouth of the Last Teller, remains.'

The sorcha flap stirred and Palansa emerged, eyes dark hollows, cheeks wet, but holding herself proudly, the circlet of chiefship glinting in her hair.

Tarkenda softened her voice. 'The Sky Chiefs have prepared us well for this moment, as they have in the past. When they called my join-husband Chief Ergardrin home, they ensured *his* seed lived on in Erboran, and now they have ensured that Erboran's seed lives on in his join-wife's belly. Once they honoured me as guardian of the new Chief until he was of age, *now* they honour Palansa.'

A murmur ran through the gathering and Tarkenda's heart faltered as she heard the voices of those who were enemies of Erboran raise in protest. Erboran had held Arkendrin's followers to his chiefship by honouring the long seasons of Shargh ways, but also with sword and spear. What hope did two weaponless women and an unborn child have? She forced herself to remain calm, even as Irdodun screwed his head round and stared down the slope. Arkendrin must be near; time was short and she must bring the Shargh behind her.

'Chief-mother, what if the Sky Chiefs send a daughter?'

Tarkenda started; it was the loyal Erdosin asking a question she would have expected from one of Arkendrin's followers. Had he turned or had she missed something? Palansa's claim to the chiefship rested on her carrying a son. What did Arkendrin's claim rest on?

Tarkenda's heart quickened. Irdodun had said nothing about the Healer's death. Surely if she'd been killed, Irdodun would have bragged about it by now.

The Shargh were beginning to murmur again, but she raised her hand, commanding silence.

'Will the Sky Chiefs break the line that stretches from the Cave of Telling to this moment?' she asked slowly. 'Always the first-born son has carried their will and spoken their voice, but if they send a daughter? Then it can only mean that it's their will that a second-born son rules, that they intend a second-born son to be the tool of our salvation by ridding us of the creature of the Last Telling. I do not think it will be so.'

Many of the Shargh were muttering, clearly unconvinced.

Tarkenda took a deep breath. 'Irdodun!'

The Shargh turned to look at him and he squirmed slightly. 'Has my second-born son led you well?'

'Yes, Chief-mother. Erb . . . Chief Erboran was killed early in the fighting. We didn't know that treemen had hidden themselves around the Healer-creature's sorcha. They attacked us, but Arkendrin gathered us once more and we killed many treemen. We burned their main sorcha to the ground, and Arkendrin himself killed the leader and his sons. It was a mighty battle and Arkendrin a mighty leader.' Irdodun's eyes shone and he seemed to grow taller.

'Ah, you should have spoken sooner, Irdodun. It would have lessened our grief to know that the shadow of the Last Telling had been scoured away forever.' She raised her voice and her gaze swept the crowd. 'Let us rejoice in Arkendrin's leadership. He has killed the gold-eyed Healer.'

An excited babbling broke out, but Irdodun shuffled from foot to foot. 'I did not say that, Chief-mother.'

Tarkenda felt like swooning with relief, but she remained expressionless, silencing the crowd with a sweep of her hand.

'Are you saying that Arkendrin *failed* to kill the creature of the Telling?'

'Yes, but . . .'

She considered him with eyes of stone.

The gathering stirred but no one spoke and then a marwing swept up from the plains and over the sorcha roof, crying thrice in quick succession as it arced away over the Grounds. Women screamed and many of the men dropped into fighting crouches.

Tarkenda seized the moment. 'The Sky Chiefs have spoken! To dishonour the way of the firstborn will surely bring bloodshed and death to us all.'

Tarkenda bowed to Palansa and brought her palm to her forehead; after an excruciatingly long pause, she heard the creak of leather and skins as the Shargh followed suit. Then, with a final imperious look at the crowd, she held the flap open for Palansa and followed her back into the Chief's sorcha.

Tarkenda took two steps, staggered, and had to clutch at the wall to keep herself upright. She hung there panting, the world blotching with blackness and her stomach roiling, and when her sight cleared all she could see was Palansa's furious face.

'You knew he was going to die, didn't you?' she whispered hoarsely.

Tarkenda nodded.

'You knew he was going to die, and you did nothing! You let him go to his death! And all the time you were planning for this!' Palansa slammed her hand down on the table. 'All the times you walked me to the Thanawah to gather basket reeds; all the times to the targasso groves. Parading me! Showing me off! Up and down the slope! Flaunting the next Chief! Knowing your son was going to his death! Knowing and doing nothing!' Palansa choked and turned away.

Tarkenda still sagged against the wall, thinking not of Erboran, but of her long dead join-husband Ergardrin.

'Had you no feelings for him?' hissed Palansa, turning on her again. 'No love? Answer me!'

'I carried Erboran in my belly, even as you carry your son, and you ask me this?'

Palansa's hands clenched and unclenched. 'Then why didn't you stop him? Why did you let him go?'

'The Sky Chiefs can't be gainsaid.'

'The Sky Chiefs!' spat Palansa, tearing the circlet from her head and hurling it at the wall.

'They've shown me what's to come.'

The heave of Palansa's chest stilled. 'They showed you Erboran's death?'

'They've shown me many deaths. What's happened in the tree-lands is just the beginning.'

Palansa's skin had whitened to wood ash and sweat glittered on her upper lip. 'How will it end?'

'That is still hidden, but this I do know. You will raise your son to be Chief, even as I raised Erboran.'

'And Arkendrin?' asked Palansa, her hands clutching convulsively at her belly.

Tarkenda lowered herself gingerly onto a stool. 'To be Chief, Arkendrin must kill the gold-eyed Healer, or Erboran's son. To strengthen his claim on the chiefship, he will seek to do both.'

Palansa groped her way to a stool and sat down too. Silence fell, disturbed only by the sound of wailing on the slope.

'I want him back,' said Palansa hoarsely. 'I want him in my arms, I want his flesh next to mine. I want to feel the softness of his hair, to smell him, to hold him . . .' She choked to a stop and looked up at Tarkenda. 'He'll never know his own son . . .' She collapsed forward and Tarkenda pulled her close. 'I loved him,' sobbed Palansa.

Tarkenda's arms tightened round her and tears stained her own face. 'We both loved him,' she said.

24

Kira came to her senses with a sickening surge of terror. Moonlight sliced down from above and tree branches formed a jagged mesh between her and the sky. She stared at them unblinkingly. Somewhere, on the edges of her mind, she knew that everything was gone but her brain was as bloodied as a wound and incapable of moving beyond the feel of leaves under her back. Her captors were crouched nearby, their harsh whispers punctuated by the raw panting of their exertions. There was another sound, too, a rhythmic scraping, like grit under stone.

After a while, the hiss of her captors' speech resolved itself into words. Shargh speaking Tremen, she thought nonsensically.

'She shouldn't be breathing like that,' said the first speaker.

'It's shock. She'll be all right.' The second speaker sounded older, and more authoritative.

'They've hurt her!' The first speaker, angry.

'She'll be all right, just keep her quiet.'

'I hate this!' The first speaker again.

'We have her, that's all that matters,' said the second speaker, the voice cracking with emotion. There was a brief silence then the voice sounded again, calm now. 'She must be kept safe. She holds the greatest healing knowing now.'

The scraping sound quickened, like an avalanche of stones, making the sweat pool in her eyes and her head swim. She was lifted again and the image of the Shargh running with their burden came back to her, bringing another surge of terror. Then the avalanche of stones became a torrent, sweeping her away.

It was the smell of dankness that drew Kira back the second time and she came reluctantly, some part of her knowing that waking would bring only misery and pain. Her mouth was full of the dregs of a herb – sickleseed, her Healer self told her as she dragged her eyes open.

It was gloomy, the room full of shadows, but the walls were clearly of stone, not wood, and she was lying on a mattress on the floor, not in her bed. Her eyes moved sluggishly over her surroundings. Sacks of scavenger leaf lay in massive piles at her feet, and casks of oil and dusty bundles of falzon took up most of the space along the walls to either side. Her thin mattress had been squashed in among the stores and a table with a water jug and basin pushed into one corner. There was no lamp set but a faint wash of light intruded from the cavern beyond, illuminating pits and hollows in the stone and the occasional wink of crystal.

Thirst burned, chapping her lips and thickening her tongue. Sickleseed was known for it, a side effect of its more useful properties of deadening pain, dulling feeling and bringing sleep. Kira could see the page detailing it in the Herbal Sheaf, except the Herbal Sheaf no longer existed, gone with everything else into the ruination of the flames. She struggled awkwardly from the bed and poured herself a cup of water, gulping it down, refilling the cup and gulping it down again. The water was dank, almost musty tasting, but she was greedy for it, drinking with eyes closed, intent only on the slide of the liquid down her throat.

There were voices, harsh whisperings of an argument ill-suppressed and she recognised one of them. Relief swept over her as the realisation that she'd been taken by Tremen *not Shargh* finally penetrated her dazed mind.

The voices intruded again. The speaker from last night was Tresen, and the person he argued with was Kest. The subject of their dispute was audible too: it was her.

She put the cup down and tried to smooth her tunic, but it was crumpled, torn and stained. The floor tilted and she grabbed the table for support, struggling to hold back the flood of images, knowing that if she let them come she would be utterly lost.

'For the sake of the 'green, leave her to sleep.'

'There are injured!'

Kira shook her head savagely, grappling with the flashes of smoke and fire filling her mind.

'She's injured herself! And exhausted. She needs to rest!'

Injured? She clutched at the word, imagining a falzon bandage binding a wound, the gaping flesh disappearing under the cream, fragrant cloth. Her breathing slowly steadied and she was able to let go of the table and move in the direction of the light, the voices growing louder as she went.

'Men are dying, Tresen! The Sheaf's destroyed, we must have –'

Kest saw her and froze mid-sentence. They were sitting at a table, Tresen with his back to her. Kest was still clad in his finery from Turning, but his tunic was grimy, one side hanging in tatters. Tresen turned, looking as old as Miken, his skin sallowed by the lamplight. No one spoke, but Kira kept her feet moving until she was almost to Kest, keeping her gaze on him, not trusting herself to look at Tresen.

'How many injured are there?' she said, her voice croaky.

Kest stood, his face full of pity, and for a horrible moment she thought he was going to offer condolences.

'How many injured are there?' She could bear being thought

half-witted by repeating herself, but she couldn't bear words of comfort, for that would mean . . .

'I . . . twenty-five, Healer Kiraon,' said Kest, his gaze on her cheek.

'Where are they?'

'In the third training room.'

'It's close to the herbal stores and the Water Cavern,' volunteered Tresen. 'We've made it into a Haelen.'

Like in the Bough. Images of the inferno surged back and she screwed her eyes shut, struggling to visualise falzon bandages until she was able to open her eyes again. Kest was exchanging glances with Tresen, but his face flicked to neutral.

'I'll need help,' she said, her voice scarcely audible. She coughed to clear her throat. 'How . . . how many Kashclan are here?'

'Five, including Miken and Tresen,' answered Kest.

'Who?'

'Arlen, Paterek and Werem.'

Not Merek. The last of her hope guttered and she gripped the table with such ferocity that her fingers went numb. 'They're not Healers,' she rasped. 'I'll need Healers. Does Sarkash command Tresen to heal or protect?'

'I'm afraid Commander Sarkash is dead. Miken leads until the council meets, but I command the Warens. You can have Tresen to aid you and whoever else you choose.'

'Whoever else . . .' she echoed. What use would any of them be? She thought of Feseren and Sanaken and their incurable wounds and clenched her jaw.

'I'll take you to the training room, Kira, and help you arrange it to your liking,' said Tresen gently.

Kest turned his feet towards the first training room, where he knew Miken waited to speak with him. The Kashclan Leader was sitting at a table resting his head back against the wall with his eyes shut, but he roused as Kest settled opposite.

'She's gone with Tresen to the third training room,' said Kest, in answer to Miken's unasked question. 'How she's walking I've no idea, let alone functioning.' He cleared his throat and rubbed his face wearily.

'Kira's concern will be for the wounded now,' said Miken. 'They will take all her intent and all her strength for a time. Her grief will come later.' He paused. 'Patrols are now in place?'

Kest nodded. 'Protectors are at the longhouses and, with the clansmen there rotating through protecting duties, the longhouses should be secure. At least there's been no argument about patrols guarding gatherers or gathering being limited to the First Eight.'

'It's not sustainable in the long term,' said Miken.

'No,' said Kest, reminded abruptly of his own objection to Sarkash's orders in the Water Cavern. It seemed a lifetime ago.

'Of course, we don't know what the long term is,' said Miken.

'My first duty is to secure what remains,' said Kest. 'The Bough is gone and the dead are beyond our aid, but the longhouses remain *and* the wounded. I need as many Healers as possible within the Warens. You, of course, must return to your longhouse, but I want Tresen here to help Kira, and Werem, Arlen and Paterek. Send Brem too – if you're agreeable.'

'While we have enough clansman at the longhouse, it's best he serves here,' said Miken, rising. 'We must keep the healing-knowing safe till it can be written again.'

The Kashclan Protectors sat quietly, grim-faced and armed, but more intent on the alwaysgreen in front of them than on the trees at their back. Pekrash's men patrolled there as discreetly as possible given their need to create a protective circle around the alwaysgreen and its grieving Kashclansmen.

Miken was barely aware of his kin as he stood with his palm against Sogren's gnarled trunk, his attention on the patchwork of sods between its massive roots. Maxen, Merek and Lern lay here, but not Kandor, though it was unheard of to separate a family in this way.

Never had so many members of a family died at one time in Allogrenia and Miken daren't risk disturbing Sogren's roots further. Kandor rested with Fasarini under the great alwaysgreen Wessogren instead; mother and son together again in death. Likewise, the other Kashclan dead had been buried under their bondmates' alwaysgreens.

Miken straightened and rubbed the soil from his hands, repelled suddenly by the knowledge of the death it held: Maxen, Merek, Lern, perhaps even the very future of the Tremen; certainly of the sweet rituals of farewell that brought comfort, for the risk of attack remained too great. No burial was easy but the embrace of clan-kin and their songs softened the pain of those left behind. There had been none this time, just the words of ending, delivered while his clan-kin stood, swords in their hands. There had been no women present either, for he'd ordered they remain within the Protector-guarded longhouse. Even Kira was absent, despite it being her right and duty to lay the first sod, to sing the first mourning-song and to lead the words of parting.

Miken hadn't seen Kira since he and Tresen had carried her to the Warens, and now his duty to his dead clan-kin was done, he had a sudden and overwhelming need to reassure himself that she was well. Nodding to his clan-kin, he set off through the trees, passing Pekrash's men but declining their offer of an escort. He had a sword but no fear he'd have to use it, for it was broad daylight and a waning moon would soon rise, not the full moon the Shargh clearly favoured for their filthy work.

His pace quickened. Their stinking swords hadn't reached Kira, nor would they while he drew breath! Not that they hadn't caused her terrible injury. Kira's loss was shocking, and the wound of Kandor's death in particular would be long in its healing. Miken took a steadying breath. Praise the 'green that she was stubborn and single-minded, qualities that had infuriated Maxen, but which would now ensure her survival. Despite Kest's concerns, she'd not be turning away from life while there were injured to be cured.

And if there were no cure? Miken's feet slowed. *Fire with flatswords brings the bane, fire without brings life again.* One indecipherable rhyme was all that lay between them and the rot that would inevitably come. And Kira knew this, for she'd seen it already in Sarnia Cave. How would she deal with so much death?

Miken cursed and shoved a shelterbush branch out of his way; he was thinking like a man defeated *and* a fool! The rhyme proved there was a cure for Shargh wounds, but they'd lost it. They'd grown lazy in their fastness of trees, that was their problem. They'd confused seasons of peace with an absence of enemies. It wasn't a mistake Kasheron had made.

Miken shrugged savagely. What was the use of dwelling on past errors; they must work now to save what Kasheron had founded.

A flowerthief danced through the foliage, its yellow eye comical against the ring of green plumage, and Miken's heart lifted. The forest was still beautiful, despite the darkness that had descended on them and, in the one thing that mattered most, fortune had been kind. The only person in the whole of Allogrenia capable of rewriting the Herbal Sheaf had survived.

But how? His belly growled and he broke off a spray of pitchie, forcing himself to chew the dusty seeds as he contemplated the attack. He and his clan-kin had been set upon as they'd neared the Arborean, but that was just the backwash of the fighting at the Bough. And suddenly, there was Kira, running towards the flames and *towards* the Shargh. The sight of her in such danger had almost been worse than the sight of the Bough burning, and it had only been her momentary pause and Tresen's younger legs that had allowed them to snatch her back from certain death. But they had been too late to save Kandor. That failure would haunt him for the rest of his days.

Miken shook his head and spat out a husk. None of it made sense. If Kira had fled the attack on the Bough, she'd have taken Kandor with her, and there was no reason for her to leave *before*. Indeed, as the only woman in the Bough, she was responsible for hosting the evening and ensuring the smooth running of the feast, duties Maxen certainly wouldn't have let her relinquish. *And* she'd escaped from the Shargh's clutches with nothing worse than bruising, when even fully trained and armed Protectors had succumbed.

There had been no warning. Kest had outlined to him the events within the Bough, telling him that Maxen wouldn't have noticed anything amiss, even if he'd believed there *was* danger. Maxen was too busy fuming over Merek bonding with a Morclanswoman – and Kest's sister of all people. Miken smiled sourly. Maxen wouldn't have challenged his eldest son and chosen successor; he was more likely to have vented his anger on Kira. Miken had seen him berate her often enough before. Then his blood ran cold.

What if Maxen's anger had gone beyond words this time? What if he'd actually struck her? Miken glanced back over his shoulder in the direction of Maxen's chill corpse, and shivered. The notion was unthinkable! He was letting his dislike of the man cloud his thinking. As Leader, Maxen most of all was bound by the Tremen strictures forbidding violence. He shrugged but the idea remained firmly lodged in his head; it gave explanation for Kira's absence from the Bough, and the bruise on her face, in a way nothing else did.

The forest thinned then gave way completely as he reached the Arborean, the air taking on a sooty scent. The trees ringing the blackened earth were fading to yellow, as if it were autumn rather than summer, but their colour had nothing to do with the gentle change of seasons. Scorched leaves littered the ground, crunching under Miken's feet and rattling from the canopy, framing a sight no less shocking than it had been after the last of the flames had been beaten out.

He stopped, despite his intention to pass through quickly, and he was unsure whether it was the devastation of everything Tremen that held him there, or the fact that so little of the building remained. Even the birds had fled. Normally the air would be alive with springleslips and tippets attracted by the rich pickings of bark beetles, stickspiders and flutterwings the clearing provided, but the Arborean was silent. Even the sky was bereft of clouds.

He started off again, moving slowly over the open ground until he felt something shift under his foot. At first he thought it was just a stick, but there was a smoothness and symmetry about it that was unnatural. Extricating it from the earth where it had been pressed by many feet, he used his thumbnail to clear the mud from the delicate scroll of carving, blinking as his vision blurred. Old Benam had given Kandor this pipe when the boy had first shown an interest in music. Kandor had barely been four seasons and Benam already an old man. Now the alwaysgreens sheltered both of them.

Feeling suddenly old, he sighed, and turned his feet north, towards the Warens.

Time in the Warens wasn't measured by sunlight or shadow, nor marked by frost or dew. Nothing gave song or lent flashes of colour like tippets or springleslips, or scented the air with leaf or blossom, berry or bark. The Warens were unchanging stone: dark and often dank, but safe, and safety was paramount now. Kest grimaced. He missed the open world above.

Footsteps sounded ahead and his sword was in his hand before he realised it, but it was only Karbrin replenishing one of the lamps. Kest sheathed his sword and nodded to him as he passed, feeling faintly foolish. The Shargh had reduced him to jumping at shadows. Better to jump than die, he thought grimly. He'd not gone much further when footfalls sounded again, but these reverberated with the precision of a patrol and he flattened himself against the stone until Pekrash's men had passed. The four patrols Kest had sent out had now returned, and they all told the same story; the forest seemed empty of Shargh. Was it possible?

The air sweetened and a yellow glow ahead announced the opening to the third training room. He braced himself; this was where they'd brought the injured, screaming with pain, vomiting and sobbing, straight after the fighting. Two had died as they'd carried them and three shortly after. Kest took several steadying breaths, fearing what he was about to see, but it was quiet now and the air sweet, no longer stinking of sweat and blood.

Mattresses had been laid in neat rows, lamps set at regular intervals to give the Healers light, and tables shifted from other caverns to serve as shelves for water jugs and basins, pots and grinding stones, and stacks of herbs. The scent he'd noticed in the tunnel was more intense, reminding him abruptly of Feserini's birthing room, and of scooping the unconscious Kira from the floor. *Leader Feailner Kiraon*, he corrected; she was going to have to accept the title now, whether she willed it or not.

Kira was at the other end of the cavern, bent in tending, Tresen beside her, but Kest turned the other way to where those with lesser injuries lay and those whose wounds were inflicted by the agony of loss. Kesilini's face was peaceful now, the savage grief smoothed away with sickleseed, and he knelt beside her and took her hand, its warmth bringing him relief as intense as pain. When he'd fought his way through the choking smoke in the Bough, he'd believed he'd never see her again, and he still had no idea how she'd managed to escape when so many hadn't.

The further caverns were being emptied of their dead, their clan-kin taking them away under Protector escort for burial. Seven Protectors had lost their lives in the battle in the trees outside, including Sarkash, who'd arrived near the end of the fighting, and sixteen Protectors and clansmen and women who'd been celebrating the Turning. The Shargh had killed all their swords could reach and scarcely a clan had escaped untouched. Clanleader Farish had perished and members of Sarclan, Sherclan and Barclan longhouses, but the greatest single loss had been from Kashclan: Mern, Stinder, old Dera, Maxen, Merek, Lern and Kandor.

He smoothed the covering over Kesilini, his gaze on Kira again. The treegems in her hair caught the lamplight as she worked, but the bruise on her face was hidden. His men had told him that Kandor had been killed after most of the Shargh had withdrawn. The Shargh had hunted him down, passing other Tremen in pursuit of him. Had their quest been to destroy the Tremen leadership? Was that why they'd ignored the longhouses in their path, striking at the heart of Allogrenia? If so, they'd all but succeeded: Maxen, Merek, Lern and Kandor were dead, and Kira was carrying their foul mark on her face.

He kissed Kesilini on the forehead, then moved towards the entranceway. Most of the more severely injured were sleeping, either from the effects of sickleseed or everest. Kira should have been sleeping too, her paleness clear from where he stood. But since Kandor's death, she had thrown herself into healing, and even when she *did* rest, Tresen said, she tossed about in nightmares, crying Kandor's name.

Kest sighed. Kira was the holder now of all the healing they had left – Kasheron's legacy reduced to one exhausted girl. How had it happened? *Why* had it happened? At that moment she looked up, but there was no flicker of recognition, and even from a distance, he could see that there was no gold left in her eyes.

25

A single column of smoke rose above the landscape, visible the length and breadth of the Shargh Grounds. No wind blew and no wing-beat frayed or softened it, so that it reached almost to the clouds before skewing sideways, staining the sky. The pyre had been set on the edge of the Grounds, where the land began to rise and break into the stony steps of the Cashgars, and where a single cave-mouth gaped, marking the place of the Last Telling. It was the place where the Sky Chiefs' breath came closest to the earth; where their thoughts had seeded the minds of Tellers; where the spirit most easily quit its human shell to make the journey skyward.

Shargh swayed and muttered, their wailing stilled by the ritual lighting of the pyre. The gather-wood was brittle from countless days under the sun, and the flames devoured it swiftly, their tongues licking at the wolf-skin enclosing Erboran's corpse, his flesh thickening and souring the smoke. The acrid plumes engulfed Arkendrin, who'd positioned himself too close to the pyre, but he stood his ground, eyes smarting, clamped mouth silencing a gurgling cough. His brother's profile was dark against the bright orange of the flames, and as the wood broke and settled, his jaw sagged open in a macabre grin. Arkendrin's teeth clenched. Even in death Erboran mocked him!

Arkendrin's gaze swung to Palansa at the head of the pyre, shimmering like a spirit-shadow in the heat-warped air, chin high, her cursed belly ripening like ground-fruit. She stood in the Chief's place, in *his* place. How could a thing unborn be Chief? He sucked in a lungful of smoke and was racked by a hacking cough. Only two thrusts of a flatsword lay between him and the chiefship, and his muscles ached to take what was rightfully his. Erboran's skin blistered and cracked, but Arkendrin barely noticed, his thoughts buzzing like blackflies. If he claimed he'd bedded Palansa before she'd joined with his brother, then the seed growing in his belly would be his, *and* the chiefship. But he'd not be believed – his cursed mother had seen to that! She'd made it known among the sorchas high and low that Palansa had bled in Erboran's bed at their joining.

Tarkenda had always sided with Erboran against him. And now she was using Palansa to take the chiefship for herself! His fingers twitched and he rocked forward on the balls of his feet. Half the Shargh already favoured him becoming Chief and it would take little to bring the rest behind him: just the death of the Healer-creature, or the miscarry of his brother's seed. Killing the creature of the Telling would be simpler, and then he'd take Palansa whether she willed it or not. Death of the young during birthing was unfortunate but not uncommon.

He felt his mother's gaze on him and he licked his dried lips, forcing his face into an expression of suitable solemnity. The air was unbearably close, the stale end of another hot day, and the craving for the touch of rain against his face was overwhelming.

Well, he'd danced attendance on the great dead Chief long enough! With the slightest dip of his head and briefest touch to his forehead, he strode off across the Grounds, breaking into a run when he was clear of the gathering, ignoring the slide of sweat over his body as he forced his feet into rhythm with his thudding heart.

The cracked margins of the Thanawah stretched ahead, and he turned along it, running parallel with its sluggish flow till he came to the stands of slitweed, the blood roaring in his ears as he came to a stop. He stood, chest heaving, until slowly the sounds of the Grounds intruded: the hungry lowing of ebis behind him; the rattle of the slitweed; a water-toad croaking. A shrunken moon bobbed on the water, shifting and blurring with the Thanawah's movement. Arkendrin glared at it. So it was with the Sky Chiefs! Their intent seeming one thing but turning out another; birthing him into the Chief's family, a season behind the firstborn, then taking the first-born to the cloudlands, and leaving his seed behind.

But no more! Before the moon was full again, he'd be back under the cursed trees and this time he'd not fail in capturing the creature. Not that the fault was his that it still lived. Erboran had led badly, thwarting him even in death by forcing him to abandon the attack to bring his body home. Well, the sending ceremony was over, and he'd not be idling away the three mourning moons watching Palansa's claim on the chiefship grow as big as her belly. The sooner the thing of the Telling was dead, the sooner he'd prise the chiefship from Palansa's fists.

Something moved and his hand went to his knife. It was only a water-toad, its eyes as yellow as those of the foul thing of the Telling, jumping closer, muscles bunching under glistening skin. Arkendrin waited, then slammed his heel down, the toad's skin popping as he ground the quivering mass to jelly, then booted it into the water. The moon shattered, then the slivers drew back into a whole, the toad's blood drifting across its face like funeral smoke.

Irdodun sat in the quiet night attending the makeshift spit, salting the peeling skins of the grahens, his gaze more often on Arkendrin's back than on the tasks at hand. The flames glanced off the eyes of the wolf Arkendrin had slain, making them glow in a hollow imitation of life as its body stiffened in the cooling air. The pelt was lush and

Irdodun wondered whether Arkendrin would claim it. He'd made no move to skin the beast, seemingly content with its hunting, and now stood staring out over the Grounds. Irdodun poked at the coals to spread the heat more evenly, imagining the pelt strewn across his sorcha floor or fattening his bed covers.

Urpalin's coughing jerked him from his reverie.

'Will I skin the beast for you, Chief?' asked Urpalin, his eyes on the wolf.

Irdodun scowled down at the fire, not trusting himself to look at the scrawny face of the younger man. He sensed Orthaken tense too, but Arkendrin was barely aware of any of them, his body still pulsing from the chase and kill, the wolf's blood still wet on his shirt. The rocky hill of the Last Teller lay at his back, and the sky was pierced with a moon as sharp as ebis horn, giving little light. Not that he needed light to know the place of each sorcha on the slope, each pool and eddy within the Thanawah, Grenwah and Shunawah, each rock and roothold of burrel, targasso and stone-tree.

Cooking fires dotted the Grounds but he stared beyond them to the south-west, to where the gold-eyed creature lived and breathed and prospered.

'I won't be waiting three moons,' he said, turning. 'I won't let my people suffer merely to honour a man who now takes his ease with the Sky Chiefs.'

'The Chief-mother will say that Erboran must have his three moons of mourning,' said Irdodun. 'She will use it against you.'

Arkendrin paced to and fro on the edge of the fire. 'The curse of the Last Telling grows stronger by the day. We cannot afford three moons of waiting on a corpse; the creature must be destroyed before we are destroyed.'

'You speak as a Chief should,' said Irdodun.

'We need to know where the creature hides. It wasn't in the place we burned. We must know where it is.'

'We could send watchers,' suggested Urpalin.

Arkendrin's teeth flashed. 'When Urgundin was taken, the Sky Chiefs granted me a boon. It's often the case with those they favour, I've heard tell.'

'A boon?' Irdodun leaned forward.

'When first we found the creature, the treemen shouted a word. It's the creature's name. We don't need to find the creature, only a treeman who knows where it is.'

'It'll be simple to make him speak,' said Urpalin, patting his dagger. 'But we don't know their tongue. How are we to understand what the treeman says?'

Arkendrin's gaze swung to Orthaken and he started. 'Your blood-tie Irason told me what the word meant, for he once traded with our Ashmiri brothers. He knows northern words, for the Ashmiri trade far. Bring him to the edge of the trees and wait for us there.'

Orthaken blanched. 'Chief Arkendrin . . . Irason's old. There's much he doesn't remember. What if . . . it's not enough?'

'It will be enough.'

Palansa wrung the water out of the last of her clothes, dumped the damp bundles into her basket and struggled upright. There were many women at the Grenwah's washpools, their chatter ebbing and flowing on the sunny air. Palansa nodded to them as she turned up the bank, glad to be done with her chores. Her belly made crouching by the water awkward and she was relieved to be away from the curious eyes of the other women. She stopped at the top of the bank and swung the basket onto her other hip. As she did so, Ormadon suddenly appeared at her side.

She glanced at the old warrior in irritation. Didn't Tarkenda even trust the washer-women?

'I'll carry the basket for you, Chief-wife,' he said.

'There's no need.'

They walked for a while in silence, Palansa scanning the sky, which was cloudless, *again*, and feeling the crisp grasses underfoot. Why did the Sky Chiefs not send rain?

'And what do the washer-women say?' asked Ormadon.

'Only the usual gossip. I'm sure it's of no interest to you . . . unless you've come to like women's work.'

'Gossip is always of interest, Chief-wife. Women speak loudly of what their join-husbands whisper. The one furthest upstream; whose blood-tie is she?'

'Ermashin's. She's joined to his uncle's second son.'

'Of what did she speak?'

'She was complaining that her join-husband gives her no pleasure in bed. She says he should just be called a husband because he's no longer capable of joining with her.' Ormadon's ruddy face remained impassive.

'She says she might try a younger man tonight, as her join-husband's away,' added Palansa mischievously.

'Did she say where her join-husband was?' asked Ormadon, his eyes narrowing.

'No, but . . . I've noticed that Arkendrin's sorcha has been empty these last few days. I know he goes beyond the Grenwah hunting, but it's his habit to be back by nightfall.'

'Perhaps he returns when you're sleeping.'

'The fire-circle's cold.'

'It's good you're observant, Chief-wife, it bodes well for the health of your son – the next Chief.'

Palansa shifted her basket back to her other hip and gazed about the brown pasture lands. 'What does it mean, Ormadon?'

'Erlken tells me that Orthaken has taken Irason to the southwest forests.'

They were coming to the first of the sorchas and Palansa lowered her voice. 'Irason can scarcely walk, so crippled is he with old-man's ache. His join-wife spends half her time grubbing for oil-root in the targasso, but it doesn't seem to do him any good.'

'I don't think they've taken him south-west for his swiftness,' murmured Ormadon, his eyes flicking between Orthaken and Urpalin's deserted sorchas as they passed. Marwings flapped overhead and Palansa saw Ormadon's hand move to his flatsword. She tightened her grip on her basket but said nothing, concentrating on navigating the steep path winding up the slope.

'Before his bones were eaten, Irason travelled far,' said Ormadon. 'He learned other tongues.'

Palansa stopped to catch her breath, the babe squirming and pummelling at her lungs, making her pant. She set the basket down, feeling inclined to accept Ormadon's offer to carry it after all, but then decided it was better that his hands were free. She squinted out over the sun-bleached pastures while her breathing steadied. There was only one reason why Arkendrin would take the slow-moving Irason all the way to the forests.

'He seeks the gold-eyed Healer of the Last Telling,' she said softly. 'He thinks killing her will give him the chiefship.'

'Killing her or killing the next Chief,' said Ormadon, his gaze following hers. 'He thinks it will be simpler to kill her, but if that fails . . .'

'I'm not afraid of him,' said Palansa, turning on Ormadon fiercely.

'There are many who aren't afraid of the red scum infesting the Thanawah's drinking holes but it still injures them,' said Ormadon.

'What should I do?' asked Palansa, her hands moving protectively over her belly.

'Let the Chief-mother guide you and I'll send Erlken to keep you company for a while. I think it's time I listened to what the sorchas tell.'

26

Kira rolled onto her side, trying to find ease for her aching bones and failing. Her mattress was the type used by Protectors, stuffed with sere grass that poked at her no matter which way she turned. Though Tresen had secured a hanging across the alcove to give her privacy and a place to sleep, there was no sleep to be had. Jarin and Marakin's groans were audible from the training room beyond and her mind was filled with images of Kandor begging her to take him with her on the night of Turning. She sat up, hugging her knees close and tugging the sleeping gown back over her shoulder. It was too big, but at least it was clean.

She clutched at the image of the falzon bandage binding a wound, managing to quench the scene of death and fire in her head before it took hold. It was almost habit now, this cutting off of memory, a reflexive response to something she knew had the power to destroy her. If only this mental sleight of hand could be used for what was to come. Everest still held the most severely wounded but those with lesser wounds were already burning, their breathing becoming like Feseren's, each gasp screaming that she'd failed, *again*.

There *must* be a cure, the old Tremen rhyme proved it! Tossing the covering aside, she paced around the alcove. *Fire with flatswords brings the bane.* Fire was fever; Feseren's death had taught her that. He'd burned, just as those beyond the hanging now burned. *Fire without brings life again.* Fire without what? It made no sense! How could fever bring life? Fever burned the flesh as surely as flames had burned the Bough. There *must* be something else!

But what? *Where?* Two steps to the wall, two to the bed. Kasheron's people must have suffered Shargh wounds and they'd survived. The cure hadn't been in the Herbal Sheaf or in the Writings. And it hadn't been in any of the many caverns she'd managed to explore so far. If she *were* to find a cure, she must search for the answer deeper in the Warens.

Wrenching the gown over her head, she pulled the dirty Protector garb back on and grabbed her jacket and pack. Tresen was at the far end of the training room, his attention on a thrashing Protector. Just as well, for she didn't have time to argue with him about her safety. Moving swiftly through the rows of wounded, she snatched one of the tunnel lamps and set off into the darkness.

Miken edged round Nogren's trunk into the outer cavern, nodding to the Protector who sprang from the shadows. It was Darmanin of Kenclan, one of Kest's men. They were all Kest's men now, he corrected, and it was fitting. Kest was a strong fighter with a good strategic brain. But more importantly, he had the men's trust.

As he hastened on along the first tunnel, the air grew danker and Miken's nose wrinkled. The ventilation was better in the training rooms, but it was no place for the ill. Still, they couldn't risk moving them. Also the bee's-comb of tunnels kept Kira safe, which was the main thing. A staccato of footsteps filled the cavern ahead and the bobbing glow of lamps appeared, requiring Miken to flatten himself against the wall. It was a patrol, their leader shouting orders in preparation for Nogren's passing.

'Commander Kest,' called Miken, having to bawl to be heard above the noise of their passing.

The patrol came to a halt and a lamp was passed along the group.

'Clanleader Miken, what brings you to the Warens?' asked Kest.

'I come to speak with Kiraon,' said Miken, his words carrying to the back of the patrol.

'I might come with you, Clanleader,' said Kest slowly.

'By all means.'

Kest called one of his men forward and they conferred briefly, then the patrol moved on, leaving him and Miken alone.

'I'm calling a Clancouncil for the morrow,' said Miken as they walked. 'The Clanleaders will formalise your command of the Protectors and appoint Kira Tremen Leader.'

'Do you think that's wise so quickly?'

'What? You or her?' asked Miken dryly. 'Kira's our best Healer,' he added after a moment, when Kest failed to respond.

'I don't doubt Kira's healing skill but she's still very young,' said Kest. 'She lacks the ability to think before she acts. I . . .' Kest stopped. 'I beg your pardon, Clanleader, I didn't intend clan insult.'

'I think you and I can put aside such niceties in the interests of honesty,' said Miken. 'Kira's lacked the hand of good guidance and, as you've no doubt noticed, is fond of going her own way. But the gift of healing's strong in her, along with the passion for it that true Healers possess. As for the rest of it . . .' Miken shrugged. 'It will come in time.'

Kest wondered whether she'd be given that time, but said nothing, and for a while the only noise was the grit of their boots over the cavern floor.

It was Miken who broke the silence. 'Has she spoken of Kandor?'

'I've had little time to visit the training rooms,' said Kest regretfully. 'But Tresen says she's neither wept openly nor spoken of anything that happened that night, and he daren't raise it with her.'

'Kira had great love for Kandor. She . . .' Miken's voice cracked and he slammed his hand against the stone. 'He was only a boy, yet the stinking murderers ignored Protectors to kill him!'

Kest waited for the heave of Miken's breathing to quieten before speaking. 'Since last we met, I've received the reports of the Protectors who fought that night.'

Miken's head flicked round. 'And?'

'The Shargh left their dead where they fell, except for one.'

'They took a body back?'

'Yes.'

'You think it was their leader?'

'Who else? No others were accorded the privilege.'

There was a brief silence while Miken digested the news.

'I've been thinking about the manner of their attack,' continued Kest. 'They passed Barclan and Kenclan longhouses to reach the Bough, making it a journey of over four days from the Sentinels. If they were simply intent on killing Tremen, they could've sated their appetites with far less trouble. Clanleaders Tenedren and Ketten had set no guards.'

'I've had the same thought,' said Miken. 'Go on.'

'Then there's the first attack. They'd choked Kandor unconscious but they were clearly intending to kill Kira.'

'What are you saying?'

'Why didn't they kill Kandor then? A hand over his mouth and a sword across his throat. It would've been easy, and then when Kira came to his aid, kill her too.'

Miken's blood ran cold. Kest's words held a terrible logic. 'You think they had no real interest in killing Kandor because they were hunting Kira? And that having failed to kill her then, they came to the Bough for her, ignoring the longhouses along the way?'

'Yes.'

'I don't suppose you've thought of reasons for any of this.'

Kest shrugged helplessly; the lamp-glow from the training room ahead illuminating his discomfited face.

'Have you spoken of this to others?'

Kest shook his head. 'To be honest, now that I've voiced my thoughts, they seem improbable.'

'It's best they remain between us for the time being,' said Miken softly, his eyes on the cavern opening, 'and that Kira remains in the Warens until the Shargh's intentions are clearer.'

The training room was little changed since Kest had last seen it, the wounded still lying in neat rows and the air carrying the familiar scent of morning-bright. Tresen got to his feet as Miken and Kest approached, Miken embracing his son. The attack had left them all with a deepened appreciation for those they loved. Kest scanned the room, tensing as he saw the mattress where Kesilini had slept was empty, and there were two other mattresses with their coverings folded neatly on top.

'Kesilini's helping Arlen prepare herbs in the last training room,' said Tresen, seeing the direction of his gaze, 'and we've had two deaths since you were last here.'

'Who?' asked Miken sharply.

'Renclansman Marakin and Tarclansman Jarin.'

'But they weren't badly wounded,' exclaimed Kest.

'No. They only had need of sickleseed, not everest, but we're finding that everest staves off the rot longer.'

'Then give them all everest,' said Kest.

'There's a risk with everest that the sleeper won't wake,' said Miken.

'And in the end, everest only postpones the rot, not destroys it,' added Tresen, his face grim.

Kest had to remind himself that Tresen was only in his first season of protecting.

'Where's Kira?' asked Miken, propping his pack against the wall.

'Sleeping,' said Tresen, nodding towards the far end of the room.

'She refused to leave the wounded so I set up a bed for her here. It's the first real rest she's had since this started.'

'I should check on her,' said Miken, moving off.

'How is she, Tresen?' asked Kest softly.

'The same. She does what she must for the injured, but barely eats or speaks. Kesilini was working with her earlier.'

'Kesilini?'

Tresen's expression eased. 'Kesilini's idea, not mine. I suggested she be escorted back to your longhouse but she refused, saying Kira is her bondsister after all. I was hoping Kesilini's grief might help Kira with hers, but it hasn't. Kira loved Kandor more than anyone else in the world.'

And you loved him too, thought Kest, remembering how, as a young Protector, he'd seen them at play among the trees. He hadn't known who they were then, just three Kashclan children, but they were always together.

There was a stifled exclamation and Kest turned to see Miken weaving his way back through the wounded, clearly perturbed.

'Kira's not there!'

'She must be!' said Tresen, frowning and starting forward. 'She said she was going to sleep.'

'Is there anywhere else she could be?' asked Kest.

'The Herbery in the last training room, or the latrines, but if she'd gone there, she wouldn't have . . .'

'Slipped out while your back was turned?' finished Kest for him. 'Well, the entrances to the Warens are guarded, so she's still here somewhere. She may have gone further into the Warens looking for a cure for Shargh wounds.'

Miken's eyebrows shot up and Kest felt scarcely less surprised at his own certainty.

'I think you might be right,' said Tresen.

Miken rubbed his face wearily. 'The further caverns are unmapped.'

'Yes, but I know Kira's been to at least some of them before, and I have too since the first attack. There are Writings there, very old and all but rotted. If there is a cure for Shargh wounds, it would be there.'

'If,' echoed Miken. 'That's less of a concern now than the possibility of her losing herself.'

'She once told me that she had a good memory of the way,' said Kest.

'That was before her heart was torn out,' muttered Miken, striding over to reclaim his pack.

Kest hastened after him. 'I'll go, Clanleader.'

'And what makes you think *you* won't get lost?'

'On my last visit I took the precaution of drawing myself a map.'

Miken stared at him for a moment, then his face cracked into a smile. 'That was very wise of you, Commander Kest.'

Kest picked up one of the lamps from the table and checked the oil. 'Don't wait up,' he said, by way of farewell.

Kira sat back on her heels, stretching her aching back and wiping the mottled fragments of paper from her fingers. There was nothing more here, but she'd wanted to be certain. It was little wonder the Writings were decayed; even the walls had growths upon them, though what they were she had no idea. Certainly not moss, for there was no light for it to grow by, and these were slimy and rank-smelling. Grimacing, she wiped her hands on her leggings, then froze as she remembered her father's harsh rebukes. For a moment she was caught, a mouse under owl-shadow, then life returned to her limbs and she struggled to her feet.

Which way should she go? Ahead the tunnel disappeared into thick blackness, while behind her, the wounded lay dying. She had to keep looking. Once she would have scorned a light, finding her way by touch and practising her remembering, but she carried the lamp before her now, too tired to trust herself. At least the floor was smooth and the journeying easy; the drip of water occasionally breaking the silence and drafts of air reminding her that there was a world above.

There were no forest scents and she felt their absence keenly. In fact, there was nothing at all here to ease her heart or to distract her from thoughts of the dying; even the slimy growths had given way to bare stone.

How much further could she go this night? Or was it day? It seemed an age since she'd heard a springleslip or seen a mira kiraon in flight. She pushed the images away. Keep moving; that was all that was important, just keep moving. She was a Healer and there were wounded to be healed. She was of Kasheron's seed and he'd sundered a people to heal. Healing was all that mattered. Her steps kept time with the mantra in her head, the tunnel ahead narrowing, the ache in her bones growing. Surely Kasheron hadn't come this far; any caverns here would be too distant to be convenient for storage, or for anything else.

Unless he'd wanted to hide something precious.

She stopped and leaned on the wall as she considered the idea; at least it was dry here, the stone unexpectedly gritty under her shoulder. Soot! She swung the lamp high and blinked the sweat from her eyes. There was a hole in the stone, a place where once a bracket had been fixed. A bracket meant that people had come here often. Right on the edge of the yellow circle of light, a shadow yawned, and she hurried forward.

The cavern was huge and she could see other entrances off at the edge of her lamp-glow. Closer to her though were two lots of wooden shelving running from floor to ceiling, each stacked high with cloth-wrapped bundles. Her heart raced, her hope rising. Kasheron's people had established a worthy hiding place indeed.

Setting the lamp down, she lifted a bundle and carefully unwound the oiled cloth from the sheaf, heart fluttering. Kasheron's

228

followers may have been the last people to touch this, perhaps even Kasheron himself! Some of the paper was fine, lacking the ridges of patchet paper, and confirming that at least some of it *had* come from the north.

Kira's excitement gradually cooled as she skimmed page after page – the provisioning and placement of the longhouses, records of what each octad offered as gathering, lists of storage space assigned to each clan. It was written in Tremen, but strangely spelt and phrased, and at the top of each page, in faded ink, was a date: *Season twenty, Allogrenia.*

Twenty seasons after Kasheron had come south? The Tremen no longer measured time from their arrival in the forest. Still, the date held her gaze. What else had changed in the north apart from the way words were phrased? Had Terak's legacy of barbarity endured in the same way as Kasheron's healing had? Both brothers had been strong-willed, neither able to compromise. Was the Terak way still to kill . . . like the Shargh? She stared at the rows of wrapped sheafs and a horrible realisation came to her; no matter what herbal lore lay in the yellowing paper, it couldn't stand against the sword. Only a sword could defeat a sword; Terak's barbarism had defeated Kasheron's healing.

Kira snapped the sheaf shut, bundled the oiled cloth round it, and thrust it back on the shelf, angry with herself. Killing could never be mightier than that which gave life! The thought was abhorrent, ridiculous, seeded by weariness, nothing more. She jerked another sheaf from the shelf but it too, was full of lists. And the next and the next. In the end she gave up looking at every page, flicking the paper over quickly and scanning for herbal or healing words. She was on her fifth sheaf when a loose page fluttered out. At first she thought her carelessness had torn it loose, but it was unlike the rest of the sheaf; it was a drawing of some kind. The lamplight flickered and she screwed up her eyes, lines resolving into patterns, then into something she recognised: a map – of the Warens.

She brought her nose almost to the paper. Here were the stores and the training rooms, there the Water Cavern and the tunnel she'd travelled to reach this cavern. And there it was – the *Sarnia Room*. The same name as the cave Sanaken and Feseren had died in. Her skin pricked. Why call the cave and this storage cavern by the same name? Then she noticed that the map showed the tunnel going on beyond where she now was, a dozen more caverns opening off it, and other entrances to the outside world, *if* that was what the open-ended lines meant. She counted quickly: one entrance to the north, and two to the north-west.

The light dimmed and she glanced up. The lamp-wick was leaning drunkenly, sucking up the last droplets of oil, and even as she stared at it, the flame shuddered and went out. She sat, frozen, the darkness so intense she couldn't even see her hand before her face. Where was the entrance she had come in by? Which way had she been facing? For a moment her mind was as dark as the cavern, then she forced herself to visualise the cavern's layout, remember her last movements.

Rising carefully, she stretched out her arms and, holding her breath, took two large strides to her right. Nothing. She took another; nothing. Maybe she was wrong, maybe . . . Then her knuckles jarred against the rough cloth of a sheaf and she felt like swooning with relief. Turning slowly, she brought her left hand into contact with the shelf, then moved forward, sliding each foot along the floor, her hand trailing into air again, her teeth chattering in panic. Two more steps and her fingers found the cool stone of the entranceway. She edged round it gingerly, keeping it at her left shoulder. The way back now lay before her. The relief was immense and she half slid down the wall, her legs robbed of rigidity.

For a while she lay on the stone, panting as if she'd sprinted between the Eights, then she steadied, becoming aware of the absolute silence. She rolled onto her back, not caring about the dust. Was this what the dead endured? No light, no sound, no warmth, no birdsong, no rustle of leaves in summer winds, no scuttle of gold and green across the forest floor. Nothing.

She wanted to weep for Kandor, for all those she'd lost; to weep for herself. But she'd forgotten how; she was lost, too, an empty shell like the stone around her. Hugging herself, she closed her eyes and slept.

Kest came to a stop, chest heaving as he stared from the dwindling bulb of nut oil to the vast darkness ahead. If he didn't turn back soon, he'd be making the return like a blind man, *if* there *were* a return journey. He'd come to the end of the rough map he'd drawn eleven caverns ago, and was now compelled to count the openings on his left in an attempt to keep his bearings. He'd never had reason to come this far before and he was surprised at how dry the air was. Dry air but no Kira! Perhaps she'd slipped through some crevice he'd missed, or looped back and was now safely in the training rooms. He started forward again. He was a fool if he believed that. She'd have only turned back if she'd found the cure, and the chances of that were remote.

Curse this stinking darkness and her stubbornness! Miken must be mad to even be thinking of making her Leader! She was like a child, going her own way with no regard for anyone or anything else. His feet pounded over the floor and his arm ached from holding the lamp aloft. Then he thought of how she'd woken in his bed, the scent of her as she'd stood beside him in his rooms caressing the chimes, the way she'd laughed as they'd danced together. What if she *were* lost? The thought was like a wood grub in his brain, and the deeper he went into the darkness, the fatter it grew. If she were lost . . . if she were lost. There was no one else. A bare half dozen in Kashclan had healing skills that set them apart, but there was no one like her, no other *feailner*.

He continued, for want of something better to do, and finally the lamp picked up a tumble of stone ahead, the first rockfall he'd seen in the otherwise smooth tunnel. And then the stone resolved into a prone figure. Stinking heart-rot! Her face was white, her braid dust-dulled. He ran forward and dropped to his knees beside her, expecting to feel the coldness of death, but she was warm.

Relief flashed to anger. 'Get up,' he ordered, shaking her.

Kira came awake, recoiling in terror.

Kest felt a pang of remorse. 'I'm sorry, I startled you,' he said grudgingly.

Kira pushed back her hair, leaving a dusty smudge on her forehead. 'I ran out of oil,' she said, as if that were the only thing of importance.

He hauled her up. 'Come. You're needed.'

'We have to search the cavern,' said Kira, gesturing to the gaping opening behind her.

He tightened his grip on the lamp, struggling to keep his voice calm. 'You've been away a long time, Kira, and I'm almost out of oil. We don't have time to argue; the wounded need you. Come.'

'No!'

Kest wrenched her forward, so that her face was close to his. 'It's not what you want anymore, Kira! Don't you understand? It's what the Tremen want. You're not free to go traipsing off when the mood takes you; you're not free to risk yourself. You're all we've got left. You're Kasheron's blood and Kasheron's legacy. That gives you obligations! That gives you responsibilities. Responsibilities, Kira! Something I know you're not familiar with. Now we're going back, whether you're willing or not!'

His grip on her arm was punishing, the bulk of him as he loomed over her reminding her of the moment in the Herbery with her father, before the blow. With desperate strength she jerked backwards, her feet going from under her and one boot catching him in the groin as she went down, breaking his grip as she landed on her backside with a painful thump. He bent double, struggling to keep hold of the lamp, the tunnel filled with the wheeze of air being sucked in and out of his lungs.

'That . . . was a . . . neat trick,' he said finally. 'Who . . . taught you that?'

'I . . . no one. I'm sorry I hurt you.'

'That is a . . . great comfort.'

He had managed to straighten a little and she took a step towards him. 'If I go back now it'll make no difference to the injured; they'll die anyway. I know it, you know it, and probably most of the Tremen know it too by now. But this cave,' she jerked her head towards it, 'is filled with Writings. I think it was Kasheron's main store. If the cure for Shargh wounds isn't here, then I don't think it's anywhere.'

'We're going to . . . run out of oil,' panted Kest, still having trouble drawing breath. 'We'll find nothing in the dark . . . including our way back.'

'There are holes in the wall where lamps have been fixed; people must have come here and stayed; there must be a store of oil nearby. I need your help, Kest. I need your help to save the wounded. Will you give it to me?'

For a long moment Kest simply stared at her, then his face kinked in a half-smile. 'Maybe Miken's not mad after all,' he said slowly.

27

Tresen yawned and hauled himself up from his position on the floor next to Farek's mattress, rubbing his numb backside and forcing his cramped legs to straighten. His Protector comrade had slid into a fretful sleep some time ago, but Tresen had been too weary to shift, unlike his father who'd gone back to his longhouse. Now Tresen hobbled off towards Kira's alcove where he knew there was a jug of water and a bowl. The pins and needles in his foot gradually dissipated as he walked, but not his sense of dread. Kira should have been back by now. Where in the 'green was she?

The jug was full, for Kira hadn't had time to do anything but tend the wounded. Looking down, he grimaced at the sight of his grimy cuffs. What he'd give for a proper wash, clean clothing, and the chance to sleep in a bed not determined to jab him to death. Why the Protectors persevered with sere grass was beyond him; perhaps it was some sort of traditional test of endurance.

He had no right to complain, though; he'd had his chance to return to his longhouse, Arlen having offered to take his place for a time, and there was no reason why he shouldn't have gone. The

Kashclansman was a careful and competent Healer. But he'd chosen to stay so he could keep an eye on Kira. Well, a fine job he'd done of that!

He stared at her mattress, with its small pile of clothing at one end, and then at the wooden bench and bowl and jug. There wasn't even a chair in the room, the alcove's emptiness seeming to amplify what had happened to her. What if *he'd* lost everyone? What if he'd seen Miken and Tenerini dead and Mikini murdered before his eyes? How did she draw breath, put one foot in front of the other, go on?

Hot tears spilled onto his cheeks and he picked up the jug of water and emptied it over his head, gasping as icy trickles found his collar and zigzagged down his back. Well, that had certainly woken him up!

'Protector Tresen?'

He started, looking around. Kesilini's tunic was crisp and her hair gleamed in the lamplight. Tresen mopped ineffectually at his face with his sleeve. 'You're looking better,' he said, then regretted his allusion to Merek's death. 'Are you looking for Kest?'

'No . . . yes. I was looking for you, but if you know where my brother is, I'd be pleased if you told me.'

'I think he's with Kira.'

Kesilini nodded, her face remaining carefully composed. 'Actually, I've come to help you . . . to offer my help, at least . . . I was helping prepare the herbs earlier and I've spent some time with women in childbirth. I know it's not the same, but . . . I could prepare bandages or clean wounds . . . if you show me how, or watch while you get some sleep . . .'

She had Kest's eyes, but so much sadder. 'Thank you, Kesilini. I'd be glad of your help.' He led her back to where the most severely wounded lay. 'The men here have been given everest and will sleep at least another day, but you can help me give the others honeyed water.' He ladled a dollop of honey into a jug and began to stir.

235

'Only honeyed water? I would have thought . . .' She coloured. 'I'm sorry, I didn't mean to question . . . I'm not a Healer.'

Tresen tapped the last of the honey off the spoon on the side of the jug, and lowered his voice. 'You thought we'd be doing more for them? You're quite right, Kesilini. We've cleansed the wounds with sorren and stitched them and bound them with falzon. Ordinarily that would be enough. But these are Shargh wounds, and Shargh wounds rot despite our healing. All that's left for us is to stave off thirst.'

Kesilini's eyes widened. 'Are you saying there's no cure?'

Tresen hesitated, having already said too much.

Kesilini came closer. 'Are you saying Healer Kiraon cannot heal them?'

Tresen looked at her, considering. 'I won't lie to you, Kesilini, not after what's happened, but what I say mustn't go beyond this room.'

Kesilini nodded.

'The Shargh use something on their blades that causes wounds to putrefy. Even small wounds rot. Kasheron's people knew of a cure, but the knowing's been lost. Unless we find it again, we can't heal the wounded.'

Kesilini's face blanched. 'So they'll all die,' she whispered.

'There's hope. Everest seems to slow the fester, and even now Kira searches the further tunnels for old Writings. Kest's gone after her.'

'Isn't that dangerous?' She'd caught his arm without realising it.

Tresen shrugged. 'The Warens are full of caverns and tunnels, and completely dark, and they've never been completely mapped. Kira's very tired; she's barely slept since the attack.'

'Then why did you let her go? If she gets lost . . . if they *both* get lost, or injured, or . . .'

'Do you think she asked my permission?' he asked, his voice sharp.

'You should have –' started Kesilini.

236

'Seen her go and stopped her? Yes, I *should* have. And Maxen *should* have heeded Sarkash's warning and postponed the Feast of Turning. And the Protectors *should* have been patrolling the First Eight.' He slammed the jug down on the table. 'All these things *should* have happened, Kesilini, but they didn't, and they can't be undone. Kira's choice was to stay here and watch the wounded die or go into the darkness. Kest's choice was the same. Which do you think they *should* have chosen?'

Kesilini dropped her head and a tear slid off her cheek onto her tunic.

'I'm sorry,' said Tresen, pushing his hand through his hair. 'It's probably best you go back to your longhouse.'

'No, I want to stay. I . . . I thank you for telling me these things. They were right to go.' She raised her head and gave a tremulous smile. 'Maxen was planning on making Merek Leader after him, but I never thought it was right. It should always have been Kiraon. I've seen her heal. She *fights* to heal in the same way Kest fights.' Tears started afresh and she wiped them away. 'It's just that I'm frightened of losing Kest too.'

Tresen touched her hand briefly. 'We're all frightened of losing those we love, Kesilini.'

Miken stood at the door of his longhouse, the dawn air chill on his face. All but one of the Clanleaders were within, breakfasting on the nutbread and dried mundleberries Tenerini had set ready, and drinking freshly brewed lemonleaf tea.

Tenerini was now busy on the edge of the trees, filling the cups of the Protector escorts gathered there and sending Mikini and Mira back and forth to the longhouse on all manner of errands. Miken heard snatches of the conversations behind him: 'the routes of Protector patrols', 'gathering', 'the likelihood of further attack'. The Clanleaders were anxious about leaving their longhouses even for a short time.

237

He glanced back, catching Marren's eye. The Morclan leader's brows rose in an easily guessed question: would the Clanleaders support Kira as Leader? It was a question Miken had spent the night pondering. Meetings to appoint Leaders were inevitably difficult, but it was doubly difficult this time. Maxen's death had been untimely, with no time to prepare, and they were now in a time of threat, not peace.

Miken rocked on the balls of his feet, trying to contain his impatience. At least Dakresh was consistent, always being the last to arrive. Perhaps it had been a mistake for him to call a council at all. Perhaps he should have waited for someone else to do it. He was widely regarded as Maxen's adversary, and the Clanleaders might withhold support for Kira simply because she was his clan-kin.

There were other sensitivities too. Most of the Clanleaders had agreed with Maxen that no threat existed. They would now have to justify themselves or admit they were wrong. He thought of Tarclan's new leader Kemrick. Who would Tarclan blame for their previous Clanleader's death? Certainly not Farish himself. It was always easier to turn away from the pain of a self-inflicted wound.

There was movement in the trees as a new patrol appeared and Dakresh hobbled stiffly towards him.

'Kashclan welcomes Sherclan,' said Miken formally.

'Sherclan thanks Kashclan,' said Dakresh, peering up under silvered brows. Miken escorted him to his seat and took his own, gulping down his tea without tasting the lemonleaf's tang, his attention on what was to come. If only there were time to let Tarclan grieve, to let them *all* grieve. But they couldn't afford to wait. New Leaders must be appointed, both for the Bough and the Warens, and a formal strategy of protection put in place. Clearing his throat, he rose, and the murmured conversations died away.

'Kashclan welcomes Clanleaders Dakresh, Kemrick, Tenedren, Ketten, Berendash, Sanden and Marren to council,' he began formally, putting Marren last so as not to highlight their usual accord.

He waited for the gathering to finish its traditional response, then, bowing to Kemrick, said: 'The Clancouncil mourns the loss of Clanleader Farish. May he rest easy beneath the 'green.'

Kemrick rose. 'Tarclan has given him to Wesgren. He is the sun and air; he is the roots and soil.'

'May the alwaysgreen Shelter him,' responded the council.

Kenrick resumed his seat and Marren rose.

'The Clancouncil mourns the loss of Tremen Leader Maxen. May he rest easy beneath the 'green.'

'Kashclan has given him to Sogren,' responded Miken. 'He is the sun and air; he is the roots and soil.'

'May the alwaysgreen Shelter him,' returned the council.

Miken stood again, surveying the gathering solemnly. 'All our clans have suffered loss. We have much to decide today, councillors. Let us begin.'

Kest pushed the sheaf back onto the shelf, swearing under his breath. His neck was stiff, he was as dry as a husk, and there were still at least two-thirds of the cavern's contents to check. It must be midday outside, or so the growl of his stomach told him.

'How many lists of gatherings do you need?' he asked of the air. *Season eleven, season twelve, season eighteen, season twenty-three . . .*' He squinted through the gloom at Kira, who was crouching motionless over a sheaf. 'Found anything?'

She didn't respond and he dragged himself upright, the pain in his groin reminding him of their earlier encounter.

'Kira?' Was she asleep? No. He crouched beside her and peered at the Writing. 'What is it?'

'Deaths,' she said softly. 'Babes and their mothers. So many . . .'

'*Season five*,' noted Kest, 'the early days of Allogrenia. They would have hunted out the silverjacks by then and were probably trying to live solely on pitchie grass. Not the best diet for a woman carrying.' He looked at the pile of discarded sheafs to her side. 'Nothing on healing?'

Kira shook her head. 'Not yet.' She peered up at him. 'We have to keep going, Kest. We won't have time to come back.'

'I know.' Did she think he was going to argue? He knew as well as she did that they only had a couple more days before the wounded would be beyond their help. And then it would be Feseren all over again.

'Have you got any food?' he asked irritably.

'No, I didn't think to bring any. I didn't think I'd be away this long.'

'The problem with you is that you *don't* think.'

Her eyes flashed. 'And I suppose you do? Well, I'm waiting for you to offer me a nice slice of that nutbread you've brought with you, *Protector* Leader Kest.'

Kest quelled a retort and grabbed another armful of sheafs from the shelf. At least the store had held a large cask of oil, *as she had predicted*, and they wouldn't have to fumble their way back. He threw the pile on the floor.

'You realise that the council's meeting today to make you Leader,' he said.

Kira stiffened, but kept her gaze on the sheaf in front of her. 'I won't accept the leadership.'

'You won't have any choice.'

'I'm not worthy of it. They'll have to find someone else.' She gathered up the sheafs she'd been looking at and pushed them back on the shelf.

'There *is* no one else, Kira.'

She kept her back to him. 'I'm not worthy,' she said.

Kest got to his feet. Had he been a fool to broach the subject? Would the grief she'd somehow managed to contain spill out again, robbing her of her wits, or worse, of her healing? They *must* have a strong Leader! Someone who took no action – or worse still, vacillated – would be useless, no matter how extraordinary their healing.

'I killed Kandor.'

For a moment he thought he'd misheard her, then he wrenched her round to face him. 'The Shargh killed those of the Bough, not you.'

'I killed him!'

It was almost a shriek. Perhaps she was becoming unhinged with the grief of Kandor's death and the battle to heal the injured.

'He wanted to come with me, but I made him stay in the Bough. Don't you understand? *I made him stay!*' Her eyes were as bright as metal, the lamplight making them other-worldly.

'Why did you leave . . . ?' Kest began, then stopped, his eyes going to the bruise on Kira's face, fading now to yellow-green, the cut under the cheekbone healing. Maxen had been furious at Merek's bonding, and he remembered well the Tremen Leader's cold gaze on him as he'd danced with Kira. The last piece of the puzzle fell into place.

By the 'green which Shelters us! He took a steadying breath. 'I know what happened that night, and I know how you got this.' He touched her face gently with the back of his fingers. 'And I say this to you, Kiraon of Kashclan, that none of it is your fault. It's not your fault that your father had no love for you, or that he put his own ambition and pride before the good of the Tremen. It's not your fault he broke every tenet of Tremen law against violence.'

Kira caught his hand in hers. 'Pledge that you won't speak of this, Kest. Pledge!' she pleaded.

'I seem to be spending a lot of time pledging to remain silent on things that everyone should know.'

'My father was appointed Leader by the Clancouncil and accepted by the Tremen people. Speaking of this will only bring shame on us all. We need to work together now, not squabble among ourselves. We need to remember what makes us Tremen, and to fight for its survival.'

'Spoken like a Leader.'

She flushed, but held his eyes. 'Will you pledge?'

He took a deep breath. 'I'll pledge if you accept the Clancouncil's decision, whatever it might be.'

Kira's eyes surged gold again as she nodded.

Kest brought her hand to his lips. 'I shall enjoy working with you, Tremen Leader Kiraon.'

28

In the hall of the Kashclan longhouse, the arguments surged to and fro like the Drinkwater in flood, showing neither signs of abatement nor resolution. Half the councillors were passionate that Kira should become Leader and the other half were equally passionate that she should not. Watching them, Miken felt as if he'd been confined in his longhouse for days rather than since dawning, and there was no release in sight. He refilled his cup and stared out the window, the light telling him that it was well past midday. The Clanleaders' escorts were no longer visible and the still morning had given way to a breezy afternoon, the castellas and severs dipping and swaying.

Dakresh was on his feet now, waving his finger under Marren's nose.

Time to call a halt. The debate had reached the stage where everything had been said anyway, and was now simply being repeated using different words. Miken set his cup down so that it chinked loudly and rose. 'Councillors. Councillors!'

The noise faltered and faces turned to him.

'I think it's time we made a decision,' he said.

'It was time mid-morning,' growled Dakresh.

'We needs make a good decision,' retorted Marren, glaring at him, 'not any decision, and good decision-making takes time.'

'So can bad,' muttered someone.

'I could have called for a division some time ago,' acknowledged Miken, 'and I would have if we'd been debating foraging rights or the fair exchange of goods between longhouses. But I need hardly remind you that we're deciding something far more important, and that whoever we appoint today must have the support of all of us, not just half of us,' he said, looking at each councillor in turn.

'It's clear you haven't got the numbers, Clanleader,' said Dakresh. 'Let's just get on with it, so we can move on to the Warens' leadership and be getting back to our longhouses.'

Marren's chair grated back. 'It's not just a matter of numbers, Clanleader Dakresh, but of who's best fitted to head the Bough.'

'Precisely,' snapped Dakresh, 'and a girl of barely seventeen seasons, even if she is a good Healer, is certainly *not* fitted. The next Leader should have been Merek; *he* was the only one of Maxen's seed to have inherited the healing power along with the strength of will to see us through this. It's one of the great tragedies of this whole sorry mess that he was taken too.'

Miken opened his mouth to protest but shut it again. Nothing he could say now was likely to improve the situation. Another figure rose. It was Kemrick of Tarclan, Farish's replacement, and until this moment he'd been silent. Miken had known nothing of Kemrick before his appointment, but had learned since that he was an intensely private man, spending most of his adult life in solitary wanderings. It was a strange choice by Tarclan, especially after the outgoing brashness of Farish.

'Clancouncillors,' began Kemrick, 'forgive me if I seem naive, for I've spent little time in these debates, whereas you are all obviously well-practised. It seems to me that the issues debated here today are really quite simple. As a Tremen, my understanding is that the Bough is the centre of all healing. Is that not so?' His gaze shifted slowly round the councillors, and there were nods of agreement. 'And it is also my understanding that Kiraon of Kashclan is the best surviving Healer in Allogrenia.'

Again came the murmurs of assent.

'Then it follows that she be made Leader of the Bough.'

'It's not as simple as that, Clanleader Kemrick,' said Berendash. 'It's not Kiraon's healing that is in question here, but her strength and strategic ability.'

'Strength and strategic ability? I rather thought that they were the preserve of the Warens,' said Kemrick, smiling to ease the bluntness of his words. 'I am, as I said, unpractised in the way of debates, but I am well versed in the history of Allogrenia. How and why we came to be here has always been of particular interest to me, and I've spent a considerable time studying the sheafs stowed in the Warens.

'What they tell me is that Kasheron gave his heart to healing, but that his head understood the wisdom of keeping the sword. We've been fortunate to have had so many seasons of peace to enjoy his legacy of healing. But now we must call upon the other half of what he has bequeathed us.

'It seems to me that the decision facing us is not who will lead the Bough – Kiraon, we agree, is the best Healer – but who will lead the Protectors in the Warens.'

There was absolute silence, then Kemrick nodded to each councillor in turn. 'I thank you for hearing me,' he said, and sat down.

Miken schooled his face to blandness. 'I thank you, Clanleader Kemrick. Are there any further contributions? No? Then I suggest we divide.'

'I see no reason to waste time in two divisions when one will suffice,' snapped Berendash, glancing around the table. 'I take it that we are in agreement in appointing Kashclanswoman Kiraon to the Leadership of the Bough?'

There was a mutter of assent.

'Then let us focus on the leadership of the Warens. The Protectors of my longhouse tell me that their preference for Commander is Kest of Morclan.'

'As do mine,' added Tenedren.

'And mine,' said Sanden.

'What say the other clans?' asked Miken.

'Kest obviously has the confidence of Morclan,' said Marren, his eyes sliding to Dakresh.

'I have no objection,' grunted Dakresh. 'He's young in seasons, but old in his thinking. The men like him and that's important if they must spill their blood for him.'

'For us,' corrected Kemrick.

Miken stood at his doorway once more, this time watching the last of the Clanleaders' escorts disappear among the trees, still not quite believing what had taken place.

'So, Kira's to be Leader,' said Tenerini, coming to his side.

Miken slipped his arm around her. 'And Kest's to replace Sarkash.'

'He's a good choice.'

'But not Kira?'

Tenerini was intent on the springleslips hunting bark beetles among the castellas, but the kink in her brows told him she was troubled.

'Kira,' she sighed. 'Kira needs time to grieve, to heal herself, but if she's Leader of the Bough, there'll be no time, even if . . . *when* this is over, there'll be no time.'

'*When* this is over, there'll be less need for healing. She'll be able to visit Sogren and Wessogren, to come to accept what has happened, to say her farewells.'

'It might be too late. Kandor was everything to her.' She looked up at him. 'We should have fought harder to have her here with us, Miken; *and* Kandor.'

Miken ran his finger down her cheek. 'Yes, how well we see when we look over our shoulders. But we both know that Maxen would never have relented. The more we asked, the more he delighted in refusing.'

'Yet he had little love for either of them.'

Miken's arm tightened round her and he kissed her head. 'No, but he enjoyed having power over them, particularly Kira. And while he had Kandor, he had all the power in the world.'

Tenerini snorted. 'Well, he has none now, and I'm glad. The only good that's come of this, may the 'green forgive me, is that Kira's free of him at last.'

Miken looked at her in surprise. 'That's an unworthy thought, Tenerini.'

'Yes, I know, but an honest one. And you're the only person I'd voice it to.'

'Ah, then it's fortunate we're bonded and bound to keep each other's secrets.' Miken stared out into the fading light, the foliage flickering with birds seeking their roosts. Somewhere to the east came the voice of a mira kiraon, its call sending an icy breath over Miken's skin.

'I need to go back to the Warens,' he said abruptly.

Tenerini's head jerked up. 'What? Not this night surely? You were there only yesterday.'

'I know, but Kira had gone off into the tunnels and I didn't see her. I need to speak with her about the leadership.' *And make sure she is well for my own peace of mind.*

'Can't it wait? You could go tomorrow – with an escort,' said Tenerini.

'There's little risk while the moon is small.' *And I'd rather leave the men here with you and Mikini and the others of my longhouse.*

'You think the next attack will come with the full moon?' asked Tenerini.

Miken hesitated, but Tenerini was not a child to be fed only honey. 'Both attacks have been at the full moon, which makes sense

247

for a people who are unfamiliar with the forest. Even Tremen have been known to get lost on a cloudy night.'

'The next full moon,' whispered Tenerini, her gaze flicking round the darkening trees.

Miken drew her back into the hall and shut the door. The long-house was alive with light and the comforting smells of espin smoke and of nutbread as well as the voices of Kashclan coming to prepare their evening meal. He watched Tenerini join them at the cooking place. Would the Shargh attack them here? he wondered, slipping on his pack. They'd gone straight to the Bough last time; straight to the Leader and his family. After making his farewells, he stepped out into the dusk and set off at speed. Miken was unsure where the next attack would be. The only thing he *was* sure of was that there *would* be a next time.

'I think I've found something.'

Kest's voice came from a long way off and Kira jerked upright, having no recollection of what she'd been thinking of in the last few moments and wondering if she'd actually gone to sleep.

'It's a list of herbs from Kenclan octad. Something about fireweed . . .' continued Kest.

Kira sprang to her feet, stumbling and almost falling on him as she snatched the sheaf from his hands.

'There's no need –' started Kest.

'I'm sorry, I'm sorry . . .' she muttered, reading feverishly. Memories rattled in her brain then fell into place and the sheaf tumbled to the floor.

'Kira?'

'I know what it is, Kest. I know what it is!' She gripped his arm. 'Come, we don't have much time.'

'Tell me what you're talking about!'

'Fireweed, Kest, it'll cure Shargh wounds. *And* it's in Kenclan octad. Come on!'

He stepped in front of her, blocking her way. 'It's a full day's travel, Kira, and we can't do it without food, water and rest, and we daren't do it without a patrol.'

'We don't have time. We have to go now,' insisted Kira.

'You don't have the right to risk yourself, even to save others. You are our Healer now.'

Kira turned on him furiously. 'We've had this stinking conversation before. I'm not skulking in this hole while people die, even if you're willing to.'

Kest's hand shot out and fastened on Kira's wrist, then he picked up the lamp and began to drag her from the cavern.

Her father had done this to her, thought Kira, not by touch, but by intimidation, crushing and confining her most of her life. It was almost as if he were here now, flesh cold as the stone pressing in on her, pushing the breath from her lungs. She began to gasp, unable to get enough air. The sweat poured down her neck, the lamplight disappearing into black blotches.

Kest felt her sag and thought it was a trick, but her breathing was harsh. He lowered her to the floor and set the lamp down. He'd never used force against a woman in his life, and he'd used it twice now, in the space of a day. There was nothing in his Protector training to teach him how to control a completely recalcitrant, totally unreasonable woman. He pushed her head down between her knees, holding her against him, feeling how small and fragile she was, like a bird. The mira kiraon; she was well-named, not just for her eyes, but for her claws. He tensed as she roused, preparing to hold her again if necessary.

'I . . . I've . . . got . . . a map,' she gasped, as if their conversation had never been interrupted. 'A map of the Warens. We . . . can get to Sarnia Cave from here. It's . . . quicker Kest, quicker than . . . going overland.'

She fumbled a page of Writings out of her shirt and flattened it on the cavern floor, her hands shaking. Did she never give up?

'There are three openings shown ... see? One in Renclan ... and these two, they open in the Kenclan octad.'

Kest shifted the lamp closer. It was the most extensive map of the Warens he'd ever seen. 'Where did you get this?'

'From the storeroom, before my oil ran out and you came.'

'And you never thought to tell me?' If there were maps like these, the Warens could become a real part of the protection of Allogrenia, rather than a musty afterthought.

'I forgot about it ... I'm sorry. But it means we can get to the Kenclan octad and back, within a day.'

'What makes you think that?'

'Well, we're about here,' she said, pointing to the map. 'They're only just outside it. There's the Water Cavern and the training rooms. It's about half that distance again to this entrance.'

'You're assuming that it *is* an entrance, and that it's open – not blocked by rockfall – and that this map's to scale.'

'To scale?'

'That that distance there is, in fact, equal to this distance here. And there's also the little matter of an escort. You're not wandering about all over the octad looking for fireweed.'

'I won't be wandering about, Kest. It's near Sarnia Cave.'

'And you've only just remembered this?' he said, folding up the map and helped her to her feet. 'This isn't a game or some sort of competition about who gets their own way. The Shargh could be anywhere, and we already know what their intentions are.'

'Are you accusing me of lying?' Her face had taken on the petulance of Eser at her worst.

'I'm saying it's strange that you suddenly have such precise knowledge,' said Kest.

'You're saying I'm a liar!'

'Stop acting like a child! If you expect people to understand what's in your heart, then you'd better start telling them what's in your head.'

'I read of fireweed some time ago, Protector Leader,' clipped out Kira. 'When we took the wounded to the Sarnia Cave, I saw a herb I didn't recognise. You refused to give me time to look at it further. Just now I've read a description of fireweed's properties and habitats, and they fit what I saw. Is that sufficient, Protector Leader?'

'It's an improvement.'

'And will you let me go, or will you take me prisoner again?'

Stinking heart-rot! Why did she have to ask him questions like these? Every shred of his Protector training told him it was madness to go to the Kenclan octad without a patrol. *And* they'd had no food or rest for close on two days. The way he felt now, he'd have trouble fighting off a stickspider. Yet if they went back to the training rooms to rest and eat and gather a patrol, more of the wounded would die. *His* men would die.

'We'll go direct to Sarnia Cave. If there's no fireweed there we'll come straight back. No argument, no scouting about, no excuses. Do I have your word?'

'Yes.'

'And one last thing, Kira.' He bent, so that his face was level with hers. 'If we come under attack, *at any time*, you are to run. Run and don't look back. Do you understand?' His eyes were hollow, his jaw shaded with stubble.

'I couldn't leave ...'

'*Do you understand?*'

'Yes.'

'Then let's go.'

29

The marwings circled and croaked higher and higher above the Grounds, their wings scarcely beating, the shimmering heat giving them an easy ride upon its back. Shading her eyes, Tarkenda shifted her gaze to the bleached earth below them, then to a dark blot. Was it the putrefying corpse of an ebis that had given up the struggle to live on the sparse pasture, or a Shargh warrior returning from hunt? She squinted into the glare, irritably wiping away the wetness seeping at the corners of her eyes. Maybe those the Sky Chiefs took early were blessed, not having to contend with rotting bones *and* clouding eyes.

Grunting, she continued up towards Arkendrin's sorcha, noting the empty fire circle and the smell of rancid sherat, and not needing the buzz of blackflies to know that the remains of his food were being devoured by things that stung and squirmed. It was fitting that the sorcha of a warrior who couldn't even pay his brother the respect of one moon's mourning had become the haunt of lesser creatures. How had she spawned such a son?

Was Arkendrin's jealousy and conniving seeded by his birth

order or gifted by the Sky Chiefs before he'd left her belly? she wondered. He'd always been one to secrete things away that should rightfully have been shared: the thickest wolf-skins, the season's first gathering of grahen eggs. And now he used his brother's mourning time to hunt the chiefship for himself. Would Erboran have acted any differently had he been the younger brother? She thought so. Erboran had held a love for his people that went beyond himself, *and* he'd respected the wisdom of the Sky Chiefs. Erboran had followed the old ways, and in doing so kept them safe. There were many on the Grounds who were blind to this, whose ears heard none of the tales of past suffering. They fed off Arkendrin's promises of future glory, and in turn Arkendrin fed off *them*.

A hot wind stirred, raising a squall of dust and thudding the sorchas against their struts. Arkendrin had been born on a day such as this, Tarkenda's sweat mixing with the birth-water on the bed as he'd squalled, louder than the summer wind. Ergardrin had laughed, swinging him bloodied and wet above Erboran's head. *Here I have a brother for you, little one, to test who might be Chief.* The words had chilled Tarkenda, but Ergardrin had dismissed her fears, insisting he'd spoken in jest. And he'd dismissed her wanting of a daughter too. *What is a daughter but a joining for some other man's son?* There'd be plenty of time for daughters, he'd said. But there had been no time, and no daughters. Just death and Arkendrin's hunger for the chiefship.

Erlken was crouched at the front of Erboran's sorcha, sharpening his flatsword, the whetstone rasping and the blade catching the sun as he turned it. The dazzle filled Tarkenda's eyes, and in its glare she saw the flash of many blades, the plunge and scream of horses and the faces of fair-haired men. In a blink the vision was gone, and the thud of hoofs became the flapping of sorchas in the wind. Erlken was still working his sword and the marwings still circled overhead.

Tarkenda no longer questioned why the Sky Chiefs sent her such visitations while those around her remained untouched, instead spending her strength in trying to understand the meaning of what she saw. This struggle now held her motionless under the harsh beat of the sun, and it was some time before she became aware of Erlken squinting up at her, his hand to his forehead in respectful greeting. His face still held a boyish softness, but his body was that of a man.

'Where goes your father?' she asked.

'He didn't say, just asked that I be with the Chief-wife. She sleeps,' added Erlken, as if to prove that he hadn't been remiss in his guarding.

Tarkenda frowned. Ormadon had barely left Palansa's side since Erboran's death and must have good reason for doing so now. She flicked open the door flap and was greeted with a wall of stifling air, thick with the scent of ripe cheese, ebis fleece and burrel cones. Hobbling across the pelt-strewn floor, she loosed a vent flap, letting a gust of warm air sweep in and wake Palansa.

Palansa jerked up, pushing the damp hair from her forehead.

'You'd be dead now, if I were an intruder,' said Tarkenda acerbically.

'You would've had to kill Erlken first,' replied Palansa.

Tarkenda poured herself a bowl of water and gulped it down. It was warm and slightly muddy. 'Simple enough,' she said, wiping her mouth. 'He may be Ormadon's son, but he lacks his fighting skills.'

Palansa came to the table. 'He wouldn't die quietly, and I'd have time to prepare.' She patted the dagger under her dress. 'Arkendrin might kill me, but I'd make sure he never became Chief.'

Tarkenda's eyes hardened. 'There'll be no victory if you lose your own life, and that of your son.'

For a while the only sound was flapping hides and creaking struts.

'Sometimes I hope that the babe is a girl,' said Palansa wearily, lowering herself onto a seat. 'Then it would be safe, and I would be safe.'

'Do you think Arkendrin would let his brother's seed live, even if it were a girl?' She poured Palansa a bowl of water and passed it to her. 'If the babe *is* a girl, then Arkendrin *will* be Chief, and none will dare raise their voices against him, no matter what he does.'

Palansa's knuckles whitened on the bowl. 'Then I hope misfortune befalls him and he never returns!'

'Hope will serve us less well than action.'

Palansa said nothing and Tarkenda cleared her throat, determinedly lightening her voice. 'I've spread word of Arkendrin's breach of his brother's mourning time.'

'That won't dissuade his followers,' muttered Palansa. 'Even if he used Erboran's bones for blackfish bait, they'd still be licking at his heels, waiting for his fortunes to drag theirs up the slope.' She got up and wandered back to the bed, picking up the part-finished keep-pot she'd been weaving when sleep had overtaken her.

'The wolf chases only what it can catch. We won't waste our strength on those who have tied their futures to Arkendrin's, but on those who waver, waiting to see which way things turn.'

Palansa turned the pot over, tracing the pattern of flatswords she'd worked into the side. 'What if Arkendrin kills the gold-eyed Healer?'

'I don't think he will.'

'Do you doubt his hunting skills?'

'The Sky Chiefs have sent me more visions,' said Tarkenda, her face grim.

The pot dropped from Palansa's hands. 'You know my son will be safe?'

Tarkenda sighed. 'Do you think if I knew that I'd have kept it from you? Do you think Ormadon would be like a shadow at your back?' She poured herself another bowl of the muddy water; she was drier than a beetle husk. It seemed an age since she'd drunk clear, sweet water.

'Then what . . . ?'

'I've seen fighting.'

'That could mean anything,' said Palansa.

255

'Fair men on white horses.'

'Northerners,' hissed Palansa, 'but why . . .?'

Tarkenda moved to the door and pushed the flap wide. She felt suffocated, as if the sorcha held insufficient air. 'It may be that I see echoes of old visions, of things that have already come to pass.' She leaned out, peering across the Grounds, searching for anything amiss.

Palansa came to her side. 'Do you believe that?' Her hand had crept to the knife hilt under her dress.

'No.' She let the door flap fall back into place. 'I think it's yet to come. The Last Telling speaks of horses in the south-west.'

'*If horses graze in forests deep.*'

Tarkenda whirled. 'You know the Telling?'

'I . . . I asked Erboran for it. I told him I should know what our son must carry forward.'

Tarkenda winced as she lowered herself back onto her seat. 'And what did Erboran say to that?'

'That I was a troublesome woman who gave him no peace.' Palansa smiled but her eyes glistened.

'Yet he told you as Ergardrin told me,' said Tarkenda. Perhaps they both sensed they wouldn't live to raise their sons.

'Northerners fighting us,' Palansa's voice intruded. 'It makes no sense, unless . . . the horses of the Telling are theirs.' Her brows drew into an intense frown. 'In which case the first part of the Telling must come to pass and the Healer *will* see the sun set. But that would mean she has to leave the forest, which would mean Arkendrin failed.'

'Not necessarily. Arkendrin might kill her after she leaves the forest.' Tarkenda shrugged. 'Assuming the Healer of the Last Telling *is* the Healer of the forest, and the gold *is* the gold of her eyes. The Sky Chiefs are not renowned for the clarity of their sendings. It might mean that Arkendrin takes us north, beyond the Braghan Mountains, as he's long wanted to do. Then there'd certainly be fighting. The Northerners aren't going to tolerate us on the plains.'

'There would be much blood spilled,' said Palansa grimly, 'and the Telling says it will be ours.'

'Fire will be the flatsword's bane and bring the dead to life again,' said Tarkenda.

'How can fire destroy flatswords other than by melting them?' demanded Palansa. 'Was there fire in your visions?'

'Yes,' said Tarkenda, her brows knitting in a heavy frown. 'But what the Sky Chiefs send is not like the view over the Grounds, but fragments of this and that, flowing together like weed under water.'

'It's strange the Sky Chiefs speak to you in this way,' said Palansa. 'Perhaps they aid us, intending my son to be Chief.'

'I'm not sure it's aid they send.' Tarkenda was old enough to know that the Sky Chiefs favoured no one, but she didn't want to crush Palansa's hope, remembering all too well how important hope had been in the long nights after Ergardrin's death. 'Did Ormadon tell you that Arkendrin has taken Irason south-west?' she asked. 'No doubt he intends to use him to speak to one of the treemen.'

'The treemen will be on their guard now and unlikely to be wandering about alone in the trees,' pointed out Palansa, rising and rubbing her back. 'Arkendrin will have trouble finding the Healer, which bodes well for us.'

Tarkenda's fingers drummed the table. 'I don't think any of it bodes well,' she said. 'Spilt blood has a habit of drawing more.' Her shrewd gaze fixed on Palansa. 'Have you heard tell of how Erboran died?'

'No. Only Arkendrin's braggings about his own valiant efforts.'

'You'd think it would be simple to kill a single, unarmed girl, wouldn't you? Yet Erboran's dead and she lives,' said Tarkenda. As if the Sky Chiefs favoured *her*, Tarkenda thought.

'What are you saying?' asked Palansa.

'That the Last Telling might be a warning.'

'But of course it's a warning. The Healer mustn't be allowed to see a setting sun, or else the rest of the Telling will follow.'

'Or *we* will cause it to follow.'

'You speak in riddles,' said Palansa irritably. She'd settled on the seat again.

'Arkendrin boasts that the loss of Erboran's life was avenged by the deaths of many in the forest; that he slew those who had stood with the Healer at their wooden sorcha,' said Tarkenda. 'The Healer might flee the forest to escape us.'

'You think the Sky Chiefs have tricked us?' said Palansa.

'It's not for us to judge the Sky Chiefs,' said Tarkenda with sudden solemnity, 'nor to question the moons of honouring owed to those who have now passed into their realm.'

'You'll seed the sorchas with the idea that the Telling can be read two ways?' asked Palansa, not put off by Tarkenda's sudden change of tack.

Tarkenda eyed her approvingly. Erboran had chosen his join-wife well. 'I think it's time you called a Speak. Such an important possibility needs to be debated.'

'And the warriors need to be reminded of the importance of honouring the dead,' said Palansa. 'We can hardly expect the Sky Chiefs to lend us the wisdom to fathom their Tellings, if we with-hold the respect owed to them.'

'Yes,' said Tarkenda. 'It would be good to remind the likes of Irdodun and Urpalin of the cost of licking at Arkendrin's heels.'

Palansa's face hardened and she cradled her belly in her hands. 'Two moons of mourning, little one; two more moons for you to grow strong.'

30

Kest had stopped again and was holding the map up to the lamp. 'We should have been out by now,' he said, chewing on his lip thoughtfully. 'Of course, this might be totally inaccurate.'

Kira resisted the temptation to sit down, fearing she'd never get up again. 'It shows the training rooms and the Water Cavern in the right places, and the Sarnia Room.' Even speaking had become an effort.

'Then it can't be to scale. We should've come to the opening by now.' Kest stared back the way they'd come. 'Unless we've missed it.'

'We haven't missed it, Kest.'

'How can you be certain?'

'We've got a lamp and two sets of eyes.'

Kest grimaced, refolding the map.

'It can't be much further,' said Kira, starting off again. 'I hope,' she added under her breath.

She trudged on and after a while the tunnel began to climb, imperceptibly at first, then more steeply. 'It must be ending,' called Kira over her shoulder.

'Keep your voice down,' warned Kest, hurrying after her, 'and don't get too far ahead.'

Kira nodded and slowed her pace. Once she had the fireweed, they'd need to get back to the training rooms as swiftly as possible. It would probably be best administered by a paste directly on the wound. The sheaf had described the fireweed as highly potent, so she wouldn't need much . . . Then her eyes widened and she came to a stop, Kest all but cannoning into her.

'What –' Then he saw what she'd seen. 'Stinking heart-rot!'

The tunnel had broken, one branch going left, the other turning sharply right.

'Look at the map,' said Kira.

'I don't need to. It doesn't show any stinking junction.'

Kira stared at the walls but there was no soot, or brackets for lamps, or markings of any kind to show which way to go.

'We could toss a stone for it,' suggested Kest sourly.

'We'll try the tunnel on the right,' said Kira.

'Why the right?'

Kira sighed. 'The first entrance was easterly, remember?'

'It might loop back west, or south or north for all we know.'

'Well, let's find out.'

Kira strode forward with more confidence than she felt, but the tunnel twisted back on itself and her heart sank. She kept going, for want of a better alternative, and after a little it swung east again and started to climb.

'It looks like –' she began, then froze.

'What is it?'

'Did you hear that?' It sounded like the clash of metal against metal.

Kest shook his head and his sword whispered free. They stood straining into the darkness, their hearts thudding. Nothing. Kira wondered if she'd imagined the noise and was about to suggest going on when it sounded again.

Kest thrust Kira behind him and Kira's heart roared, drowning all thought. Then the noise came again, sounding oddly familiar now, and she breathed again.

'I think it's birds,' she whispered.

'No bird sounds like that,' Kest hissed back.

'I think the stone's distorting it.'

'Wait here,' said Kest, setting down the lamp and moving away, the gleam of his sword the last thing Kira saw before the darkness swallowed him.

Silence closed in and after a while Kira started pacing up and down, feeling that doing anything was better than simply waiting, and hugging herself despite the mildness of the air. What if Kest didn't return? What if the Shargh were lying in wait? They might already have killed Kest and be creeping back down the tunnel towards her. She felt vulnerable exposed in the pool of light. Her scalp prickled and she imagined she could hear stealthy footsteps. Then she *could* hear stealthy footsteps! She looked round wildly but there were no weapons! Snatching up the lamp, she drew her arm back. Hot oil in their faces should give her a few moments before their blades plunged into her back.

She sucked in her breath, bracing herself, then Kest emerged from the murk. With a choking gasp, she collapsed into his arms.

'Kira! What is it?' He extricated the lamp carefully from her grip.

'I thought . . .' She was shaking, the tremors making speech difficult. She buried her face in his shirt, drawing in the scents of sweat and dust and burned espin as his arms tightened round her.

'I thought you were dead,' she mumbled, drawing away and busying herself by smoothing her crumpled shirt.

'Pecked to death by a nest of tippets. You were right, the stone does do strange things to sound. The entrance can't be very far ahead – I could see light. We need take care. Come.' He took her hand, for which she was grateful, and they went forward, the tunnel bending

261

twice more before the light began to grow, the stone going from black to brown to the silvery sheen of dusk. The noise they'd heard resolved itself into the chirp of tippets, then the sounds of springleslips and leaf thrushes intruded, the air losing its dankness and taking on the myriad scents of the forest. But instead of the tunnel opening up as they'd expected, it came to an end.

Kest held the lamp aloft, illuminating the tumbled rock-wall confronting them and the pale sun-starved tendrils of sour-ripe vine falling from a small opening above.

Kest stared up at it. 'We've come all this stinking way for nothing.'

'I can fit through,' said Kira.

'No!'

'Kest . . .' she protested.

'Absolutely not! I forbid it.'

'We agreed you wouldn't hold me prisoner again.'

'We agreed we'd stay together.' His hands came to his hips. 'You're asking me to break every tenet of Protector training, to toss aside every rule I've obeyed for eight seasons – and that I've forced my trainees to obey on pain of incarceration! I can't do it, Kira. I won't do it.'

Kest's face was haggard, his eyes dark with exhaustion. We're the same, Kira realised abruptly. Kest needs to protect in the same way that I need to heal. The revelation calmed her and she laid her hand on his arm.

'Kasheron never intended protecting and healing to fight each other, but to work together to make the Tremen strong. Most of the wounded in the training rooms are Protectors, Kest. Kesilini lives because of them. I live because of them. They did what they were trained to do. Now let me do what I'm trained to do.'

'Don't ask me to do this, Kira.'

There was a long silence.

'I'll need your help to reach the opening, Kest.'

262

He shook his head. 'How did you get to be so cursed stubborn?'

His voice was ragged and she made a determined effort to lighten hers. 'Perhaps it's the company I've been keeping.'

He didn't smile. 'Our agreement stands. You go straight there and come directly back. If there's no fireweed, you don't go looking for it, and you're to wait till dark.'

Kira nodded. 'It's almost dark now. Give me a leg up.'

'Wait,' said Kest, drawing his sword. 'I'll clear the sour-ripe.'

'No. It's better the opening stays hidden,' she said. 'A few scratches won't kill me.'

'But the Shargh will.' His warm hands cupped her face, forcing her to meet his eyes. 'You have no love for yourself, Kira, but you are loved by many. Remember that.'

Kira nodded, her throat too tight to speak. Then Kest linked his hands and she placed her foot in them, bringing their faces close together.

'Take very great care, Kira.'

She nodded again and he hefted her skyward, so that she was able to grab the edge of the opening, and kick her way forward. The sour-ripe dragged her back, as if intent on preventing her exit, but she pushed it aside and wedged her shoulders through, finally scrabbling clear of it into the leaf litter. Her hands were horribly scratched but she'd kept the worst of it off her face, and there was a major compensation for her pain and effort: the sour-ripe was loaded with fruit.

'A fair trade,' she muttered, stuffing her mouth and filling her pockets, 'your flesh for mine.' She ate greedily, the sweet juices slaking her thirst and sating her empty belly, then crawling back to the opening, called softly to Kest.

'Yes?'

'Catch.'

There was an exclamation and a muffled chuckle.

'I'll get some more when I come back.'

'Be swift,' whispered Kest, but she was already gone.

Kest lowered himself onto the dusty floor and quenched the lamp to save the oil. It was completely dark outside now, the edges of the opening limned by star sheen and light from the waning moon. It would be a good time to get some sleep, but his mind was squalling. He shouldn't have let her go. The totality of Kasheron's dream was now held only by Kira, and he, Kest of Morclan and would-be Protector Commander, had sent her off alone into a forest that might well be crawling with Shargh. He rested his head against the stone and shut his eyes. Yet what was the alternative? Backtrack until they'd found the second opening? One that he could fit through too? If there was one. Force Kira back to watch the wounded die, like he'd intended? He sighed. What was the point of fretting? For good or ill, she was gone and he'd just have to wait for what was to come.

In the trees above, Kira ran with a mixture of fear and desperation. The fear kept her scanning constantly, avoiding the crack and snap of brittle windfall and keeping to the darkest blots of shadow. She concentrated on tricking her mind into believing that the pain in her body didn't exist. But she couldn't dispel the doubt that threatened to overwhelm her.

If she were right in her reckoning, and if the opening to the Warens were where she thought it was, then the lands bordering Sarnia Cave should be close by. *Should be!* Yet she recognised nothing. The leaf litter near Sarnia Cave had been dry and thick while here it scarcely covered the simpleweed. Maybe the opening she'd scrambled through wasn't in Kenclan at all; maybe the map was completely wrong. Panic bubbled as she scanned frantically, seeing nothing beyond the walling trees. Perhaps higher ground would help her to orientate herself.

She started up the slope, then stopped, suddenly remembering that there had been white stone poking from the ground near the cave, and even with only a part moon, she should be able to see it.

But the ground was dark. Maybe it was the next slope, she thought quickly, stilling the surge of panic. Or maybe she was completely lost. Gritting her teeth, she turned and forced her trembling legs down into the shallow valley and up the other side. She had to stop often to catch her breath and sleeve the sweat from her eyes, and when she finally reached the next crest, she rewarded herself with the last of the sour-ripe, sucking it down between pants.

A nearby bitterberry thrashed sideways and she stifled a scream, barely aware of the leaf thrush winging away. All around her the leaves whispered, and scuttles in the undergrowth took on the sounds of hunting footsteps, so that she had to fight the urge to continually look over her shoulder.

She went on, straining into the gloom, and seeing a pale glimmer on the adjacent slope. Micklefungus or stone? She struggled down through the bitterberry and up the other side, the rich smell of leaf-fall quickening her heart. It was stone and the contorted sever tree to her right looked familiar too, as did the stand of shelterbushes.

She picked her way carefully between the stones, the litter so thick it reached her ankles, then stopped, her mind suddenly as blank as the night around her. The memory she'd boasted to Kest about was gone. For a moment she simply stood, sweat oozing down her back, her legs aching as if bone rubbed on bone. Then, more by instinct than anything else, she turned back and, as the leaf litter deepened further, dropped to her knees and began raking about in it. Nothing. She trawled forward, ignoring the jab of a stick in her calf, and the possibility of turning up something unpleasant, but still there was nothing.

Sweat stung her eyes and she blinked ferociously. It must be here! Then her fingers stabbed into slime and she recoiled in disgust. It didn't make sense, unless . . . there were small soaks scattered among the stone. That would explain the withyweed she'd seen. Wiping her face on her sleeve, she crawled onward, her left hand connecting with something spongy. Very gingerly she pushed aside the litter, exposing a row of fingers, the smaller ones pale, the larger ones dark-tipped. *The fireweed darkens to a deep red at maturity when its potency is greatest.*

Kira gave a sob of relief and, with shaking hands, took out her herbal sickle and began harvesting. The larger fingers came away cleanly, as if they were ripe. Lacking her herbal sling, she laid them gently in the front of her shirt. They grew in a run, and she followed their trail, smoothing away the leaf-fall, harvesting, and reburying the immature plants, collecting more than a dozen before the run came to an end. Would it be enough? The Writings had said nothing about quantities, or about storage, and her Healer sensitivities rebelled against wasting even a sliver of it. Stowing the sickle, she got slowly to her feet and turned to go, just as a figure stepped from the shadows.

Terror rooted her to the spot, turning her legs to water and emptying her lungs of air. It came closer but still she couldn't speak or move.

'I greet you, clansman.'
The customary greeting of one Tremen stranger to another.

Kira's mouth formed a word but nothing came out. He was little more than a boy, despite his height.

'I . . . I'm sorry, Healer Kiraon, I didn't realise it was you in the dark.'

'You startled me,' she choked out at last. *More like scared the life out of me.* She took a ragged breath. 'I didn't expect to see a Kenclansman beyond the First Eight.'

'I'm Sherclan. My name's Bern.' He straightened, clearly proud.

'A Sherclansman? You're a long way from home. I would have thought Clanleader Dakresh forbade such travelling.'

'Clanleader Dakresh believes that the danger of another attack before the full moon is small, and I agree with him. He's happy enough for us to continue to travel until the moon is bigger.'

'In *your* octad.'

Bern shrugged. 'I'm not gathering, I'm reconnoitring. I know every clump of simpleweed in my octad *and* the Barclan octad, but it's different here: there are caves.'

Kira didn't know whether Dakresh was right but Kest believed the threat was real *and* immediate, and she wondered abruptly if she had the authority to order Bern home.

'Have you been to the caves?' pursued Bern, his enthusiasm overcoming his initial shyness. 'They're massive, with white stone that goes on forever. One of them's even got water in it, and I've slept there many times. You can roast blacknuts at the front and see the trees swaying in the wind as far as the Third Eight.' His voice rang with excitement, reminding her of Kandor suddenly, and of her own delight in wandering.

'The Protectors prefer that people don't journey on their own, especially outside the First Eight. It would be safer if you went back to your longhouse.'

'You're journeying alone,' pointed out Bern resentfully.

'I'm gathering.' There was an awkward silence.

'I just want to spend a couple of nights at the caves,' said Bern contritely. 'Then I'll go home.'

Kira nodded and prepared to go, but Bern lingered. 'You won't tell the Protectors you saw me, will you?' he said, jiggling from foot to foot.

'Why?' asked Kira, noticing his bulging pack for the first time. '*Have* you disobeyed their orders?'

'No . . . my father's.'

'Your father's?'

'Dakresh.'

'*Clanleader Dakresh?*'

Bern nodded.

Kira stared at him in astonishment. Miken had once described Dakresh as a tardy man, as stuck in his ways as a root through rock. He was also old, and it surprised her he had a son as young as Bern. Maybe he'd bonded more than once; it was said that the

267

Sherclan changed bondmates more often than the withysnake its skin.

Bern was still waiting anxiously and she came to a decision.

'I'm living in the Warens at the moment and unlikely to see your father in the next few days. As long as you're back in your longhouse by then, I see no reason why I should mention you.'

She sensed his delighted smile and he gave a clumsy bow before bounding off up the slope.

If only her legs would carry her as fast, thought Kira dourly, trudging off in the opposite direction and starting to search for the landmarks she'd passed along the way. Here were the twin-crowned castellas, there the tangle of shaggyman clinging to a bough next to the micklefungus; there the sequence of shelterbush and bitterberry. She should run, but she was having trouble walking. She trudged on.

31

Dawn was silvering the canopy before Kira arrived back at the vine-covered hole. She numbly filled her pockets with sour-ripe fruit again before hissing Kest's name through the tangle, and shoving her feet through the opening. She inched forward until her bottom was on the edge. Then, folding her arms around her face, she dropped. There was a grunted oath as Kest's arms closed around her, crushing her to him and enveloping her in the comforting smell of his jacket.

For a long while he simply held her. 'Praise to the alwaysgreen which Shelters us,' he said, his voice ragged. 'You took long enough.'

It was dark in the tunnel after the dawn-lit forest above and Kira could barely make him out. 'Have you run out of oil?' she asked.

'No, I'm conserving it.' Flints scraped and light flared, revealing Kest's haggardness with shocking clarity. He looked as if he hadn't slept in days and Kira's heart faltered.

Kest was almost as familiar to her now as Tresen; no longer just the aloof man she'd first met near Nogren, nor the one who'd held her to his will on the nightmarish journey to and from Sarnia Cave. He was the companion who'd run with her through the rain-filled night in search of sorren; the friend who'd now searched in the darkness with her for the Writings on fireweed; the man who'd just hugged her in relief at her safe return.

And she'd seen the other side of him, too, his head thrown back in joyous laughter as he'd danced with her in the Morclan longhouse in celebration at the birth of Feseren's son. She wanted to tell him how much he meant to her, but instead blurted out: 'You should've rested while I was away.'

Kest was busy packing away the flints. 'Rested? With you out there, with the 'green knows how many stinking Shargh . . .?' He cleared his throat, and when he straightened his face was devoid of expression.

'You *did* get the fireweed?' he asked as they walked.

Kira patted her shirt.

'And with no trouble?'

'It took me a while to find it. I don't know Kenclan octad as well as I thought.' Kira's face warmed.

He hadn't actually asked her if she'd seen anyone.

'Was there much there?'

'Enough for two more harvests,' said Kira, her exhaustion returning with crushing suddenness.

'Only two?'

'The Writings say it's potent, and I didn't search for more,' mumbled Kira, dragging more air into her lungs; even speaking had become an effort. 'Now I know its habit, I might be able to harvest it closer to the Bou . . . to the training rooms.'

'Or the Protectors will.'

Kira didn't argue. The lamplight was blurring, giving the illusion that they were somehow walking in a yellow bubble. They trudged on in silence, finally passing the gape of a large cavern.

'The storage room,' said Kest thickly.

Kira nodded. How much further? And when she got back, how much longer before she could sleep? The Writing had told her little about the fireweed's preparation; no doubt it was written elsewhere, but there'd been no time to search. No time, no time, no time. Her toe caught and only Kest's reflexive grab saved her, his hand remaining on her arm. The drag on her eyelids was unbearable. Was it possible to sleep and walk at the same? Kest's grip shifted to her waist and she sagged against him, comforted by his strength and scent. Eventually he was almost carrying her over the ground but she was too tired to even thank him. Finally, as if in a dream, the darkness and emptiness dissipated and she was surrounded by light and people: Tresen and Miken and Kesilini.

'We've found something we think might cure Shargh wounds,' mumbled Kira.

Tresen gave a yelp of excitement.

'It's the fireweed I told you about . . . before . . .' Kira slurred to a stop and carefully extricated it from her shirt.

'It looks more like fungus than weed,' said Tresen, turning it over curiously.

'But how –' began Miken.

'Make a paste,' said Kira, focusing her remaining strength on Tresen.

'What makes you think –' began Miken again.

'I'll need bandages, Tresen.' She paused, considering sluggishly. 'How much sickleseed's left?'

'Kesilini made up two pots in the last night, but I'm not sure how much leaf is still there.'

'Wait for me,' said Kira, staggering off towards her alcove.

Miken turned back to Tresen, but he was already heading for the Herbery, leaving only Kest, now being supported rather than embraced by his sister Kesilini. There was much Miken needed to say, but again it seemed that he would have to wait.

Kira collapsed onto her mattress and dragged her pack onto her lap, pushing a clumsy hand into its depths. The pouch was double-wrapped

271

and had been there since last summer. Carefully she tipped the hard glossy seeds into her hand. Morning-bright. The leaves gave the training rooms their cheerful smell, but the seeds were poisonous, or so the Tremen believed. Kira rolled them back and forth in her palm. The Writings said that in the north those who took morning-bright seeds had no need of sleep, running and fighting for days, sometimes until their hearts stopped, and they dropped where they stood.

She didn't want to run or fight, just heal, and she'd only take one little seed; surely it wouldn't be as punishing? A groan sounded from beyond the curtain and, screwing her eyes shut, she placed the seed on her tongue. The effect was almost immediate, as if she'd swallowed a fire-spark. Heaving herself up, she gulped down a cup of water, but far from quenching the fire, it seemed to add fuel, heat spearing through her chest and arms, making her cough violently. She dragged in air, sweat pouring from her skin as the heat redoubled, sending tears streaming down her face. Her head felt like a furnace confined by her skull, set to explode. Then, just as suddenly as it'd begun, the heat drained away and she sagged backwards, crying in relief.

She felt normal again; well, not exactly normal, but nothing ached or begged for rest, and the crushing exhaustion was gone. Pulling off her filthy clothes, she dressed in clean ones from the pile, scrubbed her hands and face then dried herself. Two more days, she promised herself, stowing the seeds safely, then she'd rest.

Tresen had already unbound Fedren's wound, the putrid smell forcing Kira to breathe through her mouth as she knelt beside him. The bowl of pinkish red paste sat ready, but for the first time since setting out to find it, she hesitated. What did she really know about it apart from Writings transcribed by those sharing blood with the Terak Kutan?

'Why do you delay?' demanded Tresen.

Gritting her teeth, she ladled the paste into Fedren's wound, covering every part of the raw, rancid flesh, before moving on to

Berik. Tresen worked behind her, binding Fedren again, while Werem hovered beside them with a basket of fresh bandages.

What if Fedren died anyway? thought Kira. Or worse still, what if the fireweed made his passing agonising? Was this strange paste to be their salvation or bane? Her hands stilled. 'Maybe we should wait.'

'For what? Death?' said Tresen. 'Don't delay me, Kira, I'm almost finished here.'

Reluctantly Kira smoothed the paste into Berik's wound and moved on to old Miren. Next to him lay his grandson, his face as pale as wax, then Narek, Pirten and Sorosen, Dorn and Firgen, then those with lesser wounds. She toiled on in silence, losing herself in the ghastly rhythm of stripping away oozing bandages and coating stinking flesh. Finally she came to the last of the wounded and sat back on her heels, putting the bowl aside.

Chimes chinked and it took her a moment to realise that such a thing was impossible, for the Warens lacked wind. It was the chink of cups she heard, Kesilini having returned and set one of the side tables with thornyflower tea and plates of nutbread.

'Come and eat, Kira,' said Kesilini, 'then you must rest.'

Kira scrubbed her hands in a wash bowl and settled at the table. It must be close to midday but she felt no cramps from kneeling, or aches from bending.

'Drink your tea, Kira, you must surely need it.'

Kesilini's likeness to her brother was startling. She had the same white-blonde hair and the same blue eyes, which were now clearly puzzled.

'I can't understand how you're still healing when Kest sleeps as if dead,' she murmured.

'It's because she's taken something,' said Tresen, pulling his chair alongside, his voice as hard as his eyes.

'Taken something?' said Kesilini.

Tresen's hard gaze remained on Kira. 'The green and growing

273

give us herbs that mend flesh or knit bones. There are some that even make flight seem possible ... or bring death. A *good* Healer knows which is which; a *good* Healer doesn't misuse their knowing.'

Kira's head came up. 'I didn't have a choice.'

'Of course you had a choice! Why do you always think you have to do everything on your own? *I* could've tended the wounds and Kesilini could've bound them, *and* there's Arlen *and* Paterek *and* Werem. Who do you think healed while you were away wandering in the Warens?'

Anger roared, as explosive as unexpected. Kira slammed her cup down, slopping the liquid and scalding her fingers. 'I gave them the fireweed! *I* gave them something we know nothing about! It's *my* task to mend what might come of it, this night, or tomorrow, or the day after!'

'The day after? What in the 'green have you taken?' He caught her wrist and his expression turned to horror.

'What is it? What's wrong?' Kesilini's trembling hands had gone to her mouth.

Tresen's voice was sharp with fear. 'Your heart's thrashing like the Drinkwater in flood! Do you know what you're risking?'

Kira snatched her hand away and shoved her chair back. 'It's nothing to do with you ...' She was interrupted by a shuddering groan and spun. 'Who?'

Tresen was on his feet too. 'I didn't see ...'

'Serdric, I think,' said Kesilini.

Serdric was one of the last Kira had treated, and his head was now tossing from side to side, his skin florid and slick with sweat. Kira hastened to his side.

'He's burning!' She felt for the pulse in his neck and his arm flailed sideways, catching her a stinging blow across the face and knocking her backwards. Another groan erupted from the other side of the room and Kira scrambled upright, looking round wildly.

'Maybe we shouldn't have treated them all at once,' said Tresen, struggling to restrain another tossing man, while a choking sound erupted behind him.

'It's made them worse,' exclaimed Kesilini.

'Fetch all the sickleseed we have,' ordered Tresen, 'and the other Healers. We're going to need everyone.'

Tresen had no idea how long it was till the screams and thrashings had given way to the quiet of uneasy sleep. All he knew was that he never wanted to endure anything like it again. Fireweed had certainly burned the rot from their wounds, but it had brought with it a ferocious fever, barbed with a pain so severe that even sickleseed had struggled to subdue it. And it had come too late for Miren and his grandson.

He glared at Kira, still bent over the wounded. He didn't know what angered him most: her abuse of herbs or her refusal to acknowledge her mistake in doing so. It was as if she'd closed off, as if all their time of growing together had ceased to exist.

A hand gripped his shoulder and he jumped.

'I hear I've missed some very strange happenings,' said Miken.

'Giving a room full of wounded a fever-bringing herb at the same time is not a good idea,' conceded Tresen.

'But it worked?'

Tresen nodded and his father's grip tightened, bringing home to Tresen the enormity of what they'd achieved. They'd cured Shargh wounds!

'It's spoken of throughout the Warens, but I hardly dared believe it possible,' said Miken. 'This is a great day for the Tremen.'

'But not for Miren and his grandson – or Kira.'

Miken's smile drained away. 'Tell me.'

Kira blinked as the wavery form of Miken picked his way towards her, looking as though he was swimming under water. She blinked again, resisting the urge to giggle.

'Come,' he said, taking her arm and lifting her. He supported her back to her alcove and twitched back the bed cover. 'Lie down.'

Obediently she stretched herself out on her bed, Miken taking off her boots and pulling the cover over her.

'What have you taken?' he asked.

'Morning-bright seed.'

'I thought it was poisonous,' he said, bringing his hand to her neck. Kira watched as he appeared to float away, reappearing and pushing a rough sack of some herb under her legs. 'That will take some of the strain off your heart,' he said. 'You are to stay like this till I tell you that you can move.' Wood scraped against stone as he settled on a chair. 'How do you feel?'

'Like my head's at the First Eight.'

Miken grunted. 'Anything else?'

'I'm having trouble seeing.'

'What about your hearing?'

'I can hear.'

'Good, because I'm going to talk, and you're going to listen. The council has appointed you Tremen Leader and Kest, Protector Commander. I think they've chosen well on both counts.'

Kira felt like protesting but the cover was warm and Miken's blurring outline had given way to blackness. 'I've never wanted the leadership,' was all she managed to muster.

'I know, but the leadership is assigned to the best Healer in Allogrenia, and you've long been that. Your role will not be greatly different to what you're doing now. You'll continue to heal and keep healing-knowing safe while Kest ensures the protection of the Tremen. Neither of you will have to do these things alone, for you'll have the support and help of the council, and of all who dwell in Allogrenia.'

Kira said nothing, feeling Miken's hand on her neck once more.

'I think your heart's slowing. Are you feeling calmer?' he asked.

'I'm tired.'

Rough fingers smoothed back her hair, stroking rhythmically. He'd stroked her hair like this when she was a child: comforting her after the death of her mother and later cleaning the bark scuffs from her face, healing her small hurts, holding her as she wept.

'I've got something for you,' he said, his voice reverberating, like the sound in Sarnia Cave. Kira felt a smooth cylinder of wood being put into her hands.

'It's Kandor's pipe,' Miken's voice said gently.

The darkness became a storm of sleet-snow. 'I don't want it.'

Miken's warm hand closed over hers. 'Remember his smile, Kira, and his love of music, and his love for you,' his voice whispered like wind through the canopy and his lips brushed her forehead. 'Sleep now, dear one.'

His words slipped away to nothingness as Kira tightened her grip on the pipe, tears wetting her face. At least she could still feel, she thought vaguely, then that sense was swallowed too.

32

Arkendrin grunted impatiently as he flicked the flies from his face. The flies that lived under the trees were smaller than the blackflies of the Grounds, but just as greedy. They were thick now, feeding off the mess that spattered the leaves and coated the churned earth. The treeman screamed and sobbed, still bucking under Ermashin's grip, his breeches dark where he'd wet himself. Arkendrin's lip curled. The treeman was tall like the rest of his ilk but blubbered like a babe denied the teat. Urpalin slid his dagger over the treeman's shoulder, teasing him before slicing again. The treeman shrieked, his gurglings forming the word he already knew meant *owl*.

'I need more than *owl*,' growled Arkendrin. *And I need it now*. With each passing day Palansa's belly swelled with the thing that would supplant him, and the waverers on the Ground swayed more in her filthy direction. The Sky Chiefs had granted him the creature's name earlier – *Kiraon* – and he knew its meaning. But he was no closer to finding the cursed creature.

'Find out *where* the Kiraon-owl is,' ordered Arkendrin.

Irason leaned forward once more, his belly heaving as the smell of blood filled his nostrils. The day was hot and he'd had a long wait under the trees for Arkendrin to bring the treeman, but Arkendrin had offered him no water and he daren't ask for any. He wobbled, almost tipping onto the blood-soaked treeman, and Orthaken caught his arm, steadying him.

Irason dredged around desperately for more words from the north. 'Is Kiraon-owl where?' he said carefully.

The treeman's eyes were wild and unfocused and Irason doubted the treeman heard him.

'Where is Kiraon-owl?' he tried again, wondering if a different word order would help.

Urpalin raised his dagger again and blood dripped onto Irason's sleeve. Irason had to clench his teeth to stop their rattle. The treeman cried and screamed, and there was a new word in the sobbing babble.

'*Warens*,' said Irason tentatively. The word was strange to him. 'Warens,' he repeated, looking at Arkendrin.

Arkendrin's expression of frustration deepened and Irason shrank back.

'What is this cursed *warens*?' demanded Arkendrin, his hand going to his flatsword.

Irason wiped his sweaty brow and turned back to the treeman. 'Warens where place kiraon-owl is?'

The treeman was panting now, his sobs reduced to harsh whimpers, and Irason wondered if he were dying. The treeman's shirt was sodden and rivulets of blood pooled on either side of him. Irason glanced at Ermashin. Ermashin's face was blank but Arkendrin's face was like thunder now, his sword half drawn.

'What is *warens*?' bawled Arkendrin.

Irason cringed and Urpalin's lips drew back. He brought the knife down again and blood spurted from the treeman's neck, showering Irason. The treeman gurgled a single word then convulsed.

'Hole,' Irason managed to croak before his belly emptied itself onto the grass. Orthaken held him until his retching quieted, and he became aware that the treeman was quiet too. Wiping his mouth, he looked up in time to see Arkendrin's fist come down into Urpalin's face, sending him sprawling. Then, cursing viciously, Arkendrin strode about, trampling the undergrowth and slashing at the trees.

It was a long time before Arkendrin felt the storm of fury drain from his veins. Three stinking days following their slashes into the trees; three more stumbling about looking for a stray treeman; three dragging him back to the forest's edge, all wasted because that fool Urpalin didn't know the difference between pain and death. The first gave information, the second nothing! All they had for their trouble was that the creature lived in a hole. A hole! Surely Irason was mistaken? Arkendrin glared at the old man crouched next to his blood-tie Orthaken and he seemed to shrivel even further.

Arkendrin could afford to delay no longer in this filthy tangle! Thrusting his sword into his belt, he heaved on his pack, and without a backward glance, strode off through the trees.

Never had the forest smelt so wonderful or looked so beautiful, thought Kira, drawing the air deep into her lungs. Everything was scent-drenched and sun-dappled, with flutterwings spiralling in glittering columns and flowerthieves chattering high in the sever trees. *This* was where she needed to be, not in the Warens! There was nothing in the Warens except darkness and dankness; this was where she wanted to live, even if it meant being hunted down and dying beneath the trees!

But she was no longer just a Healer, free to wander at will; she was the Leader, off to her first Clancouncil, off to rule over a group of old men, half of whom didn't want her as Leader.

Her belly lurched uncomfortably and she dried her palms on her sagging leggings, watching the Protectors slipping through the trees around her. The tunic was too big too, the sleeves reaching to her fingertips, but beautifully embroidered with alwaysgreen leaves – the mark of Kashclan. Miken had told her that Tenerini was busy with her needle making her new clothes, but that they weren't yet ready, so she'd sent her own for Kira to wear to her first council. Miken's pride in Kashclan again providing the Tremen Leader was obvious, but Kira wondered whether his pride would soon turn to shame.

Her belly increased its churn and she broke off a stem of sweetchew, concentrating on peeling back the horny bark. It was always difficult to start, but once a corner was lifted, it usually came away cleanly. The bark slipped off and she popped the sweetchew into her mouth. Tresen loved it: *as sweet as honey*, he always said; *sweeter than honey*, Kandor had always retorted. She stumbled and a nearby Protector caught her arm, steadying her.

'Please take care, Leader Feailner Kiraon.'

'I . . . I will, thank you. And I am just Leader Kiraon.' The Protector was an older man Kira didn't recognise, and he was now clearly puzzled.

'Your pardon, Leader Kiraon. It's many seasons since we've had the honour of a woman Leader, and Commander Kest himself instructed us on the appropriate way to address you.'

Kest obviously still wanted her ability to take pain recognised, despite his pledge to keep the knowing to himself. Kira snapped off some more sweetchew, taking her irritation out on the bark. He probably meant well, she acknowledged grudgingly, and the last thing she should do was to undermine his authority.

'Commander Kest's quite correct,' she said carefully, 'but I don't think it's necessary to remind people I'm a woman by including *feailner* in my title.'

The Protector gave a small bow. 'As you wish, Leader Kiraon.'

They walked on, the only sound the pad of their footsteps and the calls of tippets jousting in the treetops. The Protector nearest wasn't the only one of Kira's escort she didn't recognise, in fact there were only a couple of faces of the twenty or so men who *were* familiar. Most of them were older than the Protectors who'd brought her back from the nutting expedition and older than those who dwelt in the Warens. These men were broad-shouldered and well-muscled, their faces stern and uncompromising. Kest had chosen his most experienced Protectors as her escort. Yet, rather than making her feel safer, she found herself nervously searching the trees.

'Which clan are you from, Protector?' she asked, in an effort to distract herself.

'Renclan, Leader Kiraon.'

'I've not been there,' admitted Kira, feeling inadequate again. How was she to lead a people she'd never met?

'We've been blessed with good health and few accidents, at least in the seasons of your growing, but your mother visited us often, for she had a taste for Renclan song.'

'She sang?' asked Kira, wishing she knew such things.

'Oh, she had a very sweet voice, and graced us with it many a time. Do you sing, Leader Kiraon?' asked the Protector, smiling.

Kira shook her head. Her father had insisted on a quiet decorum in the Bough, and her time had been taken up memorising herbal lists and remedies, not learning song-words.

'I'm surprised,' he said kindly, 'for your mother's bequeathed you her face, and it's said that the voice and the countenance go together.'

Kira ground the sweetchew between her teeth, waiting for the constriction in her throat to ease. 'What are you named, Protector?' she asked, when she was able.

'Lethrin, Leader Kiraon.'

'When things are more settled, Lethrin, I'd like to visit your longhouse and hear the music my mother enjoyed. Do you still play it?'

'Most nights, Leader Kiraon. And you would be a most honoured guest.'

*

They stopped to eat at midday, Kira settling under an ashael to take her meal of nutbread and fruit. As a child she'd imagined ashaels speaking to each other, their words whispering from tree to tree the entire length and breadth of Allogrenia, with news of courtings and pledgings and birthings all passed from leaf-tip to leaf-tip. But she'd never imagined them as messengers of death. It was strange. Her mother had died and others too, her father joining their processions through the trees. She'd even seen the newly turned earth when her wanderings had taken her to the Eights. Death had been all around her, but she'd never noticed it.

She got to her feet: the ashaels' song this day was lonely, almost a keening. Seeing her rise, the Protector Leader gave a short command and the men came back into formation.

The council meeting was taking place near a new moon, rather than a full one, for Miken said it was important to deal with the concerns facing the Tremen as soon as possible. It was to be held at the Sherclan longhouse, although being the first for a new Leader, it could have taken place at any of the eight longhouses. Miken had warned her not to appear to be favouring Kashclan, and not to seek advice or assistance from him or Marren at the council. It made sense that the first council wasn't at Miken's longhouse – now for a while her own. But surely as Leader she should be able to seek advice from whoever she chose? Her father hadn't liked Miken or Marren, because they'd disputed what he said. She hoped the divisions within the council between those who supported her father and those whose views accorded with Miken's and Marren's did not endure after her father's death.

There was so much she didn't know about how the council worked, Miken only being able to spend a single morning instructing her. Maybe if she made a terrible mess of the leadership, they would appoint someone else. A feeling of relief swept over her, tempered by the knowing that she was at least going to have to attend this first meeting. Clancouncils began with formal welcomes and after that Kest would probably outline his plans for the protection of the longhouses, followed by discussions on any issues Kest or the Clanleaders raised. Her role would be to ensure that any discussions were orderly and to call for a division when they'd run their course. It had sounded simple enough when Miken had described it, but now it seemed overwhelming.

What if the councillors ignored her? Tenedren and Ketten would probably be courteous, but not Dakresh. Maybe Miken had chosen Dakresh's longhouse to appease him. Marren could be relied on to be polite as well, and probably Kemrick too, since his simple words had ensured her appointment. Miken had said that Kemrick and Berendash would probably agree in most decisions, because there'd always been an alliance between the two octads. What sort of alliance she hadn't thought to ask.

Then there was Sanden, who she knew nothing about. In fact, apart from Miken, she knew very little about any of the Clanleaders. They'd come to the Bough barely twice a year, either at the Feast of Turning or at Thanking, and she'd taken no interest in them or her father's and Merek's discussion of them, or their discussions of Clancouncil business.

She spat the sweetchew out and sucked the sugary remnants from her teeth. From what Miken had said, each of the Clanleaders had their own wants and needs, and she began to see that despite the fact they were all Tremen, each clan was distinct. How had her father managed to hold them together? *And* take over the Warens? He'd obviously had skills she didn't, and this was soon going to be horribly apparent to everyone. She hoped her brief stint as Leader didn't turn into a costly mistake.

Smoke threaded the trees and there was an excited whoop and scatter of leaves as a child scampered off, rousing Kira from her reverie. The young lookout had beaten his own longhouse's Protectors to the news of their arrival. Smoke thickened, heavy with the scent of fallowood – hardly surprising given that fallowoods were

284

thick about the longhouse, and the Protectors drew in about her, more for ceremonial reasons than protection. The silvered wood of a building emerged, roofed in shaggyman and mottle-crested shingles, its shutters thrown wide to the summer air.

Voices echoed, a hubbub composed of the giggles and shouts of children and the sterner tones of adults quieting them. Sherclansmen and women had gathered in front of the longhouse and along the path to the entranceway. Kira quelled the urge to flee back into the forest as a hush fell. Then people smiled, extending their hands in welcome, and Kira slowed, refusing to scurry past them rudely despite her shaking knees.

'Kashclan thanks Sherclan, Kashclan thanks Sherclan,' she repeated over and over again, until she reached the heavily carved door and the silent Sherclansman waiting there. He was too young for Dakresh, standing stiffly in formal Sherclan clothing, light brown hair to his shoulders in the Sherclan manner, and oddly familiar, though she knew she'd never met him before.

'Sherclan welcomes Tremen Leader Feailner Kiraon,' he said carefully, bowing low.

'Tremen Leader Kiraon thanks Sherclan,' replied Kira, glancing around furtively, wondering if Dakresh's absence were some sort of insult and if so, how she should react. But there was no sign of contempt or cunning in the face of the young man who'd greeted her, just sombre respectfulness.

'I'm Clanleader Dakresh's elder son Sener. Please accept my father's apologies for not being here to welcome you himself.'

Kira smiled, realising that he was the brother of the boy she'd met near Sarnia Cave.

Sener stood aside and she moved past him into a hall decorated with garlands of starflower and lissium, the white and pink striking against the darker wood of the walls. A large table stood at its centre. Seated round it was a gathering of stern-faced men, whose conversation came to an abrupt halt as Kira appeared. There was a brief hiatus, then they rose as Sener led her to her seat at the head of the table and withdrew. All the chairs were taken except one, obviously Dakresh's, and she wondered again whether his absence was a sign of displeasure. Kest wasn't there either. Perhaps protocol demanded he join them later. After all, he wasn't a Clanleader. She took up her position, staring stolidly ahead, fighting the urge to seek out Miken.

There was a clearing of throats and then the council spoke as one.

'The Clanleaders welcome Tremen Leader Feailner Kiraon. May her healing be strong, her hand gentle and her ears open to the thoughts of her people.'

The greeting was clearly part of a traditional welcoming ceremony; the problem was that Miken had neglected to describe it to her, and so she had no idea what to say in response.

'I thank the Clanleaders for their welcome. I will heal with all my heart, gather without harm to the green and growing, and listen to those who would have words with me.'

There was a pause and Kira felt her palms moisten. Something more was obviously expected, but to mumble something inappropriate just for the sake of it wasn't going to mend the situation, so she remained silent. The silence stretched, becoming uncomfortable, then the Clanleaders sat down. Kira was about to follow suit when one of them rose again. He wore the reddish-brown tunic of Tarclan, but her mind had gone horribly blank.

'Clanleader Kemrick,' he said gently, introducing himself.

Kira felt like falling on his neck with gratitude, but all she did was nod.

'As we are enjoying the hospitality of Sherclan,' he began softly, 'it is Clanleader Dakresh's task to carry out the next part of the welcoming ceremony. However, as he has been delayed, I hope there will be no objection if I continue in his stead.' He glanced around the assembly and there was a murmur of approval.

'You have come to the leadership suddenly and tragically, Tremen Leader Feailner Kiraon, but none here doubt your strength to do it. We understand therefore that you may not be familiar with the small doings of the council, and I hope you will take no insult if we,' Kemrick gestured to those present, 'help you in these early meetings. I too am new to this role, so I know how puzzling it can seem.'

'I thank you for your words,' said Kira.

Kemrick's face was full of kindness and she sensed that he wasn't the only Clanleader who wanted her to do well, her plan to renounce the leadership at the end of the meeting beginning to seem churlish.

'The mark of the Tremen leadership is the ring of rulership,' went on Kemrick solemnly. 'The ring is older than Allogrenia and carries upon it the running horse, mark of our kin in the north, and the alwaysgreen, beloved of we who have chosen to make our home beneath its shelter. In giving this ring, the Tremen entrust themselves to their Leader. In taking it, the Leader accepts that trust, and the responsibilities that go with it. Will you take the ring?'

The question took Kira by surprise and Miken was clearly nonplussed too. Having paved the way for her appointment, Kemrick was now giving her the chance to escape it. Could it be that he wanted a good Leader, and to be a good Leader she had to be willing? The silence was stretching; she must give an answer.

'I have never sought the leadership,' she began hoarsely, then cleared her throat. 'I've always been content in gathering, in making herbal pastes and potions, in tending the sick and injured. I had thought I would heal and do nothing else. I had never imagined life beyond that.'

By the 'green, she was doing this poorly; feet were shuffling and glances being exchanged. She took a deep breath, and continued. 'The gathering of herbs and the making of potions are small things perhaps in the affairs of the council, but they are what Kasheron broke a people for, they are why he brought our forebears south, and they are why the eight clans laboured to establish our gentle, beautiful Allogrenia.'

Her throat tightened but she made herself meet the gaze of each of the councillors; at least she had their attention now.

'I cannot force my will upon you, nor will I try. I am a Healer, that is all. But I pledge to you that I will never stop striving to heal and that I will never stop struggling to keep healing strong, and that I will fight to the end of my strength to rebuild and reclaim all that the Shargh have tried to take from us. If that is not enough, then you must choose another Leader.'

Her knees felt shaky and she sat down, keeping her eyes on the table.

'It's enough for me,' said Kemrick gravely. 'Is it enough for my fellow councillors?'

There must have been nods for Kemrick's voice sounded again. 'Bring the ring of rulership.'

Kira forced her head up in time to see a small wooden box being passed from hand to hand, finally coming to rest in front of her.

'The Leader must take up her duties willingly,' prompted Kemrick.

The box was honey-coloured and heavily carved – alwaysgreen, still smelling of spice despite its age. Kira slid the lid open and froze. The last time she'd seen this ring was on her father's hand, the moment before the blow, and it rested now in a bed of brilliant red cloth. No dye in Allogrenia could make such colour. The box, like the ring, had come from the north. The cloth was as repellent as the ring, but the council was waiting and she reluctantly lifted the ring out. The metal was heavy and cold, and she had to resist the impulse to hurl it away.

'The ring can be worn around your neck if it's too large for your hand,' said Kemrick. 'I've read that Leader Feailner Sinarki and Leader Feailner Tesrina wore it so.'

Slowly Kira undid the thong Kest had given her, and slid the ring on, the ring coming to rest on the mira kiraon, the lacy wooden wings keeping the chill metal off her flesh. Then chairs grated as the councillors stood.

'The clans welcome Leader Feailner Kiraon.'

Kira stood too, scarcely believing that she'd passed up the opportunity to escape the leadership.

'I thank the clans for their welcome,' she said.

33

Kira had thought the councillors would want to spend the meeting discussing the Shargh attacks and strategies for keeping the longhouses and gatherers safe, but they seemed content to speak of more mundane matters. Perhaps they were waiting for Kest. She was tempted to ask *when*, or indeed *whether* he was going to join them, but was prevented by the thought that as Leader she should probably already know.

As it happened, Kest didn't appear until the shutters had been pulled closed against the evening dew, the day having passed in the discussion of things such as the trading of black-, brown- and bitter-nuts between the octads, the state of the withyweed harvest, and the fish stocks in the Drinkwater and Everflow. Kira had said little, for the talk had been surprisingly amiable, and there had been no need for divisions. She'd learned much.

In the past, provisions had arrived at the Bough without thought or effort: food being brought in from the octads, as well as cloth, which Sendra and the other helpers dyed and fashioned into tunics or breeches, or which Lern soaked in weatherall for boots. The Bough was the heart of healing, those dwelling there not spending their strength in gathering, or weaving cloth. Although Kira had sometimes helped Mikini weave, it was only now that she became fully aware of how much effort was involved in the longhouses supplying their own needs, as well as provisioning the Bough.

They had broken off their discussions for a time and were refreshing themselves with berries and thornyflower tea when Kest arrived. Kira was speaking with Tenedren, remembering to avoid Miken and Marren, and happened to be facing the door as it opened. Despite his clean clothing and gleaming hair, Kest looked grim and almost as tired as the last time she'd seen him. The Clanleaders turned and his grimness was swiftly replaced with careful neutrality as he exchanged greetings with those present, moving through the assembly until he was at her side.

'Congratulations, Tremen Leader Feailner Kiraon,' he said with a small bow.

'Thank you Commander Kest,' she said loudly, knowing her voice carried to the rest of the gathering. 'I congratulate you also on your promotion and ask that you simply call me Tremen Leader Kiraon, like the council. After all, the Tremen know I am a woman – I hope.'

There was a polite titter but the lines round Kest's mouth deepened. Kira bit her lip. She'd intended it as a light-hearted remark but it sounded like point-scoring and that was the last thing she'd wanted to do. She touched his arm briefly.

'Come, Commander. I will get you some tea, and then we must resume the council.'

They moved away to the cooking place, where the pot had been set back on the coals, and Kira filled a cup and handed it to him.

'There's sweetfish and nutbread too,' she said. 'You should eat.'

Kest shook his head and sipped his tea, Kira watching him.

'Tell me what's happened,' she said.

'What makes you think something's happened?'

'Your face when you arrived.'

'It seems I'll have to be more careful when I'm around you, *Tremen Leader Kiraon*.'

'I'd rather you were honest.'

'I've always been that with you,' he said, his intense blue eyes boring into hers.

Kira's face warmed. 'I know. You've often told me how stubborn and irresponsible I am.'

Kest's face remained set and Kira sobered. 'Please tell me what's wrong.'

'Dakresh's son is missing.'

'Sener? But he was here before.'

Kest moved impatiently. 'Not him. His younger son, Bern.'

Kira's breath caught in her throat. Bern had pledged her he'd return to his longhouse in two days . . . and it was long past that now.

'Dakresh thought he was visiting friends at Kenclan,' Kest was saying, 'but he never arrived. Either there's been an accident or else . . .'

'You've been searching for him?'

Kest rubbed his face wearily. 'I've mainly been fighting Dakresh. The old fool's all for storming off to the Sentinels on his own. It's understandable I suppose; Sener and Bern are all he has left from three bondings. Both his first bondmate *and* Sener's mother died of fever, and Bern's mother died in childbirth.'

'Where's Dakresh now?' Kira forced herself to ask.

'He's agreed to stay at the Kenclan longhouse in return for me sending a patrol beyond the Kenclan Second Eight.'

Kira stared at the empty seat at the table. She should have insisted Bern go back immediately, she should have told Kest she'd seen him, she should have checked that he'd arrived home safely.

Kest's hand closed over hers. 'It might yet turn out well, Kira. Bern's only thirteen seasons. Boys of that age –'

'I saw him.'

'What?'

'When I was looking for the fireweed, I saw him.'

'Stinking heart-rot! Why didn't you tell me?'

'I don't know. I . . . he said he was going to Sarnia Cave. He said he'd been there before. He was excited . . . about the cave, about seeing new things in the octad . . .' Kira's words trailed off under Kest's furious gaze.

'I *told* you how dangerous it was. Do my words mean *nothing* to you?'

'He pledged me to return home in two days. I didn't see the harm . . .' said Kira miserably.

Kest's cup slammed down and Kira was aware of the sudden silence of the Clanleaders. Kest must have been too, for his voice dropped to a hiss.

'He's probably dead!'

There was a polite cough and Kira turned to see Miken at her elbow, his gaze flicking between them. 'The council's ready to resume,' he said.

Kira made her way numbly back to her seat. How could she possibly have accepted the leadership? She must have been mad! She had no sense of responsibility, no ability to think ahead, to see the consequences of her actions, to plan, to lead! She closed her eyes. Bern! Surely he couldn't have been taken? He was only thirteen, the same age as . . .

Kest was speaking and she opened her eyes again; thankful that the councillors were focused on him – all except Miken, whose questioning gaze was firmly on her. She unclenched her hands from the table's edge and struggled to compose herself.

'. . . made up of members of each clan,' Kest was saying. 'And so, the Renclan longhouse will be guarded by Protectors drawn from Renclansmen, and the Sherclan longhouse by Sherclan Protectors and so on. This will increase the speed of foraging expeditions, because clans know their own octads best. And the quicker they can forage, the less risk there will be of attack. Foraging times must also be considered. Both attacks we've suffered have been at the full moon and it makes sense for outsiders unfamiliar with Allogrenia. I suggest each longhouse stops foraging at the waxing half-moon and doesn't resume until after the waning half-moon. As a result, Clanleaders might have to consider extra storage at their respective longhouses. Protectors will also patrol the lands circled by the Second Eight. These patrols will be made up of men drawn from all the clans, and will be concentrated in the north-east octads of Kenclan and Barclan, which are nearest the Shargh lands.'

'What of healing?' asked Kemrick. 'Is that to continue in the Warens?'

'Yes. The Warens are easiest to guard and it will take some time to rebuild the Bough, *if* it is to be rebuilt.'

There was a stunned silence, Kemrick being the first to recover. 'But surely, Commander, the Bough *must* be rebuilt.'

'That, of course, is ultimately for the council to decide,' conceded Kest. 'But remember that we have no knowing of how long the Shargh attacks will last, or indeed why they've begun. The Shargh have occupied the lands to the north-east since Kasheron's time, but there are no records of attacks *within* Allogrenia until now. Why have they begun? We don't know. What's their purpose? That's also unclear.

'To burn the Bough, they passed the Kenclan and Barclan longhouses, both unguarded. If their intention were simply to kill it would've been easy to achieve. If their intentions were to kill healing, to kill our leadership, they have all but succeeded, but again we don't know why they would want to do so.'

Kira concentrated on sucking in air, Kest's words having torn away the fragile images of falzon bandages binding wounds. *If their intentions were to kill healing, to kill our leadership, they have all but succeeded.* Kemrick quietly passed her a cup of water, which she clutched with both hands, her eyes fixed sightlessly on its patterning.

'If healing must be hidden away, they've won anyway,' said Miken.

'They haven't "won" if healing survives,' broke in Sanden. 'Everything Commander Kest's said makes sense. What's the point of spending our strength in rebuilding the Bough if the cost of protecting it leaves the longhouses vulnerable? We've already lost many Tremen and if the attacks continue season after season, and we lose men each time, there'll be too few of us to protect the longhouses, and they too will fall. It will be the ending of Allogrenia.'

Kira's head filled with the memory of the Bough burning. It would be cold ash now and bereft of life, like the dead. The darkness rose again, as choking as the smoke, and she drove her nails into the table, using pain to keep it at bay. The council had degenerated into a series of noisy debates, competing voices ringing from the rafters: Miken was gesticulating at Sanden; Kemrick and Berendash were leaning across the table to better hear Marren; Ketten and Tenedren had their heads together.

Only Kest was silent, his gaze on her, her turmoil no doubt adding to his poor opinion. If only this meeting were done with and she was away from here, leaves under her feet, the cry of the mira kiraon in her ears. But there would be none of that if Kest had his way. Instead she'd be spending her time in the Warens, eating and sleeping in its darkness until the Shargh got bored with their killing and went away. And if they never got bored?

Why had they come? To kill healing? Or to kill the leadership? It was the same thing anyway. And Sanden was right. If they continued to lose men, then in the end, Allogrenia would be no more. Feseren and Sanaken dead in the first attack, twenty-three in the fires of the Bough, five more before the fireweed had cleansed the rot and twenty still lying wounded in the Warens, some who'd take another season to recover, some who'd never fully recover. With fewer than a thousand Tremen in the forest, it wouldn't take many more attacks before Allogrenia became indefensible. Kest had a plan, but it wasn't a solution, just an eking out of existence in an ever-tightening circle round each longhouse, while healing remained buried in the Warens. Nausea surged again, and she rose, desperate to stop the storming of bleakness.

'Councillors!'

Her voice was drowned by the hubbub. 'Councillors!' she bawled, surprising even herself as every face turned to her. 'Kindly resume your seats so I can hear from you in a more orderly fashion.' *By the 'green! She was sounding like her father.*

She waited for the last chair to grate back into place. 'I've heard Commander Kest's suggestions on how we should proceed from here; now I would like to hear yours. Clanleader Sanden, have you anything to add to what you've already said?'

Sanden shook his head. She turned to Kemrick. 'Then perhaps Clanleader Kemrick can share his thoughts, followed by the Leaders on his right, until all present have spoken.'

Kira resumed her seat and the attention of the gathering swung to Kemrick. Most of the Clanleaders were in agreement with Kest's plans, although some took a long time to say so and Kira had to suppress a sigh on several occasions. Kemrick, Miken and Marren seemed to be the only ones who had thought beyond the here and now, Kemrick expressing their views the most eloquently: *To live behind a ring of swords will be to live like those in the north. Was this to be the price of their survival, and if so, were they prepared to pay it?* Many of the leaders were dismissive of such a bleak picture, but it resonated deeply within Kira.

'I thank you all for your views,' she said after the last speaker had fallen silent, 'and for your patience in allowing each other to speak.' So far, so good. 'And I thank Commander Kest for giving us so much to think about.' What next? The thought of the Shargh terrified her, but she was not prepared to spend the rest of her life underground.

'I think Commander Kest's plan is a good one ... for the present. I will remain in the Warens until the last of the wounded are well enough to be moved to their longhouses to complete their recovery. I expect this to be in three or four moons, unless we receive more wounded. During this time I will record my Healer knowing, with the help of the other Healers. There will not be just one Herbal Sheaf made but several, and these will be stowed in different places in Allogrenia. There must never again come a day when all of what Kasheron bequeathed us is held by just one person.'

There were nods and murmurings of agreement.

'But,' she continued, 'I think Commander Kest's plan of Protectors guarding their own longhouses is a poor one, and I would ask Commander Kest to reconsider it.'

Kest's sympathetic expression vanished. 'On what basis? Do you disagree that foraging will be more effective if aided by Protectors familiar with their own octad?'

'No.'

Kest's eyebrows rose in exasperation. 'Then what?'

'Because of what the forests offer, the longhouses are almost a half-day's walk from each other,' said Kira.

'You tell us nothing new, Leader Kiraon,' broke in Ketten.

'You're saying we're already isolated from each other?' prompted Kemrick.

Kira nodded. 'Assigning Protectors to their own octads will increase this isolation. We will no longer be Tremen, we will be Barclansmen and Barclanswomen, or Renclansmen and Renclanswomen.'

'That hasn't happened so far,' pointed out Kest, 'and I see no reason why it should happen in the future. The longhouses have always been separated.'

'Yes, but there's been mixing. Protector training brings young men of all clans together, seeding friendships and visitations that continue long after training has finished. They meet the sisters of their friends, and acquaintances are renewed at the Feasts of Turning and Thanking, opportunities for mingling that will largely cease.'

'I can't agree with you, Tremen Leader Kiraon,' said Kest. 'There will still be opportunities for people to forage in each other's octads as they've always done, under protection of course.'

'If the Shargh attacks continue, people might be reluctant to take the risk,' pointed out Miken.

'Surely this is a small thing,' interrupted Ketten, 'if it keeps us safe.'

Kira drew a steadying breath. 'Clanleader Kemrick raised the question earlier of what it is to be Tremen. I think that's an important question. What are we prepared to do to survive? What are we prepared to change, to trade off, to give up?'

There were mutterings and a scrape of chairs as people moved restlessly. The councillors were weary of the debate, Kira realised, and wanted to vote now simply to end the council and start the journey back to their own longhouses. The sun was sinking. At the other end of the hall, a young Sherclanswoman was quietly lighting the lamps.

'It must be time for the division,' said Ketten, his eyes on the lamp-lighter.

'It doesn't need to be one thing or the other,' said Kemrick suddenly.

Ketten peered at him irritably. 'What mean you?'

'As long as there were Protectors from their own octad guarding, *and* some from other octads, both Commander Kest's and Tremen Leader Kiraon's concerns would be met. Would they not?' He looked at Kest and Kira in turn.

Kira and Kest nodded.

'Praise the 'green,' muttered Ketten.

'Are we agreed, then, that for the next few moons, Protectors will be deployed as outlined by Commander Kest, but with mixed groups assigned to each longhouse, and that I will ensure that our healing-knowing is recorded once more?' asked Kira.

There was a chorus of assent.

'Then there is no need of a division?' added Kira, her eyes on Ketten.

'No division, Leader, please, no division,' said Ketten with a broad smile.

34

The world in the Warens was like a fractured version of the world above, rearranged in the wrong order. Night and day blended into an even grey, heat and cold became clammy warmth, sounds from nearby caverns were muffled while those from further away amplified.

Sitting at her table, Kira's senses felt dulled by the endless tedium and the repetitiveness of her task. Yawning, she set down her pen and stretched, the scratch of Tresen's pen continuing. He looked like a hanawey hovering over its prey, clean sheets of patchet paper scattered to one side, neat stacks of Writings on the other. What must be recorded seemed endless. Findings and gatherings, preparations and treatments; the signs and symptoms of fevers and chills, breaks and sprains, cuts, burns, childbirth, old age; knocks to the head; falls . . . the lists went on and on, written in Tremen *and* Onespeak.

She'd started with fireweed: the place and manner of its growth, its gathering, preparation and ministering. *Fire with flatswords brings the bane, fire without brings life again.* Fire was the fever brought on by whatever the Shargh put on their flatswords, and fire *without* was the fevered heat that came *without* flatswords, heat that came from the fireweed, which burned the flatswords' rot away. Never again would the meaning of the rhyme be lost, even if the Shargh killed every Healer in the Warens. But fireweed was just one herb in a list of hundreds.

She eased her head back and rubbed her neck. Pledging to record her knowing while sitting in a longhouse filled with sunlight and birdsong was one thing, doing it day after day – or was it night after night – in the Warens was quite another. She knew too much! Since the age of four she'd been trailing around the Herbery, looking and listening. At seven she was out gathering beyond the First Eight. She couldn't even remember when she'd first begun reading the Herbal Sheaf or felt broken bones come together under her fingers. The knowing seemed always to have been there, and now it must all be recorded.

But it was no use grumbling; she owed her understanding to the Healers who'd come before, and now she must preserve it for those who followed, no matter how wearisome the task. Picking up her cup, she gulped down the tepid water, grimacing and wiping her mouth. Why did the Warens' water taste so different to the Drinkwater? It was almost as if it had distilled the mustiness from the walls.

Tresen's hand moved from ink pot to paper, ink pot to paper, with mesmerising regularity. Kira sighed. At least they only had one copy to do, for Arlen and Paterek were busy in one of the storage rooms transcribing their Writings into others. And it would be easier soon, for there'd be fewer wounded to care for and more time to write. Two of the wounded had already been taken back to their longhouses under escort, and in the next few days another couple would be ready to leave. By late summer, the training room should be empty, *providing* there were no more attacks, and she would be free to leave the Warens, *providing* Kest allowed it. Her fingers drummed the table.

'I've almost finished the gathering sites for sorren and annin,' said Tresen. 'Do you want me to start on the mints next?'

'Yes,' said Kira vaguely, her thoughts still on Kest. 'Icemint, bluemint, silvermint, and can you include silversalve? It's similar in habit and use.'

Tresen nodded, his hand resuming its journeying.

Was Kest back yet? she wondered. It must be five nights since the council, no, probably six. If Kest were back, he hadn't deigned to visit her, which meant that Bern was probably safely ensconced in his longhouse enduring no more than Dakresh's wrath.

She rolled a stub of patchet paper along the table and gazed idly at the bundles of sorren, serewort and winterbloom stacked along the wall beside her bed. It was pointless deluding herself. If Kest *were* back, he would've come to see Kesilini, and no doubt taken the opportunity to give her another tongue-lashing over Bern. She crushed the paper under her fingers. Kest's absence could only mean that Bern hadn't been found – or Kest had come under attack. Why hadn't she insisted Bern go back immediately, or told Kest about seeing him?

Kenclan was north-easterly, and the moon must be nearly full again now, a dangerous time to be abroad, even for a patrol. Curse the Shargh! At the full moon she used to climb high into the always-green and look out over a canopy as silver as the seas of the older tales. Instead of mighty seabirds rising and falling above its waves, there was the dart of hanaweys and frostkings, and the piercing cry of the mira kiraon. Now this, too, was lost to her.

A groan sounded and she rose and went to the curtain but Arlen was already there, water tinkling as he moistened a cloth and pressed it to a wounded man's face. The restless movements of the man stilled, and she turned back to the Writings. Where should the copies be stowed? In one of the longhouses perhaps, and here, and in the more obscure caverns?

She yawned again and rubbed her eyes, not knowing whether she was really tired or simply sick of sitting. The oil was low in the lamp, the cover full of silvermoths pit-pitting against it. One had fallen in and lay moving feebly on its surface. Lifting the cover, she hooked it out with her finger, but its wings were crushed and it lay where she left it. Silvermoths would be thick in the trees outside too, drawn by the moon. What wouldn't she give to dash along the Drinkwater Path, to feel the dawn air bright against her face, to smell the wet leaf-fall and leaves and berries?

Tresen's pen had finally fallen silent and he was looking at her.

'Why don't you go to bed? You've done enough for the day,' she said to him.

His skin was sallow in the lamplight, his eyes hollow. He'd lost weight *and* his smile since he'd been confined here. He'd always been quick to tease, to joke, to laugh, but not anymore.

'You're looking pale, Tresen,' continued Kira. 'You should go back to your longhouse for a while. Tenerini hasn't seen you since this began, or Mikini. They must be missing you and you them. And what of Seri?'

'Seri's safe in her own longhouse, which is the best place for her. And it wouldn't be fair to leave you to do this on your own.'

'Arlen and Paterek can help,' said Kira.

'They don't know enough Onespeak.' Tresen recapped the ink pot and wiped his hands. 'Besides, I'm not going till you can come; it's your longhouse too, remember. Tenerini's always wanted another daughter.' He paused, and took her hand. 'And I another sister.'

'Your mother's been kind to me,' she said softly, 'and if I wasn't Leader I'd come. But I am Leader and that changes everything.'

'No Leader has to do everything on their own,' said Tresen, tightening his grip. 'You can . . .'

A rhythmic thump sounded, faint at first, growing rapidly louder, and they fell silent. The noise drew closer, seeming to pause outside the training room. Tresen half rose from his seat, then the noise passed on, receding into silence. Kira's breath hissed and Tresen slumped back.

'No more wounded, at least not yet. But the moon's waxing and Kest's still beyond the Third Eight.'

303

Kira jerked round. 'The Third Eight! How know you this?'

'Penedrin told me. You knew Dakresh's son was still missing?' said Tresen, busy gathering the unused patchet paper into a pile.

Kira nodded dumbly.

'Apparently he was sighted near Sarnia Cave, so Kest's gone looking. Personally, I doubt there's much hope of finding him; the octad's too big. It'd take a whole moon to search properly.' He pulled on his jacket and fastened it. 'Bern knew the dangers. He should've kept to his longhouse. His foolishness is risking many lives now.'

'He's only thirteen!'

'Old enough to know better. There are twenty-one men in a patrol, Kira, that's twenty-one who might be wounded or killed, and that's twenty-one who won't be there to protect their longhouses.'

'Are you saying they shouldn't look for him?'

'We lost the equivalent of a patrol – either dead or wounded – in the attack on the Bough. If that happens every full moon how long do you think we can last? Do the sums, Kira – I have.'

'Every life's important, Tresen!'

'Do you think I don't know that? Do you think . . .' He stopped, forcing a weary smile. 'I don't want to argue with you, Kira. I'm going to take your advice and get some sleep, and I suggest you do the same.' Unexpectedly, he leaned over and kissed her cheek. 'I wish you a good night, clanmate.'

The curtain fell back into place but Tresen's words remained. It was what Sanden had said at council, but Tresen had gone even further. He was suggesting having to trade one life for another, in this case, Bern's for the patrols'. She licked her dry lips and pushed the hair from her eyes. If Tresen were right, next time it mightn't be the life of a wayward boy but of a birthing woman that had to be sacrificed – Kira's own life and the lives of the patrol who must accompany her deemed worthier.

Surely it wouldn't come to that? Surely this time would pass? *And everything would go back to what it was before: summer mornings in the Herbery, the sound of Kandor's pipe?* The hope mocked her, bringing with it the unbearable, inescapable pain of Kandor's death. She curled up on her bed, cradling her head. Sleep brought no rest, just dreams of Kandor haloed in light as she'd dragged her hands from his, condemning him to death. She groaned, her thoughts going to the everest pouch in her pack, as they so often did these days. Half a leaf would bring a sleep of many days and a whole leaf send her to where Kandor now dwelt, a place empty of memory and pain. How she longed to go there. But she hadn't the right; she was the Leader, the holder of all healing, able to stop the deaths of other Kandors.

She pulled herself to her knees and then to her feet, stumbling back to the table and collapsing into her chair. Tremen and Onespeak, she thought numbly, and began to write.

Kest sat slumped against an espin, staring up at the moon. He was filthy, his shirt stiff with dried sweat, his hands gouged black with digging. Half of his patrol was secreted among the trees, the rest wrapped carelessly in their sleeping-sheets, too shocked by what they'd seen to set camp properly. Many had simply crawled into their sheets without bothering to eat, and he hadn't eaten either, the stench of putrefying flesh too strong in his nostrils.

Bern had been dead for many days, though even a couple in the summer heat would have been enough. But heat alone hadn't caused the grotesque disfigurement that had sickened them on finding him; Bern hadn't died from a single wound but from many. His death had been agonising. Kest unclipped his waterskin and took a long, slow swig. The simplest explanation was that the Shargh were barbarous, that they'd chanced upon a lone boy and enjoyed some sport. But that left too many things unexplained. The line of slashed trees penetrating to the Second Eight, where they'd come upon Bern's pack; the single boot they'd found as they'd followed the slashed and trampled growth north-east, and Bern's body dumped like refuse near the Sentinels. Why hadn't the Shargh killed him where they'd captured him?

Kest stowed his waterskin and hauled himself to his feet, picking his way between his men to the deeper darkness of the alwaysgreen. There was someone there, keeping vigil: Nandrin, Bern's clanmate. He rose as Kest approached, but Kest waved him back, settling beside him. The darkness hid the new-turned earth but the air told of where they'd cut the turf with their swords, and dug out a resting place between the roots with sticks and hands. Patrols didn't carry shovels and he wondered whether that was just one of many changes he'd have to make.

Nandrin sat with his hands hanging slackly between his knees. Kest glanced at the silent Protector next to him and at the moon-stippled shapes of his men resting under the trees.

'I hope Clanleader Dakresh forgives us for not bringing Bern home,' he said softly.

Nandrin roused, his face like a skull in the moonlight. 'At least he's safe now. The alwaysgreen Shelters him.'

'But too distant for Dakresh to visit. I don't think his old bones will carry him this far.'

'No, nor his heart,' said Nandrin, his eyes dark pools. 'Who'd do this? Who'd do such a thing to a boy?'

'People who worship death, not life.'

'Outsiders,' spat Nandrin. 'Northerners; murderers!'

The Shargh weren't Northerners, but Kest let it go, glad Nandrin was talking. Not like Kira, who'd never spoken her grief. Why did he think of her now, when so much else crowded his head?

Nandrin wiped his sleeve across his face. 'The roots have taken him,' he said hoarsely.

Kest gripped his arm. 'The tree grown strong from him, the new leaves spun from him.'

'The wind sung songs of him . . .' Nandrin choked to a stop.

'His story told,' finished Kest quietly.

As if in answer, a breeze riffled the canopy, and the alwaysgreen sighed. Kest stood. 'We leave at dawn, Nandrin; time to get some sleep.'

Kest watched Nandrin crawl into his sleeping-sheet but he didn't go to his own. He was weary, but not inclined to sleep. The bright fragments of light on the leaf litter attested to the moon's near fullness and, to make matters worse, the forest surrounding the alwaysgreen was dense with shadow. A waxing moon and heavy cover. It would suit the Shargh well. Settling with his back to a tree, he sharpened his sword.

35

In the highest sorcha on the slope, Palansa sat on the hide of rulership surveying the assembled warriors. Her fingers locked, bone against bone and greasy with sweat, as the warriors' eyes flicked over her.

Arkendrin had positioned himself directly in front, with Irdodun and Urpalin at each side. Now and again he murmured to Irdodun, and the lesser man smirked, but Arkendrin's eyes never left her.

Palansa shifted her attention to Irdodun. The man was like the stink-beetles that burrowed about in ebis droppings. Despite their grand and intricate tunnels, all they'd ever be were stink-beetles in gobs of dung. She smiled contemptuously and Irdodun dropped his eyes. Her confidence surged as if she'd struck the first blow. To her side, Tarkenda nodded discreetly and Palansa cleared her throat, waiting till the rumble of conversation ceased.

'This Speak I call on behalf of my unborn son, who, when he greets the day, will be the first-born son of Erboran himself, the first-born son of Ergardrin, continuing the line of rulership the Sky

Chiefs bequeathed us. I call this Speak because a matter of great importance has arisen, a matter that affects us all.' Palansa slowly moved her gaze from one warrior to another as she spoke, passing over her allies, Ormadon and Irsulalin and their kin, in the same unhurried way she passed over Arkendrin and Irdodun.

'The Sky Chiefs honour us with life and they take us home at its ending, so that we might dwell forever in their realm. In return, we honour them,' she said, then paused, bringing her attention back to Irdodun. 'Yet some among you besmirch that honour by hunting and spilling blood during the time the Sky Chiefs have decreed that no blood should be spilt. Irdodun, I call upon you to explain your dishonour.'

'I have no Voice, Chief-wife.'

'I grant you one for this occasion,' said Palansa.

'You cannot do that, Chief-wife, without dishonouring those you claim to honour,' said Arkendrin. 'I must speak on Irdodun's behalf, for it is I who led the hunt . . . as you well know.'

Tarkenda had warned Palansa that Irdodun couldn't speak, but she'd wanted to avoid Arkendrin. Now she kept her face impassive, resisting the urge to look back at Tarkenda as Arkendrin raised his hands theatrically.

'We teeter on the brink of our own destruction,' he began. 'Do we plunge to our doom, or do we take back what is rightfully ours? Look around you; the lands are thirsty, the pastures dying. The ebi die too, and their mothers must eat the stone-trees to keep flesh over their bones. The Grenwah and Shunawah sink and the Thanawah blooms red. Soon sickness will stalk the Grounds. The highest sorcha lies empty of Chief, although one day it might house a squalling babe.'

He got to his feet, breaking convention. 'What use is a suckling while in the fetid air of the south-western treelands, the gold-eyed creature of the Last Telling roams, plotting our destruction? Is it dishonour to hunt it? Is it dishonour to seek to destroy that which

309

will destroy us? I am a Shargh warrior! Ordorin's blood runs in my veins *too*! I, *too*, am the seed of the warrior the Last Teller chose above all others to preserve the Sky Chiefs' warning!

'Should I sit idly in my sorcha while the gold-eyed creature prospers? Should I turn my back on my people? The Sky Chiefs demand honour, yes, but they gave us spears and swords and tesat to rot the wounds of our enemies. They gave us warning through the Last Telling and the ability and strength to bring it undone. If I have dishonoured the Sky Chiefs, then in due time I will beg their pardon, but there are none here to whom I need palm my forehead.'

There was a brief silence, followed by a rising tide of muttering. Palansa's mind raced. The insult was deliberate, the challenge to her authority obvious. She couldn't call on the warriors present to defend an unborn child; an unborn child was women's business, unreal to them until born. But Arkendrin was real, chest puffed, eyes shining, painting pictures of glory that stirred their blood. Palansa stared down at Erboran's sword and spears lying before her. Why had the Sky Chiefs left her to fight this battle?

Tarkenda's voice boomed. 'Sit, Arkendrin. You insult all present by standing.'

It was a mother's rebuke, delivered to a wayward son, not an order delivered with the authority of a Chief. With a mocking smile, Arkendrin slowly sat. The exchanges died away and attention drifted back to Palansa.

'The Sky Chiefs have never left us without a Chief,' said Palansa with deliberate quietness. She couldn't out-bluster Arkendrin and wouldn't try. 'And always it's been the first-born son of a first-born son. Even when we roamed far beyond the Braghan Mountains, no second-born son has ever been Chief.'

Arkendrin's sneer now had a set quality, but Palansa felt no satisfaction. She would need to win more than a game of words if she were to protect her child. 'In this the Sky Chiefs have held true, and we have honoured them for it. Indeed, it has been our willingness to grant the Sky Chiefs their due that has allowed Arkendrin to boast that he need palm his forehead to no one, for *he* was but a babe when his own father was called home. There were those then who argued, as Arkendrin does now, that the Shargh should look elsewhere for a Chief, that Ordorin's bloodline should be broken.

'But the Sky Chiefs' wishes were respected, and in the season of their choosing, Erboran took the circlet of Chiefship and ruled wisely and well, as the Sky Chiefs themselves intended.'

Palansa paused. The warriors were quiet but she sensed they were unconvinced, her words having soothed the passions Arkendrin had roused, but not removed their cause. For what Arkendrin had said was true: the ebi *were* dying; the Thanawah's waters *were* running red. Urpalin muttered to the warrior next to him, and someone else whispered.

'I thank Arkendrin for using his Voice to bring to all our minds the troubles presently afflicting us,' she said hurriedly, then stopped, as if lending weight to what she would say next. In truth, her mind had gone blank. The child flipped inside her, pummelling her ribs as if reminding her of what she was fighting for and she flattened her palm against her belly, reassuring him.

'Life is hard now, I do not pretend it is other, but the Sky Chiefs have given us many gifts, and one of them is strength. Our warriors are mighty hunters, able to run longer than the sun's course across the sky and to track wolves when only the marwing sees their trail. Yet strength is a thing that must be tested, for without adversity it withers, becoming weakness.' She steadied, knowing what to say now.

'In withholding the rain, the Sky Chiefs test our strength. Are we to crumple before such testing? Are we to dishonour them by hunting that which should not be hunted until after the next moon and the mourning period of Chief Erboran is over? Is it too long for us to wait? Is it too much for them to ask of us? Are we not loyal enough? Are we not strong enough?'

There was absolute silence, then one of the younger warriors spoke. 'I am willing to wait. I, who have every reason to want the creature dead, will honour the Sky Chiefs.'

It was Urgasen, Urgundin's son, seated not with Arkendrin and his followers, nor with Ursulalin and Ormadon, but between. Urgasen had taken his father's place high on the spur, but he was young, his Voice untried. Palansa held her breath. There was a soft ripple of approval, growing to louder calls of agreement.

Palansa exhaled; she avoided looking at Arkendrin or appearing to gloat. The Shargh were with her for the present, and Arkendrin daren't gainsay them. She'd won more precious time for her son. And even when Arkendrin could hunt again, there was no guarantee he would find the creature quickly.

The assembled Shargh were moving restlessly, some even beginning to rise, and she spoke the words of ending quickly, watching them file out. Even after the last of them was long gone, she remained seated, simply enjoying the relief of knowing the Speak was over with. It was Tarkenda who struggled first to her feet, then helped her rise.

'We're a fine pair,' she grunted. 'One gnarled with old-man's ache, the other carrying the woman's burden.'

'Not a burden,' said Palansa, smoothing down her skirt, 'but a . . .' The flap flipped open and Ormadon appeared, '. . . blessing,' she finished. She rolled up the hide of rulership and Ormadon helped her stow it under the bed, then he collected Erboran's spears and leaned them against the wall next to Erboran's flatsword. Palansa lifted the circlet from her head and rubbed her sweaty brow.

'You spoke well, Chief-wife,' said Ormadon.

'He hates me for it,' said Palansa, taking a seat next to Tarkenda.

'His hatred is not new.'

Ormadon settled opposite, taking the bowl of water Tarkenda poured for him. 'You've succeeded in making the Shargh consider the Sky Chiefs, rather than thinking of him. That's good. It's dangerous to make the Shargh choose between you and Arkendrin, better to make them choose between honouring or not honouring the Sky Chiefs.'

'I thought Arkendrin would win the argument over hunting the thing of the Telling,' admitted Tarkenda, 'and that might have been enough. It would have kept him away from here, away from us. I hadn't thought of doing what you've done.'

'The result is the same,' said Palansa, sipping her water. 'It gives us more time.'

'Not as long as you think,' said Ormadon. 'Arkendrin knows much about the creature now. He knows she's called "owl", a *kiraon* in the treemen's speech, and he knows she's been weakened by her blood-ties being killed. He knows she hides in holes under the trees.'

Palansa paled. 'Irason,' she breathed. 'They must've captured a treeman so that Irason could read his tongue.'

Ormadon nodded. 'Irdodun puts it about that the hunt is now simple, and that soon the creature's body will be laid out on the spur for all to see. Then Arkendrin will take his rightful place as Chief.'

'He'll be free to do as he wants then,' said Palansa bitterly. The child lurched and quivered inside her and her eyes went to Erboran's flatsword. She couldn't run in her present state, even if there were somewhere to run to.

'He's filling the warriors' heads with grand schemes of joining with the Weshargh and Soushargh again and taking back the land north of the Braghans,' Ormadon continued. 'He wants to be Chief of all the tracts we once wandered.'

'He would lead us into a river of blood,' said Tarkenda. 'Does he imagine those lands are ours for the taking? That the Northerners will simply hand them over? The fighting would be worse than even the Older Days.'

Palansa's startled eyes went to hers but Tarkenda ignored her, keeping her attention on Ormadon.

'Arkendrin's tongue has always outpaced his legs,' said Ormadon, rising. 'I've heard from others that Urpalin was too ready with the dagger, and that the treeman man died before they found out where

313

the holes were. It's hard to tell mawkbird from marwing when Arkendrin's people talk, but knowing Urpalin, it's likely.'

'If that's true, it could take them many moons to find where she hides,' said Palansa hopefully.

Ormadon shrugged. 'Whatever the truth, Arkendrin's caught here until the next moon.' He moved to the door. 'Don't be alone, Chief-wife,' he said, and ducked through the flap.

'Will your vision come true?' demanded Palansa of Tarkenda, scarcely waiting for the flap to still. 'Is my son to be killed and Arkendrin take us north?'

'I've told you before that it's unclear.'

'Unclear, unclear!' Palansa paced up and down the sorcha. 'What's the point of having a vision that cannot be read?'

'Ask the Sky Chiefs,' said Tarkenda dryly.

Palansa said nothing and Tarkenda sighed. 'You've done well today, better than I dared hope.'

Palansa turned on her, her eyes as dark as night. 'Will it be enough?'

'That, too, is with the Sky Chiefs.'

36

Kest rinsed the stubble from his face and pushed the stub of clear-root back into his pack. He was clean now and, thanks to the clear-root, free of the itching half-beard. He'd slept in a bed last night as well, even if it wasn't his own.

Despite the awful trip via Dakresh's longhouse he felt rested for the first time in many days, and he had to admit that Miken had been right in insisting he stay the night rather than going straight to the Warens. *You falling ill from exhaustion will aid no one*, Miken had said. He must remember to use that argument on Kira, he thought, as he made his way down the passageway to the hall. He scanned the trees through the open windows as he went, seeing nothing amiss, and wondering what the returning patrols would report.

The hall was surprisingly crowded considering how early it was, children laughing as they rolled sour-ripe along the tables to each other, adults with heads close in conversation. This was what he'd missed most in the Warens; not just the soft air and chimes, but the sounds of normalcy, of happiness.

Miken beckoned him from further down the hall, and as he

moved between the tables a group of Protectors rose hurriedly and Kashclansmen and women swivelled, noticing him for the first time. He nodded and waved the Protectors back to their seats. Miken had poured him a cup of thornyflower tea and was busy spreading riddleberry jam onto nutbread for him.

'I've been thinking on what we spoke of last night,' said Miken softly, passing him the bread. 'I think you're right. The Shargh probably tortured Bern until he told them everything he knew of Kira. The question is, how much did he know?'

'She told me she'd seen him, that's all,' said Kest, taking a bite of his bread. And he'd been too angry to ask any questions; a bad mistake.

'She told you at the Clancouncil?'

Kest nodded, recalling with irritation that Miken had interrupted their argument.

'Kira's dear to me,' said Miken, noting his antagonism, 'not just because she's Kashclan, but because she's spent much of her growing here.' His gaze went to Tenerini, now taking her breakfast with some of the other women and his expression gentled.

'We would have taken her as a daughter if Maxen had allowed it.' He cleared his throat and refilled Kest's cup. 'We would still take her.'

'If we're right, she'd draw the Shargh to you,' said Kest, putting his breakfast aside. 'It would risk everyone.'

'I know. It's best she stays where she is . . . for the time being. And even the Warens might not be safe, especially at the full moon,' said Miken. He paused. 'Will you tell Kira about Bern?'

'As Leader, she has a right to know.'

Miken set down his cup. 'Will you tell her what we suspect about his death?'

'I don't know.' The answer was honest but Kest felt his face warm.

'As Commander, it is of course your decision, but forgive me now if I speak as someone who knows Kira well. She's stubborn, as you've probably discovered, and single-minded in her passion for healing, necessary qualities in a Leader and, no doubt, why the Clanleaders agreed to appoint her. But what is less obvious is her lack of self-interest.'

'Surely that is a good quality in a Leader, unlike her recklessness . . .' Kest faltered, recalling too late that Miken was Kashclan.

Miken nodded, taking no insult. 'Perhaps what I should have said is that Kira has no sense of self-preservation. She puts others first.'

'I would have thought that was a good quality in a Leader too.'

'It is up to a point,' agreed Miken. 'But beyond that it's destructive. If Kira believes she's the reason for the Shargh attacks, the reason for Tremen suffering . . .'

Kest gulped his tea, scalding his throat. 'Are you saying she'd offer herself up to the Shargh to protect the Tremen?' The thought was appalling and difficult to believe, in spite of what he knew of Kira.

'Not offer herself up in the way you mean, although it could amount to the same thing.' Miken leaned forward. 'Kira lived and breathed for Kandor. Into him she poured all the love her mother didn't live to give her and her father wouldn't. Now that Kandor's gone, there's nothing to hold her.'

'She has affection for Tresen,' pointed out Kest, struggling with what Miken was saying.

'That's constrained by clan-tie,' said Miken dismissively. 'Is there no one in the Warens she's shown interest in?' he asked, eyeing Kest speculatively.

Kest gaped. Was Miken suggesting that Kira could only be saved by bonding? *With him*? The idea was startling, but not without its attractions.

'Tresen, Werem, Paterek and Arlen are the only men who spend any time at all with her,' said Kest, putting the idea aside. 'And they're all Kashclan. She heals and prepares pastes and potions and records her knowing largely on her own. Eating and sleeping she does only when forced,' he added dryly. The Kashclan leader's face remained heavy with worry.

'I won't tell Kira what we suspect about Bern's death,' said Kest, coming to a decision. 'Instead, I'll emphasise the danger she'll put Protectors in if she acts recklessly and remind her how essential her Healer skill is to all our futures. If, as you say, she puts others before herself, that should be enough.'

'For the present,' said Miken, dourly.

Kira stomped around the bed, taking out her frustration on the cavern floor. She'd accorded Tresen the *courtesy* of informing him where she was going, *as a Leader should*, and now all she was getting for her trouble was an argument.

'I don't think you should be going so far into the Warens on your own, and neither does Kest or else he wouldn't have left that advice with Protector Leader Pekrash.'

'The Protectors won't let me leave the Warens, and now *you're* saying I shouldn't leave the training rooms. Maybe I should just sit here and not move. Would that make you happy, Tresen?'

'I never said that and neither did Protector Leader Pekrash. It's advice, that's all. If you go off and get lost, then Protectors will have to search for you instead of protecting the longhouses.'

'Why in the 'green would I get lost? I've been to the Storage Cavern and back before.'

'Kest brought you back last time.'

'We came back together!' exclaimed Kira, plonking herself down on the bed. 'I might go anyway. The Warens don't command the Bough.'

Tresen's eyes flashed. 'That sounds like something worthy of your father!'

Kira faltered as the images of smoke and flames filled her head, then the mattress rustled as Tresen settled beside her and pulled her close. His arms were warm and she shut her eyes.

'I'm sorry. I didn't have the right to say that.'

'Maybe not,' she muttered, 'but it's true.'

He smoothed the hair from her face. 'Kira –'

Then the curtain was flicked back and Tresen sprang to his feet. Kest stared at them, nonplussed. If it had been any other couple he would have sworn they were courting.

'Tremen Leader Kiraon, I was looking for you,' he said tightly, his eyes flicking between her and the stiffly standing Protector.

'Well, you've found me,' said Kira, barely looking at him.

Kest turned to Tresen. 'I've spent the last night in your long-house, Protector. All's well there and Kashclanswoman Tenerini sends you some clothing, also some for you Tremen Leader Kiraon. I've left it in the outer cavern.'

'I thank you, Commander,' said Tresen.

Kest dismissed him with a nod. Tresen glanced to Kira as he left, something indecipherable passing between them, making Kest wonder again if he'd stumbled into something he oughtn't.

'We need to speak,' said Kest.

Kira gestured to the chair next to the bed, but Kest shook his head; a bedroom was hardly an appropriate meeting place.

'Where else in this cage would you suggest?' she said, chin tilted, her eyes flashing gold. He'd thought they'd developed a level of accord but perhaps he was wrong.

'We can speak where you prepare the herbs if you like,' said Kest.

'No, we'll speak outside.' She scrambled to her feet, standing like a Protector about to start sword practice.

'As you wish.'

'You're letting me go outside?'

'As Tremen Leader, you're free to go wherever you like.'

Her face softened and her eyes flashed to gold, the change astonishing, then she moved past him and he followed her through the wounded and out into the tunnel. From the back she looked

319

like a child and he wondered how anyone so slight could hold such power.

'It's a trick really, isn't it Commander?' she said, as they walked. 'I can only go where it's *responsible* to go, where I don't risk anyone else.'

'You can describe it how you wish, Tremen Leader. If it's a trick then I'm caught in it too. We're both obliged to put the Tremen before our personal wishes.'

There was an echo of marching feet and he stopped and pulled her close to the wall as shadows snaked towards them. A patrol led by Merenor appeared through the murk. He looked tired and pleased to be back, but the news was as Kest hoped: no slashed trees and no sign of Shargh, despite the nearness to the full moon. Merenor finished his brief report and Kest clapped him on the back.

'Where have they come from?' asked Kira, as the footfalls faded into the darkness.

'Renclan Octad.'

'Renclan? I thought you were focusing your patrols to the north-east.'

'Not all.'

The map showed two openings in Kenclan and one in Renclan, but he already knew from his journey through the Warens with Kira, that the map wasn't totally accurate. The Renclan and Kenclan octads shared similar stone, the type that had produced the Sarnia Cave and underground streams in Kenclan. It was likely that the stone also formed more openings in Renclan. Having Protectors there might dissuade the Shargh from searching for a way in. Then again, the presence of Protectors might suggest that there was something *worth* searching for.

'You have bad news for me,' said Kira.

'What makes you think that?'

'Your face.'

320

'I was thinking of something else,' said Kest, mentally cursing his lapse. It was the second time she'd read him like a sheaf.

'So the news is good?'

By the 'green, she was persistent. 'We will speak of it outside, as you requested, Tremen Leader.'

Kira flicked back her braid and stomped across the last of the caverns, a figure suddenly stepping from the shadows and making her jump. Only a Protector, praise be to the alwaysgreen, obviously on entrance-guarding duty. Kest spoke to him quickly issuing some quiet commands. How sure he was of himself. He was growing into his role of Commander more quickly than she was adapting to being Leader. Then again, he'd been a Protector Leader first, whereas she'd only gathered.

The sounds of the forest intruded and Kira jiggled impatiently behind Kest as he edged around Nogren, following him quickly, then coming to a stop. It was dusk. For some reason she'd assumed it would be morning, like when she'd journeyed to the Clancouncil. She'd kept the sights and smells and sounds of that day in her head, savouring and replaying them all through the long days of writing, and she'd expected to experience them now.

'You seem disappointed, Tremen Leader.'

His tone was mocking and she wondered whether he was still smarting from her less-than-warm welcome earlier.

'The forest never disappoints me, Commander. Even as day dies, the dew is born and silvermoths rouse. Dusk is hunting time for the mira kiraon, and the signal for stickspiders to work their webs.' She ran her hand over Nogren's mighty trunk peering up into the branches. 'When the moon rises, the canopy turns silver. Have you ever climbed to the top of an alwaysgreen, Commander, and watched the canopy ripple like a vast silver ocean?'

'Not lately.'

'Shall we climb together?'

'Not this night.'

'You disappoint me, Commander. It seems I must climb alone.'

'We came to speak!'

'We can do so at the top of Nogren.'

Kest caught her arm. 'You're being foolish, Tremen Leader.'

'As long as I'm not being irresponsible, it doesn't matter.' She looked down at his hand on her arm. 'I'm a bit confused, Commander. If I were to call for help now, would the Protectors aid me or you?'

Kest swore and dropped his hand. 'What has got into you Kira? I thought at council that you'd stopped acting like a child.'

'Climb with me, Kest. I need to remember what I'm fighting for.'

Her eyes were burning gold, but there was no anger, just a strange combination of power and vulnerability. Swearing again, he unlaced his scabbard and tossed it at the base of the tree. 'I must be mad contemplating doing this.'

Kira was already swinging herself up into the lower branches, going quickly hand over hand, barely hesitating, never slipping. He went far more slowly, finding the spice of the tree overpowering and the foliage closer to the trunk than he remembered, or maybe it was just that he was a lot bigger.

'Take care with the thinner branches,' he panted. They were already a considerable way up, Kira barely visible above him in the thickening dusk. The return climb would be in complete darkness, he realised suddenly. He *was* mad.

Her voice floated down. 'Don't worry. No alwaysgreen has ever broken under a Kashclan climber.'

'I'm Morclan.'

'I'm sure they love Morclan too.'

He grinned in spite of himself. The bole began to taper, then sway, and he had to force himself not to look down.

'This is far enough,' he yelled.

'Only a little further.'

Finally he swung himself up to where she was waiting.

'Put your back like this, and brace your feet there,' she said, pointing.

Kest manoeuvred himself gingerly into place but she didn't settle beside him.

'I need to create a window,' she said. She stood up and Kest's heart jolted.

'Kira!'

She turned and he saw the flash of her teeth. 'One slip and I become my namesake, except I can't fly.'

Kest was too far away to stop her and was forced to watch her step out along the bough and weave the foliage into an opening. Then she came nimbly back, taking a seat on a branch slightly above him.

'Imagine the mighty oceans of the north,' she related. 'There our forebears landed, with the running horses of the far lands and, coming south, took the many-treed mountains and the plains for their own. And there they lived, loving both the forests and the plains, the speed of the running horse and the slow growth of herbs, until . . .' She shrugged. 'Terak's lust for power tore them apart, and broke the first Kiraon's heart.'

'That was an act of stupidity,' gritted Kest, his neck slicked in cold sweat.

'Kasheron would have been insulted to hear you describe his words thus.'

'I speak of your stupidity, not his. Why do you court death?'

'Perhaps death courts me. Tell me your news, Commander.'

'Bern is dead.'

'Ah.' She was staring out over the treetops, just enough daylight left to sheen her face. 'Another I have killed.'

'You're a fool if you believe that. Bern told his father one thing and did another. He brought about his own death.'

'No boy of thirteen brings about his own death!'

Kest grimaced. Kandor was always there between Kira and those who sought to comfort her. How could the dead have so much power?

'You're right,' he conceded. 'In the past, it wouldn't have mattered. A boy who loves to wander, who tells his father he's going to his friend's longhouse and goes elsewhere. But those days are gone.'

A breeze woke and the branch he was sitting on swayed gently. It would have been pleasant if he hadn't been so far off the ground.

'We cannot survive this, Kest.'

'They're hardly the words of a Leader,' he said, managing to keep his face impassive.

'Tell me what I say is untrue . . . Commander.'

He shrugged. 'We don't know the Shargh's intent. They might tire of their sport and leave us in peace.'

'I've read many things in my search for fireweed, Kest. The Shargh are hunters, following their prey on foot for days on end. They do not give up until they've killed whatever it is they seek.' Kest could think of nothing to say that wouldn't be a lie.

'Was it you who found Bern?' she asked.

Kest braced himself for the questioning to come. 'My patrol.'

'Where was he?'

'Near the Kenclan Sentinel.' Now she would ask how he came to be so far from the Sarnia Cave. The wind stirred again and the tree sighed.

'Did they cut his throat, too?'

Kandor again; he should be grateful. 'No . . . he was stabbed.'

She said nothing for a long time and Kest began to feel cold. His shirt was damp under his jerkin, and the breeze had freshened. 'Time to go.'

'I want to wait for moonrise.'

'Kira . . .'

'Please!'

Kest sighed. 'As you wish.'

She said nothing more, and in the silence that followed he became aware of myriad small sounds: the heart of the tree creaking, the whisper of leaves, the scratching of some small creature above his head. In the distance, a bird gave voice, then another, closer, wings scything the air.

'The hanawey hunts,' she said softly.

'And a frostking?'

'Perhaps. It sounded more like a hanawey hatchling. Often the parent bird and its young hunt together.'

'We see a lot of hanaweys on patrol. They're not as striking as the frostking, but quicker in flight. Which do you like best?'

'Neither.'

'Ah, let me guess. You favour the gold-eyed mira kiraon.'

'Yes, but not for its eyes, for its freedom.'

Kest peered at her, the moon at last lighting her face. 'Is it so bad in the Warens?'

'Kasheron never intended people to live there. He built the Bough to house healing and the longhouses; the Warens were only for storage and training.' She moved restlessly and her branch rattled and creaked. 'I've finished the Writings, and Arlen and Paterek are more than halfway through the other copies. Almost half the wounded have now gone back to their longhouses too. I pledged the council to remain only until they're all gone. I understand that the Bough can't be rebuilt for the present, Kest, but I won't live my life in the Warens.'

Tendrils of moonlight were drifting through the leaves, painting her hair and skin silver.

'You will be easier to protect, *as Leader*, if you remain there,' he said carefully.

'The Leader should endure the same hardships as the rest of the Tremen. I can hardly claim Leadership if I skulk underground.'

'You wouldn't be skulking, you'd be keeping healing safe and lessening the risk to those who must protect it.'

Kira's branch jerked up and down. 'I've recorded my knowing and copies will be hidden around Allogrenia. Tresen or even Arlen or

Paterek could now heal as I do. Healing is safe, irrespective of what happens to me.'

'You know that's not true. For one thing, no one else can take pain.' There was a short silence. 'I'm taking Tresen back on patrol,' said Kest suddenly, taking the opportunity to change the conversation's direction. 'It's time he resumed his training, and as you say, the need for healing is less now.'

Kira was silent but Kest pretended not to notice. He needed every man he could get for the patrols, but that wasn't the only reason he wanted Tresen out of the Warens. He knew of no instances where clanmates had defied their clan-ties to be together, but it could happen . . . if the circumstances were right.

'Miken will be glad to have his son back in his longhouse too,' he added. 'I know he's been missed there.'

'Yes, he's greatly loved.'

Kira's voice was sad, but Kest resisted the urge to reach out to her. His task was to keep her safe, both from breaking Tremen law and from the Shargh – at all costs. 'The moon's up,' he said, craning forward. 'Almost full. Very impressive.'

Kira was looking out over the trees too, but there was no pleasure in her face. 'It's a Shargh moon, a hunting moon,' she said, swinging herself down from the branch. 'Let us go.'

37

The Storage Cavern still elicited equal amounts of excitement and dread for Kira, no matter how many times she visited it. What else could be hidden in the shelves of Writings? Cures for the aching bones of the old? Concoctions to stop a babe from coming too early? Salves to replace the skin that flame peeled away like sweetchew bark? Or tales of the Shargh and the Terak Kutan, and other scarcely guessed-at barbaric peoples? Searching through it was like looking for glitterstones in the Drinkwater. Each Writing contained a potential treasure waiting to be extricated from the detritus of records upon records upon records.

But at least she had time to look now, and no one to ask leave of. The only good thing that had come from Kest ordering Tresen back to his longhouse was that Kest had lost his spy. She wondered if Kest had realised this. There was no one to argue with about going to the Storage Cavern or even deeper into the Warens, no one to point out the reasonableness of Pekrash's commands. She thumped another sheaf down on the floor, flicking over the pages and sighing. How many times did the harvests of Allogrenia need to be recorded?

And its births, deaths and bondings? *And* the goings-on of the Clan-councils? It must have been Kasheron's bent to have everything noted and accounted for. *And* his sons had been record-keepers too, although they seemed to have tired of it once he'd died for there was nothing after season forty-three.

Still, their keenness for record-keeping was puzzling. Surely such meticulousness wasn't a trait of a people who'd spent their lives riding, hunting and fighting? She pushed the sheaf back onto the shelf and dusted herself down. Her clothes were grimy and her other set was yet to be washed. Not that it mattered, there were few in the Warens to see her *or* miss her. Arlen and Werem had gone gathering and Paterek was readying one of the wounded Sherclansmen for removal to his longhouse.

She wondered what Tresen was doing now? Taking his midday meal with Miken and Tenerini? She could see the sunlit walls of the longhouse and imagine him teasing Mikini across the table. Or was he patrolling under the trees that now hid Shargh swords and daggers? She hugged herself, feeling suddenly cold. How she missed him! His jokes, his smiles, his easy familiarity . . . Nothing had to be explained to him, unlike Arlen, Paterek or Werem – why she'd chosen this herb over that, why she'd prepared a salve in a particular way. Kesilini had gone back to Morclan, back to her people as well. No doubt Kest was glad to have her in his longhouse again.

Wrenching another sheaf off the shelf, she sneezed repeatedly and then swore. More records! Nothing on the Shargh, or the battles the Northerners had fought; nothing of any use. She stood with hands on hips, surveying the shelves opposite. Perhaps she'd start there, even though the sheafs looked newer. Taking one at random, she slid it off the shelf, but it seemed to give way under her hand, the pages fluttering like leaves all over the cavern floor.

Stinking heart-rot! They must be older than they looked, the stitching decayed. Now she'd have to spend valuable reading time putting it back together again. Then she stilled; these weren't Writings at all, but maps like the one of the Warens she'd found earlier – which Kest had taken. They weren't just of the Warens either, but of rivers and mountains and forests, all drawn on large pieces of paper carefully folded to fit within the covers of the sheaf.

Her hands were shaking as she laid them out. There were settlements with strange and exotic names: Kessom, Maraschin, Talliel – words she rolled round in her mouth, tasting them like food. One map even had an ocean called Oskinas marked on it. Putting it aside she unfolded another: *Allogrenia and lands*. The floor bit into her knees but she barely noticed, craning forward, for it showed the lands west, north and east of Allogrenia. Her eyes darted over it eagerly, and the flowing script resolved itself into a familiar word: *Shargh*.

Even in the safety of the cavern, the word had the power to make her tremble. So close! Only a little north-east of Kenclan's Sentinel, where Bern had been killed. It didn't make sense. The Sentinel was a long, long way from Sarnia Cave. Perhaps the distances weren't the same. What had Kest called such things? Scale? Yet the Eights seemed to be shown correctly, evenly spaced, a day's march apart.

She sat back, hugging her knees. Why had Bern gone to the Sentinel anyway? It was a three-day trek from where she'd seen him and he'd been excited about exploring the caves. Yet he'd broken his undertaking to her to return home after a couple of days, going off to the Sentinel instead . . . or been taken! She shuddered, chilled by the image of the terrified boy being forced through the trees. But why would the Shargh take him all the way to the Sentinel when they could have killed him where they found him? She peered down at the map. It looked about a two-day walk from the Sentinel to the Shargh lands. Maybe they'd intended to take him all the way back but got tired of his struggles. But why take him there anyway? Surely Shargh came to kill, not kidnap.

The cold stone closed in around her and she sighed, tired of asking questions that had no answers. Gathering the maps, she returned them to the sheaf. Third shelf down, fifth partition from

329

the entranceway, she noted, as she picked up the lamp and made her way to the tunnel. With a final glance back at the Storage Cavern, she extinguished the lamp and placed it just inside the entranceway, then set off into the darkness.

Kest would be most displeased. Lamps, or the lack of them, had been the topic of their very first conversation and similar ones since: no wandering off, no wandering alone, no being irresponsible, no being immature, no risking of healing. Still, she couldn't be angry with him. His concern for Allogrenia and for those he now commanded was etched into his face. When was the last time she'd seen him smile? After she'd delivered Feseren's son? Yes, he'd been happy then, his eyes sky-blue, not the blank grey they often looked now. And how grim he'd been in Nogren when he'd told her of Bern's death.

The stone disappeared under her fingertips and her hand sailed into nothingness: the first left turning. There would be two more, roughly two hundred paces apart, before the tunnel swung west, rejoining one of the better-used tunnels. She concentrated on counting her steps, allowing herself a small smile each time the stone gave way and her memory was vindicated. How many others had found their way by touch, here in darkness, or walked this way by lamplight? Tremen Protectors certainly, but who else? Had people lived in the forests before Kasheron and his followers had come? The sheafs spoke of no one, nor did the Tremen, but that proved nothing. There was much she'd learned in the last few moons that no one spoke of. And there was probably much still to be learned, things only the Protectors knew.

The walls whispered and she stopped, every nerve awake. There were voices, but how far away? The main tunnel must be close and the speakers could be very near or they could be many tunnels distant, but they were still a long way from their rooms and from Nogren. She chewed her lip. Most of the guarding was centred round the longhouses now, except for the patrols in Renclan and Kenclan,

Kest had mentioned. Perhaps he had sent a patrol into the further reaches of the Warens to test the accuracy of the map she'd found. She had no wish to meet Protectors in her present grubby state, or to endure another dressing-down if it *were* Kest, for he'd be greatly displeased that she was so deep in the Warens, *and* without a lamp. It would be better to wait to see if the patrol came her way, and if so, to follow quietly behind.

She went on until the wall gave way to the main tunnel, then carefully took several steps backwards and settled on the floor to wait, her back against the wall and her knees drawn up for warmth.

The voices continued to ebb and flow, but no one appeared. The sweat under Kira's shirt cooled and the cold stone bit into her behind. She was parched, having run out of water, and all she wanted to do now was to get back to her alcove and have a drink, wash and think. Curse this waiting. Maybe the men were actually back in the training rooms and she was simply sitting in the dark like a fool, wasting her time.

She pulled her feet under her, intending to go on, when abruptly the sound intensified, the rasp of steps suddenly very close, the blur of sound resolving into individual words: '. . . sleep in a decent bed . . .', '. . . old enough to know better, still you can't tell a Morclansman anything . . .', '. . . best ale I've had . . .', '. . . since the last one . . .' a new voice chimed in. There was a grunt of laughter and Kira grinned. A glow appeared, elongated shadows snaking in advance of their owners, and she smelt burning nut oil as the first of the Protectors passed her line of vision. They were strung out, the tunnel being narrow here, and she didn't recognise the Leader. They strode by, those nearest their Leader holding their silence but conversations increasing towards the rear:

'. . . heartily sick of this darkness . . .', someone grumbled. So am I, thought Kira. '. . . not a place you'd want to live.'

'At least she's safe here,' a second voice broke in, and Kira stiffened.

'She's not safe anywhere anymore,' the first speaker said. 'There's an opening in Renclan, and two in Kenclan, and who's to say there aren't more. And the cursed Shargh'd know all about Nogren, after what they did to Bern. Poor Bern . . .'

There was a shout from the Leader, ordering them to hurry, then the rapid staccato of feet as the men complied, the echo of their passing fading, leaving only the smell of lamp oil behind. Kira scarcely noticed, frozen against the wall, everything suddenly, appallingly clear. Bern had been taken to the edge of the forest to elicit information about *her*. The Shargh didn't speak Tremen, but there must have been someone with them who knew it, or Terak, which was the same anyway. Bern had been stabbed, Kest said, and now she knew why; cutting his throat would have been too quick. They'd tortured him for information about *her*. By the alwaysgreen which Shelters us!

Her stomach churned. Kest knew this or else how did the Protectors know? The Shargh didn't hunt healing, or food, or extra land, they hunted *her*! Kest was sending patrols through the Warens looking for other entry points, not to keep healing safe, but to keep *her* safe. But the Protectors were right; there was no safety. Sooner or later the Shargh would find their way in, hunt her down in the darkness and kill her. How many others would die too? How many Berns? How many Kandors?

Vomit spilled from her mouth and she rocked on her knees, sweat and tears mixing with the liquid on the floor, until empty, she rolled away from it, lying on her back like a husk in the darkness. Her very existence put every Tremen at risk. Surely *her* death would be better? Death came to everyone and everything; even the alwaysgreens fell, giving their essence back to the earth so that new things might grow. It was not death she feared so much as the moment of death: the slice of the blade through flesh, the blood in the lungs, the drowning; the loss of everyone and everything. Her face grew wet again and she wiped at it angrily. She was a coward, that was all, huddled here in the darkness feeling sorry for herself.

She hauled herself up into a sitting position and dried her face on her shirt. Kest had hidden the truth from her. Had Tresen too? Who else knew? Miken? All the Protectors? Was she to live her life surrounded by liars? Maybe the Shargh were hunting healing and through their eyes she and it were the same thing. But in that case, why had they left the Kashclan longhouse alone? After torturing Bern, they must have known healing was strong there. And there'd been no attacks in the last two full moons, which meant they were most likely after her, not healing. On the other hand, maybe they simply wanted to destroy the Tremen leadership, not her in particular. It amounted to the same thing anyway. Maybe, maybe! Maybe she was just grasping at straws.

Her choices were, in fact, horrifyingly clear: stay in the Warens until the Shargh inevitably found her, or leave. There would be a lot of killing if she stayed. Kest would send every last Protector to his death, including himself, before surrendering her. And if she left? She had a vision of running through the trees, the pound of Shargh feet, the flash of metal in sunlight. Would the Shargh leave the Tremen in peace with her dead? If only she knew for sure, the choice would be simpler.

She forced herself up and moved off slowly, using the wall to support as well as guide her. Was there nothing else she could do? The maps showed other places and other peoples beyond the trees, perhaps they would help. But why should they? What were the Tremen to them? Did they even know of their existence? Kasheron had hidden them too well, that was the problem. The trees that had sheltered them from likely enemies had sheltered them from likely friends.

She stopped, hope firing as she thought of the possibility of seeking help from the Terak Kutan. The Terak Kutan were kin, blood-linked, but to go begging to them would be to betray everything Kasheron had fought for: healing kneeling before the sword. No! It was abhorrent, unthinkable! There had to be another way! She was

333

tired, that was all; once she'd eaten and slept and perhaps spoken to Kest or Miken, things would look different. And there were many more Writings yet to be read; surely they would hold things that would help them. Powerful salves to make the Shargh disappear; to unburn the Bough; to bring the dead to life? She pushed the thought away, refusing to give way to despair again; food and sleep, that was what she needed, and time to think.

38

Pain always wore the same face whether it be that of a birthing woman, a turned ankle, or a sword wound. Under her fingers, in the flame-dark world Feseren had shown her, it wore the same face. Now, as she ran her fingers lightly over the part-healed wound, pain smiled its ghastly smile, though Brithin's face remained unchanged.

'Does it hurt here?' she asked.

The young Protector shook his head.

'Here?' Her fingers fired, but again the headshake.

Kira flicked her fingers slightly to dispel the heat, glad that her only witness was a young Protector who didn't understand what he saw, not that she understood her increasing sensitivity to pain either.

'Another few days,' she said, easing his shirt back over his shoulder.

The Protector's disappointment was plain. 'The wound feels well. I'm strong enough to go.'

She slipped the buttons through their holes, the wood smooth and cool like the buttons on Kandor's shirts. Pain fluttered again and she busied herself collecting her salves.

'Tenedren has enough to do guarding the Kenclan longhouse without having to worry about you –' she started, then seeing his face fall, paused. He was the last of the wounded and it was understandable that he'd want to be among his clanmates again.

'You can start taking some gentle exercise to build your strength when Arlen comes back. He'll help you.'

His expression lightened and he nodded.

Kira rose and went to the table at the side, crushing some morning-bright leaves into a bowl of water, the leaves turning the water a faint red and sweetening the air. The vapours should soothe Brithin's impatience a little, she thought as she made her way back through the empty mattresses to her alcove. The room seemed strange now without its rows of wounded, each neatly folded cover a testament to the fact her work was almost done. The alcove was the same though, small and dingy. Tossing the salves on her bed, she wandered restlessly round the cramped space, wondering whether she should go back and take a deep breath of the morning-bright herself.

It was quiet beyond the curtain and she peered through the slit, then went back and lifted the mattress. The coarse filling rustled dryly, sending grassy scents into the air as she drew out a map and laid it on the cover. She didn't open it but, half-closing her eyes, mentally retraced the Warens' route that would take her close to the Renclan Second Eight. Only when she'd finished visualising the way did she open the map and pore over it with intense concentration, raising her head at last with a satisfied grin.

She'd remembered accurately; her knowing was complete. The map could go back to the safety of the Storage Cavern, all she need do was rehearse the route occasionally so as not to forget. Sliding the map back under the mattress, she drew out a second one showing the lands north of Allogrenia and as far as the Oskinas Sea. She hadn't bothered committing it to memory as she intended to take a copy with her. It wouldn't matter if the Shargh found this one, for they probably knew about the northern lands, but she couldn't risk them finding a map of the Warens.

Kira didn't know when the resolve to leave Allogrenia had crystallised, but it was there now, as hard as sun-baked sap. If she somehow escaped the Shargh blades and reached the edges of the forest, where to then? The possibility of going north to the Terak Kutan lurked on the edges of her mind, abhorrent though it was. In her explorations of the Storage Caverns she'd come upon many references to their blood-thirst, to their love of horses, and to the massive stone city of Sarnia they had been building at the time of the Sundering. Both Kasheron and Terak had been birthed by the first Kiraon, a mighty Healer. Surely some shred of healing lived on in the Terak Kutan.

She stared down at the rivers and mountains she'd have to pass – if she went north – and wondered how much food she would need to carry. Her pack wasn't large and she must take her Healer's pastes and pouches. She calculated quickly. The Warens map had shown an opening in Renclan – near the Second Eight – that she could use. There were also two openings in Kenclan, but she needed to go north, not north-east towards the Shargh. If she *were* able to come out of the Warens beyond the Second Eight, it would take her another three days to reach the Renclan Sentinel. She knew gathering was plentiful between the Renclan Second Eight and the Renclan Sentinel. Abutting the forests, the map showed a lightly treed plain; *if* the small blotches of ink represented trees, at least some of these should be blacknuts. *The Dendora Plain*; it was a pretty name and, unlike many of the other names, had no 'S' or 'T' following it.

Many of the rivers and mountains had two names, each with an 'S' or 'T' after it, and the only reason she could think of was that different peoples had named them. If the 'S' stood for Shargh, did 'T' stand for Terak Kutan? Many of the places were a long way from

337

the Terak lands. Maybe there were other peoples living nearby whose name began with 'T' as well. She'd long known that Onespeak had come into being because different peoples lived beyond the forests, but seeing the evidence before her eyes was extraordinary.

The Dendora Plain lay west of the Shargh lands and maybe the absence of the 'S' meant the Shargh didn't go there. After all, why would they have a word for something they had no *need* to name. Hope fired and she scanned excitedly, but the massive mountain range she must cross had two names: Azurcades (T) and Braghan (S). If the scale were as she thought, it would be at least eight days before she even reached it. Eight days with the Shargh at her heels!

It would be better to stay here; the Shargh would never find her, it was safe here . . .

No! She scrambled to her feet and strode up and down the tiny space. If she stayed more Tremen would die. If she were to be Leader in more than name, she must go north and beg aid of the Terak Kutan. She came to a stop. The idea was just as appalling as when it had come to her nearly half a moon ago. She'd probably be dead long before that anyway. That was a comfort, she chided herself sarcastically, and not much practical use to her planning.

She took a steadying breath. Suppose the Shargh didn't catch her, and there were nuts or other types of gathering on the Dendora Plain, how was she to cross the Braghans? Azurcades, she corrected, refusing to use a Shargh word. They appeared to have trees as well, so there'd be shelter and possibly nuts or vine fruit, but there might also be ravines and rushing rivers and many days of climbing. Did people live there? If so, were they friends or foe of the Shargh? And even *if* she made it across the mountains, there was another massive plain on the other side, the Sarsalin, which was, she calculated, another ten days across. At least it was only followed by a (T).

She slumped back, staring despondently round the room. What was the use of looking so far ahead? Better to take each day as it came: reaching the Third Eight, reaching the Fourth Eight, reaching the Sentinel, completing a day's travel across the plain, then another. To think of the whole journey was akin to watching a heart-rotted tree crash towards her.

'Leader Kiraon?'

She started violently. Kest's shadow was distinct through the curtain. 'One moment, Commander.' Silently cursing that she hadn't noticed his steps, she quickly folded the map and slid it back under the mattress, hoping that Kest would think the rustling some private female matter. He'd developed an irritating sense of propriety recently, refusing to come into her alcove, which at least had saved her from discovery.

Kest looked fresh and relaxed: his face lightly tanned, his eyes a startling blue despite the poor light. He even smelt of sun-tinged air. Kira smoothed down her crumpled over-sized Protector shirt, aware of how unkempt she must look, but her other clothes were still drying near the very small fire the vents allowed.

'Only one wounded remaining,' he commented.

'Yes, Brithin of Kenclan. There's still pain in the wound, so it's best he stays here till it fades.'

'Is that his view too?' asked Kest with a smile.

Kira shrugged. 'He's young. It's natural he misses his clan and Protector-mates.'

'He's nineteen, Kira. Two seasons older than you.'

Kest's face had gentled and she shifted uncomfortably. 'I'm sure you didn't come here to discuss my age, Commander.'

'No, I came to see how you were,' he said, smiling.

'I am well, as you can see,' she replied.

'What I see is someone who's too thin and too pale.'

'Ah, you've learned healing since last we spoke,' she said.

Kest refused to bite. 'I think it would be a good idea for you to go the Kashclan longhouse for a while.'

Kira stared at him in astonishment. She must really look awful. 'I still have a wounded man to care for,' she said.

339

'Then go after he's well. A few more days, you said.' His hand had closed over her arm in the same way she held the wounded as they took their first steps.

'Come to the second training room, it's a pleasanter place to talk and we can eat there as well.'

'I prefer Nogren,' said Kira, resenting his gentle but firm pressure as he escorted her between the mattresses.

'My turn to choose,' said Kest lightly.

He really was in a good mood. Surely he didn't believe the Shargh attacks were over with? Whatever his beliefs, he hadn't shared them with her, which meant it was time to test her theory.

'I've been thinking about all that's happened,' she began. 'I think there's a pattern to what the Shargh are doing.'

In the passing pool of lamplight, she saw Kest become guarded.

'What mean you?' he said.

'The Shargh let the longhouses be in their journey to the Bough, and they killed Bern because he was wandering alone. I think they mistook him for a Healer out gathering. I think they want to destroy healing.' They turned into the main tunnel, their footsteps echoing hollowly.

Kira waited till the next lamp to examine Kest's face. His expression had eased again.

'Do you agree?' she asked. Thank the 'green it was a little way to the next lamp and Kest couldn't see her face. She was sure her ruse was written plain upon it.

'It's possible,' he said, fingers tightening on her arm.

'If I go to my longhouse, it might suggest that it's a place of healing. I don't want to risk those who are there,' she said, feeling his fingers relax. 'Do you think I'm right, Commander?'

'You could be.'

'But do *you* believe it?'

She held her breath. What he said now would almost determine

340

whether she stayed or went. If she couldn't trust Kest to tell her the truth, then it was time to go.

He was a long time answering, but finally he said, 'Yes.'

Kira's knees sagged and his grip tightened again.

'Are you unwell?' he asked.

They came to another lamp and she turned her face away. 'Just a little tired.'

Tired of the darkness and dankness and dust; of being old enough to lead but not old enough to hear the unpalatable truth; of being afraid, but most of all, of being alone.

The second training room was bright with lamps and full of men lately come in off patrol, talking noisily and joking as they jostled each other round plates of nutbread and sweetfish, and steaming pots of tea. Pekrash and Merenor were there, sitting with two other Protectors who looked like Leaders but who Kira didn't know. The shouted conversations of the men quieted as Kest steered her between the tables towards the Leaders, then picked up again as they passed. They came to a halt and the Protector Leaders stood to greet her.

'Protector Leaders Merenor and Pekrash I believe you know,' said Kest to Kira. 'This is Protector Leader Senden of Kenclan and Protector Leader Bendrash of Sherclan.'

'Kashclan greets Kenclan,' she said, bowing to the first. 'Kashclan greets Sherclan.' She had no idea whether the normal clan greeting was appropriate between Protector Leaders, or between the Tremen Leader and Protector Leaders. All she could think of was her too-big crumpled Protector shirt, and her half unravelled braid, which she hadn't thought to redo that morning. In contrast, the Protector Leaders looked as fresh and clean as Kest.

'Would you join us?' said Pekrash, with a small bow.

'I thank you,' said Kest smoothly, before Kira had time to reply, 'but the Tremen Leader and I have things to discuss.'

Kest still had hold of Kira's arm and she had to resist the urge

341

to shrug him off as he guided her to the table furthest away from the rest of the room's inhabitants. 'I'll get us some food,' he said, making his way back to the throng.

Kira watched the Protector Leaders eat, their faces serious as they exchanged words she couldn't hear. They knew what Kest knew, as no doubt did the young Protectors opposite, busy dipping their straps of dried sour-ripe in honey. In fact everyone in the room probably knew things about her she didn't know. Even as she looked at them, one of the young Protectors turned and caught her eye, then glanced towards Kest, now taken up with a tired-looking older man who'd just entered the room. The young Protector pushed his chair back and made his way over to her.

'Tremen Leader Kiraon,' he said, bowing low, his already ruddy complexion going a deeper shade of red.

Kira went to rise but he'd taken both of her hands, making any movement awkward.

'Protector . . . ?'

'Protector Arin of Tarclan,' he said hurriedly, his eyes flicking to Kest again.

'Kashclan greets Tarclan,' said Kira automatically. Was the young Protector about to tell her something Kest wouldn't want her to hear?

'Tremen Leader . . . I come to thank you for saving my brother Eresh,' said the young Protector, bowing again, his eyes glistening with tears.

'I'm a Healer, Arin, there's no need for thanks.'

His head bobbed once more, his grip on her hands tightening. 'He said you healed his pain. He said –' His eyes went to Kest again, now clearly moving back in their direction, and Kira took the opportunity to extricate her hands.

'I thank you for your words, Arin.'

Arin straightened and with a final bow made his way back to his comrades, bowing to Kest as they passed.

'What did Protector Arin of Tarclan have to say for himself?' asked Kest, as he juggled a platter piled high with nutbread, sweetfish and sour-ripe onto the table, then two cups of thornyflower tea.

Normally Kira would have found such an enquiry innocent but now she found it intrusive. Did Kest imagine that Arin had told her something he shouldn't? Like the fact that the Shargh hunted her, not healing.

'He thanked me for healing his brother,' she muttered, sipping the tea.

'Protector Eresh,' said Kest thoughtfully. 'He's one I didn't think would survive, and of course he wouldn't have, if you hadn't found the fireweed.' His voice was gentle, his words clearly intended as a compliment, but Kira kept her eyes on the table. There was a short silence and she heard his fingers begin to tap. It never took Kest very long to become irritated with her.

'Aren't you going to eat?' he asked at last.

'I'm not hungry.'

'When was the last time you *did* eat?'

Kira shrugged, and his hand shot out and seized her wrist, pushing the shirt cuff high. 'Look, all bone and no flesh, Kira. Is that how a Healer looks after herself?'

'Don't,' she said, but he was as angry as she was, his grip on her wrist solid.

'Then eat,' he said, releasing her, his eyes like ice. 'If *you* sicken, then who will heal? You don't have the right –'

'Don't tell me my rights! The healing's recorded, Kest. There's a copy in the training room, three in the reaches of the Warens, one in the Tarclan longhouse, one in the Kashclan longhouse. Tresen's a gifted Healer, Brem's good, Werem, Arlen and Paterek are improving. You don't need me anymore, Kest; the Tremen don't need me anymore!'

'What are you talking about?' he said, leaning across the table, his shrewd eyes searching her face.

She felt her cheeks warm. Shrugging, she picked up a piece of nutbread, taking a large bite to appease him.

'You'll always be needed, Kira, you're the Tremen Leader. Even if . . . *when* this is over, *when* the stinking Shargh have gone, you'll be needed.'

Kira swallowed the moist lump and looked up. 'Tell me, Kest, is it the task of the Tremen Leader to save the Tremen people?'

His eyes narrowed. 'By healing?' he asked.

Kira nodded. 'By stopping their suffering.'

Kest's eyes were still searching Kira's face, looking for hidden meanings. 'Of course,' he said finally, 'why do you ask?'

'Sometimes in the Warens I need reminding, that's all.' She forced a smile. 'It's easy to forget, in the darkness.'

The day was dying, flutterwings spiralling to the forest floor, just the occasional chirrup filtering from the canopy. Kest scarcely noticed; in fact he was so preoccupied he was almost to the Kashclan longhouse before he realised it. Four days in Kenclan octad with Senden's patrol and another two returning through Morclan – it was little wonder that his bones ached. He'd walked further in the last moons than he probably had in the previous twelve, but at least the news was good. No more slashed trees in any of the octads, no sightings, no Tremen unaccounted for. The third full moon since the last attack had passed and the night forest was growing dimmer again. The Shargh were waiting, but for what?

His hand played over his sword hilt as his thoughts turned to Kira. Perhaps it was his concern for her, rather than the Shargh, that fed his unease. It had been some time since her eyes had flashed that extraordinary rebellious gold, but in some ways she seemed even less in accord with him than before. At that age Kesilini had been cool when upset with him and overly loving when pleased with him. But Kira wasn't like Kesilini, or like any other woman he'd ever encountered. She was more like an enthusiastic new Protector if anything, full of an exuberance that must be moulded into a useful shape, and with lots of inclinations that had to be curtailed.

When she'd insisted they climb Nogren she'd been as wild as a bird, eyes smouldering, and then she'd walked out on the branch. The cold sweat broke out on his brow even at the memory. Her sudden turns of recklessness boded ill, almost seeming to hint at some sort of death wish. He wondered whether it stemmed from the loss of her family, and of Kandor in particular, or whether it had always been part of her nature.

He hadn't known her at all before the Shargh attacks and the problem was that those who had known her best were dead, except for Miken and Tresen, which was why he was here instead of in his bed. He was worried, though, that seeking advice from a Clanleader who'd been no friend of Maxen's was doing nothing to enhance his command, and even risked alienating those who *had* been Maxen's allies. If they were to fight off the Shargh, the Tremen must be united, not fractured along old lines of allegiance.

He rapped on the door and it swung open almost immediately to reveal Tresen, clearly surprised at seeing him. 'Commander Kest . . . I . . . Kashclan welcomes Morclan.'

'Morclan thanks Kashclan,' replied Kest, stepping into the longhouse.

'Is your father within?'

'He's beyond the Second Eight gathering with a patrol.'

And so would not be back before the morrow, realised Kest.

'Would you like me to send message to him to return?' asked Tresen.

'No. I . . .' He stopped. He'd wanted to consult with Miken about Kira, and Tresen – mostly to be reassured that there was no risk of Tresen and Kira breaking Tremen law by bonding if Tresen returned. But it seemed he would have to think for himself after all.

'I know you're on a few days' leave, Protector Tresen, but I have a favour to ask.'

345

'By all means, Commander. But please, come in and eat with us first.'

Kest peered past him to where Kashclan were taking their evening meal, the inviting smell of new-baked nutbread drifting towards him. He shook his head regretfully. 'I thank you, Protector, but I must be back in my own longhouse before dawn.' He lowered his voice. 'I'd like you to return to the Warens.'

Tresen's eyes narrowed.

'Call it guarding duty if you like, but I want someone with the Tremen Leader,' said Kest.

'Isn't Kesilini there?'

'Kesilini's been back in my longhouse since the new moon and the training room is all but empty of wounded. Arlen and Paterek are there, of course, and I know that Kira spends much time reading the Writings in the Storage Cavern, but the Warens is a lonely place for her. Soon the council must decide on how and when the Bough is to be rebuilt. In the meantime, I'd feel better if she had the company of someone who knew her before all this began.'

'I'll leave at dawn,' said Tresen.

'I'd prefer it if you went now.'

'Then I'll go immediately, Commander.'

'Thank you, Protector. I'll be in Renclan octad with Clanleader Sanden for the next few days but back in the Warens by the new moon. We can discuss your duties more fully then.'

39

The sun slid clear of the world's curve, glancing off the eastern walls of the sorchas and sending the spur's shadow snaking to where ebis slumbered, propped on rigid legs, heads low. But there was no sleep to be had by Palansa, confined in the highest sorcha on the spur, the stifling interior and her aching back both ensuring wakefulness. Ormadon had insisted the flaps be shut when they slept, but it meant the air pooled like the scum-filled puddles in the Thanawah, sticking her shift to her back and breasts, and plastering her hair across her forehead. Finally she got up from her bed and went to the vent and loosed the flap.

The dawn air was scarcely fresher than the fetid air inside, but she stayed there, shifting on swollen feet and rubbing her back as she stared across the Grounds. Already the day was heavy with the smell of dust and dry grass, the ebis beginning to shamble towards the Thanawah in ragged lines, tails flicking at the blackflies.

She turned, her gaze following the slope beyond the Cave of the Telling and the Cashgars, towards the distant blue of the Braghans, until the press of her belly against the wall prevented her from seeing further. She was tighter than a drum and a lot heavier, but at least the babe was quiet now after spending the entire night kicking her! Perhaps she'd go back to bed and snatch some more sleep, but pain jabbed and instead she paced slowly to the table and back, since the pain usually grew less when she walked.

Window to table, table to window, taking care not to nudge or kick anything that might disturb Tarkenda. Two days ago the older woman had laid her rough warm hands over Palansa's belly and proclaimed the next Chief ready to be born, then fetched sweet-oil and rubbed her back.

When Palansa had woken later, she'd found the swaddlings Tarkenda had used with Erboran and Arkendrin next to the bed, and a sleep-sling fastened to the roof.

None of it seemed real, thought Palansa, clasping her hands under the mountain of her shift. The babe that had flickered inside her as light as button-flower seed now bulged her belly with foot and fist, and would soon be in her arms. Erboran's son. She smiled at the thought before new pain speared, making her gasp and double over.

'What is it?' said Tarkenda sitting up, tucking her hair back into her grizzled plait.

'Just my back,' said Palansa, lowering herself onto a stool and screwing her eyes shut as the pain stabbed again.

'I'll rub it for you.'

The mattress rustled and the uneven pad of Tarkenda's crooked feet crossed the pelts, then there was the clunk of wood hitting wood as she retrieved the oil from the basket of ease-pots. 'Come and lie down.'

Palansa heaved herself up and retched, having to hold the table till the nausea ebbed. 'My back's making me ill,' she muttered.

Tarkenda peered at her. 'I think the babe's coming.'

Palansa retched again and Tarkenda fetched a bowl, helping Palansa to the bed again and setting the bowl beside her before ducking out through the door flap. The air was thick with midges but all was quiet in the other sorchas. Ormadon was the only person awake, leaning on his spear surveying the slope. He'd already discarded his cape.

'There's a storm coming, Chief-mother,' he said, his eyes squinting against the glare.

Tarkenda followed his gaze towards the Braghans. The sky was clear but she felt the same faint tingling as he did. 'Has Arkendrin returned yet?'

'No, Chief-mother, nor those who accompany him. Most of the lower sorchas are empty.' Ormadon's black eyes held hers. 'Since the moons of mourning finished he's made sure those who follow him remain in the northern and eastern parts of the forest. This is where Irdodun first saw the creature, and where she escaped Arkendrin before. The treemen have recently been favouring these reaches too. Arkendrin knows time grows short.'

'Shorter even than he thinks. Palansa's taken to her bed.'

The furrows of Ormadon's face deepened. 'Then it's better he's not here, Chief-mother. Will the Chief-wife birth this day?'

'I don't think so. I laboured for two dawns to birth Erboran, and a babe will often follow its father in such things.'

Ormadon turned the spear over in his hands, as if testing its strength. 'I'll summon those loyal to the blood-born Chief to ensure the Chief-wife births in peace. And I'll tell Gensana to start her baking. The Sky Chiefs will have their squaziseed and shillyflower cakes to keep them content.' His face broke into a smile. 'It will be good to have a Chief again, even if he does squall.'

A long, shuddering groan sounded from the sorcha and he touched his brow and stared skyward. 'May the Sky Chiefs send her strength.'

'And a cool day,' replied Tarkenda.

Tresen let the curtain to Kira's alcove fall and wandered around the empty training room. He'd journeyed through the night, buoyed by the thought of sharing hot tea and fresh nutcakes with her. Kest had clearly been worried, and he'd half feared that he'd arrive in the Warens to find her hunched in a corner, silent and uncommunicative. But all that had greeted him when he had arrived was a deserted alcove and a solitary jug of water.

Kest said she spent much time in the Storage Cavern and no doubt that's where she was, her nose buried in a dusty Writing, but he'd feel better if he could get hold of someone to confirm her whereabouts. He scratched at his stubbly jaw and, taking a cup from the side table, poured himself some water, gulping it down before the taste hit him. After a few days back in his longhouse and on patrol under the rustling leaves, hearing birdsong again, he'd forgotten how bleak this place was. But Kira hadn't had the chance to forget. Was that why Kest had sent him?

Footsteps echoed, the unmistakable pound of Protectors, and he tensed as a command was shouted and they came to a halt outside the cavern. Surely not more wounded? A single set of footsteps detached itself and Tresen braced himself.

It was Penedrin, still sweat-stained and grimy from patrol.

'The Leader is here?' asked Penedrin.

His lack of greeting added to Tresen's sudden unease. 'I've just arrived myself, on Commander Kest's orders. I'm assuming the Leader's in the Storage Cavern. Have you wounded?'

Penedrin ignored the question, hurrying back to the cavern entrance and barking another order. The patrol marched on. Then he came back into the cavern, his face grim.

'I've sent the patrol to the Storage Cavern, but we must ascertain exactly where the Leader is,' he said. 'There are slashed trees in Renclan octad. I returned via the Renclan longhouse and left a message for Commander Kest, who is due there shortly. If the Leader returns or you learn of her whereabouts, send message to me immediately at the Storage Cavern.'

Then, nodding briefly, he strode out.

Renclan had only one Warens opening, thought Tresen, trying to reassure himself. But the Shargh might still find their way in, and if they did . . .

There was the soft fall of footsteps and he whirled in relief – but it was only Arlen, the Kashclansman's face reflecting his own surprise but not his disappointment.

'Tresen! Welcome. I didn't expect to see you here.'

'Why not?'

'Well . . . I thought you'd be guarding our longhouse, since the Leader's there.'

Tresen's heart jolted. 'What makes you think the Leader's at Kashclan?'

'I . . . I assumed it was so. It was said among the men that she'd go there when the last of the wounded went home, and when Brithin was released and the Leader left, I thought that's where she'd gone.'

'Left? When did you last see her?'

Arlen stood, considering with maddening slowness. 'It must be near two days,' he said, 'though it's hard to track time here.'

'And you didn't tell anyone? Stinking heart-rot, Arlen! She could be lying injured in the Warens!' *Or already taken by Shargh.*

Arlen looked startled. 'She hasn't gone into the Warens, Tresen.'

'What makes you so sure?' demanded Tresen.

'She's taken her clothing and a sword.'

Tresen gaped at him. 'A sword?'

'She came to the training rooms and asked for one,' explained Arlen. 'Paterek sharpened a practice sword for her; they're lighter. I . . . we assumed she'd carry one since she was going back under the trees.'

Tresen rushed back to the alcove, Arlen close behind him. Her pack was gone, but she always carried it anyway, and she owned so little it was impossible to tell whether anything was missing. He gazed about wildly. The bed was neat, the cover pulled smooth, but there was a sprig of something on it that he hadn't noticed before.

351

'Cinna,' said Arlen helpfully, 'it must have fallen from her pack.'

'Herbs don't *fall* from Kira's pack,' snapped Tresen. Why had she left it? He racked his brains. Cinna was the first herb to poke its leaves through the soil in spring, and the last to die away. The clans hung it in the longhouses in winter as a reminder that spring would come back. There was even a children's rhyme about it: silvermint to calm, bluemint to smooth the scar, icemint to balm, *cinna to remember*.

He seized Arlen's arm. 'Send message to Penedrin in the Storage Cavern. Tell him Kira's been gone two days and is leaving Allogrenia.' He thought feverishly. She'd exited the Warens through Kenclan before, but Kenclan was north-east, towards the Shargh. He guessed she'd choose the Renclan opening instead. 'Tell Penedrin she's leaving through Renclan and that I've gone after her. Penedrin will send scouts to Kest.'

Arlen stood staring at him, mouth agape and Tresen shook him violently. 'Go!' he shouted, waiting only to see Arlen flee before grabbing his pack and sword and sprinting out of the cavern. By the 'green, he hoped his guess was right!

He still had nutcake and a full waterskin and while it'd be quickest to go through the Warens, he didn't know the way well enough. Cursing as he ran, he swerved back down the tunnel towards Nogren. He should have seen it coming – he knew Kira best of all. Even Kest had suspected something, but all too late! He pounded through the last cavern, ignoring the guarding Protector's exclamation, and flung himself past Nogren, before sprinting off again. It was dawn, a small moon still in the sky, not a full one; she might be safe. He cursed again, the spit hot in his mouth, his lungs screaming. Slashed trees in Renclan! He thought of Bern and forced his legs to greater speed.

Kira shifted restlessly, making her sleeping-sling jiggle and creak. She felt like she was the only thing awake in a forest drowsing in the quiet heat of midday. The journey through the Warens had been longer than the map suggested, and it had certainly taken more time than the journey she'd taken to the Kenclan octad with Kest. She'd slept on the hard floor of the Warens several times, but sleep eluded her now, driven away by her roiling thoughts. Why did the Shargh hunt her? Was it hatred of her, or hatred of healing or of something else? Why would they hate her anyway? They didn't even know her. Yet Kest believed they hunted her, and he was no fool, and it *did* fit with what had happened.

Her heart started racing again and she turned over, the sword jabbing her hip. Why had she brought it? Was she turning into some sort of Terak Kutan or was she fooling herself into thinking that she could actually use it, striking them down before they struck her? She'd long outgrown the sword-fighting games she'd once played with Tresen in the Warens, and stabbing at effigies bore no resemblance to plunging a sword into a real flesh-and-blood person.

She rolled onto her back, cupping her hands behind her head and trying to still her panic by watching the lumbering progress of a bark beetle along the bough above. What was Tresen doing now? And Miken? And Tenerini? Would they mourn her passing? Her eyes burned and she swore; instead of fretting over things she couldn't change, she was now wallowing in self-pity. Not very impressive, *Tremen Leader Kiraon*! She began to list the herbal requirements of each of the salves, where the herbs grew, their flowering, the manner of their harvest, of their preparation, of their storage, and slowly she began to drift. Then her eyelids flew open again.

Twigs snapped and cracked as something drew near. Voices! They were still a little way off but coming in her direction. It seemed that even the forest held its breath, nothing rustling or creaking or calling. Then the scattered fragments of sound came together, clear, unequivocal. It was Shargh speaking Shargh words!

How close? How many? Two speakers? Three? Eventually they passed somewhere to the left of her, leaving Kira rigid. She was barely halfway to the Third Eight and already there were Shargh! What hope did she have? How was she ever to reach the edge of the trees?

A springleslip fluttered onto the bough above her head, trilling and preening, its eye flashing as it tilted its head at her before darting forward and disappearing into the foliage. The leaves shivered and stilled, then it gave voice again, as springleslips always did. No one knew why they sent this second song. Maybe it sang of its joy in flight, a song which was as much a part of Allogrenia as the song each tree composed with its leaves and twigs and branches. Kira plucked a sprig of foliage, inhaling its sappy breath. The Tremen left no footprints in the green and growing, but the Shargh trampled and crushed, so were easy to hear coming and to track where they'd gone. They were intruders, ignorant and uncaring of the forest's ways. And though her sword might be useless against them, her knowing wasn't.

She caressed the sprig of terrawood, determination hardening. Allogrenia was worth fighting for, but she'd fight as a Healer not as a Terak Kutan. Terak Kutan swords she must have to meet the Shargh swords, and she'd give them healing in return, but when it was ended, the Terak Kutan would leave, the paths grow over and the wounds of the Tremen mend, and then they could be as they were before. She unlaced the sword and pushed it deep into her pack, then hauled herself out of the sling and stowed it too. Every one of her senses was shivering, as if she'd lost a layer of skin. Staying here was wasting time; instead she'd travel through the day and the night as well, until exhaustion ensured she *did* sleep.

The terrawood trunk was rough and warm under her hands as she came down it, pausing on the lower boughs to listen, keeping a layer of leaves between her and the ground. The forest spoke of a breeze and a roosting bird, and the air touched her hands and face with nothing more sinister than pockets of cool and warmth. She dropped to the ground, briefly placing her palms and forehead against the bole.

'I thank you for your Shelter,' she whispered, then moved quickly away.

Arkendrin tore a strip of smoked ebis fat and chewed on it as he glowered at the man standing in front of him. It was some nameless kin of Irdodun's, face shiny with sweat, chest heaving with running, his message punctuated by hoarsely drawn breaths. Arkendrin ground the fat between his teeth, considering the long and ill-favoured day they'd endured, trawling through the murk with no sightings of treemen, a day now turning into a stinking, windy night.

But at last the news was good, despite the man's lowly status. There was a swift movement of treemen towards them, different to their usual aimless wanderings, and that could only mean that there was something or someone here of interest to the treemen. And as the treemen had never spent time in hunting *them,* it must be something *or someone* the treemen wanted to protect.

He'd been right to delay, he thought, swallowing the fat and tearing off another strip. The Sky Chiefs had gifted him the foresight to wait, and were now sending the creature to him as a reward for his forbearance. He rose and the air sang as he slashed the surrounding foliage, striding to where Irdodun and his kin took their food in the lee of some bushes.

'The Sky Chiefs send treemen this way.'

Several of the Voiceless men laughed uneasily, and Orthaken seemed to shrink. 'Maybe they seek us, Chief Arkendrin,' he said, peering up, his chin shiny with grease. 'Some from the lower slope hide themselves as ill as mawkbirds on sorcha roofs.' He turned the small joint in his hands, nipping at it with nervous bites. 'Maybe the treemen come to fight us.'

Arkendrin's legs splayed and his hands came to his hips. 'Do you fear them?'

Orthaken blinked. 'I welcome the chance to work my flatsword,

Chief Arkendrin, but they'll be less sport than wolves. At least wolves have teeth.'

Arkendrin grinned. 'Urpalin, do the treemen have teeth?'

'They graze like ebis, so it seems likely.'

Arkendrin threw back his head and laughed, leaning on his flatsword as he turned to Irdodun. The older warrior was silent, busy smearing tesat over his dagger.

'Do your lesser kin speak for you this day, Irdodun?' asked Arkendrin.

'The treemen fought last time, Chief Arkendrin, and they'll fight this time. The creature's important to them.'

'And important to us,' said Arkendrin, 'or why else would the Sky Chiefs have granted the Last Teller his vision and my blood its guardianship?' His eyes glittered and he stabbed at the greenery again. 'The treemen come this way. They mean the creature to see the sun setting; they covet our doom.'

Urpalin sprang to his feet. 'It'll not happen while I live, Chief Arkendrin! Not while I've a flatsword in my hand!'

Arkendrin's hand slammed down on his shoulder, all but buckling Urpalin's legs. 'It'll be the *Chief's* blade that blinds her, and the *Chief's* blade that kills her,' he said, thrusting his face close to Urpalin's.

'I . . . I meant only that I would kill those who aid the creature,' stammered Urpalin.

The trees thrashed in a sudden squall and Arkendrin's grip tightened, making Urpalin blanch. 'There'll be plenty of killing, even for you of the lower slope,' he said, his eyes burning into him. Then he dropped his hand and Urpalin staggered backwards.

'Tesat your flatswords,' growled Arkendrin to the gathering. 'Then we go south. We have work to do.'

Kira stopped in the lee of a castella, pulling her cape close against the stinging shower of twigs. The canopy roared and broke, revealing then hiding the faint scud of clouds. Somewhere ahead something crashed to the ground, making her jump. The night was so thick it was impossible to see more than a few paces ahead and the wailing wind and rattling branches blotted out all other sounds. There could be Shargh all around but there was nowhere to shelter: no caves, no dense stands of bitterberry. Not that she had time to crawl into some hole if she were to reach the Fourth Eight by dawn.

Turning her back on the wind, she took a swig from her waterskin before going on. The wind grew but it didn't rain, which was unusual; such winds usually brought downpours or even hail. Perhaps it was only the edge of a storm that was shedding its water elsewhere, or maybe it was simply drier here. The ground was hard underfoot and the only annin she'd seen was brown-edged and spare.

The last time she'd been here, she'd been less than ten seasons and it had been spring. The journey had taken her over six days each way, a long trip for a child, and yet she couldn't remember her father reprimanding her or confining her as punishment; he hadn't cared where she was until her healing had begun to rival his.

The night had turned before Kira stopped again, settling in a tangle of undergrowth to remove something from her boot. She shook the boot out, then sagged back against the bushes, enjoying the brief hiatus out of the wind. The scrubby growths of bitterberry and lissium provided a surprising amount of shelter and she was tempted to stay there, but she pulled her boot on reluctantly and glanced at the way she must go.

Something wasn't right, and her skin prickled. She was inexplicably reminded of the Drinkwater, of the leaves floating on its surface. They swirled and eddied where the bank curved in or where stone protruded, but in the end they all went the same way. The shadow she watched was at odds with its fellows. She blinked hard, wondering if it were a trick of the light. The trees bent and thrashed under the wind's hand, then came upright again, so it made sense that shadows ran both ways, but still she crouched lower, keeping her eyes on the blot of darkness. It was motionless now, and that more than anything kept her frozen and watchful. Then another blot joined it and voices spoke: harsh, disjointed, unmistakable, and coming her way!

Now she could see the glimmer of their eyes! Surely they could see hers? But to drop her gaze would mean not knowing where they were. They moved inexorably closer: twenty paces, fifteen, ten, their swords and knives clearly visible. Memories tore at her mind, clamping her eyes shut in reflex. Suddenly, there was a tearing crash as a branch was wrenched from the canopy and thrown to the forest floor. She saw them drop to the ground, and swords flashed. There was another exchange, the words completely alien to her, and they moved off in the direction *she* must go.

Kira stayed where she was. Maybe she should spend the rest of the night in the trees. They were tall enough, but there were no terra-woods. Maybe the Shargh wouldn't think to look up. Then again, the way things were crashing down in the wind, they'd be fools not to. A horrible image came to her of Shargh crowded round a tree staring up at her sleeping-sling, then soundlessly climbing up to slay her. What she really wanted was a dense stand of bitterberry or shelterbush to crawl into, but there was nothing.

Finally she crept from her hiding place and into the next pool of darkness, stopped and scanned, and crept on. Her progress was excruciatingly slow for a time, until her fear lifted enough for her to quicken her pace.

The night wore on but the wind didn't ease, carrying with it strange, pungent scents that Kira guessed came from the lands beyond the trees: the Dendora Plain. The realisation that she was actually going to leave Allogrenia began to close in with a crushing dread, and she had to force herself to keep going. Her legs were aching and her back cramping from the unaccustomed weight of a pack bulging with not just her Healer's kit but nutmeat, dried fruit and clothes.

The dark faded and she looked up often, searching for a terra-wood to sleep in, but finding only severs and castellas, now silvering in the dawn's first light. The trees were sparser here, and she peered about as she walked. She must be near the Fourth Eight but could see no darker foliage of an alwaysgreen through the trees. There were plenty of springleslips, though, their shrill calls now filling the canopy. Only a springleslip could compete with the wind, she thought dryly, watching them dart above her. Then she glanced back to the way ahead.

Shargh! And she was a full three paces from the shadow of the last sever. To step back now, or even move, would risk drawing their attention. She remained frozen to the spot. There were two of them, only about twenty paces in front of her, busy with their water-skins. If either glanced round, they'd see her. Neither appeared in a hurry, the taller talking and the other nodding at regular intervals. Sweat trickled down her back and she took a cautious step back. The speaker fell silent and his partner gave a final nod and half turned.

Terror tore the strength from her limbs, but in the same instant a figure burst from the trees in front of them and the Shargh exclaimed and swung back. Kira gasped in horror. It was Tresen, alone, travelling fast and several paces into the open before he sensed the watchers' eyes and spun, drawing his sword in the same swift action. Then his head lifted fractionally and Kira knew he'd seen her too. For the briefest of moments he hesitated, then he thrust his sword back into its sheath, turned and ran. The air rasped as the Shargh drew their swords and sped after him.

Tresen! Her legs had gone wobbly, so her first few strides of pursuit were more a stagger than a sprint, but then desperation lent her strength and she sped through the tangle of roots and broken boughs, her eyes on the backs of the pursuing Shargh. Branches whipped her face and vines tore at her breeches. The Shargh weren't going as fast as Tresen, but their pace was relentless. The air burst from Kira's lungs in grunts and sweat blurred her vision as the steepness of the land increased. She scrambled up the slope, gripping at shelterbushes to haul herself forward and dashing the sweat from her eyes. Suddenly her shoulder clipped a sever and she fell sideways onto her knees. By the time she'd clawed herself upright, only one Shargh was in sight. Where was the other? Running in front or looping round to cut Tresen off?

Something launched at her from her left and she ducked instinctively, then the world disintegrated into shouts and screams and the explosion of metal against metal. A hand fastened on her arm and she was wrenched backward so violently that her shoulder muscles screamed.

'This way!'

'Penedrin!' One hand held her, the other a sword, and he was dragging her back down the slope. She clawed at some passing bitterberry but it was ripped stinging through her fingers. 'Penedrin, no! Tresen's ahead.' She had no air in her lungs, no air to speak. 'Tresen's . . .'

'Stinking heart-rot!' He thrust her behind him and she landed with a thud on her back, scrabbling her heels in the litter to get clear. Metal clanged as Penedrin's blade thrust towards Shargh flesh and bone and was turned aside at the last moment. Sweat was acrid in the air and they were both panting, great sobbing breaths drawn in and out of heaving chests as they circled and clashed. Then Penedrin's blade sliced the Shargh's arm and a wash of blood sprayed over them both. Penedrin was lighter and more agile, but the Shargh was stronger, his expression murderous. As the fight brought him round, his eyes flicked to hers: black and cold and filled with hatred.

Kira scrambled to her feet and fled back up the slope, reaching the top and scanning wildly. There were two other fights going on, a scatter of Protectors darting through the trees and flashes of movement the way Tresen had gone.

'Kira!'

She whirled.

Kest was clambering up the slope towards her, his shirt torn, the end of his sword brilliant with blood. Then a scream sounded, low and guttural, and she flung herself down the hill, pelting between trunks and slicing her face and hands in a thicket of sour-ripe. Tresen was on his knees, his sword resting slackly on the ground, his shoulder laid open from blade to breast, and before him a Shargh stood with his sword raised high.

The sword started its descent and Kira launched herself forward. The Shargh half turned, and in a single, smooth action, snatched the dagger from his belt and slammed it into her back. The force of the blow knocked her to the ground and blotches of black distorted her vision. The Shargh was smiling and something warm dripped on her cheek as he raised his sword again. Tresen's blood. Then his smile flashed to astonishment and his eyes jerked to a point beyond her, as if seeking someone, then widened in terror. There was the sound of a sword cutting flesh and a crunch as it found bone, then the thump of a body hitting the ground.

The sounds of fighting still rang out, but they were drawing away from her, like the light. With her remaining strength, she crawled to where Tresen lay. He had fallen backwards, his face turned towards the sky. Looking at the trees, she thought, collapsing against him. A good way to die.

40

Tarkenda pushed the vent aside and looked out, a deluge of rain striking her face. The Braghans had been eaten by the layer of cloud lying like dark fleece over the sky, the only sign that the sun had risen a silvery glow in the east. The heaving sides of the sorcha groaned under the force of the gusting wind, and the billowing roof emptied sloshes of water down the side.

The wind had howled like a wolf pack all night, bringing a pounding, soaking deluge. Surely it was a good omen to finally have rain? The slope was awash with rivulets streaming down to the grazing lands. Was it too much to hope that the ebis range would soon be green with new pasture and the river's red scum flushed away?

She let the flap fall and came back to where Palansa lay with her eyes closed, her hands clenching the cover each time a wave of pain took her. The birthing-woman had gone back to her own sorcha to sleep. *Another day*, she'd said. Tarkenda remembered well the long agony of Erboran's birth. She settled back on the edge of the bed, smoothing a tendril of hair from Palansa's forehead. At least Palansa had stopped vomiting.

'Do you want to walk again?' she asked.

Palansa's head shook imperceptibly. 'I want it over with.'

'Erboran took two dawns to birth,' said Tarkenda, her hand stroking Palansa's hair gently, 'and all I wanted was to die. It takes many moons to grow a child, and while he's in your belly he belongs only to you, and you to him. There's nothing sweeter than that closeness. I've wondered sometimes whether birthing's painful because neither mother nor babe wants to let go.' She sighed. 'Men never know that sweetness. Perhaps that's why they're so ready to take their swords to the children of others.'

Tears squeezed from under Palansa's lids. 'I want Erboran.'

'I know,' said Tarkenda.

Palansa shifted restlessly, pulling her knees up hard against her belly. 'I want him here with me! Why should I have to do this without him? Why should –' She stiffened and clenched her teeth, waiting for the pain to pass. 'Why should I have to *fight* Arkendrin to try and keep . . . the loyalty of those as hollow as slitweed?'

'You're not doing it alone, Palansa, though it might seem so. Erlken sits at that door now, his spear across his knees. He's as sodden as a newborn ebi unlicked by its mother.' Tarkenda smiled but Palansa's face remained set. 'Squaziseed and shillyflower cakes have been set for you. In sorchas up and down the slope, people call on the Sky Chiefs to send you strength. Ormadon himself spends his entire waking hours plucking the whispers from the air and listening to what's said of the trees, and there are many others who use their strength in smaller ways to protect you.'

Palansa said nothing and Tarkenda went back to the vent, silently cursing the damp air, no friend to rotting joints. 'It's well that Arkendrin's deep in the trees, and even if he starts back now, the babe will be snug in its sleep-sling before he returns. There will be peace for the next Chief's birth.'

Palansa's weary face turned to her. 'And then?'

'It's as we've discussed,' said Tarkenda carefully. 'If Arkendrin finds the creature of the Telling and brings her back here to kill, it will sway many of those presently content to wait. A Chief with fire in his belly and a spear in his hand is always preferable to a babe in his swaddlings.'

'Then he will kill my child.' Palansa's eyes were huge in her pale face.

Tarkenda came back to the bed and closed her roughened hand over Palansa's damp one. 'He can't do it openly. We're strong. We'll protect him.'

Palansa gasped, her hand balling under Tarkenda's grip. '*You're* strong,' she said, when she was able, '*I* fear everything.'

Tarkenda stood for a moment listening to the steady tattoo of rain. 'An ebis cow will defend her young against a wolf pack, one pair of horns against many slashing teeth. That's all we see, but it's not all there is. The ebis loves its young and love gives strength. When Ergardrin was called home, I despaired as you do now, but I loved Erboran and Arkendrin, and that love became my horns, defeating the doubters and even the spears of the hollow-hearted.'

Her grip on Palansa's hand tightened. 'The babe that struggles to free himself is my blood, too, and we have horns enough between us to keep him safe.'

Palansa said nothing but her fingers relaxed. 'Now,' said Tarkenda, giving her hand a final pat, 'I'll mix you some honeyed water and then you must try to sleep.'

Something was tapping Kira's face and she turned away, nonsensically thinking of a bat's wing, soft and membranous. There was a smell of wood-smoke, spicy and clean, but also the smell of sweat and blood. The tapping continued and she opened her eyes reluctantly, to see Kest looming over her.

'I'm sorry to wake you, Kira, the 'green knows you need rest, but we've got wounded we need to get up on their feet and away from here.'

Kira raised her head as appalling memories flooded her mind, and her breath caught in her throat. Every bone in her back felt like it was crushed. Kest pulled open her sleeping-sheet and eased her up, the pain shooting to the top of her head. She shut her eyes again.

Kest gave her arm a gentle shake. 'We need you, Kira.' His voice seemed to be coming from far away and she had to struggle to focus on it. 'We've stopped the bleeding, but he must be stitched and you're the best person to use the fireweed, too. We've boiled the stitchweed and made bandages. We've done as much as we could before rousing you.'

Kira struggled to clear her mind. '*Who?*'

'Tresen.'

The air stuck in her throat, thick as tree-sap. 'I thought . . . I thought he was dead.' Her voice broke and she palmed away tears, powerless to stop them. 'I'm sorry . . . I . . . he's all I've got left.'

'There are many who love you, Kira,' said Kest, gently pulling her into his arms. 'Never think you're not loved,' he muttered, before releasing her. There was a pause while Kira sleeved her face dry and Kest cleared his throat. When he spoke again his voice was even.

'Brem doesn't think anything's broken in your back.' He held up her cape, sticking his fingers through the rent. 'Straight through this, straight through your pack and into this.' He held up a shattered pot of bruise-ease, and unexpectedly grinned. 'Strangely enough, it was the bruise-ease that did you the damage. Apparently it has the opposite effect to usual when it's driven into your back.'

Tossing the pot aside, he helped her up, supporting her as she hobbled to where Tresen lay. She could see no other wounded and she wondered whether they were already dead.

'Others?' she reluctantly mouthed, her tongue still feeling awkward.

'Two dead. The other wounds are minor and Brem's dealt with them.'

Tresen was ashen, even the firelight failing to give him colour as she knelt beside him, every bone in her back feeling as if it had been wrenched out of place and put back wrongly. Amazingly his eyes opened and his hands moved feebly.

'You forgot to say goodbye,' he whispered, his breathing shallow pants, wincing with every breath.

Kira's eyes burned again. 'Has Brem given you anything for the pain?' she croaked.

'Sickleseed.' He half raised his head, his pallor increasing. 'No everest . . . Kira . . . too dangerous for . . . the Protectors . . . to carry me. We will need to leave . . . at dawn. Shargh are . . . near. I'll put up . . . with . . . the pain.'

'I have to cleanse the wound with fireweed and stitch it and you've already lost a lot of blood, Tresen. We both know the shock could kill you.'

'No everest.' He smiled weakly. 'I'm . . . not intending to die. I'm Kashclan, remember, as stubborn . . . as you are.'

'We're renowned for it,' she said hoarsely, then coughed to clear her throat. 'I'm just going to check the wound.'

Peeling back the sleeping-sheet she placed her hands over his heart. The wounded she'd tended in the Warens had taught her that the pain was strongest there, perhaps because . . . Her fingers warmed, then the wave of fire broke over her, burning until she could bear it no longer, then ebbing, leaving her panting and nauseous. She rocked backwards and Kest's strong hands steadied her, careful not to touch her back; then he passed her his waterskin, watching her drink.

'Better now?' he asked.

Kira nodded.

'It's the strangest thing . . .' said Tresen. 'The pain's gone . . .' His gaze moved from Kira to Kest and back to Kira. 'You took the pain,' he said incredulously, 'but how . . .'

'She's a feailner, like in the Writings,' said Kest proudly, 'a taker of fire.'

Kira said nothing and Kest rose. 'Your clanmate will explain it to you,' he said, moving away.

'How long have you known?' asked Tresen.

Kira began unwinding the bandages Brem had used to staunch the bleeding, the outer ones stiff with dried blood, those nearest the wound sodden.

'Since the first attack, but I didn't understand it then.' She put the bandages aside and reached for the fireweed Brem had set ready.

'So long,' breathed Tresen, 'and so many secrets. You didn't tell me you were leaving the Warens, either.' Kira said nothing, her attention taken with the wound. It was deep but, thank the 'green, clean-edged. She picked up the fireweed and Tresen's good hand caught her arm. 'I thought we were friends.'

Kira's eyes flared. 'So did I! Yet you didn't tell me how Bern died, or why I needed to stay in the Warens. And you weren't there.'

Tresen's grip tightened. 'I was under orders.'

'We're *clanmates*, Tresen, clan-kin. Didn't that mean anything to you? All the time we've spent together, everything we've shared.' She jerked her arm free. 'You and me and . . .' She clamped her mouth shut and began easing the fireweed into the wound.

'It was to keep you safe,' he said hoarsely, 'to keep you from this.'

'There *is* no safety!' she gritted out, keeping her eyes on the wound. She took a ragged breath. 'I'm going to stitch this now, and take the pain again, then you must sleep if you want to walk out of here and not be carried.'

Tresen's hands plucked at the sleeping-sheet, his brief moment of strength spent.

'Don't leave, Kira, don't let it end like this.' His voice was slurring, his eyes unfocused. 'You weren't the only one who loved Kandor.'

Clenching her teeth, Kira pulled the edges of the wound together and started to stitch.

'Pledge me you won't leave . . . without saying . . . goodbye,' whispered Tresen, his chest heaving with the effort to speak. She

367

pulled the stitchweed taut and passed the end back through the flesh.

'Pledge me.' It was more a harsh exhalation than a word, and it forced Kira to stop.

'I pledge,' she said.

It was almost dusk but Kest still stood, his sword in his hand. The burial party had returned without incident but he felt in no mood to lie down in his sleeping-sheet and rest. He'd sent off six of his men the short distance to the Fourth Eight, four on the bearers and two guarding, to lay Bisren and Cadrin to rest beneath the nearest alwaysgreen. It was Renclan, despite Bisren being Barclan and Cadrin Sherclan. They were safe in the Fourth Eight's Shelter now, and that's all he could do, not being prepared to risk the living by carrying the dead back to their own octads. The Tremen tradition of burying the dead only under the alwaysgreens of their own clans was one of the many things the Shargh had destroyed, and he had no doubt that the Shargh were still looking for them in the forest, watching and waiting, regrouping their strength.

Those of his men not sleeping stood as he did, guarding Kira and Tresen, and Darmanin, who'd badly wrenched his ankle. Penedrin stood as he did, despite a shallow cut to the hand, and his own shoulder burned from a dagger score. Six Shargh dead and two Tremen; a better ratio than the first time they'd clashed. He grunted. Was this how it was to be from now on? A good day when more Shargh died than Tremen? He was beginning to sound like a stinking Terak Kutan. All death was bad, no matter whose.

He sensed rather than saw the methodical movement of Nandrin and Jonkesh round the northern perimeter of their camp, and Saresh and Deran round the southern. Nearby, the bodies of the fallen Shargh still lay, unclaimed by their comrades. Presumably this meant that no leaders had died.

It had been hard to tell who, if anyone, had been in charge of the attack. Two Shargh had clearly been pursuing Tresen, but the others had simply appeared in ones and twos, and in no particular pattern, apparently drawn by the shouts.

Protectors moved silently but the Shargh blundered about in the undergrowth as if at war with the trees. He'd known of their presence long before he'd seen them, not that the advantage had served him well, not with Tresen running for his life and Kira in the middle of it. Not one of his better leadership moments, he conceded, but then no previous Commander had confronted what he now faced. Sarkash had trained them to fight in formation, each man protecting his comrade, not engage in mad scrambles where you never knew which direction the next sword blow was coming from. And at dawn he'd have a different sort of fight on his hands; that of convincing Kira to return to the Warens, or of taking her there by force.

Kest woke as a silvery haze was creeping through the trees. It lit Tresen's deathly countenance and Kira's weary one. She looked older suddenly, the childlike roundness honed from her face making her less like Kandor and more like a woman. She was lying on her side facing Tresen, her outstretched hand touching him. *He's all I've got left*, she had said.

He grimaced. She hadn't included him as someone close to her heart, and he could scarcely blame her. She had been with Tresen since childhood, and they were clan-linked, whereas she'd known him only a few moons, and for much of those he'd been in conflict with her. And now he must take her back to the Warens. Kest remembered all too well the previous occasions he'd tried to get Kira to accompany him to safety. It wasn't an experience he wanted to repeat, but he had no idea how he was going to convince her to come back to the Warens of her own free will.

He rose and moved a few paces away, nodding to Nandrin and Jonkesh as they came off guarding duty. Maybe he could argue that Tresen needed her and that without her his wound wouldn't mend. Or that the women of Allogrenia needed her, for her birthing skills surpassed even those of the oldest birth-wives, or . . . She was waking, her first concern for Tresen, then her gaze moving to him. She pulled open her sleeping-sheet and winced as she got to her feet, limping over to him.

'We must speak, Commander,' she said.

'As you wish, Tremen Leader Kiraon.'

He led her away from the mutter of the other Protectors now rousing, to an ancient castella with a trunk broad enough to shelter them from any spears thrown beyond the guards, and sat down. Kira settled beside him, her gaze on the canopy.

'The wind's dropped and I've only just noticed,' she said.

'It was while you were unconscious. It disappeared as quickly as the Shargh.'

'They haven't gone far.'

'No,' agreed Kest. 'Now, Kira . . .'

Her gaze swivelled to his shoulder. 'You're wounded. Why didn't you tell me?'

'It's only a scratch, it'll wait. Now, I . . .'

'It won't wait, Kest. Whatever filth the Shargh put on their swords is already working its way into your flesh. Unlace your shirt.'

'This isn't necessary,' he said in exasperation.

But she had already gone back for her pack.

'I'm the Healer, remember,' she said when she returned, taking out three small pots and setting them carefully on the bough.

'And I'm the Protector.' He unlaced his shirt. 'I'm glad you've reminded me of the distinction, and of my task, which is to protect the Tremen, including you.'

She ignored him, her face filled with the intensity he noticed whenever she healed. He felt the cool touch of salves then the scorch of pain.

'The rot's started and I'm afraid the fireweed will make it worse before it makes it better. I'll take the pain before I go any further.'

'I'll put up with the discomfort, *Feailner*, I've seen what taking pain does to you.'

'It's part of healing,' she said, recapping the pot and grimacing as she stooped to her pack.

'And after you've seen to me I'll get Brem to salve your back.'

'There's no need.'

'I think there is.' He paused. 'It's part of healing.'

She flashed a smile and Kest started. For a brief moment the planes of her face had softened and her eyes were as luminous as honey, then the weariness reasserted itself.

'I could bandage your shoulder,' she said, 'but it's not really necessary and it might restrict the movement of your sword hand.'

'Ah, now you're sounding like a Protector.' It felt like fire coals had been placed on his wound, and he struggled not to groan.

'Burning?' she asked.

'Yes.'

'*Fire with flatswords brings the bane, fire without brings life again,*' she quoted. 'If I'd been quicker in my understanding, many of the wounded would still be alive.'

'And if I'd been quicker learning how to fight, there'd have been *fewer* wounded. It's been a hard learning for both of us.'

Kira picked up a small branch of castella and began turning it over in her hands. 'You should have told me the Shargh were hunting me, Kest.'

'Yes. In retrospect it was a mistake. Miken feared you might throw your life away to save the rest of us . . . *and* I agreed. As it's turned out, he was right.'

'Leaving Allogrenia's not throwing my life away.'

'The chances of you reaching the Sentinel are small, and of getting beyond it, highly unlikely. There's more grass than trees there, Kira, and fewer places to hide. You won't be able to outrun them either. The Shargh aren't fast, but they have great stamina – the Writings speak of them hunting on foot for days upon days.'

Kira said nothing, but the castella was a ragged stem. 'It's safer in Allogrenia,' he finished quietly.

'For me, yes,' said Kira, her eyes firing, 'but not for anyone else! I can't live out the rest of my days in the Warens, Kest, and if I go to the longhouses, I'll draw the Shargh there. At least if I leave, they'll follow me.'

'We don't know that. We know little about the Shargh and less of why they hunt you. After you're dead, there's nothing to say they won't resume their attacks on the rest of us.'

'Is that what you believe?' she demanded.

Kest hesitated. 'Whether they'd be satisfied with your death, I don't know. What I do know is that I won't allow you to sacrifice your life in the hope that they'll stop their attacks. I'm sworn to protect all the Tremen, Kira, but the Leader most of all, for the Leader holds healing, and it's healing that makes us what we are. My oath is binding and that means I'm going to have to take you back.'

She rose and took several paces away from him. When she turned, her eyes were a softer gold and her voice calm.

'The Warens don't command the Bough, nor the Bough the Warens, despite what my father tried to do. You don't have the right or authority to command me to do *anything*, nor me you. Using force against me wouldn't be protection, it'd be an attack on the Bough. On our return, the Clancouncil would be forced to remove you from command. The Protectors love you and you're the best man to lead them, so there'd be widespread dissension, perhaps a schism, and even if the Protectors *did* bow to the will of the council, your loss would weaken them.

'You'd be betraying those who trust you and compromising the protection of the longhouses. You'd be breaking your oath.'

Kest came to his feet. He was a good head and shoulders taller than her, but she didn't break her gaze or step back.

'That's an interesting idea and, I admit, one I hadn't thought of. I give you credit for a vivid imagination and proficiency with words, but the more likely scenario is this: The death of Kandor and the wounding of Tresen have unhinged you. Your grief for your younger brother is well known, and it's understandable that you might yearn for death for a time. I would be remiss if I *didn't* bring you back to the Warens, so that you might have time to heal and grow strong again.'

Kira was rigid, hands clenched. 'I'm not yearning for death, I'm going to the north to get aid!'

Kest stared at her in astonishment. 'From the Terak Kutan? The descendants of a people Kasheron broke with because of their violence? It's unlikely they even remember us. Even if they do, why would they help? Kasheron's parting was bitter, and I doubt they've lost any sleep since worrying about our welfare. How many Terak have visited the Bough to see how we do, Kira? Precisely none.'

'They're blood, and I'll go there as Leader to call upon their Leader to honour the blood-link.'

'And how do you intend to get to the north? It's a journey of many, many days,' snapped Kest.

'I have a map.'

'Oh, and that's going to be wonderful protection against spears and swords.'

'Stinking heart-rot, Kest! I'm Leader and it's my duty to seek help for my people. Your duty is to stay here and protect the longhouses. I suggest you concentrate on that!'

'Don't presume to tell me what my duty is!' he hissed, lifting his hand to remonstrate. Kira flinched, and for a moment neither of them moved, then Kest stepped back. *Curse Maxen for being as ill a father as a Leader*, he thought. He rubbed his hand through his hair and half turned, noticing for the first time that his men had ceased any semblance of resting or eating, and were openly watching them. He glared and there was a hurried averting of heads and a sudden rumble of small talk, then he felt a hand on his arm.

'It's not you. I don't fear you.'

It was a strange sort of compliment, but he took it as one.

'I've been thinking, Kest.'

'That's a good start.'

'If the Shargh believe I'm with you, they'll follow the patrol. That'll give me time to get ahead of them, even leave the forest before they know I've gone.'

'Why would the Shargh believe you're with us?'

'Well, Nandrin isn't much different to me in height, and if you travelled more at dusk and dawn, and he wore a cape, and checked on Tresen regularly, even walked beside him and seemed to be looking after him, you might trick the Shargh.'

'Nandrin doesn't look anything like you and he certainly doesn't walk like you.'

'How do I walk?'

'Not like a man,' he said irritably. He took several steps away and pulled at his hair again. 'You're assuming I'll let you go.'

'I'm assuming you've accepted the Warens don't command the Bough.'

Kest grunted and the lines round his mouth deepened.

'If you were looking for me in a crowd of Protectors, what would you look for?' she pursued.

'Someone small and finely built,' he answered grudgingly.

'That could be Nandrin.'

'*And* your hair. Nandrin doesn't have a long, fair braid.'

'That's easily solved.' She fumbled in her pack and pulled out her herbing sickle, then caught her braid, and with two quick strokes, severed it.

'Kira!' said Kest, horrified.

'Now Nandrin will look like me and I'll look like an ordinary Protector,' she said with a grin, holding it up. 'You *will* guard Nandrin carefully, won't you?' she asked, suddenly serious.

Kest ran his fingers over the heavy silk. 'Your beautiful hair.'

'Am I so ugly without it?'

The cutting of her hair seemed ominous, as if the Kira he'd known was already gone.

'Not ugly. Different.' *Like Kandor.*

Her hand touched his arm again. 'Don't be angry, Kest.'

'You can hardly expect me to rejoice in sending you to your death,' he said, bundling up her hair and pushing it into his pack. 'And if you're determined to go ahead with this charade, we'd better start now. Pull your hood up and keep your eyes down, and when I address you, put your hands to your sides and straighten your back. If you must speak, deepen your voice, and call me *Commander*, followed by a respectful bow of the head. I suggest you spend time practising the respectful part; it won't come naturally to you.'

Kira fastened her hood, straightened and dropped her head. She knew Kest's anger stemmed from his anxiety for her, but his manner was stirring her own resentments.

'Yes, Commander,' she clipped and, giving a short bow, turned on her heel and strode back to the fire.

41

The men slept with their sleeping-sheets unfastened and their weapons unsheathed and close to their hands. In spite of their preparedness for battle, though, they *did* sleep, unlike Kira, who lay tense and fearful, listening to their snores and snufflings.

Her fear had grown with the ending of the day and multiplied with the darkness. The realisation of what she was finally about to do lay on her chest like a stone, crushing all hope. No matter how much she chastised herself for being foolish or self-pitying or cowardly, she kept coming back to the thought that this might be her last night alive. At dawn the Protectors would go, taking Tresen with them and leaving her behind. She rolled onto her side and ran her fingers through the leaf litter. If the Shargh killed her in the forest, would she feed the hanawey and frostking, perhaps even the mira kiraon, before her bones became litter as well?

Her hand closed over the leaf litter, holding it entombed, like the earth now held Kandor. He was safe from the beaks and claws of birds but did it really matter once you were dead? She clenched her hand and let the leaf fragments sift through her fingers. Her thoughts were wild and strange; maybe she was unhinged as Kest had suggested. Surely it was madness to leave Allogrenia when she had no hope of outrunning, out-hiding or outwitting the Shargh. Maybe what she really wanted was to be with Kandor but, lacking the courage to swallow everest, was pretending some heroic quest north. She rolled onto her back, gritting her teeth at the burst of pain from the bruising.

The ground vibrated, then a sleeping-sheet was thwacked down beside her, billowing up the litter and making her blink. Kest lowered himself down and flicked the sheet over him.

The scouts had returned and he could at last take some rest.

'Not sleeping, Protector Nandrin?'

Kira pulled her own sheet closer and shook her head.

'Is your back paining you?'

'No, Commander.'

'Considering the bruising, I find that hard to believe. I notice that you didn't eat with the men. Aren't you hungry?'

'No, Commander.'

'I don't believe that either and you can drop the Commander bit and start acting like a Leader again.'

'And how should a Leader act, Commander?'

Kest bit back a retort. 'The Bough *doesn't* command the Warens nor the Warens the Bough, as you've pointed out, and that makes us partners in protecting the Tremen, which means we work together. So you can begin your leaderly behaviour by telling me what's keeping you wakeful when you're clearly exhausted. I might even be able to help.'

She was silent, digging at the ground with her fingers. 'I was thinking,' she said at last.

'What of?'

There was a long pause and he strained to see her face in the darkness.

'Of what happens after death.'

Was she thinking of Kandor or herself? Either would be enough to rob her of sleep. 'The Northerners have many gods that they believe take them back at death. The Shargh believe the same. But Kasheron spoke of the dead feeding the living, of seeds sprouting, growing and decaying, becoming food for that which follows. Even the rains that fall again rise again as mist, or are sucked back by the summer sun so they can fall again.'

Her hand gouged at the leaves, building small mounds and flattening them. 'Do you believe that?' she asked, without looking at him.

'The truth of it is all around us.'

'Do you fear death, Kest?'

He took a deep breath. 'I fear the pain that must come with sword-death,' he said honestly, 'but I don't fear what comes after. When my father died he was very peaceful, as if going to sleep.'

'A very long sleep,' she murmured, 'with no awakening and never to see the sun again or feel warmth or love.'

By the 'green she was bleak, as if preparing for her own death. Perhaps there was still a chance of persuading her to stay.

'If you came back to the Warens we could devise a better way for you to go north. If we sent a patrol with you the Shargh would still know you've gone, but you'd be safer.'

'Yes, but the Protectors wouldn't be. A single spear through the trees or sword slash would leave them with a wound full of rot and no one to bring them back. How many times would the Shargh have to attack before all the Protectors would be dead or dying? No, Kest, enough people have suffered on my behalf already.'

He caught her hand, stilling its violent movement through the litter. 'The fault's not yours, Kira. You're not to blame for their stinking blood-thirst. You don't have to pay for it!'

'I know. But I have to stop it.'

'There's no guarantee . . .'

Her fingers closed over his. 'We've been through this before, Kest; don't start it all over again.'

Kest stared down at her hand, seeing again how fine her fingers were, locked through his in the way lovers held hands. Her face was fine too, and he remembered how happy she'd been at Turning, luminous in her love for Kandor. If only she were older, more aware, ready to bond, he would court her now, if only to keep her safe.

Her slim form was visible beneath the folds of the sheet and it would easy to lean across now and caress her face, to bring his mouth to hers. He wasn't new to the art of love-making and even here, surrounded by the sleeping men, he was confident he could rouse in her a passion that might persuade her to turn aside from her chosen path. But should she bond with him? Kesilini and Merek had pledged knowing fully the gravity and consequences of what they did, but Kira knew nothing beyond curing the hurts of other. He sighed and withdrew his hand.

'We'll delay our departure for another day,' he said slowly, 'and let Tresen build his strength. Then tomorrow night, when it's fully dark, I'll take you to the terrawood grove Saresh and Deran found earlier. We'll take three or four men with us and disguise it as a gathering expedition, then you can spend the rest of the night there while we make a great show of preparing to leave. We'll go at dawn and you can stay in the terrawoods till the next night. I think it's best you continue to travel at night.'

Kira nodded. 'Another full day of rest will help Tresen greatly but I don't think he'll be able to journey all day. Will you be able to stop as you travel?'

She was being careful not to impinge on his role of Commander, noted Kest.

'There's no haste in our journey back; in fact, it will be better if we go slowly so you'll have time to get clear of the forest while the Shargh follow us.'

'And they'll attack?'

'At some point they might, if they judge our strength less than theirs. They've already lost six of their number. Of course I don't know how many more have since joined them. Time will tell.'

'The Writings are clear on how to treat the wounds and there's plenty of fireweed in the Warens,' said Kira. 'Arlen and Paterek know how to prepare it and can stitch wounds as well as I can.'

'No one can stitch wounds as well as you, Kira,' he said shortly, 'and I know your pack is full of salves and herbs. What are you intending to eat on the journey?'

'I've got nutmeat and dried fruit, which I've been saving by eating pitchie seeds and sour-ripe since I set out.'

Kest grunted. 'A Protector needs a double handful of nutmeat to march all day. How much are you carrying?'

'I'm smaller than a Protector.'

'One and a half handfuls then and, judging by what I saw of your pack, I'd say you've about five days' supply.'

'About seven days, and I can gather as I go.'

'Really? Have you read in the Writings what gathering's available beyond the trees?'

'No.'

'Neither have I.'

'Kasheron and his followers must have lived on something when they came south,' pointed out Kira.

'They came on horses and turned them loose when they reached the trees. You can carry a lot more on a horse than you can on your own back.'

Kira pulled her sheet higher and said nothing.

'I'm not trying to be difficult,' said Kest. 'As a Protector, I know how much food you need to journey. If you don't eat enough you'll lose fat, then muscle, and you can't afford to lose either. It's pointless escaping the Sharghs' blades only to die of hunger and weakness further north. Look, Kira, I can give you more nutmeat to take but you'll have to leave the salves and herbs behind.'

'I'm a Healer, Kest, I must have them with me.'

'Once you leave the forest there'll be no one to heal but yourself and the best salve for that will be food.'

'I've always carried my herbal kit,' said Kira stubbornly.

Kest wriggled slightly, making a dip in the litter for his hip. The sleeping-sheet was pleasantly warm and his eyelids were growing heavy.

'Then compromise and take less of each herb and salve. You might be able to gather more beyond the trees.'

'And where did you read that in the Writings?'

He grinned. 'Sleep,' he said, and let his eyes close.

42

Tarkenda clenched her jaw, biting back her fear. The bed's covering was drenched with birthwater and blood, and blackness from the baby's bowels was adding to the stains. Tarkenda knew what that meant, for she'd seen it before when a child had been lost – and sometimes the mother too. The babe should have been born by now! Even she had never laboured this long. It must be dawn beyond the rain-sodden clouds and long since Palansa had even the strength to groan.

The birthing-woman was silent, her hands on Palansa's belly, her head half turned as if listening. What was there to hear? The wind still screeched like brawling mawkbirds, scooping up the rain and dashing it back against the sorcha as if the Sky Chiefs were venting their fury. Having parched the lands for moons on end, they now seemed intent on drowning it.

They certainly had cause to be angry. Arkendrin had broken Erboran's mourning time and plotted to break the line of first-born Chiefs, and now, to add to his contemptuous disrespect, Arkendrin and his cronies roamed the forests instead of safeguarding the passing into life of the new Chief. Was this the cause of the Sky Chiefs' fury or . . . a terrible thought occurred to her. Supposing the Sky Chiefs had *intended* the Telling to come about. Suppose they bequeathed the Last Teller with his vision to *prepare* the Shargh for it, not to *warn* them of it? And supposing they'd sent her visions for the same reason? Perhaps, in trying to prevent their unfolding, it was *she* who was offending the Sky Chiefs, not Arkendrin.

Shaking, she lowered herself onto a chair. Surely the punishment wouldn't be the death of Palansa and the babe? Dread quickened her heart as she stared at Palansa. None of her visions had shown Arkendrin as Chief and she'd taken this to mean that Palansa had birthed a boy and both had lived, but her visions hadn't shown that either, just fair-haired men on white horses slaughtering Shargh warriors.

Why hadn't these things occurred to her before? Were the Sky Chiefs gifting her a moment of insight, or was she so addled with weariness and fear that her mind was wandering along strange and misleading paths?

'The child's big,' said the birthing-woman, jolting Tarkenda from her reverie. 'We need to get her up.'

Tarkenda looked at Palansa doubtfully. She lay as if dead.

'Take her arm,' ordered the birthing-woman.

Tarkenda gripped Palansa's arm and together they hauled her upright, Palansa groaning, her head lolling forward.

'Hold her,' instructed the birthing-woman, and Tarkenda took her full weight, grunting as her back and hips screamed in pain, and tightening her grip as a shudder passed through Palansa's body. The birthing-woman was busy between her legs, blood dripping off her elbows onto the wolf-skins Erboran had hunted. Tarkenda watched it pool in crimson puddles and faltered.

Palansa shuddered again and jerked convulsively, and the birthing-woman's heavy frown gave way to a gap-toothed smile. 'Ah, so you've decided to greet the world, have you,' she muttered, quickly changing her position.

A bloodied fist appeared, perfect in miniature, then a slide of sticky hair and a bluish back. Tarkenda struggled to hold Palansa upright as the food-bag came away and there was a single high-pitched squawk as the birthing-woman cut the cord. Tarkenda gritted her teeth as she lowered Palansa back onto the bed and pulled away the sodden coverings, turning back in time to see the birthing-woman putting on her cape. The sleeping-sling was swaying gently, weighted by a small bundle.

'What is it?' Tarkenda forced herself to ask.

'Only a man would give that much trouble,' said the birthing-woman, picking up her bag. 'And a Chief at that. Keep her abed for the next few days and send for me if the bleeding grows heavier.' Then, pulling her hood close, she turned to the sling and touched her forehead briefly. Then she was gone.

Tarkenda hobbled to the sling and carefully lifted the child out, then went to the vent and pushed the flap aside. The rain had eased at last and the clouds had peeled back, spilling silvery light over the Grounds. In the wash of watery air, the babe's dark eyes gazed back into hers.

'Son of my son,' she murmured, bringing her lips to his sticky forehead, the swell of her heart stopping further speech. Then, forcing her aching back straight, she went to the door and stepped out into the mud. Ormadon was there in the churn and those who were loyal to Palansa, as well as some of the higher-placed blood-ties of those who trailed at Arkendrin's heels. Pulling the swaddlings away she held the babe high, his arms and legs jerking convulsively and his mouth opening in a long, loud bawl. There was a murmur of approval and Tarkenda gathered him to herself again, winding him snugly into his swaddlings before going back into the sorcha.

Palansa's eyes were open, her hands fluttering towards her and Tarkenda placed the bundle carefully into her arms.

'Is he well?' whispered Palansa.

'You heard him,' said Tarkenda, smoothing the sweaty hair from

Palansa's eyes. 'He's better than you.' She heaved herself onto the bed and turned the bundle towards Palansa so that she could see him.

'Erboran's son,' breathed Palansa.

'The son of Chief Erboran, son of Chief Ergardrin, first-born son of the first-born son of the Last Teller's Mouth. What will you name him?'

Palansa gazed at him, devouring him with her eyes. Tarkenda smiled, remembering how it was with Erboran.

'Ersalan.'

'Ersalan,' repeated Tarkenda. Palansa had taken part of Erboran's name as she must, but also part of her own as was fitting, for she was now both his carer and protector.

'Chief Ersalan,' said Tarkenda softly, 'you are well named.'

43

Night had fallen again and it was time. Kira knelt beside her clanmate, speaking his name softly. 'Tresen?'

The Protectors sat quietly, taking their evening meal. Kira was acutely aware of their presence as she shook Tresen gently. Kest already waited with a group of others on the edge of the trees to begin their ruse, and she shook Tresen again. She wanted to be alone with him to say a proper goodbye, but Nandrin hovered on Tresen's other side like a concerned Healer would.

'Tresen?'

Her clanmate roused and she waited for his eyes to focus. 'Your hair?' he whispered hoarsely.

'I'm leaving now, Tresen.'

Tresen's hand moved feebly and she took it in hers. It was clammy and limp.

'Kest's letting you go?' he croaked.

'He understands I need to do it for the Tremen.'

'He's a fool then.'

Nandrin's breath hissed and Kira's heart quickened. Surely what a wounded man said wouldn't be held against him?

'Kest knows we can't defend Allogrenia on our own,' said Kira.

'Then let him take your place.'

Kira began to extricate her hand. 'I have to go now, Tresen, Kest's waiting for me. I'm going to hide in a terrawood all through tomorrow and Nandrin's going to pretend to be me. See? He's wearing my plait.'

She made an attempt at a smile but Tresen's hollow eyes didn't leave her face. 'Your death won't bring Kandor back, Kira.'

She felt a sense of suffocation and it was a moment before she could speak. 'I don't intend to die . . . I intend to bring aid.' Her words sounded empty, even to her own ears, and Tresen's fingers tightened on hers.

'I love you. Doesn't that mean anything?'

She jerked her hand free and scrambled to her feet. 'I have to go now, Tresen. May the alwaysgreen Shelter you and guide your way; may its shadow bring you home again, lest you stray.' Her haste robbed the farewell of any meaning and Tresen turned his face away. Was it to end like this? thought Kira. All their seasons of growing together, everything they shared? It might well be the last time she ever saw him, yet her mind was empty. She wanted to be enclosed in one of the intense hugs they'd shared each time she'd said farewell and set off back to the Bough.

Nandrin was trying to make himself as small as possible, clearly discomfited, and she touched his hand briefly. 'Thank you for doing this, Protector Nandrin. Stay safe.'

'May the alwaysgreen Shelter you, Tremen Leader Kiraon.' He went to bow, catching himself just in time and nodding instead.

Kira picked her way through the sleeping men and into the scrubby land where Kest and the others waited, her cape catching on sour-ripe vine as she neared them. She felt like sobbing and was glad the gloom hid her face from the assembled men.

'We'll walk apart as if we're gathering,' instructed Kest, moving away.

They were playing a game now, Kira reminded herself – Protectors on a night-time forage – and she couldn't expect Kest to notice her distress or offer her comfort when the Shargh's eyes might be on them. The vine tore at her hands but, with a final wrench, her cape came free and she followed them into the night.

A little to the east, in the Kenclan octad, Irdodun sat with his leg resting on a broken bough, contemplating the half-hidden shapes of his comrades. Most of the warriors lay sprawled in the undergrowth resting, but Arkendrin was busy applying tesat to his flatsword, the use of his running hand rather than his fighting hand the only sign that something was amiss. He'd said nothing about the wound to his shoulder, neither washing nor binding it, but his shirt was stiff with blood and he'd slept a good part of the light away.

Chief Arkendrin wounded, Urpalin and five of his lesser kin dead in the rot of leaf and root, and still the creature lived. It was as if the Sky Chiefs smiled on her rather than them. A bird broke cover and Irdodun jumped, his hand going to his flatsword as he watched it wing away, cawing discordantly. Then, to the east, foliage rustled and snapped, and his grip tightened on the cool metal as he wondered if the treemen had developed an appetite for hunting as well as fighting. But it was only Orthaken returning from a scout.

Orthaken stooped low and palmed before Arkendrin, Irdodun straining to hear if the other man had found anything of use on his long reconnoitre. But it was as he'd expected: having camped with their injured for two days, the treemen were preparing to leave. Twenty, Orthaken said, against their own eleven. Irdodun grunted as he shifted his leg again, still finding no relief. Orthaken must have miscounted, although he'd never admit it; there'd been twenty-one when Urmarchin had scouted earlier. Maybe one of them was off in the trees scavenging for the foul things they ate, though the Sky Chiefs only knew what they gathered. He'd found nothing worthy of his mouth among the trees.

He rubbed his leg absently, considering the odds. As well as the two they'd killed, two of the treemen were wounded, one so badly that he'd not left his bed since the battle, the Healer-creature staying by his side. He doubted she'd be fighting either. Eighteen to eleven then or seventeen to eleven if you believed Orthaken's boast that he'd wounded their Chief. Irdodun's lip curled. He certainly hadn't seen any sign of it, the man striding about as if sound and whole.

Pushing the crude crutch he'd fashioned deep into the rotting leaves, he levered himself upright and hobbled towards Arkendrin. His ankle was twice its normal size, the result of a branch giving way as he ran, and he wondered how he was to fight when he could barely walk. Arkendrin was on his feet too, his eyes like coals in his pale face, striding about the clearing as if preparing for battle.

'I'll not lose the creature a third time,' he muttered, as he slashed at the foliage.

He was still using his running hand. 'I'm wondering if your brother's join-wife has birthed,' said Irdodun carefully.

Arkendrin stopped in mid slash, turning to stare at him. 'What matter if she has? A squalling babe is no defence against the evil this creature intends us.'

'You're right, Chief Arkendrin, but its birth would bring offerings and entreaties to the Sky Chiefs. They may have . . . been distracted from our cause. It was a great ill-fortune to lose Urpalin and to have the creature slip away again when we were so close to ridding ourselves of it.'

'It'll be dead by the dawning.'

'I thought you intended to kill the creature at the Grounds. If there's a babe in the highest sorcha, the Chief-mother would have claimed the chiefship for it while we've been away. Those who follow like water down a hill will need to *see* the creature's blood spilled to believe the Sky Chiefs favour you over your brother's seed.'

'I'm Chief!' said Arkendrin, eyes bulging. 'I need no proof of the killing!'

Irdodun let his shoulders sag. 'It's as you say, Chief Arkendrin.'

There was a brief silence then the unmistakable sound of running feet. Warriors scrambled for their weapons and Irdodun struggled to hold both his crutch and his sword, as the thumping grew louder. Finally the bushes gave way and Urgasen appeared, sweat-stained from his long journey from the Grounds but showing no weariness in the way he moved or in his crisp gesture of honour to Arkendrin.

'I've been searching for you these past days, Chief Arkendrin, and give thanks to the Sky Chiefs for your clear trail and the scouts you've seeded in the trees. I bring important news from the Grounds: the Chief-wife has birthed a son.'

The warriors muttered but Arkendrin's face remained impassive. 'What she's birthed is of no interest to me. The Healer-creature's within reach of our swords.'

Urgasen looked at him in surprise. 'The honour of the Sky Chiefs requires your return.'

Arkendrin's jaws moved up and down as if chewing ebis fat and the warriors tensed, but Urgasen seemed oblivious, glancing round and frowning. 'Where are the others?'

Arkendrin's feet had planted wide and he was fingering his flatsword. 'They fought badly.'

The reply was little more than a snarl and Urgasen paused, becoming aware of the tension and considering his next words more carefully. 'It may be that they fought without the Sky Chiefs' favour, Chief Arkendrin,' he said steadily, 'for those who dwell above have as little liking for the stale closeness of this place as we do. Certainly the Sky Chiefs favour the bright openness of the Grounds, for they've sent rain there and a male child to the highest sorcha. For this they should be honoured in the way we have always honoured them.'

'The highest honour's the creature's blood!'

Urgasen stepped back. 'It's as you say, Chief Arkendrin, but I follow the older ways, like my father Urgundin before me. I wish you well in your hunt.' Then, palming his forehead again, he disappeared back into the trees.

44

Kira lay in the muted green cave of the terrawood's boughs, debating whether to wait or continue her journey. She'd promised Kest to wait and rest, but there was no rest to be had when her nerves were as taut as saplings under boots.

Curse this waiting! She sat up, making the branch creak and dip and peered down, but all she could see was an interlocking sea of dark foliage, which of course was why she'd chosen a terrawood to hide in. It must be close to midday. Even given the fact that he'd have to stop to let Tresen rest, Kest should be halfway to the Third Eight by now, as should the Shargh who followed him. There was really no reason for her to stay, but still she hesitated. Kest's instructions had been clear: 'Wait for a full day and travel only at night. The Shargh see less well than us in the forest, especially with a small moon.' And then, unexpectedly, he'd asked her whether she still had the small carven owl he'd given her. 'Let it remind you, Tremen Leader Kiraon, when you're far from us, of your home under the trees and of those of us here who love you.'

Kira's hand closed over the mira kiraon, hanging round her

neck next to the ring of rulership. Her eyes burned, the longing to go home an immense unsated hunger. She could wait no longer. Either she must go back or she must go on, there was nothing in between. She came down the tree soundlessly, stopping short of the final boughs to peer out and listen. The forest was still, pulsing with the ripe smells of summer, the scents of her childhood, and she leapt nimbly to the ground. All she wanted to do now was to get the leaving of Allogrenia done with and begin the next part of her journey.

She kept to the shelter of the larger trees where it was possible, passing the Fourth Eight with its new burial mounds of cut turf. *Two dead*, Kest had told her after the attack, but she'd been so concerned about Tresen that she hadn't even asked who they were. They had clan-kin, mothers, fathers, possibly brothers and sisters. She hurried on, scanning continually, ears straining for sound. The warmth of the day began to ebb and finally the sun disappeared beyond the canopy and the chuff beetles' rattle joined the jostle of roosting birds.

There were no terrawoods but it didn't matter. She had no intention of stopping. Her legs were weary and her shoulders ached from the bulging pack, but fear clothed her like a cape, and she knew that even if she did find a tree to climb into, sleep wouldn't come. There was something else keeping her moving too. The knowing that in the bottom of her pack was the pouch of morning-bright seeds. One of those would grant her at least another day and night of travel, before her senses failed her and she'd need to hide. She tried not to think about *where* beyond the forest she could safely sleep for two days, as she had after taking morning-bright in the Warens.

The small moon was outshone by the glimmer of stars, and these seemed to grow brighter as she went, for the canopy was breaking and the stands of shelterbush and bitterberry thickening. Rambling tangles of sour-ripe formed impenetrable barriers, at times even climbing into the trees. Kira had to loop around each sprawl, re-orienting herself before continuing. At least the sour-ripe's presence so close to the edge of the trees gave her hope that they'd grow beyond the forest as well, their fruit giving her food on her journey.

Kest hauled on his pack and adjusted his sword. 'Yes, we're leaving,' he muttered, resisting the urge to stare out into the forest. 'Now you can follow along behind us with your stinking swords and leave Kira in peace.'

His pack was wet with dew and chill against his back and he barked an order for his men to come into defensive formation around Darmanin and Tresen. Jonkesh provided an arm for Darmanin and Brem took most of Tresen's weight, Nandrin hovering on his other side with hood drawn close. Fortunately the heavy dew made the use of hoods necessary.

Tresen was paler than hoarfrost and the fact that he was upright at all was a tribute to Kira's skill. Tresen's wound and Darmanin's inability to put weight on his ankle made them horribly vulnerable but there was little he could do about it. They moved off slowly, Kest snapping off a sprig of silvermint and sucking the dew from its fronds as he anticipated what might be to come. The water was crisp on his tongue, sharpening his senses. The attack would be sooner rather than later, he concluded, for each step took them closer to home and the Shargh further from theirs, and if the Shargh followed their usual pattern, they'd go straight for Nandrin. Kest had once thought this denoted a perverse kind of honour but he'd since realised their desire to kill Kira blinded them to all else.

It made the Shargh single-minded and fearless but it made them predictable as well, the Protectors being able to let them pass before attacking from behind. He'd also come to understand that the honour of killing Kira wasn't to be shared. In the most recent attack, the Shargh who'd wounded Tresen had had ample time to kill her, but after stabbing her in the back he'd hesitated, clearly looking for someone else. It was a delay that had cost him his life.

Kest stared around grimly, his men equally stony-faced, their tension palpable. The castellas were old here, broad and close-growing, their ancient trunks providing good shelter from spears but limiting visibility, perhaps aiding the Shargh more than them. At least the castellas would make the Shargh's running style of attack difficult, Kest comforted himself, unlike the sparser stands of sever ahead.

Somewhere to the left, a springleslip chirruped, cut off abruptly and chirruped again and Kest's hand went to his sword. Either a hunting bird was sliding towards its nest or something else approached. He flexed his shoulder experimentally, the wound burning but, thanks to Kira, his muscles loose.

His men knew, as did Nandrin, that Nandrin was in terrible danger whichever way the attack went, as was anyone who tried to defend him, but the young Protector had accepted the risk with the same good nature as he'd accepted the teasing that had accompanied his donning of Kira's plait.

Another shrill piping erupted and Kest jerked his eyes to the trees. If the Shargh discovered now that Kira wasn't among them, they'd realise the trick and speed back. His heart thundered and he shortened his steps, allowing Penedrin to draw near before muttering a command to him. His words ran like a ripple back through the patrol to Tresen, who groaned loudly and allowed his legs to buckle. Brem called out in alarm and Kest raised his hand, bringing his men to a halt.

'We rest here for a time,' he said.

The men exchanged glances, as if wondering why they were stopping so soon after starting their journey, but formed a defensive circle and began removing their packs. Brem spread a sheet for Tresen and helped Nandrin lower him onto it, then made his way to Kest's side.

'You think they're close?'

Kest nodded and they walked on until they were clear of the guarding men. 'I think they're *very* close and unlikely to wait much longer.'

Brem stroked his stubbly chin, gazing round as if admiring the shafting sunlight. 'And if they discover our Healer's a man, they'll go back to find the real one?'

Kest nodded. 'I'm beginning to think I made a mistake in telling Kira to stay in the terrawoods for a day. If she'd set off at dawn, she'd be well past the Fourth Eight by now.'

'Or in their hands. We don't know how many Shargh have joined the rabble since the last attack but we do know they're favouring the octad the Leader's journeying in. No, she's better in the trees till the battles on the ground are decided.'

Kest was not much comforted by Brem having left the role of victor open. Perhaps he was right. Just because they'd bested them last time didn't guarantee they'd win again. He scanned the defensive formation of his men anxiously. The Shargh were raiders, harrying Kasheron and his followers in their journey south, sweeping in across the grasslands and disappearing just as quickly. But that style of fighting hadn't served them well in the trees, a fact they'd probably realised by now.

What other tactics might they use? A simultaneous attack on all sides? A wedge driven between Nandrin and his men? He dredged his memory for more of Sarkash's teachings.

'There's fire ahead, Commander!'

Stinking heart-rot! That was the answer! He spun, drawing his sword as he did so. 'Maintain defence pattern,' he bawled. His men had drawn their swords too, heads swivelling as plumes of yellow smoke sprang up around them. Were the Shargh intending to burn them out or . . .

There was a blur of movement above him, then something struck him heavily on the shoulder sending him sprawling and knocking the sword from his hand. He flung himself over as the clash and grunt of battle erupted behind him and rolled again as the Shargh blade came down, kicking up with all his strength. The man lurched sideways, then there was a crack and a scream as Kest's heel connected with the Shargh's kneecap. Kest didn't wait to see him hit the ground, already sprinting back towards his men.

And then to his right, a Shargh burst from the murk. *Leader*, thought Kest. It was stamped all over him. Kest glimpsed Jonkesh launch himself forward and be slashed down and Penedrin try to break free from the fight he was engaged in. Then things slowed. He saw the Shargh reach Nandrin, catch him by the throat and drag him upright, and he saw Nandrin's hood come loose and the Shargh's face contort in astonished fury. His sword flashed back but the stroke went awry as Penedrin, in a final desperate lunge, broke free of his antagonists and speared his blade into the back of the Shargh's leg.

The man roared and staggered and the nearest Shargh immediately abandoned their attacks, grabbing him by the arms and, with swords slashing and their comrades forming a shield, half dragged, half carried him back into the pall. The crash of their retreat faded, giving way to the groans of the wounded and the crackle of the burning forest.

Dawn was close but Kira's pace remained swift, despite having rested little throughout the night. The growing sheen of light revealed more clearly what she had seen in the darkness. The trees were dwindling, severs now mixed with slender-trunked and sparsely canopied fallowoods, and a strange grey woody tree with musty-smelling leaves. Strange vines twined about the sour-ripe, their red-black fruit already crowded with blue-breasted birds. Was the fruit edible? wondered Kira, her belly growling. She was about to pluck one when something exploded from the thicket at her feet and she jumped back. There was a flash of white and it was gone. Silverjack!

The word sprang from childhood stories of the creatures of the north and she remembered the beautifully carved chime hanging in Kest's rooms.

There was another rush of movement and Kira jumped as a

second silverjack started from the bushes. Then the blue-breasted birds darted away, leaving the vine deserted. The hair on the back of her neck stirred and then there was the pound of feet and Shargh voices. She looked around wildly – there was nowhere to hide! Dropping to her knees, she forced a tunnel into the tangle, the thorns clawing at her hands and face and dragging at her cape as she desperately burrowed deeper and deeper. The ground was now vibrating with thumps and she drew into a ball, pulling her cape over, her heart battering against her ribs. Her clothing was brown and green and if she stayed absolutely still they mightn't see her . . . unless they were searching for her, unless they slashed the thicket with swords, unless . . .

They were making a lot of noise, not just in their travel but in their exchanges. Someone was groaning loudly and shouting and another voice was responding, low and respectful. There were grunts and panting too, as if some of them were straining under a load. Kira kept her head down and the commotion finally faded before more thumpings arrived, this group without the urgency and anger of the first, moving quickly but talking among themselves like the Protectors did on patrol. Their footsteps receded and silence descended but Kira remained motionless, her face smarting with scratches, her muscles cramping.

Chirruping erupted close to her head and twigs rustled and fluttered as birds returned to their feeding. Finally Kira eased back the cape. A jagged row of thorns was dangerously close to her eyes and she squinted up through the mesh, the new sun burnishing the edges of each leaf and lighting the fruit so that they glowed like tree-gems. She began to ease herself out, the thorns no more forgiving than on her inward journey, tearing her cape and raking over her flesh. She was ragged now as well as dirty and she hadn't even left the forest.

She stared around, straining for sound.

The Shargh had veered east, leaving a trail of beaten and broken plants in their wake. They were going home, Kira thought, remembering the map, then faltered. *The Shargh were leaving Allogrenia!* Did it mean they knew she'd gone, that the attacks on the Tremen would end? By the 'green! It meant Kest had been attacked again! The Shargh had left Allogrenia carrying the wounded – for surely that was the meaning of the grunting she'd heard – because they'd fought Kest. How many Tremen had been wounded or killed? Nandrin? Tresen? Maybe Kest himself?

They'd need her: there'd be wounds to stitch, fireweed to give, pain to take. She took several quick steps back and jerked to a stop. For a moment she was caught, the need to go on and the need to go back tearing her apart like a storm-blasted tree. The Writings were finished and there were Healers who could heal nearly as well as she could, she'd told Kest so herself. Her task was in the north! She forced herself to turn, tears streaming down her face. She was the Leader; it was her task! She was the Leader! How much nobler it sounded than 'deserter'!

She stumbled on. If they'd attacked Kest, the Shargh would know she wasn't with the Protectors anymore. Did that mean they'd guess she'd gone and leave Allogrenia in peace now? At least if the Shargh had wounded, they'd be unlikely to loiter on the edge of the trees waiting for her.

The day grew older, ripe pools of sunlight on the forest floor now larger than tree-shadow. Flutterwings danced in the clearings, not just the usual green, but pale yellow and gold. The birdsong was different too. Springleslips and tippets could be heard, and the occasional flowerthief, but also high pipings and trillings. Kira gazed up at the pale-trunked trees, seeing flashes of blue and red. The red was brilliant against the foliage, reminding her of the ring of leadership in its box of scarlet cloth.

Weariness dragged at her limbs and her thoughts increasingly turned to the morning-bright seeds. And then, as day waned and she felt she could go no further, she smelt the unmistakable scent of an alwaysgreen and the Renclan Sentinel came into view. She broke into a staggering run, throwing off her pack and standing with heaving chest, her forehead pressed against its bole, her arms flung wide around it.

Gradually her breathing steadied as the scent of the spicy foliage calmed and revived her. She walked slowly round the tree, tracing the ridges and runnels of its growth, reading its story with her fingers. On the far side, straggly fallowoods stood in scattered stands, and clearly visible beyond their trunks was a sweep of tussocky grass. So close! The map suggested a greater distance but here it was, scarcely fifty paces away: the Dendora Plain, gateway to the north, to the dealers in death who she would somehow have to bring to her side.

Her sweating palm imprinted the tree and she flinched as a bird winged overhead, dark and heavy, calling with a voice as harsh as the Shargh's. All she knew of the world beyond the forest were names on a map, childhood stories of Kasheron's mighty trek, and what she could see now. Leaving the shelter of the alwaysgreen, she made her way reluctantly through the spidery shadows of the fallowoods, coming to a stop at the last one.

The sides of the world had been devoured by an immense sweep of sky, curving up into unimaginable heights and down again to the skin of the earth itself, the sight so overwhelming that she felt like swooning. Here and there trees grew in ones or twos, spare-limbed and scarcely bigger than shelterbush. Beyond them, in the far distance where the earth met the sky, the land rucked up in mighty ridges, purple against the darkening sky. A wave of dizziness swept over her and she had to grab the fallowood for support.

The Azurcades, she realised, dazed. How would she cross the shelterless expanse of the plain and then find her way over such wild and alien terrain?

'One day at a time,' she muttered, that was all she could do, and each day of journeying she survived would take her closer to the north and closer to the day she might turn her feet homeward once more. She pushed the tangle of choppy hair from her eyes and looked westward. The sun was starting to slip from view, an immense orange ball with its lower half already flattened by the earth, the cloud blazing crimson and gold.

She stood transfixed until the last sliver of sun had disappeared into the land, the fire-laced clouds dulling to grey and the vast dome of sky washing pink and finally fading. What she'd seen had been so large and empty and yet so filled with splendour that she felt shaken, almost oppressed by it. The world of the plain had no roof of leaves, no kindly mesh of branches, no Shelter.

She made her way back to the Sentinel to retrieve her pack, sucking in the tree's spicy scent until the world seemed normal again. She should go, but something held her there, and it came to her abruptly that she was the first Tremen ever to leave Allogrenia. What she was about to do was akin to dying, except there'd be no funeral rites, no one to mourn her, as she'd mourned no one: not her father or Merek or Lern or . . .

Without really knowing why, she took off her pack again and retrieved a narrow bundle, laying it gently on the leaves and then kneeling, she cut a neat patchwork of sods between the roots with her herbing sickle. The soil was rich and dark, and she used the haft to gouge out a narrow grave, then she unwrapped the bundle, and for a long moment simply held it, eyes shut and head bowed, before laying it gently in the hole.

'The roots have taken you, the tree grown strong from you, the leaves been spun from you, the wind sung songs of you . . .' She choked to a stop, scooping up the earth and letting it sift through her fingers until the pale wood of Kandor's pipe had disappeared under the fragrant soil. Then she firmed the sods back into place and rose. Beyond the alwaysgreen, the first stars were glimmering in the sky.

'Kashclan thanks Renclan,' she said softly. Then, hefting on her pack, she turned northwards.

45

Tarkenda sat leaning against the sorcha, bathed in the last of the sunlight reflecting off the hide behind her, revelling in the ease its warmth brought to her aching joints. Next to her Palansa sat holding the babe close, making small grunts as he suckled, his tiny fists pummelling her breast. Palansa's eyes were locked with his, her free hand caressing his pink wrinkled feet and Tarkenda smiled, enjoying the sounds of pleasure he made.

'You're missing the sunset,' she chastised.

'They'll be plenty more,' said Palansa, without looking up.

The clouds blazed red and then, as the earth ate the sun, the warmth began to ebb and a bessel moth fluttered past Tarkenda's face. She rose and stretched. Soon Palansa rose also, the babe nestled against her shoulder, his face dreamy with milk. She rubbed his back absently, eliciting a bubbly burp, and ducked back into the sorcha.

Tarkenda lingered, her gaze sweeping from the Grounds up to the Braghans, purpling now like the sky, then back to the Cashgars, clustered at the mountains' feet. There the Sky Chiefs had bequeathed the Last Telling, and the Last Teller had made Ordorin his mouth, seeding the lineage that had given her a join-husband, a Chief-son and Palansa's suckling. What else would come of it? Only time would tell.

She followed Palansa into the sorcha and the door flap stilled. High above, marwings circled slowly in the last of the dying light.

Read on, as Kira's adventures continue in

The Song of the Silvercades

Kira sprinted the last of the way to the trees, desperate to reach the Azurcade foothills before the storm broke. Thunder boomed then rain pounded and she crawled under a bush, chest heaving. But its shelter was poor and she struggled to her knees to look for somewhere more protected.

By the 'green! There was a man at the edge of the trees. Kira dropped back to the ground, heart thrashing, and watched him closely. He didn't appear to have seen her, and she hugged herself fearfully. He wasn't Shargh, she realised with relief, but he might be just as deadly.

She remained still and the thunder finally rumbled away, the rain easing. The stranger moved restlessly around his camp, but seemed in no hurry to depart. Kira could see from the way he held himself that he was injured, and guessed it might be the reason for his delay.

But she couldn't afford to wait any longer, her journey north urgent. Careful not to make any sudden movements, she rose to her knees again. The man swung toward her in an instant, sword in hand. Kira gasped and fumbled for her sword, even as her wits told her to run. But her cramped legs refused to move.

There was a shout behind her and Kira cringed. Then, out of the night three dark shapes raced towards the stranger. They were Shargh! The squeal of metal against metal filled the night. The stranger's sword arm flashed, skilled and agile, felling one Shargh. But two remained, and the stranger was tiring.

Conflicting thoughts hammered at Kira, holding her still. She couldn't aid the stranger by using her sword – she wasn't a barbaric Terak Kutan who took life as easily as draining a cup. But was she to sneak away and let the stranger die at the Shargh's hands? Too many of *her* people had already died at their hands. It had been a long time since she'd played at fighting with Tresen in the Warens, but his instructions came back to her: the point of the neck to aim for; a quick death, a clean death.

Kira gritted her teeth and crept forward, looking for the best angle of attack. The stranger was tiring rapidly. As one of the Shargh leapt backwards, away from a thrusting parry, Kira screwed her eyes shut and brought the blade down with all her strength. The sword sliced through flesh and bit bone. Then her arms were all but yanked from their sockets, and she was wrenched after the rolling body, landing on her back. The remaining Shargh was on her in an instant, flatsword high.

The stranger's sword struck home and the Shargh's flatsword clattered off into the bushes. There was a thud as the Shargh's body hit the ground.

'Are . . . you . . . hurt?' said the stranger, leaning over Kira and using Onespeak, low and urgent, interspersed with heaving pants. He repeated the question in a language she didn't know, then in Tremen, then in another strange tongue, but Kira was shaking too much to comprehend him.

He withdrew, then came back and pulled her to her feet. He brought a metal cup urgently to her mouth. Morning-bright mixed with strange herbs, she realised numbly. Within a few moments heat sprang from her belly to her limbs, bringing a surge of strength. Kira leaned over, spat out the dregs and struggled to control the heave of her stomach. The stranger's hand came to her arm, steadying her.

'Where there are three Shargh, there'll be more,' he said in Onespeak, his voice still ragged with the effort of the fight. 'We must leave this place.' He hauled her upright, but Kira staggered, retched and was violently ill.

Her retching had scarcely stopped before he had her upright again.

'I must wash,' she said, dredging up the words in Onespeak.

'No time,' he replied, pulling his pack on and cleaning his sword and hers on the grass.

Nearby, the slain Shargh lay like branches felled by winter storms. Kira averted her eyes, suddenly overcome by the horror of what she'd done. She'd pushed filthy metal through another living being, sliced open his flesh and stopped his heart. She'd killed! She'd betrayed everything Kasheron had fought for, everything the Tremen believed in.

The stranger looked up at the sky, brought the back of his hand to his forehead, and spoke under his breath. Then he turned to her.

'Come,' he said.

'Do you go north?' asked Kira hoarsely.

'Yes,' he replied, handing her back her sword.

Kira hesitated. The stranger had spoken Tremen earlier, but she realised abruptly it couldn't be Tremen. It must be Terak. Maybe he was Terak Kutan, since the Tremen's northern kin would have a similar tongue. But the stranger had used other languages too. What did that tell her? That he travelled a good deal? If so, he'd know where he was going. Still, she knew nothing about him except the

Shargh hated him, and that he fought well. Perhaps that was reason enough to go with him, besides the fact he was going north.

'Come,' he repeated, beckoning her.

Not knowing what else to do, Kira followed.

The land quickly steepened, the bushes giving way to boulders and broken stone among trees that soared to great heights. The ground was slick and the storm had unleashed a thousand scents. The frantic beat of her heart gradually slowed.

They toiled on, the cloud clearing and the fiery blaze of the stars eclipsing the moon's wan light. Glancing behind, Kira saw the dim outline of the Dendora Plain far below, a pale sweep blotched with trees. Were the Shargh still in the foothills or sliding through the trees behind them, she wondered.

Abruptly, the stranger stopped and turned. 'We need be careful for the next part,' he said. 'Shardos likes to shed his skin and the path changes with every climbing.'

Shardos? thought Kira. Was it the name of the mountain? And what did he mean by shedding its skin? Her Onespeak was unpractised, so perhaps she hadn't understood.

The stranger moved ahead slowly now, testing the ground with a stick and gesturing to Kira to place her feet where he placed his. The trees thinned as they picked their way forward; those that remained were gnarled with splayed roots that gripped the ground like hands. There was little undergrowth, as if only the deeper-rooted trees could survive. Even in the darkness, Kira was horribly aware of the drop that had opened beside them.

The stranger edged round a series of large broken boulders that seemed to hang in space and Kira stopped. Her pack felt as if it had doubled in weight.

'Come,' he said, his voice gentle.

Kira willed her feet to move, but nothing happened.

'Not far now,' he said, reaching out his hand.

Kira crept forward. She'd only gone a few paces when a grinding

408

noise sounded and she felt the stone under her feet move. For a single heartbeat nothing happened, then it tilted and began to slide.

The stranger's hand clamped around Kira's wrist, arresting her fall. Over the sound of the rock crashing away through the trees, his voice came to her again, calm and strong. 'Turn . . . now.'

Numbly, Kira obeyed.

'Hand on tor . . . now right foot there . . . slowly, slowly.'

Step by step, Kira followed the path he spoke for her, terror clouding her sight and roaring in her ears. But she was held by his hand and his mind, and he coaxed her safely to his side. Then her legs lost all rigidity and she clung to him, his warmth and closeness like food and rest, the sweet spice scent of him comforting.

'I thank you,' she said, when she had breath enough.

'I should thank you, for you saved my life, yet I don't know your name,' he replied.

Kira hesitated, suddenly wary.

'Perhaps the debt dictates I introduce myself first,' he said. 'I am Caledon e Saridon e Talliel.'

'Caledon e Saridon e Talliel,' echoed Kira.

'In these lands, I'm called Caledon.'

'I'm Kira.'

'The Saridon are honoured,' he said, and bowed.

Kira though it odd that he referred to himself so formally, unless she'd misunderstood him, which was possible. If only she knew more Onespeak!

'It's past the mid point of the night but we're close to a place where we can rest. Can you go on?' he said.

'Does the path continue like this?' she asked.

'I haven't journeyed here for five years and Shardos might have sent stone from above or eaten the path from below, but the ground's more solid after the sida groves,' he said, pointing to dark shapes ahead.

'We should go then,' said Kira.

The unstable stone gradually gave way to the firmness of grass and stands of small shapely trees.

The sida looked like ashaels close up, but their scent was different. Black insects buzzed in their branches though Kira could see nothing to attract them: no blooms or seeds or other small creatures they might feed off.

'Night-hovers,' said Caledon, noting her gaze on the insects. 'They pierce the stems and feed on the sap. You can too, if you're thirsty.'

Startled, she looked at him.

'You have to be *very* thirsty. Not far now,' he said, smiling, then starting off again.

Kira took three sips from her waterskin, a habit she'd developed to save water and sate hunger, and forced her trembling legs on. Kest had told her to eat one and a half handfuls of nutmeat every day to maintain her strength, but to do so would have meant carrying nutmeat at the expense of herbs. She had hoped to gather on the Dendora, but there had been nothing there – she'd never seen such barren land. As a result, she'd had to eat very little to make her food last the eight days it had taken her to cross the plain. Her breeches were already loose no matter how much she tightened them, and her shirt flapped.

The night-hovers bounced off her face and tangled in her hair, and Kira beat at them, repelled by their nearness. Caledon slowed, then veered upwards through the sidas, and all but disappeared. Kira struggled after him through the thick leaf-fall. Why couldn't their shelter be down the slope instead of up?

Caledon was making his way up slabs of stone that looked like huge steps, but Kira came to a stop before the last as her weary legs protested.

'Here,' said Caledon, offering his hand and hauling her up. He winced as he deposited her beside him.

'I thank you,' said Kira.

He nodded and led her into the deeper darkness ahead, a cave, dry and fragrant, the back of it filled with river sand. Caledon slipped off his pack and rolled his shoulders.

'The Tain call this Aurantia, for the colour of the stone,' he said. 'At dawn you'll see why.'

There was a clear flow of water tinkling down one side of the cave that pooled briefly before it disappeared between rocks.

Caledon went to the pool and scrubbed at his face and hands, then drank deeply. Afterwards he took a square of cloth from his pack and dried himself.

'The sand makes a good place to sleep, softer and warmer than the ground,' he said.

Kira's fear of the Shargh had wiped away fear of him, but now it flooded back and she tightened her grip on her pack.

As if sensing her sudden unease, Caledon made his voice gentle. 'Come. You need to wash the blood from your hands, Kira, then drink.'

Kira remained where she was, suspicion fighting with her wish to trust him.

He settled on the sand. 'I've told you my name is Caledon e Saridon e Talliel. Saridon is my family name, and I'm called that in the north. Talliel is the port city where I live. It's west of the Silvercades, the great mountains of the north. Do you know the north, Kira?'

'No,' she said, moving slowly towards the pool.

'Talliel is a beautiful place, and a peaceful one. It's many years since there was fighting. You don't need to fear me,' he went on, 'but I understand if you do. I'll sleep under the sidas if you wish and we can go on together at dawn. Or you can go on alone.'

'There's no need,' said Kira, feeling shamed. 'But perhaps **we** *should* go on. The Shargh might be close,' she said, thinking of the Writings in the Warens that described the Shargh's ability to quickly cover long distances on foot. It was a skill that had added to the brutal fighting triggering the Sundering.

'I was attacked by the Cashgar Shargh,' said Caledon. 'Like their brothers the Soushargh, Weshargh and Ashmiri, they believe their gods live in the sky. Climbing mountains insults their gods by drawing too near their god's domain. The Shargh stay on the plains.'

Caledon had spoken slowly but Kira struggled to understand the Onespeak words.

'Let's eat,' he said, pulling close-wrapped packages out of his pack. 'I've got malede, cheese, biscuit, dried figs and tachil.'

'I thank you but I have food,' said Kira.

'Eat my supper and I'll eat your breakfast,' he replied.

Her hunger proved too powerful. Kira washed, then sat opposite him on the soft sand. The food was arranged on its wrappings but it was too dark to see it clearly.

'I don't know your food,' she said.

'Cheese is made from goat's milk, biscuit from maize, figs are a fruit, malede is spiced smoked meat and tachil is a ground-nut,' he said, pointing to each in turn.

Kira took a fig, some tachil and a piece of the biscuit, eating slowly and relishing every mouthful. The fig was sweeter than any fruit she'd ever tasted and the tachil had an earthy taste, nothing like red- or blacknuts. The biscuit was strange but tasty. Maize, Caledon had called it, whatever that was.

'So you know the north well?' she asked as they ate.

'Very well,' said Caledon. 'My father trades brocades and spices, and as a boy I used to travel with him all around the north.'

For a little Kira ate in silence. 'What about the Terak lands? Did you visit those?' she asked.

'Of course. They stretch from the southern Silvercades most of the way across the Sarsalin Plain,' replied Caledon, rewrapping the remains of the food and packing it away.

Kira wanted to know more about the Terak lands, and their inhabitants, but Caledon yawned noisily. Besides, if she questioned him, he was more likely to question her.

'Kashclan thanks–' she started, then stopped herself. 'I thank you for the food,' she said instead, but what she really wanted to thank him for was his kindness.

'Sleep now,' said Caledon. 'We need go on at first light.'

Caledon found it difficult to follow his own advice. He loved to see the birth of a new day, but on this occasion the pain in his shoulder forced him from his ciraq at dawn.

He rose and went to the cave's entrance, worrying about the last few days. Was it a coincidence that he had been caught by the Cashgar Shargh twice in five days? Only Weshargh herders wandered the Dendora, and yet four groups of warriors had been there, two of which had seen him and attacked. He sensed that their sudden movement didn't augur well – and nor did the pain in his shoulder.

It was likely the wound was poisoning. It was two more days to the Pass, and three after that to Maraschin – maybe three days too far. He searched the sky for stars but the coming day had robbed them of light. He turned to consider another problem – his new companion.

The girl still slept, wrapped in what appeared to be a basic ciraq. One of her hands lay palm upward on the sand, the fingers fine like her face, but with no rings or adornment. Her hair was cut in a choppy line at jaw level and was brown, though probably fairer clean. Her shirt was brown, her jerkin a soft green. The pack under her head was rustic, with woven laces and wooden buckles. Everything he could see was coloured with plant dyes, with no leather and no metal, apart from her sword, which was of good though plain workmanship. But she was no fighter – her attack on the Shargh warrior successful only because of its suddenness.

The first rays of sunlight reached the cave and the silvery notes of an ilala sounded. Then another joined it, until the valley rang, reminding him of the bells that welcomed the sailing traders home to port.

Kira stirred and her eyes opened.

By the stars! thought Caledon. Her eyes were gold!

Kira coloured at his gaze and Caledon quickly looked back to the valley. 'You see why this place is called Aurantia now?' he said as she came to the cave's entrance.

'No.'

'Aurantia is the Tain word for flame.'

'Who are the Tain?' asked Kira.

'Peoples of the northern Azurcades. Once we start our descent, we'll be in their lands.'

'Oh,' she said, tensing.

'I have friends in their city – we have nothing to fear from the Tain.'

Her cuff slid down and exposed her bony wrist as she pushed the hair from her eyes. She'd disciplined herself to eat very little, if the meal last night was anything to go by, and that meant she'd journeyed long enough to have to ration her food. But where had she journeyed from? He knew of nothing further south but Shargh.

Her Onespeak was poor and she didn't trust him with anything else, not that he could think what *anything else* could be. She looked pure Kessomi – except for the eyes – but then why would she be so far south?

'You haven't slept,' she said, her eyes pulsing between their earlier metallic sheen and honey.

'Do I look so grim?'

'Is it a Shargh wound?' she asked.

He nodded, surprised.

'How old?'

'Three days,' he replied. Her directness was disconcerting after her earlier reticence.

'It must be salved. Undo your shirt,' she said.

He hesitated, then shrugged out of his jerkin and unbuttoned

414

his shirt as Kira pulled wooden pots and bulging pouches from her pack, a range akin to the physick stores in the Sea-Farer's Way.

'I've salved it already,' said Caledon.

She peeled back the bandage he'd managed to apply with his left hand, releasing a stench so putrid Caledon expected her to recoil in disgust. But she leaned closer, looking at the wound, before calmly reaching for a pot of pinkish paste.

'You've slowed the rot,' she said, scooping on the cool mixture. 'What did you salve it with?'

'Kalix.'

'Is that a herb?' she asked, taking a bandage from her pack and bringing it up and over his shoulder.

'It's a mixture of . . . herbs,' he said, wincing at the sudden severity of the pain.

'You can show me later,' said Kira, tying off the bandage. 'Burning yet?'

'Yes,' he said, gulping down air as sweat started beading on his face. 'What have you done?' The fire in his shoulder and back ran like boiling water into his belly and hips, and he doubled over in an effort not to cry out. Kira supported him, her hand flat against his chest and, inexplicably, the run of pain reversed. It was like a plug being pulled out of a bath, the pain draining away under her hand.

He looked up in amazement. 'How –' he started, then saw she was ashen, her eyes the colour of sida, her expression blank. She sat down heavily. She had taken his pain, he was sure of it, and it had cost her dearly.

'I am in your debt. Again,' he said.

'There's no debt,' she replied. 'Healing is given.'